"Brad Thor proves he's
the ultimate thriller writer."
—*Suspense Magazine*

Praise for
SPYMASTER

"Thor convincingly portrays Russia as a reborn Cold War–era evil empire hell-bent on reconquering its former territory."   —*The Washington Post*

"A master of action and pacing, Thor continues channeling the likes of John le Carré in crafting a thinking-man's thriller packed with as much brains as brawn, making *Spymaster* a must-read for summer."

—*Providence Journal*

"You can be certain that a thriller is going to be a great read if it's by Brad Thor. . . . Without question, *Spymaster* is Brad Thor's best novel ever. . . . *Spymaster* is a fantastic read—one of the all-time best thriller novels."

—*The Washington Times*

"Timely, raw, and filled with enough action for two books, *Spymaster* is this summer's must-read thriller and the most gripping novel of Brad Thor's iconic career."

—The Real Book Spy

More acclaim for Brad Thor

Praise for
USE OF FORCE

"His best book yet. Powerful and reads like the news of what is going on today."
—Glenn Beck, #1 *New York Times* bestselling author

"No one writes a better thriller than Brad Thor—and *Use of Force* . . . will be viewed by many as his very best."
—*The Washington Times*

"Pure thriller gold . . . well conceived, perfectly timed . . . elegantly paced, harking back to the best of masters like Alistair MacLean and David Morrell."
—*Providence Journal*

Praise for
FOREIGN AGENT

"The best thriller of the year . . . an exciting and entertaining read."
—*The Washington Times*

"A top-notch thriller!"
—Bill O'Reilly

"*Foreign Agent* is Thor's best yet."
—Hugh Hewitt

"Make sure you clear your calendar before you start . . . it's impossible to put down."
—*The Daily Caller*

Praise for
CODE OF CONDUCT

"Counterterrorism operative Scot Harvath plunges into another world-shattering plot with plenty of personal consequences in Brad Thor's latest thrilling read."
—*PARADE* magazine

"Thor tackles the fear of terrorism and makes it both a scary and an exciting read."
—Associated Press

BRAD THOR

A THRILLER

SPY MASTER

POCKET BOOKS

New York   London   Toronto   Sydney   New Delhi

Pocket Books
An Imprint of Simon & Schuster, Inc.
1230 Avenue of the Americas
New York, NY 10020

This book is a work of fiction. Any references to historical events, real people, or real places are used fictitiously. Other names, characters, places, and events are products of the author's imagination, and any resemblance to actual events or places or persons, living or dead, is entirely coincidental.

First Pocket Books paperback edition May 2019

POCKET and colophon are registered trademarks of Simon & Schuster, Inc.

For information about special discounts for bulk purchases, please contact Simon & Schuster Special Sales at 1-866-506-1949 or business@simonandschuster.com.

The Simon & Schuster Speakers Bureau can bring authors to your live event. For more information or to book an event, contact the Simon & Schuster Speakers Bureau at 1-866-248-3049 or visit our website at www.simonspeakers.com.

Manufactured in the United States of America

10 9 8 7 6 5 4 3 2 1

ISBN 978-1-4767-8942-2
ISBN 978-1-4767-8943-9 (ebook)

For Sean Fontaine
Friend, Warrior, Patriot
Semper Fidelis

NEWTON

There is very little difference between one man and another; but what little there is, is very important.

—WILLIAM JAMES

NATO MEMBERSHIP
IN EUROPE

Members *
Non-members

*Also includes Iceland

FINLAND

Baltic Sea
ESTONIA
LATVIA
Gotland
Kaliningrad
LITHUANIA

RUSSIA

BELARUS

POLAND

CZECH REPUBLIC

SLOVAKIA

UKRAINE

MOLDOVA

HUNGARY

CROATIA

ROMANIA

BOSNIA
SERBIA
KOSOVO

Black Sea

BULGARIA

MONTENEGRO
MACEDONIA

ALBANIA

GREECE

TURKEY

Mediterranean Sea

© 2016 Jeffrey L. Ward

THE NORTH ATLANTIC TREATY
WASHINGTON, D.C.—4 APRIL 1949

The Parties to this Treaty reaffirm their faith in the purposes and principles of the Charter of the United Nations and their desire to live in peace with all peoples and all governments.

They are determined to safeguard the freedom, common heritage and civilisation of their peoples, founded on the principles of democracy, individual liberty and the rule of law. They seek to promote stability and well-being in the North Atlantic area.

They are resolved to unite their efforts for collective defence and for the preservation of peace and security. They therefore agree to this North Atlantic Treaty.

CHAPTER 1

The limbs of the tall pines hung heavy with ice. When they snapped, they gave off cracks that echoed through the forest like gunfire.

With each one, the small counterterrorism team from Norway's Police Security Service, known as the PST, halted its advance and froze in place.

Seconds—sometimes even entire minutes—passed before they felt comfortable enough to begin moving again.

No one had expected the storm to be this bad. Ice covered everything and made the sloped ground almost impossible to walk on.

Several of the team members had wanted to wait. Their leader, though, had ordered them forward. The assault *had* to take place tonight.

Backing them up was a contingent of Norwegian Forsvarets Spesialkommandos, or FSK for short. Their commander wasn't crazy about hitting a target under these conditions either, but he had reviewed the intelligence and had come to the same conclusion.

The two outsiders, sent up from North Atlantic Treaty Organization headquarters at the last minute and forced onto the team by the Norwegian government, didn't get a vote. Though the American looked as if he could handle himself, and probably had on multiple occasions, they knew nothing about his background or the woman he was with. Therefore, the pair from NATO HQ also didn't get any weapons. None of the Norwegians wanted to get shot in the back.

Encrypted radios, outfitted with bone conduction headsets, kept them connected to each other and to the PST operations center. They wore the latest panoramic night-vision goggles and carried a range of firearms from H&K 416s and MP5s to next generation Glock 17s and USP Tactical pistols. Theirs was one of the best-equipped, best-trained teams the country had ever fielded for a domestic counterterrorism operation.

Their target was a weathered cabin in a remote, heavily wooded area. It had a long, grass-covered roof pierced by a dented black stovepipe. A season's worth of firewood had been chopped and stacked outside.

Even if the weather hadn't gone bad, conventional unmanned aerial vehicle surveillance was worthless. The density of the trees, combined with the shrieking, bitterly cold winds, also meant that the nano drone the FSK carried was impossible to fly. They had been left with no other option than to go in "blind."

As the team slowly picked their way through the forest, sheets of snow and ice blew at them like shards of broken glass.

The last five hundred meters were the worst. The cabin was built in a wide ravine. Maneuvering down, several team members lost their footing—some more than once.

Because of the trees, the FSK's snipers couldn't find anywhere to set up. There were no clean lines of fire, and they were forced to move closer to the cabin than they would have liked. The operation was feeling more and more like a mistake.

Ignoring the trepidation sweeping through the ranks, the PST leader pushed on.

Three hundred meters from the cabin, they could make out light from behind the shuttered windows.

Two hundred meters away, they could smell the wood smoke pouring from the stovepipe.

With one hundred meters left to go, the signal was given to halt. No one moved.

Something was wrong. Everyone felt it. Heart rates increased. Grips tightened on weapons.

And then, all hell broke loose.

CHAPTER 2

There was a chain of explosions, followed by waves of jagged steel shrapnel that tore through the flesh of the approaching counterterrorism operators.

As the antipersonnel devices, hidden waist-high in the trees, began to detonate, Scot Harvath knocked his colleague to the ground and threw himself on top of her.

"I can't breathe!"

"Stay down," he ordered.

Being stuck at the rear of the column had given them an edge, but just barely. Harvath's quick reaction had saved both their lives.

Other members of the team hadn't been so lucky. Blood and body parts were everywhere.

When the explosions stopped, those who could scrambled for cover, dragging their injured teammates behind them. Any dead were left where they lay.

As a former U.S. Navy SEAL, Harvath knew what was coming next. There wouldn't be much time. Rolling off the woman, Harvath rapidly assessed her for injuries. "Are you hurt?"

Monika Jasinski shook her head.

Pulling out the Sig Sauer pistol he had hidden under his parka, he pointed toward a slab of rock two PST agents had taken refuge behind. "I'll cover you," he told her. "Go. *Now*."

Jasinski looked at the gun and then at him with confusion. She had a million questions. Chief among them—*Where had the weapon come from and who the hell was this guy really working for?* But now wasn't the time to ask. Getting to her feet, she ran as fast as she could.

Once she had made it to the rock and was safe, Harvath raced over and joined her.

Both of the Norwegians there were in bad shape. One of them was actively bleeding out, the icy ground around him pooling with blood.

Grabbing the tourniquet from the man's chest rig, Harvath tossed it to Jasinski. "Apply it here," he said, pointing to the correct spot on the agent's injured leg.

Then, picking up the man's rifle, he turned to the other agent and asked, "Can you fight?"

Though the man's left arm looked as if it had been dragged at high speed down a gravel road, he nodded—the pain from his injury evident in his face.

As soon as Harvath asked the question there was an eruption of automatic weapons from the cabin.

The rounds slammed into trees and chewed up the ground around them. When they connected with the slab of rock, large pieces were chipped off and broken away.

Harvath hated gunfights. Both as a SEAL and now as a covert counterterrorism operative, he had seen way too many of them. A gunfight meant you had lost the element of surprise. He hated them even more when there were injured men on his side and the bad guys were holed up in a fortified position.

Quickly returning the Sig beneath his parka, he plucked out his earpiece and let it dangle over his shoulder. The radio was jammed with traffic, all of it in Norwegian and all of it only adding to the chaos.

Checking to make sure the rifle was hot, he flipped the fire selector to semiauto and peeked out from behind his cover.

The cabin was one story, with three windows along its side. The shooters appeared to know what they were doing. They had set up inside, several feet back from the windows, probably prone and atop tables or some other sort of perch. That meant they'd be very tough to take out. But it also meant that their field of fire was limited.

Focusing on the closest window, Harvath let loose with his own volley. The PST agent with the bad arm did the same.

Immediately, gunfire was returned on them, and they were forced to retreat behind the rock.

Nearby, other Norwegian operatives did the same, but it was an anemic response. There weren't enough of them in the fight. They were pinned down.

When the rounds stopped hitting their cover, Harvath leaned out again. Before he could fire, though, he noticed that the volume of smoke coming from the stovepipe had increased. They were burning more than just logs. Now, they were likely burning evidence. Targeting the same window, he opened up with another barrage of fire.

Emptying his magazine, he leaned back behind the rock and motioned for Monika to toss him a fresh one from the chest rig of the PST agent she was tending.

Swapping the mags, he tried to come up with a plan. The FSK members, though, were already ahead of him.

Unlike the PST—which was Norway's version of the FBI—the FSK were Norwegian military and kitted out like soldiers. That kit included M320 H&K grenade launchers mounted beneath several of the team's rifles. Someone had made a decision to end this thing, now.

Maneuvering into place, an operative drew fire while two of his teammates stepped into the open and each launched a 40-millimeter high-explosive round at the cabin.

Only one of the grenades needed to find its mark. In this case, both did, sailing through their respective windows and exploding in a hail of shrapnel inside.

Moments later, a fire started, and thick, black smoke began pouring out of the windows.

Harvath didn't waste any time. Stuffing the pockets of his parka with extra magazines, he grabbed a thermal scope from the severely injured PST agent and took off for the cabin.

Behind him, he could hear the Norwegians yelling for him to wait—to not go in until backup arrived. That wasn't going to happen. There was no telling what evidence had already been destroyed. If there was anything left, he wanted to get to it before it was gone.

He used the trees for concealment and moved at an angle. Drawing parallel with the front door, he raised his weapon and crossed the icy ground toward it.

Pulling off his glove, he put his hand against the door. It was already way too hot to the touch.

Slinging his rifle, he flipped his night-vision goggles up, removed his other glove, and drew his Sig. With the cabin on fire, his night vision was of no use. The thermal scope, though, was a different story.

After he powered it up, he took a step back, readied his weapon, and kicked in the door.

Fueled by the introduction of fresh oxygen, tongues of flames came racing toward him, but he had already moved out of the way. Bullets or fire, he knew there was nothing good waiting on the other side of the door.

When no one engaged him, he risked a glimpse inside using the thermal scope, which allowed him to see through the smoke. There were bodies scattered everywhere. None of them was moving.

He figured most of them were dead, killed by the grenades. Dead or alive, they were all about to be consumed by the fire.

Harvath wanted to get inside, but going through the front door was out of the question. The fire was too hot. He decided to try the side.

Crouching, he took a quick look around the corner. If someone was there, waiting to take a shot, they'd be focused higher up.

There wasn't anyone there. But there was an open window with smoke billowing out of it. Raising the thermal scope to his eye, he looked at the ground and could see the heat signature of a set of footprints leading away from the cabin.

Carefully, below the window line, he moved toward the open window and risked another glance inside. The structure was almost entirely engulfed in flames. There was no way he'd be able to find anything inside, much less escape without getting very badly burned. No matter how much he wanted to recover evidence, it wasn't worth it. Instead, he took off in pursuit of the footprints.

CHAPTER 3

This side of the ravine was just as treacherous as the side Harvath, Jasinski, and the Norwegians had come down earlier. From what he could tell, the rabbit he was chasing didn't have that much of a head start. The footprints were still glowing warm in his scope.

Based on the size of the print and length of stride, he guessed it was a man, about his size: five-foot-ten or maybe a little taller. He was hauling ass, but he wasn't very graceful. The thermal scope indicated multiple locations where the subject had lost his footing and had fallen to the ground. *But where was he going?*

Harvath had done his homework. He knew the area, had memorized maps and satellite imagery. There was an old logging road that cut through the forest about three klicks from the cabin. There was also an abandoned rail line just beyond it. He figured it was more likely this guy had a car stashed somewhere. He had to be headed toward the road.

It was a bitch using the scope to track him, but it was the only way to spot the man's heat signature. Stopping to adjust his night-vision goggles slowed Harvath down. He did what he could to quicken his pace and close the gap, but the faster he moved, the greater the chance he'd slip and come down hard. Cracking his knee, an elbow, or his skull wasn't something he was interested in.

That said, he wasn't interested in losing the rabbit either. He'd been tracking this group for months. Portugal, Spain, Greece. They'd always been three steps ahead. Until tonight.

Now, he was ahead of them. He'd arrived before they could carry out another similar attack. Momentum hadn't necessarily shifted fully in his favor, but it had looked over its shoulder and glanced in his direction.

That was good enough. Considering the stakes, Harvath would take *anything* he could get.

Checking the scope again, he tracked the footprints until they disappeared around the next bend. The rabbit obviously knew the forest, eschewing established trails for making his own way through the trees.

That was fine by Harvath. He had hunted worse than rabbits over his career. Ice be damned, he doubled his pace.

Minutes later, he caught sight of his quarry. Jeans, hiking boots, hooded jacket. Over his shoulder was a backpack.

Transitioning to his rifle, Harvath attempted to capture the rabbit in his sights, but before he could press the trigger, the man disappeared.

Fuck.

He swept the weapon from left to right. There was nothing. He was gone. Letting the rifle hang, Harvath transitioned back to his pistol to leave one hand free for the thermal scope.

Pushing deeper into the trees, he continued to follow the heat signature of the footprints. The ground was still slick, but it was less ice and more snow. Fifty meters later, there was a shot.

Harvath dropped to the ground as the bullet snapped over his head. *The rabbit was armed. Where the hell was he?*

Peering through the scope, he could see a break in the trees up ahead. And there, making his way toward the logging road, gun in hand, was the white-hot outline of his target.

Raising his pistol, Harvath took up the slack in the trigger and fired three rounds.

The rabbit went down.

For several seconds, Harvath watched for movement. Seeing none, he cautiously closed the distance.

Approaching the body, he saw a lot of blood. One of his bullets had caught the man in the neck.

After kicking the man's gun aside, he felt for a pulse. *Nothing.* Removing the rabbit's rucksack, he opened the top and looked inside.

It contained envelopes of currency, driver's licenses, and several cell phones. By the looks of it, the man had tried to sanitize the cabin. Leaving the cash, Harvath pocketed the phones. And after quickly photographing the IDs, he pocketed those as well.

Patting down the rabbit, Harvath snatched the man's phone, photographed his personal ID, and examined his pocket litter. He took pictures of everything.

Wanting to transmit it all back to the U.S. as quickly as possible, he headed for the logging road. There, he'd find a break in the trees and would be able to get a signal.

When he arrived at the road, he pulled out his satellite phone, powered it up, and connected it to his cell phone. Using an encrypted app created for the military called XGate BLACK, he compressed and reformatted his photos so that they would upload faster. The sooner they could dig in on the people who had been in that cabin, the better.

As the photos prepared to load, he drafted a quick situation report to be included in his email.

Norseman + 1, Eagles Oscar.

"Norseman" was Harvath's call-sign, Jasinski was his "plus one," and "Eagles Oscar" meant that they were both uninjured.

As he wasn't in a position to be resupplied, he refrained from giving any updates on his current level of ammunition or the condition of his weapon. He simply went straight to the meat:

Ambush. Anti-personnel devices encountered 100 meters from target. At least 4 Norwegians KIA. Multiple injuries—some critical. Took automatic weapons fire from inside target—at least 3 shooters. Norwegians engaged with 40 mms. All Tangos KIA. Target destroyed. Solo Tango attempted escape. Tango engaged and KIA. Transmitting photos of materials recovered.

While the U.S. military had switched to the term MAM, short for military-age-male, as well as EKIA for enemy-killed-in-action, his organization still preferred Tango. It didn't engage in a lot of navel-gazing.

With the photos ready to go and a strong signal from overhead, he reviewed the message and hit Send.

Moments later, his sat phone vibrated with a reply:

Message received. Full Stop. UPDATE: O.M. is worsening.

O.M. was code for Harvath's boss and mentor, Reed Carlton—someone he was very close to and someone whose health had been deteriorating. The news was not good. He kept his reply short and to the point:

Understood. Will be back in touch soon.

Once the message had sent, he powered down his sat phone, disconnected his cell, and headed back toward the cabin.

Halfway there, he encountered Jasinski. Harvath had taken his helmet off, revealing his short, sandy colored hair.

"What happened?" she asked. "I heard shots."

It took him a moment to respond. He was still thinking about Carlton, trying to put pieces together several steps ahead. "One of them ran," he finally said.

"Is he still alive?"

Harvath shook his head.

"Damn it. I tried to hail you over the radio. Why didn't you answer?"

He pointed to the earpiece hanging over his shoulder.

"You could have waited," she declared. "And by the way, who authorized you to carry a weapon?"

He wasn't in the mood for an interrogation. "Not now," he replied.

His response only made her angrier. This was *her* investigation, not his, yet for some unknown reason she'd been forced to accept him as a "consultant." Something very strange was going on and she intended to get to the bottom of it. *No matter what.*

CHAPTER 4

Lydia Ryan hadn't wanted the enormous corner office, but Reed Carlton—the firm's founder and namesake—had insisted. As The Carlton Group's new director, it was only appropriate that she take it. Considering all of the job's responsibilities, she was entitled to reap its benefits.

The view was amazing—even at night. The Carlton Group occupied the very top floor of a twenty-five-story glass office building, ten minutes from Dulles International.

They had their own private elevator, with access from the garage, which allowed them to secretly whisk people up without passing through the lobby—a must for a private intelligence agency, especially one now tasked with some of the CIA's most sensitive assignments.

Because they handled classified information, the entire space had been constructed to the strictest TEMPEST requirements. Meant to safeguard against "compromising emanations" or CE, TEMPEST regulated the mechanical, electrical, and acoustic signals from all equipment used for receiving, transmitting, processing, analyzing, encrypting, and decrypting classified information. Every possible step had been taken to prevent both active and passive eavesdropping.

The firm had been just as diligent in protecting its IT, as well as all of its communications systems. In fact, wherever they could, they exceeded the standards. It put their facility years ahead of anything the government was doing.

It had cost a fortune, but it was an investment Reed Carlton had been willing to make. He was blazing an entirely new trail with his firm and being on the cutting edge of technology was sine qua non.

Carlton had a gift for recognizing threats before they ever appeared on the horizon. He also had the type of mind that was always steps ahead of everyone else.

During his three decades at the CIA, he had traveled the world, battling everything from communists to Islamic terrorists. His greatest achievement, though, was establishing the Agency's now famed Counter Terrorism Center. There, he had dreamed up and carried out some of its most daring operations.

When the time had come to retire, he tried it, but it didn't agree with him. He missed the "great game." Part of him resented its going on without him. What's more, the threats facing America hadn't abated. They were growing. And as they grew, his beloved CIA was changing—and not for the better.

It was being overwhelmed and subverted by bureaucrats. Operations were being scaled back, or scuttled altogether. Management was obsessed with minimizing losses. An infamous maxim, pinned to the wall in one manager's office, read *Big ops, big problems. Small ops, small problems. No ops, no problems.*

Like a terrible vine, the bureaucracy had wrapped itself around Langley's throat and was choking it to death.

No longer was it a vibrant, dynamic agency carrying out some of the nation's most dangerous and necessary business. It had all but come to a halt.

The calcification had terrified Carlton. Without an effective intelligence service, the United States was in serious trouble. So Carlton had done the only thing he could do. He had come out of retirement and had founded his own private intelligence firm.

Unlike private military corporations, The Carlton Group offered more than just hired guns; it offered global intelligence gathering and analysis. For select clients, it went even further—offering full-blown covert operations.

In essence, he had created a smaller, faster version of the CIA. The United States government quickly became one of his biggest customers.

He had modeled his new company upon "Wild Bill" Donovan's OSS—the precursor to the CIA. Their guiding principles were the same—if you fall, fall forward in service of the mission. Only the mission mattered.

To staff his operation, Carlton recruited the same type of individuals as Donovan. He wanted courageous, highly effective self-starters for whom success was the only option. He focused on the elite tiers of the military and intelligence worlds, people who had been proven, people who had been sent to the darkest corners of the world, tasked with absolutely impossible assignments, and had prevailed. He had an exceptional eye for talent.

Looking across the hall, Lydia Ryan could see Scot Harvath's office. It was smaller than hers, but that had been his choice. He had turned down the Director position.

Carlton had been disappointed. His greatest asset, the foundation his company was built upon, was his wisdom, his hard-won experience, and his global network of intelligence contacts.

He had distilled his thirty-plus years of espionage experience and drilled it as deeply as he could into Harvath's bones. He had forged him into one of the most cunning weapons the United States had in its arsenal.

He had also taught him about leadership and running an organization—specifically The Carlton Group. But any time the subject of one day "taking over" had come up, Harvath had made it abundantly clear he wasn't interested. He preferred being in the field. That's what he was good at.

When Carlton was diagnosed with Alzheimer's, he pulled out all the stops. Harvath was too valuable to keep putting into the field. Scot was his protégé and he wanted him as his successor. And, like any good intelligence officer, Carlton was willing to use anything, even a personal tragedy, to get what he wanted.

He played upon Harvath's emotions—particularly his sense of duty. He used guilt, leveraging their father-and-son-like bond. He even tried to shame Scot, suggesting that he owed it to the family he was starting to stay home and to limit going overseas.

That last attempt was particularly egregious. Harvath was dating a woman whom he was very much in love with and she had a little boy. It was the perfect, ready-made family, especially for a man who had spent the better part of his adult life kicking in doors and shooting bad guys in the head. To drag them into this discussion showed him how desperate and even how fearful Carlton was of the future. Not only the future of his business, but more important, the future of the country.

Out of his love for Carlton, or the "Old Man," as Harvath affectionately referred to him, he agreed to a compromise. Harvath would keep one foot in the field and one foot in the office. To do that, though, he insisted Carlton hire a full-time Director.

After a lengthy meeting in the Oval Office with the President and the Director of Central Intelligence, approval was given to hire Lydia Ryan.

Up until that point, she had been Deputy Director at the CIA. The President had handpicked her, and her boss, to clear out the deadwood at the Agency, streamline it, and get it aggressively back in the fight.

It was a Herculean task—akin to cleaning out the Augean Stables—and they soon realized it would take far longer than any of them ever anticipated. Entrenched bureaucracy needed to be torn out, root and branch. The most difficult part of tearing it out was that it fought like hell every step of the way.

While the Director tried to rescue the CIA, Ryan came over to helm The Carlton Group. It would function as a lifeboat of sorts—a place where critical operations that couldn't be handled by Langley, would quietly be carried out until the Agency could be rehabilitated.

A handsome New Englander with a prominent chin and silver hair, Carlton had been a legend in the intelligence business—the spymaster's spymaster. He was brilliant. To have his mind taken from him was the cruelest twist of all.

It robbed the nation of one of its greatest treasures. He literally knew where all the bodies were buried— names, dates, accounts, passwords, places, times, who had screwed whom, who owed whom. . . . He was a walking encyclopedia of global espionage information and it was all slipping away—quickly.

Harvath and Ryan were in a race against time, harvesting what they could. They took turns visiting with him, never knowing when Carlton would have enough energy or lucidity.

Some days were better than others. Carlton would drop cognitively, then level off, and drop again. It tore both their hearts out, but especially Harvath's.

Then one day, out of the blue, there'd been a dangerous lapse.

CHAPTER 5

Ryan had gone to Carlton's home to sit and spend some time with him. If he felt up to talking, she was always prepared to take notes.

When she arrived, he was engaged in an animated discussion with one of his private, round-the-clock nurses. While it was wonderful to see him so talkative, he was regaling his caregiver with highly classified information about America's relationship with the Saudis. *Not good*.

Pulling out her phone, she had called Harvath first. He was at the office and told her he'd get to the house as soon as he could. Next, she called her former boss at the CIA and suggested that the Office of the General Counsel get the nurses to sign national security nondisclosure agreements. It was a temporary fix, a stopgap, but it had to be done—immediately. There was no telling what he had already revealed.

Coming back into the den, Lydia offered to sit with Carlton so the nurse could work on preparing his lunch. The Old Man immediately began telling her how beautiful she was.

She was, indeed, a beautiful woman—tall, with long black hair, green eyes, full lips, and high cheekbones—the product of a Greek mother and an Irish father. He wasn't paying her some passing, sweet compliment, though. His internal brakes were coming off. He was saying things people might think, but knew better than to give voice to.

The doctors had warned this might happen, but no one expected it so soon.

She tried to take advantage of the situation by pressing topics they needed information on; plumbing areas where his mind had gone dark too quickly.

By the time Harvath arrived, she had assembled several pages of notes. How reliable the information was, she couldn't know. It would have to be checked out. Nevertheless, the visit had been somewhat productive.

"How's he doing?" Harvath had asked.

"*He's* doing fine," Carlton answered, speaking for himself. There were moments where he appeared to have decent self-awareness. Unfortunately, if you pressed him on details, he often couldn't access them. In essence, his high degree of intelligence allowed him to bluff his way through a lot of conversations.

As if on cue, the nurse poked her head in to check on her patient. Harvath handed the lunch tray back, vegetables uneaten. Thanking her, he asked politely for some privacy. Walking her to the door, he closed it behind her and returned to Ryan, who explained everything that had taken place since she had arrived.

Harvath smiled at Carlton. "I don't know what else to call this. You're like a loose nuke. You've got all of these secrets that we have to make sure don't fall into the wrong hands."

The Old Man brushed it off with a dismissive wave. "Don't be melodramatic. I'm fine."

He wasn't fine. He had become a security risk.

To his credit, Harvath hadn't wasted time. He already had a contingency plan.

On a beautiful lake in New Hampshire was a small island with a cluster of old vacation homes—one of them built by Carlton's grandfather—where he had spent summers as a boy. As his strongest memories were his earliest, Harvath thought it would be a comfortable, familiar place to put him.

He had arranged an open-ended lease from the current owners and with permission from the Department of Defense, assembled a contingent of Navy Corpsmen to see to the Old Man's care and security. No one wanted a loose nuke to become a broken arrow. If the wrong people got their hands on Carlton, there was no telling what kind of intelligence they could extract from him. It was worth every penny and every ounce of effort to keep him safe and out of sight.

Under the cover of darkness, he was moved. Harvath went along to help keep him calm and had stayed for a couple of days just to make sure everything was running smoothly.

Carlton was delighted at being at the house he recognized from his youth. He didn't like that the décor had been changed, but he blamed his grandmother, who never seemed to be happy unless she was redecorating.

He didn't understand who the Corpsmen were or why they needed to be there. Harvath eventually gave up trying to explain.

It seemed to be enough for him. Though he couldn't afford to, Harvath stayed for one additional night. They grilled steaks, smoked cigars, and drank more bourbon than was healthy for either of them.

Not knowing how long his upcoming assignment would keep him overseas, Harvath wanted to squeeze every good moment out of the visit that he could.

The next morning, when it came time to leave, he embraced his mentor and held him for longer than he ever had. The Old Man seemed to know something serious was going on—that one of them might not be seeing the other again—and he, in return, held the embrace.

When they released, Carlton placed his hands atop Harvath's shoulders, looked him in the eyes, and said, "You've been a good son."

Then, the Old Man turned and walked back into the cottage. Had one of the Corpsmen not been close by to witness it, Ryan would likely never have heard that part of the story. It wasn't the kind of thing she could imagine Harvath sharing.

Having ducked college for a career as a freestyle skier, Harvath had barely been on speaking terms with his actual father. If not for his mother, they wouldn't have communicated at all. The death of his father, a Navy SEAL instructor, brought Harvath's world crashing down.

From what Ryan had gleaned from the people who knew Harvath best, something inside him at that moment had either clicked, or snapped.

Scot had lost his appetite for professional athletics. Quitting the U.S. Ski Team, he attended college and then followed in his father's footsteps by joining the Navy and becoming an even more accomplished SEAL than his dad had been.

It was almost two months ago that Harvath and the Old Man had embraced outside the New Hampshire cottage, and much had happened since. People were asking questions. Carlton's name was coming up in more and more conversations. It wasn't safe for him. So Ryan had made the decision to put the next phase of Harvath's plan into action.

CHAPTER 6

E ven if they could have gotten a fire crew into the woods and to the cabin, it was a lost cause. A forensics team would be left to sift through ashes. There wasn't much hope of finding anything.

Harvath and Jasinski returned to the injured Norwegians and did what they could for them.

When reinforcements arrived, Harvath slipped away. He had several loose ends to tie up before he took off. A car was waiting for him just beyond the first-responder vehicles. It was a half hour before Jasinki realized he was gone. It was an additional forty-five minutes before she was able to get her own ride back to Værnes.

Værnes Air Station belonged to the Norwegian Royal Air Force. One of its biggest users, though, was the United States Marine Corps.

As part of the Marines' Preposition Program, massive amounts of U.S. military equipment entered Norway via Værnes. From there, it was stashed in top-secret caves throughout the region in case a NATO member was ever invaded and the organization was called to war. Preventing an attack on those caves was what tonight's raid on the cabin had all been about. The equipment inside was a highly strategic stockpile. Had it been destroyed, it would have been a critical blow to an alliance that had come so far and had been so successful.

Created in the aftermath of World War II, the North Atlantic Treaty Organization had originally comprised Belgium, Canada, Denmark, France, Iceland, Italy, Luxembourg, the Netherlands, Norway, Portugal, the United Kingdom, and the United States.

It then went on to add Greece, Turkey, Germany, Spain, the Czech Republic, Hungary, Poland, Bulgaria, Estonia, Latvia, Lithuania, Romania, Slovakia, Albania, Slovenia, Croatia, and Montenegro.

It had been formed as a means of collective defense in the hope of discouraging war. Article 5 of its treaty stated that an attack on one member was an attack on all. No matter who the aggressor, member nations were obligated to come to the aid of their fellows.

Only once in NATO's history had Article 5 ever been invoked. In the wake of 9/11, the nations of NATO had joined together and gone to war in Afghanistan.

But while the September 11 attacks had demonstrated the asymmetric threat of Islamic terrorism, another threat—one far greater and far more powerful—was looming on the horizon.

As it had done in Crimea, Russia planned to take back all of its former territory. It was going to continue with the Baltic nations of Lithuania, Latvia, and Estonia. There was only one thing standing in Russia's way—the North Atlantic Treaty Organization. But ever the tacticians, Moscow had already formulated a plan to break NATO.

Harvath, though, had developed a plan as well. The United States didn't intend to be drawn into another world war in Europe. It also didn't intend to let the greatest military alliance in history be dissolved. No matter what the cost, Harvath couldn't allow the Russians to succeed.

He had been set up in an officer's quarters on the north side of the airfield in the Værnes Garrison. It smelled like stale carpet and looked as if it had been furnished for a hundred bucks spent at a local IKEA store.

He could hear Monika Jasinski coming down the hallway. Tucking his phone into his back pocket, he walked over and opened the door.

She confronted him right away. "The Norwegians are looking for you. They want to chat about the dead guy. Might have been a good idea to check in with someone before leaving the scene."

Before he could reply, she continued on. "Would you care to explain to me what happened out there? We were specifically told that we couldn't carry weapons here. How was it that you had a pistol?"

"You're welcome," he said.

His response took her by surprise. "For what?"

Fingering the rip in her parka where the shrapnel had just missed her neck, he replied, "For saving your life."

Color rose to her cheeks. He couldn't tell if she was embarrassed or growing angrier.

Turning her head away, she murmured, "Thank you."

He stood back so she could enter.

At a small table sat a gray-haired man with a thin mustache. He wore a dark turtleneck and gray trousers. A pillar of blue smoke rose from the cigarette in the ashtray in front of him.

Jasinski looked at him. "Who's this?"

Using the heel of his boot to shut the door, Harvath introduced her. "Monika Jasinski, meet Carl Pedersen. Carl is NIS. Norwegian Intelligence Service"

"I know what NIS is," she responded, confused as to what the man was doing there.

Pedersen rose and they shook hands. "Scot tells me you're with Polish Military Intelligence. Currently billeted at NATO?"

Jasinski nodded. "The terrorism intelligence cell. I don't understand. What does any of this have to do with Norway's *foreign* intelligence service?"

"Carl is our liaison," said Harvath.

"No, he isn't. This is a NATO investigation. We liaise with our local counterparts."

"Your English is remarkable," Pedersen interjected, changing the subject. "Barely any hint of an accent."

"I'm Polish, but was raised in Chicago. We moved back to Krakow when I was twelve." Noticing a pile of cell phones stacked nearby, she then asked, "Where did those come from? Please don't say they're from the dead guy who fled the cabin."

"I told you she was smart," said Harvath as he walked over to the table, picked up a bottle of aquavit, and grabbed one of the shot glasses for her.

"I'm not thirsty," she insisted.

"Drink," Pedersen urged. "You'll feel better."

"Excuse me, NIS, but you don't have the slightest idea how I—"

Harvath handed her the glass, pulled the cork from the bottle, and filled it. "It wasn't our fault," he said. "The Norwegian police had already decided they were going to go in. They had all the cell members in one place. Our being here had no impact on their decision."

Jasinski leaned against the wall, closed her eyes, and exhaled. "They got slaughtered. It was like a war zone. The Norwegians should have been warned."

"We were," Pedersen admitted.

She didn't believe him. "By whom?"

"By me," replied Harvath.

"You? I don't understand. I was told we couldn't discuss the other attacks. What's going on?"

Setting the bottle back on the table, Harvath pulled out a chair and gestured for her to sit.

CHAPTER 7

There were a lot of things he wanted to tell her—such as who he really worked for, why he had been sent, and why he had chosen her for this assignment—but he couldn't, not yet.

He had studied her file backward and forward. She had come highly recommended and he knew practically everything about her.

Monika Amelia Jasinski. Thirty-one years old. Five-foot-seven. Blonde hair, wide hazel, almost doelike eyes. Her father had been attached to the Polish Trade Commission in Chicago. After high school in Krakow, she had attended Poland's National Defense University. From there, she entered the Polish Army where she distinguished herself in military intelligence with multiple tours in Iraq and Afghanistan.

When NATO stood up its new Joint Intelligence and Security Division at Supreme Headquarters Allied Powers Europe, or SHAPE, she was tapped for a key position as an investigator in its terrorism intelligence cell. She had more than proven herself worthy.

"What's this all about?" she asked as Harvath topped off his glass, as well as Pedersen's.

"You were right," he replied.

"About what?"

"About all of it. Three attacks. Three dead diplomats. A sniper in Portugal, a car bomb in Spain, a shooter on a motorcycle in Greece. They're all connected to a larger plot. And now we add Norway."

Jasinski took a sip of the strong liquor. It was rewarding to hear someone reaffirm that she had correctly connected the dots. But by the same token, she still had no idea who Harvath was really working for.

They had met on a tarmac less than twelve hours ago. Allegedly, he had been sent by the NATO command based in the United States. The Supreme Allied Command Transformation, or SACT, was headquartered in Norfolk, Virginia. Its job was to come up with new, revolutionary concepts to keep NATO on the cutting edge.

As far as she was concerned, SACT was simply a glorified think tank. And sitting there in his jeans and T-shirt, Harvath didn't strike her as the think tank type. He didn't look like someone who sat behind a desk all day. He was too fit.

He looked like someone used to being challenged physically. There was a steeliness to him, a seriousness. He was someone who had seen bad things, and who had probably done his share of them as well.

He was also a bit too handsome. He had strong, masculine features, but she couldn't get over the intensity of his deep blue eyes.

It was shallow of her, she knew, but this wasn't the kind of man who toiled away at a place like SACT. She'd be willing to bet her career on it.

Also bothering her was that in the short time since they had met, not only had he smuggled a weapon into a foreign country, violated the chain of command, killed one of the operation's targets, and stolen evidence, but he was holding out on her. There was something he wasn't telling her. She was certain of it.

Her face must have given away her thoughts because Harvath looked at her and asked, "What's wrong?"

She shook her head. "You're not here because I was right in connecting the previous attacks to a larger picture."

"I'm not?"

"No. You're here because the United States now has skin in this game. Those other attacks weren't personal. But once this terror group decided to blow up caves full of American military equipment, suddenly it's *game on* and here you are."

He liked her instincts. They were on the money. But there was still a lot she didn't know. "Trust me," he offered. "You and I are both on the same side."

"Really? And what side is that?"

"We both want this group stopped."

Pointing at the stack of cell phones, she stated, "I think you and I have very different ideas about how best to do that."

"Right now? Maybe. But let me ask you something. Do you want to win?"

"What?"

"You heard me," he said. "Do you want to win? It's a simple question."

What was with this guy? "Of course I do," she replied. "I didn't come here to lose."

"Good. If we're going to win, though, we have to get creative together."

"*We?* I don't even know who you work for, or why I got stuck with you."

"I'm the guy who's going to help you win."

She looked at him. "Help me how? By stealing evidence? Killing suspects?"

"Monika, the enemy we're facing doesn't follow a rulebook. If we want to win, we have to do the same."

"Something tells me the Norwegians might not see it your way."

Harvath glanced at Pedersen. "Am I going to have any problems with Norway?"

Pedersen extended his hand and made the sign of the cross. "You're absolved."

Jasinski stared at both of them. "Somebody needs to explain to me what the hell is going on."

"What's going on is us getting one step ahead."

"One step ahead of who? Everyone from that cabin is dead."

Harvath set his glass down. "I'm not talking about them. I'm talking about the people behind them. The people who ultimately planned and coordinated the attacks that killed a NATO diplomat in Portugal, another in Spain, and a third in Greece."

"Are you talking about some sort of leadership structure?"

Slowly, he nodded.

"Do you know who they are?" she asked. "Or even where they are?"

"We're working on it."

"So what's the plan? Shoot and steal our way across Europe until we find them?"

"Would that be a problem?"

"What it would *be*," she replied, "is illegal."

"You let me worry about what's illegal," said Harvath. She shook her head.

"What?"

"I don't even know who you really work for," she responded.

"I told you," he began, repeating his cover story. "I'm a consultant—"

"Mysteriously sent from NATO's strategic command back in the United States. Even if I did believe that, there's just one problem."

"What's that?"

"I don't like mysteries."

He looked at her. "Let's be clear. You volunteered to come along."

Jasinski laughed. "When the Supreme Allied Commander personally calls you into his office and offers you an assignment, you take it. *Any* assignment."

"I can ask him to find me somebody else."

"Someone as up to speed as I am? Good luck. You'd be starting from square one. I bring more to this than anyone else at SHAPE."

She was correct, in more ways than she realized.

"So then are you in?" he asked.

Moments passed. He was calling her bluff.

"I'm in," she finally replied. "But understand something. The only things I like less than mysteries are surprises."

Harvath smiled. He didn't like surprises either, but unfortunately, there were many more in store—for both of them.

CHAPTER 8

The thieves worked quickly, but carefully. Wearing baseball caps and dark clothing, they expertly hid their faces from the closed-circuit television cameras.

Once the merchandise they had stolen from the truck had been transferred to their van, they exited the parking lot and made their getaway.

As far as they could tell, no one had seen them—not even the American soldiers whom they had just robbed. Even so, it only took one person to call in a report to the police. They had to be extra cautious.

In order to avoid authorities, the thieves had decided to stay off the main motorway. They used rural back roads. It took longer, but it was safer. If they were caught, it would cause a major international incident.

The theft of American military equipment on Polish soil would be extremely embarrassing for Poland, especially because this wasn't the first time it had happened. In advance of a joint readiness drill in the fall, night-vision goggles and other assorted gear worth more than $50,000 U.S. had been nicked from a cargo container at the port of Gdansk.

This time, though, the cargo was much more sophisticated and the implications for the region much more serious. Mere mention of what the U.S. soldiers were allegedly transporting had the potential to destabilize the entire region. The case could even be made that it had the potential to upend the entire geopolitical order.

The team that had been sent in to commit the robbery, though, couldn't occupy themselves with the big picture. Not now. They had to focus on transporting the cargo to a predetermined location without encountering any members of law enforcement or the military. Something much easier said than done, especially in Poland where cops had a habit of popping up in the most unusual of places, at the worst of times, and often with a keen interest in anyone and everyone, no matter how benign they might appear.

While this was likely due in part to the healthy suspicion endemic in all law enforcement agencies, it was Poland. Only thirty years earlier, it had still been under the yoke of the Soviet police state. Suspicion was woven into the DNA of entire generations of Poles. Patrol officers back then were police academy instructors and even agency commanders now. Echoes of the old days still reverberated across the country.

Not wanting to leave a trail of digital breadcrumbs as they passed from one cell tower to another, the thieves had disassembled their phones and placed them in a signal-blocking pouch. Similarly, they had chosen an older vehicle and had not employed a GPS unit to assist them in their navigation. They had gone "pre-tech." While the driver drove, the passenger navigated using a red-lensed flashlight and a detailed paper map.

With practiced military experience, the passenger called out upcoming turns and forks in the road, then repeated them for certainty. The driver parroted each direction back.

It took several hours to get to the drop-off location. Once they arrived, the passenger removed a semiautomatic WIST-94 pistol, conducted a press check to confirm a round was chambered, and exited the van.

The night air was cold. The sky was clear and crowded with stars. They were in the countryside. The chilly breeze brought with it the scent of livestock.

After taking a quick look around, the passenger reappeared, and flung open the doors to an old, decrepit barn. The driver advanced the van inside. Waiting for them was a silver Škoda Kodiaq SUV.

After wiping down the van for fingerprints, the driver and passenger unloaded the crates they had stolen from the American soldiers.

The Škoda, seats already folded down, was ready to receive the cargo. As they emptied each crate, they cast it aside.

Once everything was loaded, they covered it with blankets, and the driver pulled the SUV forward, out of the barn. Closing the heavy wooden doors behind him, the passenger got into the vehicle.

"Ready?" the driver asked.

The passenger nodded and, pulling up the onboard GPS, plotted their course for Belarus.

CHAPTER 9

Oleg Tretyakov's cell phone woke him from a sound sleep. Even in the dark, he knew which one it was. He could tell by the ringtone.

Only a handful of people had the number. But no matter who it was, they had bad news. There was no other reason to be calling that phone at this hour. Reaching over, he depressed the power button, thereby declining the call. Instantly, the phone fell silent.

He picked up his watch and looked at the time. It felt as if he had just gone to sleep.

Throwing back the duvet, he got out of bed. The apartment was cold. He put on his robe, picked up his laptop, and headed for the kitchen.

The timer on the coffee machine had been set for 5:00 a.m. Overriding it, he began the brewing now. He wouldn't be able to fall back to sleep. And whatever problem had required waking him in the middle of the night, he wanted to be as sharp as possible for it.

As the coffee machine gurgled to life, he pulled out a stool, sat down, and powered up his computer.

Russia had the largest Internet population in Europe and the sixth largest in the world. With over 109 million users, monitoring people's every keystroke was virtually impossible. To ferret out dissidents and spot potential trouble, the Russian government used highly sophisticated algorithms to monitor its citizens. The algorithms searched for thousands upon thousands of keywords and phrases. But despite their sophistication, a lot of traffic was swept up that posed no threat to the Russian state.

A colonel in Russia's vaunted military intelligence unit, the GRU, he knew how to mask his Internet usage. He didn't have anything to hide from his own government, but operational security was of paramount importance in his business. Spies within the Russian security apparatus were always a possibility, as were hostile foreign nations hacking from the outside.

Via an anonymous portal controlled by his headquarters near Moscow, he logged on to one of his dummy social media accounts. From there, he leapfrogged over to a benign photographer's profile, scrolled back through the correct number of posts, and "liked" an obscure photo. With that, his contact would know that he had received the phone call and was online.

Tretyakov stroked the manicured beard that covered his lean face. He had prominent cheekbones, dark receding hair, and dark brown, almost black eyes—gifts from his ancestors who had migrated from the Kalmyk Steppe.

Though he stood six-feet tall, people sometimes said he bore a similarity to the much shorter Vladimir Lenin—also of Kalmyk descent.

Lenin had died at fifty-three. Tretyakov was now fifty-two and had no plans to follow the great revolutionary leader and founder of the Soviet Union in an untimely demise. He had many more years of useful service to render to his country.

Throughout his career he'd been an adept recruiter and runner of spies, but he had made his true mark in the realm of subversion, sabotage, and special operations.

The son of an accomplished father who had taught applied mathematics at Moscow State University and a mother who had taught piano at the Moscow Conservatory, he had been a child prodigy. He was skilled in both mathematics and music, but had had no desire to follow either path.

When "spotted" by a university professor paid to be on the lookout for potential GRU recruits, he had jumped at the chance. The idea of being of value to the powerful Russian military appealed to him. Being recruited to work with their famed intelligence unit was beyond any dream he had ever had for himself.

He had visions of fast cars, beautiful women, and James Bond style assignments. The reality couldn't have been any more different.

His training had been brutal. Not only was it physically demanding, it was also psychologically merciless. The instructors were sadists who took pleasure in abusing the cadets. One cadet ended up hanging himself in the barracks shower and it was Tretyakov who found him.

He had never seen a dead body before and stood there for several minutes staring at it—the tongue protruding, purplish-black, from between blue lips, a bloody froth oozing from the nostrils, and saliva dripping from the mouth. The cadet's member was erect and his trousers had been soiled. The sight should have repulsed him, but it didn't.

He felt a mixture of fascination and contempt. The cadet had not only been defeated, but had allowed himself to be defeated to such an extent that he had willingly given up his own life as a result.

Tretyakov first respected, and then grew to covet that kind of power over another human being. The pursuit of it propelled him upward through the ranks of the GRU. With each new promotion and each new posting, he accumulated more. It was like a drug—the more he tasted, the more he wanted.

Now, as the GRU Chief of Covert Operations for Eastern Europe, Tretyakov was at the pinnacle of his career, and his power.

That made the middle-of-the-night call all the more disturbing. *Transept* was the most important assignment he had ever been entrusted with. If it failed, at best his career would be over. He didn't want to think about what might happen at worst. There were only two things of which he was certain. If he failed he would not only get the blame, but would also not be around to argue in his own defense. The GRU, like the KGB's successor the FSB, had a way of permanently "distancing" its mistakes.

Tretyakov didn't want to be a mistake. He believed in his mission. He was its author and wanted it to be a success. It was why he had taken such painstaking care over every detail—no matter how small. He knew how easily things could go bad.

Pouring a cup of coffee, he waited a few more moments and then entered the encrypted chat room. Though he was concerned, he wanted to maintain the appearance of confidence and control. Showing up too quickly might suggest that he was worried.

His contact was already there, and Tretyakov had been right. The news was bad—*very* bad. The Norwegian cell had been eliminated. *All of them.*

The news was devastating and would not be received well in Moscow. He needed to figure out what had happened, and then what to do about it.

At the very least, the remaining cells needed to be put on notice. There could be no mistakes, not one. The fate of the entire operation was in their hands.

CHAPTER 10

The "consultations chamber" was a smaller, less opulent meeting room than the one most people saw on television. It had a narrow, U-shaped table in the center and glass windows running down the walls, behind which headset-wearing interpreters sat and carried out their duties.

The fifteen-member Security Council was having a heated discussion about the drafting of a joint statement. A series of mass graves had recently been discovered in Syria. Russia wanted to go easy on the response. U.S. Ambassador Rebecca Strum, a tall, tough, brunette in her late forties wasn't having any of it.

"The United States will not agree to soften the language," she said in reply to the Russian request. "Absolutely not."

The Russian envoy put on his most charming smile. "Surely words matter to the United States."

"*Truth* matters to the United States."

"Perhaps," offered the French Ambassador, "we can change some of the words without changing the spirit of the statement. How does that sound?"

"It sounds like more game playing to me," Strum answered. "The Syrian regime must be held to account. Along with men, those graves were filled with women and children. The United States intends to paint this atrocity in the most vivid terms possible. The world must know."

The Chinese envoy threw up his hands. "We will be here all day. Let us finish this statement and get on with our other business already."

She looked at him and quipped, "It is so unusual to see the Chinese Ambassador agreeing with the Russian Ambassador, especially when it comes to Syria."

The diplomat bristled at the remark, but let it slide. He had tangled with Strum before and it hadn't gone well. She was like a bear in a pit. If you climbed in with her, you might make it back out, but not without suffering tremendous damage.

He had fulfilled his promise to his colleague. He had said his piece. It was up to the Russian envoy to convince the Americans to change the language.

Still smiling, the Russian tried once more. "We don't yet know, with complete certitude, who was responsible for these deaths. This is all the more reason for us to carefully craft our response."

Strum was about to respond when one of her aides stepped up behind her and whispered something in her ear. Gathering her things, she stood.

"Where are you going?" the Russian Ambassador asked.

The U.S. Ambassador motioned for her deputy to take her seat.

"Ladies and gentlemen, please excuse me. I will be back as soon as I can. Thank you."

Turning, Strum headed for the door and exited the consultations chamber alone.

Down the hall was a café known as the UN Delegates Lounge. Here, United Nations diplomats and staff could meet and chat casually over coffee. The Americans, French, and British had nicknamed it the Russian Café for the "secret" bottle of vodka kept under the bar. Throughout the day, members of the Russian delegation would pop in, speakeasy style, to fill nondescript containers with the spirit before rejoining the current meeting or proceeding to their next.

Off to the side, she saw the people she was looking for. Seated at the table were the Ambassadors for Lithuania, Latvia, and Estonia. All three stood as she approached.

"Thank you. Please sit," said Strum as she joined them. "I have bad news. And none of you are going to like it."

Across the room was Russia's Deputy Permanent Representative to the UN for Political Affairs. He was within sight, but out of earshot. As he sat sipping his morning "coffee," he couldn't help but notice the meeting.

Strum was doing most of the talking, but it was obvious that her tablemates were not happy. In fact, the Baltic Ambassadors looked deeply concerned. One was so angry that after jabbing his finger at her, he stood and stormed out of the lounge.

Something was afoot and he took careful mental notes. Any strife between NATO members was always of interest to Moscow. NATO was the only enemy Russia worked as hard to undermine as it did the United States.

He waited for the meeting to end and once it did, returned to his office and began typing up his notes. His superiors were going to have a very interesting report to send to Moscow.

CHAPTER 11

The five-star Ristorante La Perla in Georgetown was known for some of the best Italian cuisine in the city. In addition to being walking distance from Embassy Row, it was also open until almost midnight. It was the perfect spot for a clandestine dinner that wasn't supposed to appear clandestine.

As Lydia Ryan walked in, carrying a Brooks Brothers shopping bag, her guest was already waiting for her. He sat at a table in the back, facing the front. Knowing his commitment to tradecraft, she figured he had arrived at least twenty minutes early, checked everything out, and then, given his proclivity for alcohol, had begun drinking.

Artur Kopec worked under official cover at the Polish Embassy for the Agencja Wywiadu, Poland's foreign intelligence service. He had been at the spy game for decades, and he looked it.

His fair hair had gone white long ago. He carried a spare tire around his middle—the product of spending too much time behind a desk running spies, rather than just getting out and running. His red-rimmed eyes were milky with the onset of cataracts, likely sped up by a two-pack-a-day smoking habit. The end of his large nose was a sea of broken capillaries, brought on by his alcoholism.

He had high blood pressure, high cholesterol, and symptoms indicative of the onset of diabetes. He also had a doctor whom he paid handsomely to keep all his medical issues out of his file and off the radar screen of his superiors. What they didn't know wouldn't hurt them. He had plenty of years of service left in him.

The Pole watched as Ryan entered the restaurant. How such a tall, gorgeous woman had evaded marriage for so long, especially in a town like D.C., was a mystery to him. If he had been twenty years younger, he might have considered making a play for her. As it was, he was not only old enough to be her father, but he was dangerously close to grandfather territory. He stood to greet her.

"Hello, Artur," she said, smiling. "Thank you for meeting me."

"Of course," he replied, kissing her on both cheeks and then pulling out her chair. "It's been too long."

"I know. I've been busy. I'm sorry."

He returned a gentle smile as he sat down. "Completely understandable. How is he?"

Ryan sighed as she placed her napkin in her lap. "Not well."

"I was afraid of that. I tried to call him not too long ago. They told me he had been moved?"

"He's in hospice. According to the doctors, he has less than six months."

Kopec shook his head. "My God. Such a shame."

Ryan nodded solemnly.

"Did he ever tell you the story of how we first met?" he asked, a smile coming to his face as he tried to buoy her mood.

"He did," she replied. Leaning down, she removed a wrapped parcel from the shopping bag and handed it to him. "This is for you."

The Pole, who had just picked up his glass, looked at it for a moment and asked, "What is this?"

"Open it," Ryan encouraged.

Setting his glass down, he accepted the package and peeled away the brown paper.

It was a framed set of handwritten notes from one of the most dangerous operations Reed Carlton and Artur Kopec had ever undertaken together.

In the run-up to the first Gulf War, six American intelligence operatives sent to spy on Iraqi troop movements became trapped in Kuwait and Baghdad, and the U.S. had put out the call for help.

The United States asked for assistance from multiple countries, including Great Britain, France, and even the Soviet Union. Only Poland had stepped up and agreed to help get the Americans out.

The operation was dubbed Operation Simoom. And Carlton and Kopec were sent in to coordinate everything that would take place on the ground.

Because of Poland's extensive construction and engineering contracts in the region, it was uniquely positioned to help smuggle the Americans out.

All six were issued Polish passports and then integrated into various construction camps and work groups. Somehow, though, Iraq Intelligence had caught wind that something was going on with the Poles and the Americans.

There were many dramatic twists and turns. The operation almost collapsed multiple times. Even as they attempted to sneak the Americans over the border, they encountered an Iraqi checkpoint where one of the officers, who had spent time in Poland and spoke Polish, wanted to interrogate the Americans.

It seemed that no matter what the Old Man and Kopec did, the deck was stacked against them. Yet they never gave up.

Not only did they get the six intelligence operatives out safely, but the Americans brought with them secret maps and detailed notes critical to the planning of Operation Desert Storm.

One of those critical pieces of intelligence was what Kopec now held, framed, in his hands. A small, engraved plaque centered in the bottom of the frame gave the date and location of that final border crossing.

It was representative of the kinds of gifts that often passed between teammates and allies.

As soon as Kopec realized what he was looking at, he smiled.

"I thought you would appreciate it," said Ryan. "And I know he would have wanted you to have it."

"Thank you. Where did you find it?"

"Since he was moved to hospice, I've been going through all his personal papers."

"It was lovely of you to frame this for me," said Kopec, as he waved the waitress over. "But something tells me this isn't why you wanted to see me."

Ryan hesitated for a moment, visibly struggling to find the right words. Finally, she said, "I don't know how else to put this. We have a problem. I need your help."

CHAPTER 12

By *we*, do you mean you and Reed?" asked Kopec after the waitress had left their table with their order.

Ryan shook her head. "I'm talking about the United States."

"Whatever you need, consider it done."

"It's not a small problem."

Once more, the Pole smiled. "In our line of work, it never is."

"Artur, on behalf of the United States, we need your help, but we can't involve the Polish government."

"Now things are getting interesting. Why don't you tell me what it is we're talking about."

"As part of our NATO partnership, the United States has been prepositioning certain military equipment in Central Europe."

"Tanks, Humvees, and other items. We know this. What's the problem?"

Ryan took a deep breath. "There are some things we've been storing that you *don't* know about."

"Such as?"

"I'm not at liberty to say."

The Pole laughed. "I can't help you, Lydia, if I don't know what it is you need."

"Yesterday, a U.S. Army transport was robbed in Poland."

"*Robbed?* In Poland? What are you talking about? Where?"

"Just outside Warsaw," said Ryan. "The soldiers had been traveling from their base in Żagań in western Poland and had pulled off at a truck stop for a break."

"And?" asked Kopec.

"The lot was crowded and they didn't park line of sight. They thought their trucks would be safe. But while they were inside, one of the vehicles was broken into and a theft occurred."

They paused as the waitress brought Kopec another vodka and Ryan a glass of Sancerre.

"What was taken?" he asked after the waitress had left.

"Six crates."

"Six crates of what?"

Ryan demurred.

When she failed to answer his question, he asked, "Am I supposed to guess?"

"For the record, the soldiers had no idea what they were transporting. The crates had been purposely mislabeled and the paperwork altered."

Kopec took a sip of his drink and leaned forward. "Now you absolutely have my attention."

"The equipment in question never should have been delivered to Poland. Somebody screwed up."

"What are we talking about?"

Again, Ryan hesitated.

"Lydia, ask any of my ex-wives. I'm a terrible mind reader."

"Upgrade kits for BGM-109G missiles."

Kopec laughed—quietly at first, and then his laugh

grew louder. Ryan looked around, concerned that he was drawing attention.

Catching his breath, the Polish intel officer shook his head. Also known as the Gryphon, the BGM-109G was an American ground-launched cruise missile capable of carrying multiple types of warheads—including nuclear. It had long been outlawed under the Intermediate-Range Nuclear Forces treaty with the Russians.

"What you're saying is impossible," he chuckled. "There aren't any Gryphons in Europe. There aren't even any Gryphons in America. They were all destroyed under the terms of the INF treaty."

After another look around the restaurant, Ryan leaned forward. "No, they weren't."

Kopec was shocked by her admission. "Do you realize what you're saying?"

It was a rhetorical question. She didn't need to answer.

"How many of them are in Europe?" he asked.

"I can't discuss that."

"Fine. Let's back up. Are there any in Poland?"

She shook her head. "No."

"The ones that are in Europe, where are they located?"

"Artur, you know I can't discuss that either."

Kopec laughed once more. "If you want my help, you have to work with me, Lydia. How about this? How many trucks were there?"

She took a sip of her wine, using the time to weigh what she should tell him. "Three," she replied.

"Now we're getting somewhere. What was their destination? Where exactly were they headed?"

Reluctantly, she divulged the information. "The Baltics."

"Can you be more precise?"

"Deliveries were scheduled for Lithuania, Latvia, and Estonia."

The Pole let out a slow, slightly boozy whistle. "If the Russians find out, they're going to lose their minds."

"We obviously don't want that to happen. The missiles are simply an insurance policy."

"Insurance against what?"

"Russian incursion."

"Incursion where?"

"Anywhere under NATO protection. If push comes to shove, we won't hesitate to use Gryphons."

"Is there something going on that I don't know about?" Kopec asked, concerned. "Is the United States or NATO anticipating some sort of hostile action by Russia?"

"Concern is running very high—the highest it has been since the Cold War. And Russia hasn't exactly been doing anything to lower that concern."

"What do you mean?"

Ryan rolled her eyes and took another sip of wine. "So many provocative acts. How much time do you have?"

"As much time as you need," the Pole replied. He wasn't kidding. In fact, his tone was dead serious.

In no particular order, Ryan went down the list. "The annexation of Crimea, continued military operations in eastern Ukraine, repeated violations of U.S. and NATO airspace, the use of a nerve agent to assassinate a former Russian intelligence operative on U.K. soil, and the buildup of Russian troops and equipment in its western district, as well as in Russia's client state of Belarus— both of which are right on NATO's doorstep."

"We've been monitoring it, too," said Kopec. "Russia,

though, claims they're simply prepositioning in advance of a new war-gaming exercise."

"A previously *unscheduled* war-gaming exercise."

The Pole shrugged. "They're a sovereign nation. They can schedule snap military exercises. They have done it before. It doesn't necessarily mean they're preparing for an invasion."

"Is that what Poland believes?"

"Poland's position is Ronald Reagan's famous position—trust, but verify."

"Well, any trust Russia may have enjoyed with the United States has been swept away by their own actions. The current position of American intelligence, unfortunately, is to distrust first and work tirelessly to verify."

"That's not only unfortunate, but it's extremely dangerous," said Kopec. "In such an unstable climate, there's less margin for error. War becomes much more possible."

"I agree," she replied. "I wish it weren't so, but that is where we are."

"So, back to the business at hand," he said, pinching the bridge of his nose. "If you cannot discuss how many missiles there are, let's talk about the number of road-mobile launchers."

Ryan shook her head. "I cannot comment on that either."

Kopec understood that she was limited in what she could divulge. The key lay in coming up with the right questions. "What about warheads? Are any of them nuclear-tipped?"

Once again, the look on her face said it all. *Jackpot.*

"Jesus, Lydia," he muttered. "No wonder you don't want my government involved. What kind of yield are we talking about?"

"I can't go into detail."

"I'm going to need *something*. Are they strategic or tactical? How about that?"

She was slow to answer. They were on very dangerous ground.

"From what I understand," said Ryan, "they're tactical. Low-yield if that makes any difference or makes you feel any better."

"Not really." Kopec knew that the presence of smaller, low-yield "battlefield" nukes only meant they were more likely to get used. And once tactical nukes were in play, the larger, much more devastating strategic nukes were only a step away.

"Artur, if this gets out, understand that the United States is going to deny any knowledge."

"They can deny it all they want, but if even one of your upgrade kits turns up on Polish television or in one of our newspapers, you'll be in a bad spot."

"Which is why I'm asking for your help," she replied. "The car park where the robbery took place has CCTV cameras. Do you have people back in Poland you trust? Someone you can put on this?"

The man thought for a moment and then nodded.

Pressing forward with the toe of her beige pump, she slid the blue and gold Brooks Brothers bag nearer to Kopec. "I think I got your size right. You can keep the shirt. The file's underneath."

"What about expenses? I may need to spread some money around."

"How much?"

"Ten thousand for starters. If this is some low-level criminal operation stealing from parked cars, I may not even need it."

"And if it's something else?"

"I may need more. Possibly a lot more."

She understood. "You'll provide me with an account?"

Kopec removed a tiny pen and a small pad of paper from his jacket pocket. Writing down a bank name and a series of numbers, he tore off the page, folded it in half, and slid it across the table.

With that part of their business—for the moment—complete, he turned back to the subject of Lydia's boss. Raising his glass, he offered a toast. "To Reed Carlton. A fine intelligence officer and an even finer gentleman."

They clinked glasses and drank. A silence then fell over the table. An accomplished intelligence officer herself, Ryan knew better than to move to fill it.

Eventually, it was Kopec who spoke. "I'd like to see him; spend some time with him, before he passes."

She had expected the request. In fact, she had rehearsed her response. Even so, she spoke her next words carefully.

If the Polish spy-runner sensed anything was off, it would be the end of everything.

CHAPTER 13

Harvath and his team had set up shop in a semi-restored, seventeenth-century fortified "chateau." It didn't look much like a chateau to him. It looked more like an elongated, three-story farmhouse, surrounded by a high stone wall.

The property was at the end of a gravel road in the Belgian countryside, halfway between the Brussels South Airport in Charleroi and NATO's Supreme Headquarters Allied Powers Europe (SHAPE) in Mons.

"What is this place?" Jasinski asked as they approached.

"It's a rental," said Harvath. "Belongs to a Belgian businessman. He was transferred to Thailand with his family. We found it online."

As their car neared the gates, two serious-looking men materialized on the other side. After confirming the driver was Harvath, they unfastened the lock and opened the gates so the vehicle could enter.

Though they were wearing jackets, Jasinski had no doubt they were armed. Both had earpieces.

"Pool boy and the gardener?" she asked.

Harvath smiled as he drove forward into the motor court and parked.

Getting out of the car, he introduced the two men.

"Monika Jasinski, I'd like you to meet Jack Gage and Matt Morrison."

Gage, who looked to be in his forties, was an enormous man. He stood six-foot-three with a thick, dark beard and had a wad of chewing tobacco in his mouth.

Morrison was a few inches shorter and several years younger. He looked to be in his early thirties and stood about five-foot-eleven. He offered his hand first and Monika shook it, followed by Gage's. When he extended his hand, she could see a paperback novel tucked inside his coat.

"What are you reading?" she asked.

"*The Terminal List*. It's a thriller by a guy named Jack Carr," Gage answered.

"Any good?"

"Considering the author is a former SEAL and can even string his sentences together, it's amazing."

Out of the corner of her eye, Monika saw Harvath raise his middle finger and use it to massage his left temple. There appeared to be a little interservice rivalry going on here.

"Let me guess," she said. "You're Army?"

Gage nodded. "Was. Fifth Special Forces Group."

"Which makes the fact that *he* can read even more amazing," jibed Morrison.

That got a laugh out of Jasinski. "And you?" she asked.

"United States Marine Corps," he replied with an Alabama drawl. "Recon."

"Where the motto is," said Gage, "when you can't dazzle them with brilliance, just riddle them with bullets."

Jasinski laughed again.

"You don't have to laugh," Harvath deadpanned, though it was pleasant to see her smile for the first time. "Their jokes aren't that good."

In unison, both Gage and Morrison raised a middle finger and began massaging their temples.

Harvath shook his head. "Are you two joining us for lunch?"

"We couldn't get a reservation," replied Morrison.

"Sorry to hear that."

"Don't be," offered Gage. "Your chef's a little too temperamental for my taste."

Harvath shook his head once more as he led Jasinski away from the car.

In addition to the main structure, there was a garage and a small stone guesthouse. She was studying its tiny windows when the door opened and an equally tiny man, accompanied by two enormous white dogs, stepped out.

"Who's that?"

"That's my secret weapon," said Harvath. "Come on. I'll introduce you."

The moment the two dogs saw Harvath, they began wagging their tails. They never left the little man's side, though, until he whispered some sort of a command and they raced forward.

"Five minutes or five months," stated Harvath, scratching them behind the ears. "It's always the same welcome."

"I'm beginning to believe they like you more than me," said the little man, as his small boots crunched across the gravel motor court.

He couldn't have been more than three feet tall. His salt-and-pepper hair was long enough to be swept back behind his ears. He had a neatly trimmed beard and wore jeans and an Irish fisherman's sweater.

"Nicholas," he offered, sticking his hand up so she could shake it.

"Pleased to meet you," replied Jasinski, bending down. "I'm Monika."

"Are you hungry, Monika?"

"I am."

"Good, because lunch is ready. Let's go inside."

When Harvath had called her for lunch, this wasn't what she had expected. They had each left Norway the same way they had arrived—separately. NATO had arranged for her to hop a ride on a military transport. Harvath had remained behind for a day with Carl Pedersen. He wanted to see what, if anything, the Norwegian forensics team pulled from the ashes of the cabin. It turned out to be a bust.

As Harvath was a special consultant to SHAPE, Jasinski had assumed he and anyone working with him would have been issued offices on the Mons campus. Stepping into the guesthouse, she realized *these* were his offices.

The building had low ceilings with exposed timber beams. Taped to the plaster walls were countless maps, photographs, and computer-printed documents. There was a large whiteboard with notes in multiple colors of dry-erase marker. Makeshift desks held rugged laptops or keyboards and large monitors. In the corner stood a rack of hard drives. Multiple muted, flat-panel television sets were tuned to different twenty-four-hour news channels.

This wasn't a domicile. It was a control center. And at that moment, she knew her hunch was correct about who the little man was.

The Troll was infamous in intelligence circles. He was a purveyor of highly sensitive, often classified information. He bought it, sold it, traded it, and stole it. He had an amazing list of clients around the world and an equally amazing list of enemies. The intel he trafficked in had been used to disrupt covert operations, blackmail politicians, and bring down governments.

"You're the—" she began.

"Not anymore," he replied, cutting her off as he climbed onto a stepstool to reach the stove in the open kitchen—the smells from which were delicious. "Now, I'm just Nicholas."

She noticed he spoke English with a slight accent. "You're working with the Americans?"

"I *am* an American," he beamed. "Recently minted."

"I give up," she said. "I don't understand any of this."

"Don't worry," said Nicholas as he lifted the lids off several pots and pans and began plating their lunch. "It will eventually make sense."

"Or it won't," said Harvath as he examined a new photograph that had been added to the wall.

Jasinski lowered her voice. "Is he always like that?"

"Like what?"

"Such an asshole."

The little man smiled. "He's just testing you."

"For what?"

"He doesn't like people who blindly follow orders. He wants you to think for yourself, to think outside the box. Don't worry, he's a Teddy bear."

"I heard that," Harvath replied from the living room.

The little man smiled at her and, nodding at the plates, asked for her help in carrying everything out to the table.

He then encouraged Harvath and Jasinski to sit, while he fished a bottle of white Burgundy out of the fridge.

"I actually found a very nice 2014," he said, bringing the bottle over and handing it to Harvath, along with a corkscrew.

Harvath looked at his watch. As long as they didn't open a second, they'd be okay. It might also help to further take the edge off of Jasinski.

He had decided to read her in, and a lot of it was going to come as a shock.

CHAPTER 14

For a man of such small stature, Nicholas's appetites far outstripped his size. One of his most troubling predilections, at least from a security standpoint, had been Nicholas's appetite for women. Because of his primordial dwarfism, he had been accustomed to paying for sex. And not just any kind of sex.

As with his passion for food, the little man had been a gourmand in the realm of exotic sexual practices. The pool within which he could "fish" for the right professionals was quite limited. Eventually, one of his enemies had discovered the highly secretive service he employed. An assassin was dispatched and Nicholas had almost died.

Those days, though, were behind him. An intriguing woman named Nina had become a permanent fixture in his life. She understood not only who he now was, but also why.

Once his adversary, Scot Harvath had become Nicholas's friend. He had realized his talents and had given him an opportunity to go from an international fugitive to being one of the key players of his team. Even Reed Carlton, who had been highly suspicious, eventually grew to trust and respect him. In fact, it was Carlton who had convinced the President of the United States to pardon his past offenses and make him a citizen.

For the first time since his parents had abandoned him at a brothel, Nicholas had the one thing he had always wished for—people who cared for him and a semblance of an actual family.

As Harvath poured, the little man explained what he had prepared. The wine was from France, but everything else was classic Belgian. There was *tomate crevette*, ham and endive gratin, and *sole meunière*.

Before they dug in, Jasinski had a question. Ever since she had entered the guesthouse, music had been playing. It sounded familiar and she thought she recognized the artist. "Have we been listening to George Clinton and Parliament-Funkadelic this whole time?"

Nicholas looked at Harvath and grinned. "I like her. *A lot.*"

Both men were fans of funk music in general, and George Clinton and Parliament-Funkadelic in particular. The fact that Jasinski recognized what they were listening to said a lot about her. Good taste in music wasn't easy to come by.

As they ate, they made small talk. Harvath hoped to bond with her and get to know her better. In order to facilitate a conversation, he opened up—a little.

Referring to the back-and-forth that had taken place at the gate, she asked about his military background. Harvath explained that he had been a Navy SEAL.

When she asked which team, he told her. "I started at Team Two and ended up at Team Six. They now call it Development Group, or DEVGRU for short."

He described how he had caught the attention of the Secret Service and had worked for the White House, after which he gradually moved into the role he was now in.

"As a *consultant*," she repeated, the skepticism evident in her voice.

"If it flies, floats, or fights—chances are I have consulted on it," he replied with a smile, taking a sip of his wine.

There was something devilish about him. He reminded her of someone from her past—someone she had loved very much, someone who had been taken from her way too soon.

She glanced at his left hand again, as she had when they'd first met, and there was still no ring, but that didn't necessarily mean anything. Plenty of operators removed their wedding bands when they were away on assignments.

"Let's stop playing games," she said. "You've been holding out on me. I want to know what's going on."

He smiled. She was the right choice for this job. Her intelligence and her instincts were excellent.

Leaning back in his chair, Harvath picked up a folder from the credenza behind him and set it on the table. Opening it, he removed three photographs and slid them toward her. "Do you recognize these?"

Jasinski looked at them and nodded. "They're crime scene photos from the attacks on the NATO diplomats in Portugal, Spain, and Greece. In Lisbon a high-powered rifle was used, in Madrid a rather sophisticated car bomb, and in Thessaloniki a .45 handgun was fired by a passenger on the back of a motorcycle."

"Correct," said Harvath. "The victims all worked for NATO and all the attacks happened in NATO countries. What else did they have in common?"

She thought for a moment. "Allegedly, they were carried out by the same organization—some new terrorist group called the People's Revolutionary Front."

"Exactly," said Harvath. "Except the PRF isn't real."

"What?" asked Jasinski, confused.

"The People's Revolutionary Front is all made up. It isn't real."

"I don't understand."

"It's a two-pronged attack against NATO. The first part involves the attacks themselves. They're meant to create an internal panic and drain NATO resources as SHAPE moves to secure all their diplomats and facilities while simultaneously hunting down the perpetrators.

"Then there's the propaganda component. With each attack, the PRF puts out a gratuitous statement, describing NATO as an imperialist organization, propped up by global corporations, committed to war, conquest, and profiteering, among a host of other false charges. Each attack gets them even more news coverage.

"On the Internet, armies of trolls and bots repeat the lies. They attack anyone with a pro-NATO stance. They put out fake news stories to amplify their message, to appear like they are part of a broad international movement. Their goal is to throw NATO into chaos and to cause the citizens of its member countries to question the organization's ultimate value."

She was stunned. "But to what end?" she asked.

"To prevent NATO from effectively responding to an invasion."

"By whom?"

Harvath took a long pause before responding. "Russia."

Jasinski couldn't believe it. "You're telling me Russia is behind the attacks on our diplomats?"

Harvath nodded.

"And the attempted sabotage of American military equipment in Norway?"

He nodded again.

"How can you be so sure?"

He looked at her. "Because I personally put the bag over the head of the Russian embassy official who provided this information."

CHAPTER 15

"Wait," she said. "You kidnapped a Russian embassy official?"

"Technically, he was Russian Military Intelligence."

"GRU?" she asked, using the popular acronym for the Main Intelligence Directorate of the General Staff of the Russian Army, Russia's largest and most secretive foreign intelligence service.

He nodded once more. "Colonel Viktor Sergun. He was operating as Russia's military attaché to Germany, out of their embassy in Berlin."

"And you just snatched him off the street?"

"No. From his apartment."

"I can't believe I'm hearing this."

"Believe it."

Jasinski shook her head. "There's no way NATO condoned something like that."

"I wasn't working for NATO at the time," he stated.

"Then whom were you working for?"

"I'm not at liberty to say."

Jasinski shook her head again. He was exasperating—all the subterfuge, all the double-speak. "I'm going to go out on a limb and assume it was for the United States. I'm going to go even further out on that same limb and assume it probably involved more *consulting*, right?" She drew the word "consulting" out as if it was some sort of slur.

Harvath let her get it out of her system. He knew what was in her file. He knew she hated the Russians just as much as he did, if not more. She also believed in the rule of law—as did he. But she wasn't yet at the point where she was willing to bend one to beat the other.

"By the way," she continued, "what does *consulting* even mean? That the law doesn't apply to you? That you can do whatever you want, wherever you want, whenever you want—all in the name of *winning*? Is that what consulting is?"

He waited, to make sure she was finished, and then asked, "Do you remember the bombings in Turkey a little while ago—one of which killed the U.S. Secretary of Defense, along with several members of his staff as well as his protection detail? Or the female suicide bomber who hopped the fence and detonated at the entrance to the White House?"

"Of course."

"Those were Sergun. He trained and dispatched the terrorists responsible. There were other attacks on Americans as well. Suffice it to say, we felt justified in grabbing him."

"Where is he now?"

"In a very deep, very dark hole."

"From which, of course, he's not free to leave," she commented.

"That's the problem with holes," Harvath remarked. "Some are so deep that you can't get out of them."

Jasinski paused. Her head was spinning. She didn't know what to say. He was all but admitting that the United States was still running its rendition program—

a program globally condemned and one that the U.S.A. had long since claimed to have shut down.

She had several questions, but she wasn't sure she wanted the answers. *Fuck*, she thought. *Why had she agreed to this assignment?* Harvath could not only tank her career, he could also land her in prison. No one could just flout international laws the way he was.

"I'm not comfortable with this," she said.

"Well you need to get comfortable," he replied, "because this is the way it is, Monika. We fight here, on these terms, right now, or the entire continent of Europe becomes a battlefield. Poland, Germany, France, all of it."

"What are you talking about?"

Harvath reached for the tiny copper kettle Nicholas had brought out at the end of the meal and poured himself a strong cup of Turkish coffee.

The more time he spent with Monika, the more he liked her. She was the next wave. She would help steer her country and NATO going forward. She just didn't know it yet. Soon, he hoped, she would. He just needed more time to get her there.

"We interrogated Viktor Sergun for months," said Harvath. "He had been involved in a lot of different things during his career with the GRU. One of the more interesting things we learned was a rumor he had overheard at headquarters in Moscow."

"A rumor about what?" she asked.

"Russia's plan to invade the Baltics."

She was visibly taken aback. He was talking about Poland's neighbors. "The *Baltics*?" she replied. "When?"

"We don't know," he stated, taking a sip of coffee.

"What about how they plan to invade?"

"We don't know that either."

"What the hell do you know, then?" she exclaimed, exasperated.

Harvath focused on what, at the moment, he thought *she* should know. "According to Sergun, the GRU was charged with paving the way for the invasion. In addition to a full-blown propaganda campaign, they had activated what the old-time Soviets called "useful idiots"—disenfranchised nationals in NATO countries with certain political and worldviews—who were susceptible to influence.

"They based the PRF on the Marxist-Leninist terror groups of the 1970s—similar to the Red Brigades. Once promising individuals were spotted and assessed, they were recruited and indoctrinated. Then they were brought to Russia and trained in paramilitary tactics—weapons, explosives, and guerilla warfare. After that, they were sent home and told to await further instructions.

"Sergun didn't have all the details, but he warned that once attacks on NATO personnel, equipment, or installations started happening by the so-called PRF, that was our sign that Russia was preparing to move on the Baltics."

"So we basically know the PRF is a distraction. Is that it? We have no clue where they'll strike next or when, and no timetable for the Russian invasion of the Baltics?"

Harvath nodded.

Jasinski dropped her napkin down on the table and stood. Pacing, she tried to figure it all out.

Nicholas cleared the dishes as Harvath watched her. He was pleased to see her so worked up, so passionate. If she could control that, channel it, she might just exceed his expectations.

It took Jasinski a moment to process everything. Finally, she turned and asked, "How did you know about Norway?"

"The equipment we keep hidden in those caves needs to be serviced," he replied. "As part of our agreement with Norway, we hire Norwegians to do it. Whoever works in the caves has to have a background check. And because of the importance of that equipment, we routinely review the personnel files, as do our counterparts in Norwegian intelligence.

"Two weeks ago, there was a red flag and an investigation was opened. That investigation uncovered a plot to bomb the caves and destroy the equipment. When we learned that the saboteurs were all going to be at the cabin, the decision was made to move in and capture them. Obviously, everyone wishes there had been more time for reconnaissance."

"Obviously," said Jasinski. "What's also obvious is that you took Sergun's rumor seriously."

"Only when the attack in Lisbon happened, then our antennae went up. Then once the attack in Madrid took place, we had a high level of confidence that we knew what was happening."

"A confidence that you never shared with NATO. In fact, you didn't do anything until your equipment was targeted."

"Wrong," corrected Harvath. "We looped in the Supreme Allied Commander from the start."

That was a piece of the puzzle she hadn't been aware of. "Then why didn't he do something?"

"Communiqués were sent to all NATO personnel after the first attack. Everyone was warned. You know that."

"But the communiqués didn't contain all of the information. I saw them. None of us knew what you knew."

Harvath shook his head. "It wouldn't have made a difference."

"You don't know that," she pushed back.

Harvath could see the deaths weighing on her.

"Maybe the diplomats wouldn't have been able to do anything with it," she pressed, "but on the intelligence side, it could have helped the investigation. Maybe *I* could have done something with it."

"There's nothing you could have done."

"You don't know that."

"Maybe. But we couldn't risk it."

"Why not?"

"Because NATO is shot through with Russian spies," said Harvath. "It has been since the beginning. That's its greatest weakness. It's like Swiss fucking cheese. For every Russian you uncover, there are two more hiding somewhere else. We couldn't risk their learning what we know."

Monika looked at him defiantly. "How do you know I'm not a spy?" she demanded.

"To be honest, I don't."

She glared at him. "Then why am I here?"

It was a fair question, but one that he wasn't going to answer—at least not fully, and certainly not yet. "Because the powers that be want my team working with someone from SHAPE," he said. "And that someone is you."

"*What* powers that be? The Defense Intelligence Agency? The Central Intelligence Agency? Who do you work for? And don't tell me again that you were sent by SACT. You don't work for NATO. And him," she added, pointing at Nicholas. "He definitely doesn't work for NATO."

Though Harvath had no idea why, he glanced at his little friend. For his part, Nicholas simply shrugged as he set down three dessert plates, each with a piece of *Makowiec*—a traditional Polish poppy seed pastry cake, normally served at the holidays. He knew well enough to stay out of this. Harvath was on his own.

"Our job is to represent the interests of the United States government," Harvath stated.

"So which interests would those be?" she asked.

He thought for a moment. "Anything related to the North Atlantic Treaty."

He was still lying. She could sense it and pressed further. "What's your objective?"

This time, there wasn't a pause. Harvath replied immediately. "Per the treaty, to promote stability and well-being in the North Atlantic area."

"How, *precisely*?"

"By doing *everything* in our power to prevent an Article 5," he stated. "To make absolutely certain that the United States and its armed forces aren't dragged into war, any war—no matter what it takes."

At that moment, everything clicked for her.

CHAPTER 16

Jasinski was intimately familiar with Article 5. She could practically recite it by heart. It was the cornerstone of the NATO treaty:

The Parties agree that an armed attack against one or more of them in Europe or North America shall be considered an attack against them all and consequently they agree that, if such an armed attack occurs, each of them, in exercise of the right of individual or collective self-defence recognised by Article 51 of the Charter of the United Nations, will assist the Party or Parties so attacked by taking forthwith, individually and in concert with the other Parties, such action as it deems necessary, including the use of armed force, to restore and maintain the security of the North Atlantic area.

She had been wrong about Harvath and his involvement. This wasn't simply about American military equipment. This was about the American *military*.

Out of twenty-nine NATO countries, only six—the United States, the United Kingdom, Greece, Romania, Poland, and Estonia—were annually expending their required 2 percent of GDP on defense.

In light of what she now knew about Russia, it was no

wonder the United States had been so angry about the other twenty-three members' not living up to their military spending agreements. That went double for Lithuania and Latvia, two of the three Baltic countries, which were sitting right on Russia's doorstep.

America's debt was in the tens of trillions of dollars and had exploded since the September 11 attacks. Its annual deficits were also out of control. Its budgets showed no signs of balancing. Would the United States willingly incur even more debt to go to war in the Baltics? After nearly two decades in Afghanistan, eight years in Iraq, and multiple years spent chasing ISIS in Syria, would Americans agree to expend additional blood and treasure to defend the tiny Baltic countries of Lithuania, Latvia, and Estonia? Could a majority of Americans even find those nations on a map? Or, had Americans had enough?

And what about Poland? she thought. Poland was an exceptional partner to the United States. It *had* met its NATO spending requirements and was a staunch U.S. ally. But if Poland were attacked, would Americans see it as far away and inconsequential as the Baltic nations? Would the United States honor its commitments and come to Poland's defense?

Jasinski wanted to believe America would, but if she had to be honest, she wasn't 100 percent sure. She was even less sure about the United States defending the Baltics.

Though she hated to think it, she could envision a scenario in which America sat things out.

Via fake news and information warfare, she could imagine a fervor being whipped up where Americans might be swayed to believe it was better to let nations like Poland, Lithuania, Latvia, and Estonia fall, rather than have the U.S. go to war with Russia on their behalf.

It had happened before. She had studied it while at the National Defense University. In 1938, Hitler annexed Austria. Instead of coming to Austria's defense, the rest of the world did nothing.

Emboldened, Hitler then pressed for, and was awarded, a strategic chunk of Czechoslovakia populated by "ethnic Germans," referred to as *Sudetenland*. The Europeans, hoping to "slake Hitler's thirst and avoid a Europe-wide war," agreed to trade away the sovereign territory of Czechoslovakia for a false peace and empty promises.

Winston Churchill had seen it for the folly it was and had sent a strong warning to his countrymen, as well as the Americans. His words were so chilling to her that she had committed them to memory. "And do not suppose that this is the end. This is only the beginning of the reckoning. This is only the first sip, the first foretaste of a bitter cup which will be proffered to us year by year unless by a supreme recovery of moral health and martial vigor, we arise again and take our stand for freedom as in the olden time."

Things moved quickly downhill from there. In March of 1939, Hitler took the rest of Czechoslovakia and annexed a slice of Lithuania. On September 1 of that same year, the Nazis invaded Poland. Two days later, Britain and France declared war on Germany. Two weeks after that, the Soviet Red Army invaded Poland from the east. On September 27, 1939, Warsaw surrendered to Germany. It would take fifty more years for Poland to fully recapture its freedom.

And while history didn't necessarily repeat, it did rhyme. What was now making sense to Jasinski was that with its invasion of Ukraine and the annexation of the Crimean peninsula, Russia was taking on the role of Nazi Germany.

The arguments made for the Russian invasion were practically identical to those that had been made by Adolf Hitler and the Nazis. Russia was simply acting to defend ethnic Russians.

Despite having assurances that the United States would defend Ukraine if it agreed to denuclearize, when Russia seized its territory, the United States did nothing but impose sanctions and uselessly saber rattle at the United Nations. It was 1938 all over again.

By allowing Russia to invade Ukraine uncontested, America had emboldened Russia. With a revanchist President intent on returning his country to the power, influence, and territorial integrity of the days of the Soviet Union, Poland and the Baltic nations had every reason to worry that Russia wouldn't stop at Crimea. Not knowing if America or NATO would come to their aid only deepened that concern.

If Russia invaded even just one of the Baltics and the Americans sat it out, that was it. Not only would it be the end of NATO, but Russia would have nothing further to hold it back. It would be the end of a free and democratic Poland. Poland would be Russia's next target.

Harvath didn't have to do any more convincing. Sergun's rumor clearly made sense as far as Jasinski was concerned. The fact that Harvath and his team had been sent to Europe demonstrated how seriously the Americans were taking the threat. Avoiding a war by taking the fight to Russia, before Russia could bring the fight to them, made sense.

What also made sense was Harvath's attitude that to do so might require operating outside the bounds of the law.

Looking at him, she asked, "How are we going to stop Russia?"

Harvath liked that she was using the word "we." "Our main focus has to be figuring out who's running the operation," he replied. "If we can uncover that, we can begin to take it all apart."

"So what's our next move?"

Glancing at Nicholas, he responded, "We're going to have to take another trip."

"Where to?"

"Gotland."

"The island off Sweden?" she asked.

He nodded.

"Why? What's on Gotland?"

Climbing down from the table, Nicholas shook his head and answered for him. "Trouble. Very serious trouble."

CHAPTER 17

Colonel Oleg Tretyakov needed to get out of his office. It was stifling—too many people, too many telephones ringing. He needed to think.

He had relocated to Kaliningrad—the Russian exclave along the Baltic—twenty-four months ago in preparation for the invasion of neighboring Lithuania, Latvia, and Estonia.

Of course, no one in his government would dare refer to it as an invasion. They were taking back territory they saw as rightfully theirs. Publicly, they planned on calling it a "peacekeeping" mission aimed at protecting "ethnic" Russians. It was a dubious term at best, as most of Central Europe was, until the collapse of the Soviet Union in the 1990s, under Russian control and thereby still contained people of Russian lineage, or "ethnic" Russians.

The plan was simple and had worked for Russia before—foment dissent, encourage uprisings, and use their permanent position on the Security Council to defeat any vote for UN peacekeepers to be sent in.

Instead, Russia would magnanimously offer to send in Russian Special Forces soldiers who would provide "security" until referendums could be held and political solutions arrived at.

Of course the referendums would be bogus, would break in Russia's favor, and the Russian government would use the "democratic" results to justify officially annexing the Baltic States.

To help create an environment of chaos, local intelligence assets—as well as "useful idiots"—were being paid, trained, and directed to create as much anarchy as possible. Their efforts were being amplified by legions of online trolls, armies of Internet bots, and hordes of fake news sites—all of which were run out of a secret facility in the Russian city of St. Petersburg, called the Internet Research Agency.

A GRU cyberespionage group called Fancy Bear rounded everything out. Fancy Bear hacked sensitive information and passed it on to the Internet Research Agency. The Internet Research Agency then used the information to create yet more fake news stories. Fellow travellers, also known as "fifth columns," in the targeted countries acted like repeater stations, boosting anything and everything the Internet Research Agency and Fancy Bear put out.

This basket of espionage and propaganda tactics was called "special," or "hybrid" warfare, and the Russians were masters of it. By the time NATO could realize what had happened, or could even respond, the Baltic States would already be lost. Tretyakov's job, though, was to make sure that if NATO did respond, that response would be as weak and ineffective as possible.

This meant knowing as much as possible about NATO's operations. To do that, he had developed a vast network of spies—both inside and outside of the organization.

The creation of the PRF anti-NATO terror organization had been his idea—and its cells hadn't been limited to just NATO countries. Cells had been created not only in nations that were currently considering membership, but in ones that might be sympathetic to NATO and provide staging to NATO forces or other strategic military support.

Moscow considered it a clever plan. Diverting attention away from any Russian involvement by making the world believe the PRF was a genuine grassroots uprising across NATO was brilliant.

There had been no equivocation. Moscow had made it crystal clear that his mission was of critical importance. And that importance was driven home by the size of his budget. In his decades in military intelligence, he had never seen anything like it.

But with exceptional responsibility came exceptional accountability. News had broken about Norway. His superiors back at headquarters were not happy. They wanted a report. How was that PRF cell discovered? Did any of its members survive? Was there anything linking them to Russia? What did the Norwegian authorities know? What was the status of the other cells? What changes did he plan to make?

They were overthinking it—reacting, instead of acting. The truth was, he didn't plan on changing anything. Not without a good, solid reason. The rest of the cells were still in place and ready.

He didn't know how the Norwegian cell had been uncovered. He was just as confused and angry as his superiors were.

Putting that cell together had taken a tremendous amount of work. Getting them into positions where they could be hired to service equipment in those caves had taken even more work. It had been a good plan, a solid plan.

Something, though, had gone wrong. Someone had talked, or had slipped up somehow. And while the GRU had plenty of spies across Norway, the information was slow in coming in.

Only a small piece of intelligence had made its way to him so far. At the last minute, just before the raid on the cell had been conducted, two investigators from NATO had been added to the assault team.

His source didn't have any more information than that, but he was working on it.

Tretyakov was not surprised. There had been three attacks on NATO personnel up to this point. Per his instructions, the People's Revolutionary Front had taken credit for each one. He wanted NATO chasing the organization down, wasting its time and energy—racking up bad press at every possible turn. What he needed to be careful about, though, was NATO making too much progress too quickly.

In the case of Norway, he had many questions. How had the authorities uncovered the cell? Had they done it on their own? Did they have help? And if they did have help, where had that help come from? NATO? The Americans? Finally, was there anything in Norway that could lead to the other PRF cells that had not yet been deployed?

There were countless moving parts, but that's where Tretyakov excelled. His brain was incredibly flexible and its gears moved smoothly in concert with each other. That was until now, which was why he needed to escape the cacophony of his office.

Exiting the building, he walked down the broad Leninskiy Prospekt toward the Pregolya River.

It was cold. The sky overhead steel-gray. Snow was predicted soon. He turned the collar of his leather jacket up against the chill.

As he moved down the sidewalk, his dark, narrow eyes swept from side to side, taking everything in. He had been in the intelligence game for decades and there were certain habits that you never lost—even on your home turf.

He kept his dark, receding hair cut short—not military short, but rather businessman short. When he traveled from country to country on a range of different passports, businessman was his preferred cover.

For a man of fifty-two, he was in decent shape. He ran and did calisthenics almost daily.

Like most Russians he was a drinker. But unlike so many of his countrymen, he didn't drink to excess.

He rarely drank in public and almost never with his colleagues or subordinates—unless he was trying to get one of *them* drunk, so he could squeeze information out of them.

When he drank, it was solely to unwind, and he always knew when he'd had enough.

Alcoholism was rampant in the Russian military. It was such a problem that soldiers' field rations even included small bottles of vodka.

He saw it within the GRU as well. Empty bottles could be found on windowsills and toilet tanks in every men's room. No doubt many full or half-full bottles were hidden away in desk drawers throughout the building as well. It was a national sickness—the means by which the masses numbed themselves while the politicians and oligarchs avoided having to answer for the people's shitty existence.

Russia was better than this. His countrymen had lost

their pride. The USSR had been a global superpower. It had demanded respect on the world stage. It had launched the first earth-orbiting satellite, had put the first man into space, as well as the first modular space station. It had introduced the world's first regional jet and had invented the first artificial heart. It had carried out the first heart transplant, the first lung transplant, and the first liver transplant. It had grown to be the world's second-largest overall economy.

As far as Tretyakov was concerned, Russia would not only be great again, it would be united again. And for that to happen, every Russian had to do his or her part. Tretyakov was committed to doing his.

Taking the long way around, he crossed the short Honeymoon Bridge where newlyweds came for photos and to fasten a padlock to the railing symbolizing their undying love.

Tretyakov was no romantic. He was a realist and found the practice ridiculous. There had to be thousands of rusting locks along both sides of the bridge. He could only imagine the weight it added. It was a trend he saw repeated throughout cities in Russia and across Europe.

Before World War II, the city of Kaliningrad had been the German city of Königsberg. The Soviets annexed what was left of it in 1945, and gave it its new name in 1946.

The twenty-five-acre island on the other side of Honeymoon Bridge was known as Kneiphof Island. Home to Königsberg Cathedral, it was also the final resting place of philosopher Immanuel Kant.

Tretyakov had always found the island's walking paths, as well as its quiet cathedral, good places to collect his thoughts. The fact that Kant was entombed there was a bonus. Marxism, the philosophy of the Soviet

Union, was built upon Kant's work, which only made it feel more special.

Crossing the bridge, a sense of calm usually befell him—as if magically, his troubles couldn't follow him onto the island. Today, though, that wasn't the case.

With each step he had taken since leaving his office, his problems, like the locks, had only weighed heavier upon him. In addition to wanting a full report, his superiors were considering moving up his timetable. They were concerned over two pieces of intelligence that had recently come in.

One was about an odd meeting that was observed at the United Nations in New York City. It had involved the U.S. Ambassador, as well as the Ambassadors to Estonia, Latvia, and Lithuania. No one knew precisely what to make of it, until another piece of intelligence had come in.

A small U.S. military convoy, leaving Poland for the very same Baltic nations, had been robbed. Allegedly, the cargo that had been stolen included upgrade kits for land-based, incredibly hard to defeat Gryphon cruise missiles. These were the same missiles that had been banned under a previous treaty between Russia and the United States. None of them should have existed, much less have been in Europe.

Even more troubling was the fact that Gryphon missiles were capable of carrying nuclear warheads. According to one of their Polish spies, a covert Polish intelligence team had been tasked with trying to recover the stolen upgrade kits. If the intelligence was accurate, and he had no reason to doubt it, the missiles represented a significant obstacle to the invasion. It was no wonder his superiors were nervous. Their entire calculus could very well be in jeopardy.

But if they were thinking of beating the upgraded missiles to the battlefield by accelerating his timetable, such a move wasn't without risk. It was when one sped up operations that mistakes happened—often deadly mistakes—and he felt certain that would be the case here. It was a recipe for potential disaster.

Nevertheless, he was a soldier. It was his job to follow orders, not question them—no matter how poorly conceived he believed them to be. If headquarters wanted to accelerate the timeline, he would do what they commanded.

There would be consequences, though, of that he was sure. And he had a pretty good idea of where some of the worst might take place.

Removing his encrypted cell phone, he began to compose a message. The cell in Sweden needed to be warned.

CHAPTER 18

The prospect of flying back to Scandinavia, especially on another military transport, wasn't very appealing to Jasinski. On the plus side, though, at least the flight would be short, less than two hours.

After thanking Nicholas for lunch, Harvath had driven her back to SHAPE. On the way, she had asked again why they were going to Gotland. Harvath told her he would explain once they were in the air. Dropping her at the front gate, he instructed her to pack a bag and meet him at Brussels South Airport at 7:00 p.m.

When she arrived at the address he had given her, she was shown through the lobby of a fixed-base operator and escorted outside. There, standing on the tarmac beside a sleek white business jet with gray pinstriping, was Harvath. He had his back to her and was sipping from a Styrofoam cup of hot coffee as he admired the aircraft.

"Nice ride," she shouted, loud enough to be heard over a commercial aircraft taking off nearby. "Gulfstream G650?"

Harvath was impressed. "G650-ER," he clarified,

turning to greet her. "Extended-range package. Seven thousand five hundred nautical miles. Sleeps ten, can travel at Mach .90, has a kick-ass espresso maker and comes with cup holders and free Wi-Fi."

"How'd you swing this?"

"Like I said—if it flies, floats, or fights—I'm your guy."

"Apparently," Jasinski agreed, as the copilot approached, politely took her bag, and added it to a stack of much bigger luggage near the tail. Much of it was hard-sided, plastic Storm cases. She could only imagine what was inside. She doubted they were full of toothpaste, razorblades, and clean underwear.

Looking back at Harvath, she asked, "How long are we planning on being away?"

"Those belong to the rest of the team."

"Team?"

"They're already on board. I'll introduce you."

Harvath led the way up the airstairs and into the cabin of the G650-ER. The first thing she noticed was how luxurious it was. The white leather seats were trimmed with gray piping and had individual controls for heating and cooling. The tables were crafted from highly polished Makassar ebony veneers. Plush gray carpeting with a swirling black design ran end to end. The fixtures were polished nickel. It even had the new-plane smell.

Scattered throughout the cabin, in various stages of shoes off, feet up relaxation, were four men and one woman who made up the "team."

Leaning in close to her, Harvath confided, "They still refuse to wear nametags so I'm probably going to get a few of these wrong." Straightening up, he pointed as he worked his way down the aisle and said, "You've already met Gage, Morrison, and Nicholas, who are holding down the fort back at HQ, so let me introduce the rest of the team. Everyone, this is Monika Jasinski. Monika, this is, Gimpy, Grumpy, Dopey, Drippy, and Sparkle."

Each of the passengers held up a middle finger in response. Some of them held up two.

"Be especially nice to Sparkle," Harvath added. "The entire cabin—lights, music, temperature—runs on an app and she's the only one who has been able to figure it out."

Rolling her eyes, the woman Harvath had identified as Sparkle stood up, came forward, and introduced herself. "Nice to meet you, Monika, I'm Sloane Ashby."

She was a very attractive woman. In her late twenties, she had blond hair, smoky gray eyes, and distinctly high cheekbones.

"It's a pleasure to meet you," Monika said, shaking Sloane's hand.

"If you haven't figured it out yet, Harvath's superpower is being a smartass."

"It's pronounced *jackass*!" someone yelled from the back.

Sloane chuckled and continued. "So, like I said, I'm Sloane. Let me introduce you to everyone else."

Gesturing with her hands as if she was giving an airplane safety demonstration, she pointed to each team member and gave their real name and background as they walked down the aisle. Each stood and politely shook her hand as they were introduced.

"First up," said Sloane. "Mike Haney, USMC Force Recon."

"Pleased to meet you," the six-foot-tall, forty-year-old Marin, California, native said.

"Next, Tim Barton, US Navy SEALs, DEVGRU."

The stocky fireplug of a man was in his early thirties.

Despite only standing about five-foot-six, he looked tough as hell. He had reddish blond hair and a full beard to match.

"Then we have Tyler Staelin, Combat Applications Group, or simply CAG. Which used to be called Delta Force, but is still referred to as the Unit. I think. I can't be sure. There may have already been another name change since we got on the plane."

The thirty-nine-year-old from downstate Illinois smiled as he shook her hand. He stood five-foot-ten and had a book on the table in front of his seat called *Beirut Rules* by Fred Burton.

"I've heard of that book," said Jasinski. "Is it any good?"

"That bearded refrigerator you met earlier today gave it to me," he replied. "I'm only a couple of chapters in, but so far it's excellent."

"I'll make sure to add it to my list. Thank you."

Staelin smiled again and sat back down as Sloane introduced Monika to the plane's final passenger.

"And last but not least," she said, "we have Chase Palmer, also of Combat Applications Group, Delta Force, or whatever they're calling themselves over the next half hour."

"You forgot handsome," Palmer stated, his voice identifying him as the one who had called Harvath a jackass.

He was in his early thirties and actually looked so similar to Harvath that the two could have passed for brothers.

"And what's your background?" Jasinski asked, once Sloane Ashby had finished the introductions.

"U.S. Army, THTH," she replied.

"THTH?"

"Too Hot To Handle," Sloane explained. "The first

soldier to ever be pulled from combat for being too damn good at her job."

"You mean killing as many of the enemy as possible?"

"That's what I thought I had signed up for, but being a woman in a—"

"Long story," Harvath said, peeling Jasinski away from Sloane and steering her toward a seat near his up front. "Do you want anything before we take off?"

"Can I get a water?"

"Sure."

Walking to the rear of the cabin, he pulled a bottle from the galley fridge, prepared another espresso, and returned as the jet began to taxi to the runway.

"Here you go," he said as he handed the water to her.

"Thank you," she replied.

Sitting down across from her, he placed his espresso atop the table between their seats and asked to see her cell phone.

"Why?"

"I'm going to give you a superpower of your own."

"Smartass?" she asked, handing it over to him. "From what I hear, I'm already okay in that department."

Removing a small piece of metal from his pocket, he popped open the cover for her SIM card and replied, "No. Invisibility."

It only took him a couple of seconds to swap out her card and replace it with a brand new one that didn't have a history and couldn't be traced back to them.

"There you go," he said, closing everything up and returning her phone.

"What about my original SIM card?"

"We'll all swap back when we're in the air on the way home."

It seemed to her a pretty elaborate precaution—one

that you would take only if you were doing something you shouldn't be. "The Swedes know we're coming, right?"

He took a moment before answering and when he did, it was his pause, not his words, that unnerved her.

CHAPTER 19

As the twin Rolls-Royce BR725 engines roared to life and the G650-ER began to race down the runway, Jasinski tried to get clarification. "Either they know, or they don't know. Which one is it?"

Harvath picked up his espresso and settled back in his seat. "Like I said, the appropriate agency has been made aware."

"What does that mean?"

"It means they know."

Jasinski doubted that's what it meant, but she let it go and changed the subject. "Why Sweden?" she asked as the jet lifted off. "Technically, they're not a NATO member."

"Correct," he replied. "But they are a NATO 'affiliate.' They're also strategically important. In particular, Gotland is very important. If the Russians want to take and hold the Baltics, they have to control the Baltic Sea. To do that, they need the Swedish island of Gotland. It's small, which means a large invasion force isn't necessary. And its position near the middle of the Baltic Sea would allow Russia to prevent any NATO ships from reinforcing Lithuania, Latvia, and Estonia. If they control Gotland, they control everything."

"But I thought Sweden was already handling concerns over Russia. Didn't they bring back conscription?"

"They did. They have even permanently garrisoned several hundred soldiers on the island, but it isn't nearly enough. Three years ago, thirty-three thousand Russian troops rehearsed an invasion of Sweden. Gotland fell in less than an hour."

"So if Gotland is so important, why hasn't more been done about it?" she asked.

"The Swedes have pumped a lot of money into infrastructure," said Harvath. "But infrastructure isn't their main problem. Troop strength is. We've been working with them, conducting joint training exercises and encouraging them to build up their forces on the island, but they simply don't have enough soldiers to go around."

"So what happens if Russia invades?"

"The Swedes think they can move troops in from the mainland."

"In under an hour? You can't even mobilize, much less move troops in under an hour."

"That's what we're worried about. There's a concern the Swedes might not even defend Gotland at all. They might choose to focus their resources on Stockholm and other key areas, in hopes of limiting the invasion and holding out until the United States and other NATO members come to their aid."

"By which time, control of the Baltic Sea will have already been ceded to the Russians, giving them exactly what they want."

Harvath nodded solemnly. "Swedish politicians may not think they fully need NATO, but NATO absolutely needs Sweden if it wants to protect the Baltic States. That's why Russians can't be allowed to take Gotland."

"I still don't understand why Sweden hasn't joined NATO yet."

"Russia has made it very clear that if Sweden does, it will be seen as an act of aggression against them."

"So?"

"So, I think Sweden is spooked. They're trying to remain neutral, if they can, and thread the needle in order to hopefully have their cake and eat it, too."

"Sounds like a pretty dangerous gamble to me."

Harvath nodded again. "Believe me, we agree. If war broke out with Russia, we couldn't afford to have our forces divided, fighting on both sides of the Baltic."

"Suppose the Russians did seal off the Baltic, then what?"

"To get to any of the Baltic States, NATO's ground forces would have to move up through Poland. Normally, most of the equipment would be put on trains. There's just one problem. Western Europe adheres to a standard gauge. Once you leave Poland and head up into Lithuania, the width of the tracks change. It's a logistics nightmare."

"Not to mention the transition points being prime targets for sabotage."

"Exactly," replied Harvath. "We're looking at weeks, possibly even a month, before an effective response to a Russian invasion of the Baltics could be launched."

"During which time, Lithuanian, Latvian, and Estonian forces would be cut to ribbons. Russian forces would have ample time to fortify their positions, dig in, and prepare for any NATO attack."

"Along with the additional troops NATO rotates through the Baltic States, as well as the standby force it maintains in Poland."

"But what about air support?" she asked. "Couldn't allied aircraft launch from Sweden or Finland?"

"Depends on whether they grant us permission, or whether they play the neutrality card and stay out of it. Finland, as you know, isn't a member of NATO either. The U.S. has been doing a lot of training with them, weapons sales, and things like that. But until bullets start flying, you never really know what people are going to do.

"What's more, NATO air superiority isn't guaranteed. Russian attack fighters and antiaircraft systems could make it very difficult for our pilots."

"Sounds pretty dire."

"I deal in worst-case scenarios. Like I said, my job is to prevent an Article 5 from happening."

"So why are we going to Sweden?"

Harvath took a sip of his espresso. "To see a man in a hat."

Jasinski looked down the length of the luxury plane, studying all the players assembled aboard. "Must be one hell of a hat."

"Second-best thing to ever come out of Sweden."

"Really? What's the first? And don't say ABBA."

"Okay, I won't."

The NATO investigator smiled. "Seriously, what's in Sweden? Besides this man in a hat."

Harvath took another sip of espresso. "Nicholas cracked three of the phones from the cabin in Norway. They led us to a person of interest on Gotland. We have a contact in Swedish intelligence. He has been running it to ground for us."

"Is that what Nicholas meant by Sweden might hold *very serious trouble*?"

"He has a lot of history with the Russians. He doesn't think they'd waste an anti-NATO cell here. What he does think is that they might place a deep-cover Spetsnaz team, highly trained in reconnaissance and sabotage, to harass and tie up Swedish troops during a Russian invasion."

"What do you think?"

"I think it could go either way. But regardless, we need to find out."

"Is that what all the Storm cases are about?" she asked. "What's inside them?"

Harvath winked at her. "Pens, pencils, paper—that sort of thing. This is a fact-finding trip. We're just here to learn."

"Right." She laughed. "And I've got a big, beautiful bridge to sell you in San Francisco."

"Too dangerous."

"Bridges?"

"No, San Francisco," he replied.

She laughed again. He smiled back.

Slowly, he was winning her over. That was important, because he needed her. In truth, he needed a hundred more like her, a thousand.

The threats faced by Western Europe were rapidly changing, evolving. Unfortunately, Western Europe wasn't.

By not leaning in, by not being aggressive, they were encouraging more acts of violence upon their nations and their citizens. They had forgotten that civilization lives, thrives, and survives only when it is willing to wield a very sharp sword. If you didn't meet the barbarians out on the road, soon they'd be at your gates. And once at your gates, be they Islamic terrorists or Russian soldiers, they would soon be inside.

Simply put, Western Europe's enemies did not fear them. They did not fear them because they did not respect them. And they did not respect them because the Western Europeans would not fight.

The Europeans, like any noble society, prided themselves upon what set them apart, what made them better than the barbarians—their laws. The barbarians didn't care for laws. They only cared for brute force—*What can I take, whom can I subjugate, what can I make mine through sheer force of will?*

Law and civilization were supremely important things, but without strength, and a willingness to engage the enemy, they were worthless.

Harvath had always appreciated the maxim of an Army Lieutenant Colonel named David Grossman. In Grossman's mind, there were just three categories of human beings—sheep, sheepdogs, and wolves.

To those three categories, Harvath had added another—wolf hunters. That was what the world needed more of.

The sheep had only two speeds—graze and stampede. They needed sheepdogs to keep them safe in case of an attack by the wolves. Wolf hunters, though, were needed to find and kill the wolves, whenever possible, before they attacked.

Harvath was a wolf hunter. His whole team was composed of wolf hunters. He saw the potential for Jasinski to be one, too. That's why it was important that she experience what they did and understand why they were necessary. He and his team couldn't be everywhere. There were too many hot spots, too many threats.

But when they did appear, only for the most serious of threats, they acted as a force multiplier. And in those situations, like now, the more wolf hunters they helped create, the more endangered the wolves became, and the safer the places the hunters protected.

"So," she said, breaking into his thoughts, "what do I need to know before we land?"

Harvath thought about it for a moment. "You're with an exceptional team that's on the right side of this fight," he replied. "No matter what happens, just remember that."

CHAPTER 20

They landed at Visby Airport on the west side of the island. Seeing the town's name emblazoned upon one of the hangars, Jasinski said, "Visby's an interesting name. I wonder where it comes from."

"It's Old Norse," Harvath replied. "It means the pagan place of sacrifices."

"Seriously?"

"Seriously."

"What a delightful omen," she stated.

Harvath grinned.

At one hundred miles long and thirty miles wide, Gotland was Sweden's largest island and was known as the Pearl of the Baltic. It lay ninety miles from the mainland and was home to sixty thousand inhabitants, twenty-three thousand of whom lived in the main town of Visby.

Surrounded by the Baltic Sea, its coasts were craggy and windswept, covered with limestone pebbles, while its interior boasted lush pine forests, dramatic grass marshes, sprawling meadows, and fertile, verdant farmland.

As the jet rolled to a stop, a private aviation ground crew materialized and laid down a red carpet.

Looking out the window, Harvath didn't see his contact. What he did see were two uniformed police officers—one tall, one short, along with a man in a leather coat, exiting the FBO building and walking in the direction of their plane.

"What's going on?" Jasinski asked, as she looked out the window at the men who were approaching.

Picking up his cell phone, he dialed the man in the hat. It went immediately to voicemail. He tried again with the same result.

"Do me a favor," he said, pulling out his Sig Sauer and handing it to her. "Hold this for me until I get back."

"What's up?" Sloane asked from the back.

Chase, who could see the cops approaching through his window, said, "Karma. I've got a hundred bucks that says Harvath dated at least one of their daughters."

"Time to face the music, Norseman," Barton joked.

Harvath ignored them as he grabbed his North Face jacket and moved forward. Sticking his head in the cockpit, he told the pilots, "Keep the engines hot."

Then he disarmed the forward door, opened it up, and extended the airstairs. They hit dead center at the top of the red carpet. The chilly, salt-tinged ocean air blew through the open doorway.

As he zipped up his jacket and prepared to walk down to speak with the men, Jasinski changed seats so she could get a better view of what was happening. Sloane came up and joined her.

"Any idea what this is all about?" the NATO investigator asked again.

"I don't know," Sloane replied. "The man in the hat was supposed to meet us. Apparently, he's not here."

"Why do you keep calling him that? Doesn't he have a name?"

Sloane smiled. "Lars Lund. He works for Sweden's Military Intelligence and Security Service."

"MUST," Jasinski replied, using its acronym. Part of the Swedish armed forces, MUST was the country's main foreign intelligence service and reported to both the government and the military.

Sloane nodded. "Lars is known for his good looks—tall, blond, and Nordic. But he is even better known for his vanity. When he started to go bald, his friends began buying him hats. His trademark is one of those small Alpine-style caps made out of felt."

"A Tyrolean?"

"That's the one. He has all kinds of them."

"Which division of MUST is he from?" Jasinski asked.

"Now you're going to stump me," Sloane replied. "I'm not up to speed on all the acronyms yet."

"It's okay. What does he specialize in?"

"Espionage and clandestine operations."

"He's probably in KSI then."

"That's the one," said Sloane.

Also known as the Office for Special Assignment, KSI was the darkest corner of Swedish intelligence. In all of the country's civil law system, there was only one mention of it.

Jasinski was intrigued. "How is it you know him?" she asked.

"I don't. Not personally. I only know of him. He and my boss go way back together."

"Lars and Harvath do?"

Sloane smiled. "I should rephrase that. Lars and my boss's boss go way back."

"And who is your boss's boss?"

Sloane smiled once more. "Now we're getting into things above my pay grade."

"So you're not going to tell me?"

"It's better if you ask Harvath," she replied as she glanced back out the window.

Jasinski realized that she had likely hit a dead end. Changing the subject, she, too, looked out the window and asked. "Are we in trouble?"

"Only if they search our luggage."

Shit, Jasinski mumbled under her breath.

"And knowing Harvath," Sloane continued, "he probably did date one of their daughters. So we're probably totally screwed."

The joke made her smile. "Where'd he get the Norseman call-sign?"

"In the SEALs. He had a thing for flight attendants from Scandinavian Airlines. Dated quite a few of them. The name started as a joke, but stuck."

"And now?"

"Meaning what?" Sloane replied. "Is he dating? Married?"

Jasinski nodded.

Sloane grinned. "Yeah. His friends refer to her as the 'underwear model.' Her parents are from Brazil. She's gorgeous. Super smart, tough as hell, and really sweet. Why? You're not interested in him, are you?"

"Me?" Jasinski scoffed. "No. Not at all. Just curious."

She's a liar. And not a very good one, Sloane thought. But better for her to know up front. Harvath was as close to marriage as you could get without actually being married. The joke around The Carlton Group was that if he ever came back home long enough for there to be a wedding, he'd probably be married already.

As far as Sloane was concerned, Harvath would be an idiot not to marry Lara. They were made for each other. She'd never seen two people click as well as those two.

But what truly amazed her was how Harvath could put his entire personal life in a box, slam the lid shut, and not let it intrude on his thinking while he was down-range on a mission.

He had an iron will. It was the only way she could describe it. Only half-joking, she had teased that she hoped to grow up and be just like him one day.

She made a lot of jokes at Harvath's expense, especially about his being older, but he took them all in stride. He was like the older brother she never had.

Harvath made his share of jokes at her expense as well. One of his favorites was that she was just young enough and good looking enough to be a rich country-club doctor's perfect idea of a third wife.

That had cracked Sloane up. Outside their age difference, she and Harvath were very similar personality-wise. Both had been accomplished winter athletes before joining the military. They were also hard chargers who employed a lot of take-no-prisoners humor to buoy morale in order to get through tough assignments, as well as just the day-to-day.

It had always impressed her that he had never come on to her. Many men, even in leadership positions, had, but not him. It was one of the many reasons she respected him.

"I have it on good authority," Sloane joked, "that he sleeps with a light on and leaves the toilet seat up. You can do better. *Much* better. Believe me."

Jasinski laughed and tried to appear blasé. He was off the market. His teammates liked his significant other and apparently the two were a good match. She had been foolish to allow her mind to even explore the possibility.

You got one really good chance in life and she'd had hers. It had been wonderful, while it lasted. That kind of person didn't come around twice. She consoled herself with the thought that at least she had her work.

Concentrating on the scene unfolding outside, the two watched as Harvath descended the airstairs and approached the man in the leather coat flanked by the pair of police officers.

Despite the jokes that had been made at Harvath's expense, suddenly the situation didn't seem funny anymore.

CHAPTER 21

Halogen lights illuminated the revetment area. The man in the leather coat had stepped away from the uniformed officers and was making his way forward. He met Harvath halfway across the tarmac. Removing a set of credentials, he held them up and asked, *"Pratar du svenska?"* *Do you speak Swedish?*

Harvath shook his head. "English."

The majority of Swedes were bilingual, and the man seamlessly switched over. "My name is Chief Inspector Anders Nyström. Swedish Police, Gotland."

Nyström was thin, like a distance runner, and stood about five-foot-eight. He had a head of short blond hair and a closely cropped blond beard—both shot through with streaks of gray. He wore a trendy pair of glasses, behind which a pair of green eyes took everything in. On his right wrist was a large digital watch.

Harvath knew that in any encounter with law enforcement, the first test was the attitude test. If you failed the attitude test, everything went downhill from there.

Smiling, he extended his hand and replied, "Nice to meet you. Is everything okay?"

"That depends," said Nyström. "May I ask your name, please?"

Harvath didn't want to give this guy anything. The

man in the hat had not only failed to meet their plane, but had also failed to answer his phone. Something was wrong. And until Harvath knew what was going on, he was going to be very careful about what he revealed. "My name is Stephen Hall."

The Hall alias was one Harvath had created in honor of a courageous OSS member who had been murdered by the Nazis.

"May I see some identification, please?" the Chief Inspector requested.

"I'm sorry," said Harvath. "Did we come in on the wrong runway or something?"

"No, nothing like that."

Having come from Belgium to Sweden, this was an inter European Union flight. That meant no border controls, passport checks, or customs inspections. Being met by national police like this was highly unusual.

Harvath removed his own set of credentials, which had been fabricated for him back in Virginia, and showed them to the officer.

"NATO," the man remarked as he examined them. "Supreme Headquarters Allied Powers Europe. Interesting. What is your purpose in Sweden?"

"I collect ABBA memorabilia."

The joke made the Chief Inspector chuckle. "I see."

"Can you please tell me what this is all about? You're obviously here for a reason," Harvath said.

"I was hoping you could tell me. There was a car accident tonight. The driver was carrying a piece of notebook paper with the Visby airport code, a time of arrival, and the tail number for your aircraft. I assume the driver was on his way here to meet you."

A bad feeling began to build in the pit of Harvath's stomach. "Is the driver okay?"

"Unfortunately, no. He was killed in the accident."

"Have you identified him?"

Nyström nodded.

"And?" asked Harvath.

"First, please tell me. Were you expecting someone to meet you here tonight, and if so, whom? Their name."

"Lars Lund," said Harvath, the feeling in his stomach climbing into his throat.

"I'm sorry to inform you that Mr. Lund died this evening as a result of the injuries he suffered."

Harvath masked his feelings. He was highly skeptical of car accidents, especially when they involved skilled intelligence operatives in the middle of assignments. He felt the same way about plane crashes and hit-and-runs.

Experienced people in the espionage game tended to be very careful. As a rule, they checked and then double-checked everything. They didn't take unnecessary risks.

When they did end up the victim of an "accident," foul play always had to be considered. "What can you tell me about it?" Harvath asked.

"From what we can surmise, Mr. Lund was traveling at a high rate of speed and lost control," said the officer. "Is there a reason why he may have been in such a hurry?"

Harvath shrugged. "None that I can think of."

"Exactly why was Mr. Lund coming to meet you?"

"He was supposed to have been our host."

"Host for what?" asked Nyström.

"Mr. Lund worked for the Swedish Defense Force back in Stockholm. We were going to tour the island with him and discuss logistics for an upcoming multilateral training exercise."

Harvath knew that Swedish authorities, particularly those on Gotland, were alert to potential Russian infiltration. At the same time, they had also become increasingly accustomed to military training exercises with NATO. That meant the closer he stuck to the truth of why he and his team were here, the less chance their presence would raise any alarm.

"Can you tell me more about this exercise?" the Chief Inspector inquired.

"Unfortunately, not without approval from higher up. What I can say is that it's an unannounced drill designed to test joint readiness. Participants, including the garrison here on Gotland, would be given a scenario and then be graded on how quickly they mobilized and how well they responded."

"So the exercise is a secret?"

"That's a good word for it, but I think *surprise* would be more accurate. By surprising them and not giving them time to prepare, we're better able to measure how they would react in real life."

Nyström seemed to buy it, and handed Harvath his credentials back. "Should I not alert the garrison commander about claiming the body then?" he asked.

Harvath had to think quickly. "That should probably be up to the Swedish armed forces. It's their choice if they want to inform the garrison commander or not. They might decide to send someone from Stockholm to quietly claim the body."

"Indeed," replied the Chief Inspector. "Speaking of which, did you know Mr. Lund personally?"

"I did."

"As he's from the mainland, we don't have anyone on Gotland who can confirm his identity. Would you be willing to come with me to the hospital?"

"Now?"

"Yes," said Nyström. "If it is not too much trouble."

"Of course," replied Harvath. "Give me a couple of minutes to inform my colleagues inside the plane about what has happened."

"Absolutely. Take your time."

"What's the story, boss?" Haney asked, as Harvath came back aboard the aircraft.

The team had all assembled up front as they watched the conversation unfolding on the tarmac.

"Allegedly," said Harvath, "the man in the hat was involved in a car accident tonight. According to the police, he died of injuries sustained in the crash."

A silence fell over the plane.

"They have asked me to go to the hospital with them and identify the body."

"Bad idea," stated Staelin.

"Agreed," replied Chase. "On the way to meet us, the man in the hat dies in a car crash? Now three strangers show up and want you to drive off someplace with them? How do we even know they're real cops?"

"I don't like it," added Sloane.

"I don't like it either," Harvath responded. "But I want to confirm the body is Lund's. If this is legit, we might need the local police."

"And if it's not legit?" Jasinski asked.

"Then make sure Nicholas gets all my vinyl."

She rolled her eyes.

"Relax," he continued. "Everything is going to be fine. But in case it isn't, I'd like to have my Sig with me."

"Good call," she said, handing his pistol back to him.

"Let's find room for this, too," said Haney, holding

up a small GPS tracking device and tossing it to him. Harvath tucked it in his pocket.

"The man in the hat was supposed to hook us up with vehicles. How are we going to follow you?" Sloane asked.

"If worse comes to worst, Gotland has Uber. We're only a few kilometers from the city center, so there should be plenty," replied Harvath. "For now, though, I want you to send Ryan an update on our situation and have her reach out to Carl Pedersen. He has some good contacts in MUST and knows what's at stake. He'll help put a lid on this.

"Chase, I want you deplane and see if you can secure a courtesy car from the FBO. Barton, we're going to need at least two permanent vehicles while we're here, so check what the airport rental agencies have and try to nail something down. Haney, no one touches our gear but you. It stays onboard this plane until you're sure the police are gone. In the meantime, Staelin, I want you to figure out where we're going to bunk."

"How long do you think we're going to be here?" he asked.

"As long as it takes," Harvath stated. "Okay, that's it. Everybody get to work. Let's go."

While the team jumped up to do as he had directed, Jasinski stopped him. "Sloane explained to me that Lund was close to Pedersen and your boss. I'm sorry for your loss."

"Thank you. He was one of the good guys. Took a lot of risks over the years. Those risks made a difference."

"Does MUST really know we're here, or was Lars Lund the only one who knew?"

Harvath wasn't sure how he wanted to answer her

question, but decided to tell her the truth. "Lars was the only one who knew we were coming. I doubt he shared it with anyone else."

"That makes what we're doing, what *you're* doing, even more dangerous." Placing her hand gently on his shoulder, she warned, "Be careful."

CHAPTER 22

Harvath carried his Sig Sauer in a neoprene Sticky brand holster, tucked inside his waistband at the small of his back. It was uncomfortable, and he wanted to adjust it. He didn't dare to, though, for fear of tipping off Nyström that he was armed. Instead, he tried to focus on the sights and sounds of Visby by night.

It was a medieval city that functioned as the island's capital. A UNESCO world heritage site, it was the best-preserved fortified commercial city in Northern Europe. Its Old Town looked like something out of a movie.

Strung with painted cottages, cobblestone lanes, and the ruins of Romanesque and Gothic churches, its most dramatic features were the largely intact thirteenth-century ramparts surrounding it. Harvath could only imagine what a draw it was at the height of summer.

Right now, on a Friday night off-season, it was still doing very well. Bars, restaurants, and cafés conducted a brisk business. People walked up and down the sidewalks and there was plenty of car and bus traffic.

As the Chief Inspector slowed down to allow a group of pedestrians to cross up ahead, Harvath asked, "What more can you tell me about the accident?"

"Not much. It happened in the countryside about thirty kilometers outside of town. Based on the tire marks, we believe Mr. Lund was traveling in excess of 120 kilometers an hour. The speed limit in that area is only 70.

"Mr. Lund appeared to have lost control of his vehicle, whereupon the vehicle left the roadway, rolled, and hit a tree. He was pronounced dead at the scene."

"Who reported the accident?" Harvath asked.

"A passing motorist saw taillights in the brush, stopped to investigate, and then called police."

"Do you see a lot of vehicular fatalities on Gotland?"

Nyström shook his head. "They are very rare. But when they do happen, the victims are usually holiday-makers and alcohol is involved. Was Mr. Lund a drinker?"

"Not that I'm aware of," replied Harvath.

"Any medications?"

"I have no idea."

"That's okay," said the Chief Inspector. "They will do a toxicology screen at the hospital."

"Any evidence that Lund may have been forced off the road?"

The Swede thought about it for a moment. "*Forced?* Why do you ask? Are you aware of someone who wished him harm?"

Harvath shook his head. "Just wondering."

"Perhaps he swerved to avoid an animal. Gotland is predominantly rural and roe deer are a real hazard throughout the island."

"Was there any unusual damage to Lund's vehicle? Anything that would suggest he came in contact with a deer, or anything else?"

"The car was very badly damaged. If there was such evidence, it would be incredibly difficult to ascertain. Have you much experience with automobile accidents?"

"Some," Harvath replied. "Where is Lund's car now?"

Nyström looked at the clock on his dashboard. "A wrecker was dispatched to retrieve it. It will be kept at the wrecking company's lot while we finish the paperwork and file our initial findings. Sometimes, if a claim is filed, an insurance representative will come out from Stockholm. They may conduct their own investigation. When that's complete, the car will be released."

"And then?"

"In a case like this, where the vehicle is unsalvageable, it is sold for scrap. It will be loaded on the car ferry back to the mainland and disposed of there."

"I'd like to see the vehicle myself. Would that be possible?" Harvath inquired.

"I suppose something could be arranged," said Nyström. "But I must ask. What is your interest in viewing it? Are you looking for something? Something you think my team may have missed?"

"I'm sure your team did an excellent job. I only ask because my superior was quite fond of Mr. Lund. They were friends, as well as colleagues. He will be glad to know that I took an additional look."

"You said you had *some* experience with automobile accidents. Were you a police officer previously?"

"In a prior career, I was a federal law enforcement officer."

The Chief Inspector knew a thing or two about American law enforcement. Judging by the look of his passenger, he asked, "U.S. Marshals?"

"Secret Service," Harvath replied. "Like I said, my superior will be happy just to know I took a look."

"So this is a request, *cop-to-cop*, as you Americans say?"

Harvath nodded. "A professional courtesy. Cop-to-cop."

Up ahead was a sign for the Visby Hospital. Nyström applied his turn signal and turned down a narrow residential street. Beyond, Harvath could already see the lights of the parking lot.

When they pulled in, the Chief Inspector found a space near the emergency room entrance and parked.

The hospital was much bigger than Harvath had expected. It was a sprawling three-story complex, built of orange brick, overlooking the ocean. The pale green of its multiple rooftops was echoed in the pale green of the window mullions. Harvath noticed a windsock, which told him there was a helipad nearby as well.

Entering the ER, they approached an intake desk, staffed by a pretty young nurse with spiky red hair who knew Nyström on sight. After a friendly back-and-forth, she laughed and waved the police officer and his guest past.

"Friend of yours?" Harvath asked as they walked down the hall.

"We're in a local trail-running club together on Facebook," the Swede replied. "She was teasing me about my recent time. She says that if they released criminals on the trails, maybe I would run faster."

"And what did you say back that made her laugh?"

"I told her that I would definitely run faster if they released *redheads*."

Harvath grinned. "Good line." He had been right about the Chief Inspector being a runner.

Approaching a bank of elevators, Nyström reached out and pressed the down button. When an elevator arrived, they stepped inside and rode it to the basement.

As soon as the doors opened, Harvath got a blast of one of his least favorite smells. Morgues had a very distinct odor. No matter how far the actual room was from the elevators or a stairwell, the minute he arrived on the same floor, he knew it. There was no disguising the scent.

"I assume you are familiar with the identification process?" the Chief Inspector asked.

Harvath nodded. He'd been through the process before.

Walking into the morgue, Nyström paused briefly to chat with one of the technicians. Once the discussion was complete, he led them to an autopsy table at the end of the tiled room. Atop it was a black body bag.

The Chief Inspector looked at him. "Ready?"

Harvath nodded again.

Reaching out, the morgue technician zipped open the bag enough to reveal Lund's head and upper torso.

The trauma was horrific and the corpse was in bad shape. But the disfigurement wasn't so extensive as to render it unrecognizable.

"Is this Lars Lund?" Nyström asked?

"That's him," said Harvath.

The Chief Inspector nodded at the technician, who then zipped up the body bag.

"What kind of personal effects was he carrying with him?" Harvath continued.

Nyström nodded once more and the technician stepped away to a cabinet. When he returned, he was carrying a police evidence bag. Setting it on an adjacent counter, he unpacked the contents.

Harvath examined the items—*wallet, watch, keys, reading glasses, money clip, and a small tin of mints*. "That's all?"

The technician nodded.

Harvath looked at Nyström. "Where's his cell phone?"

"We didn't find one."

"Don't you think that's a bit strange?"

The Chief Inspector shrugged. "He may have been in such a hurry that he left without it. Or it might have been ejected from the vehicle. I'll have a team search the area again in the morning."

"Was there a briefcase or a laptop in the vehicle?"

"No."

"Were you able to open the trunk, or was the vehicle too badly damaged?"

"We checked the trunk," said Nyström. "What you see in front of you is everything he was carrying."

"I'd like to see his car now, please."

The Chief Inspector looked at his watch and then back at Harvath. "Let me make a call."

CHAPTER 23

Lydia Ryan was in the middle of preparing an updated briefing for U.S. Ambassador to the U.N. Rebecca Strum, as well as running down all of Scot Harvath's requests, when a call came in from Artur Kopec. He had an update for her. He claimed it was urgent and he needed to see her right away.

It was two o'clock on a Friday afternoon. Whether his update was truly urgent or not, she figured it was probably no coincidence that it would take him out of the office for the rest of the day. Her suspicions were all but confirmed when he suggested that they meet at a particular D.C. watering hole. Though the traffic would be a pain in the ass, she told him she was leaving right then and would get there as soon as she could.

Kopec wasn't exactly subtle with his choice, but considering the cuisine and ambiance dovetailed with Poland's, she supposed he could be forgiven. Even so, the Russia House Restaurant and Lounge near DuPont Circle at Connecticut and Florida avenues was a bit over the top.

She parked at the Washington Hilton and went the

rest of the way on foot—careful to make sure she wasn't being followed.

The Russia House Restaurant and Lounge was like escaping back in time to czarist Russia. It was decorated in rich mahoganies, ornate carpets, red silk draperies, and ornate gold brocade.

The only thing that outdid the décor was the menu. It included every Russian staple imaginable—from borscht and wild boar to kulebiaka and shashlik.

Not to be outdone in the food department, the Russia House boasted an astounding collection of vodka. It was not only one of the best in D.C., but it was one of the best in the United States.

The vodka menu listed more than forty different kinds from Russia and twenty from Poland, and included vodkas from Moldova, Ukraine, Lithuania, Estonia, England, Sweden, Holland, and even Israel.

On top of everything else, the Russia House was less than a mile and a half from the Polish Embassy.

She found Kopec at a small table on the second floor, in the cozy, seductively lit "Czar's Bar."

In his typical fashion, he had started without her. A bottle of Chopin potato vodka sat next to a silver serving dish filled with crushed ice and chilled caviar. It was encircled on a plate by small Russian pancakes known as blini. A colorful trio of minced red onion, chopped egg, and sour cream sat on a plate to the side.

When Ryan entered, Kopec stood and watched her as she walked over. She looked stunning.

Though he wasn't an expert on designer labels, he assumed the suit she was wearing was Italian. If he had to guess, Armani. It was sleek and black and complemented her long, thin frame.

Her hair was pulled back in a tight ponytail, her full

lips accentuated by the peach lipstick she had chosen. He never got tired of looking at her. She was a vision.

After giving her a quick kiss on each cheek, he pulled out her chair and assisted her in sitting down.

"I hope the traffic wasn't too awful," he said as he re-took his seat.

"Friday in D.C.," she replied, putting her napkin in her lap. "I'm sorry I wasn't able to get here sooner."

"That's quite all right. I hope you don't mind. I started without you."

"It depends. What kind of caviar did you order?"

Leaning forward so that no one could overhear him, he whispered, "Royal Osetra."

Two hundred bucks a tin. Ryan wondered how much of the money she had wired into Kopec's account was funding this gourmet outing, but she kept her curiosity to herself. She hadn't believed all of the money would go to tracking down the missing missile kits. A certain amount, undoubtedly, would wind up in Kopec's pocket and be justified as "handling."

Figuring she, or rather The Carlton Group, had helped pay for it, Ryan availed herself of a large serving, but demurred when the Pole attempted to pour a shot of vodka for her. "I have to drive back to the office after this."

"Then just have one," he said, using the bottle to gently brush her hand aside.

Next to cash, alcohol was the lubricant that greased the wheels of the espionage world. Drinking was just part of how the great game was played, especially with older operatives. Retracting her hand, she allowed him to pour. Ryan could handle her liquor.

"To Peaches," he said, raising his glass.

In addition to being a brilliant intelligence officer,

Reed Carlton had also been known as a ruthless inter-rogator. It wasn't something he relished, but it wasn't something he shied away from either. When tough work needed to be done, his colleagues knew he could be counted upon. His most aggressive interrogating was reserved for the worst actors.

Because of his ability to break the toughest, most evil of men—by any means necessary—Carlton had been given the amusing sobriquet Peaches. In time, it grew to be a term of endearment.

"To Peaches," Ryan replied, clinking her tiny glass against Kopec's and throwing the vodka back in one shot.

The Pole refilled his glass, but before he could do the same for hers, she slid it away and turned it upside down.

"Na Zdrowie!" he cheered with a smile, To health, and then knocked his back.

He was an amazing drinker. She could only imag-ine what his liver looked like. They probably could have used it for a doorstop back at the embassy, which got her to thinking.

"Aren't you concerned someone from work might see us here together?" she asked.

"Concerned? I'm *counting* on it!" he replied. "Do you know what being seen with a beautiful woman like you would do for my standing in the diplomatic corps? In fact, I'm not allowing you to leave until someone *does* see us."

Ryan smiled politely. "Even you are not that care-less, Artur."

"True. But, being seen with the recent Deputy Di-rector of the CIA is a resume enhancer. The fact that she is also very attractive is a plus."

"Thank you."

"You are welcome," he said. "And don't be worried. No one at my embassy has the courage to leave before five o'clock—especially on a Friday. Most are career civil servants with the lingering fear of authority beaten into them during the Soviet days. Besides, it's cheaper for them to stay at the office and drink. This way, when five o'clock rolls around and they're ready to go out and party, they're already drunk."

Ryan laughed. She had had lots of overseas postings, and drinking before going out, in order to save money, was the rule, not the exception.

Knowing that Kopec would keep her here boozing with him as long as possible, perhaps indeed hoping they'd be spotted together, she decided to professionally move things along. "So, what is the urgent update you have for me?"

She had caught him just as he was putting a blini loaded with caviar, red onion, and sour cream into his mouth.

It took him a minute to chew it all and swallow. She was relieved to see him reach for his ice water, rather than another vodka, to wash it all down.

Finally, the Polish intelligence officer spoke. "I think we may have found the upgrade kits for your illegal missiles."

CHAPTER 24

S he didn't like that Kopec had used the word "il-legal," nor did she like the way he had said it. He was setting her up for something; she could sense it, but she didn't let on. "What did you find?" she asked.

Taking out his phone, he opened a folder, and then slid the device across the table to her. "Feel free to scroll through."

Ryan did. There were multiple still photos, beginning with the CCTV footage of the theft. Though the thieves' faces were not visible, their robbery was. The cameras had made it all possible. The van the thieves were driving, as well as its license plate, could be seen as clear as day.

"This is terrific," she remarked. "Were you able to trace the vehicle?"

"It turns out that it was stolen, but keep going."

Ryan scrolled through the pictures of a barn that followed. Inside was the van. "Oh, my God, you found it."

He shook his head. "It had been abandoned. They hid it inside the barn, hoping to delay its discovery. Keep going."

Ryan did, and in the next series of photos saw a stack of empty U.S. Army crates that had been left behind.

"I had my people go over everything—the van and

the crates," said Kopec. "They wiped everything down. They couldn't find any clues."

"How did they find the barn in the first place?"

"I had put a flag on the stolen vehicle. When a local reported finding it, my team was alerted and they stepped in."

Ryan lowered her voice. "Have you told anyone what was in those crates?"

"No, but we had to pay the local police to forget they had ever been called to the barn."

"Money well spent," she replied

"Indeed," said the Pole, nodding as he poured himself another shot.

"So what do you think happened?" Ryan asked.

"I think they had another vehicle waiting. I think they transferred the upgrade kits and took off."

"For where?"

Kopec shook his head and raised his hands, palms up. "Who knows? It could be anywhere."

"Come on, Artur. You must have some idea."

"All I have are guesses."

"So guess," she encouraged.

"Belarus."

Ryan looked at him. "You think they left Poland?"

"The spot where the van was discovered is near a known smuggling area. It's not as bad as parts of your border with Mexico, but we have some of the same problems—drugs, sex trafficking, those kinds of things."

"Damn it," she replied. "If those upgrade kits were taken into Belarus, they might as well have been taken into Russia."

"I agree. It's not good. But it's also not hopeless."

"What do you mean?"

"There may be something we can do," said Kopec.

"In Belarus?"

The Pole nodded. "It won't be cheap, though."

"I'm listening."

"I'm going to need ten times the money."

Ryan didn't bat an eye. "I'm still listening."

"And I'm going to need a piece of insurance."

"What *kind* of insurance?"

As he had done when identifying his luxury caviar, Kopec leaned forward and lowered his voice. "You're going to need to give me Matterhorn."

CHAPTER 25

R yan quickly glanced around the lounge to make sure no one was listening to their conversation. She then focused back on Kopec and said, "I don't know what you're talking about."

The man laughed. "Which is why your entire body tensed at the mention of his name and you quickly looked around the room."

"Are you crazy? We can't talk about this out in the open."

"We don't have a choice. Not if you want to prevent those upgrade kits from finding their way to the Russians."

Ryan fixed him with an icy stare. "This is blackmail."

"This is business."

"You know what, Artur? I thought we had a better relationship than this."

"Our business is built on favors, Lydia. You are asking me for one and in return, I am asking one of you."

"Certainly. But *Matterhorn*? I can't trade favors for that."

"You have asked me not to tell my government what I am doing for you. Further, I now need to send my people into Belarus and very carefully exploit my network there. And let me tell you, it will not be easy. If word gets out, the Russians will outbid, outmuscle, and out-destroy anyone who stands between them and proof that the United States has reintroduced cruise missiles into Europe in violation of the INF treaty. That alone could kick off World War III. But couple it with the fact that an untold number of your missiles are nuclear-tipped? That could very well be game over."

"Pick something else, Artur. Anything else. You've said this will cost one hundred grand. Make it five hundred. We won't care where the money goes. Do with it as you see fit."

The Polish intelligence officer shook his head as he loaded another blini. "You can't put a price on an asset like Matterhorn, especially for Poland."

"I understand," replied Ryan. "But Matterhorn is not mine to give."

Popping the blini into his mouth, he let her words hang in the air above the table, as he took his time chewing and then swallowing.

"There has to be another arrangement we can come to," she said, breaking the number one rule about not rushing to fill uncomfortable silences.

"The missiles are your insurance policy against the Russians," Kopec insisted. "Matterhorn will be ours."

Ryan began to argue, but the Pole held up his hand. "Think about what you are asking me to do. Matterhorn is *one* asset, Lydia. That's all, but he could be the difference between life and death for Poland."

"I can't bargain with you over Matterhorn because we don't know who the hell Matterhorn is."

Kopec, who was normally quite good at playing his cards close to his vest, appeared genuinely startled. "That's impossible."

"Well, welcome to my new world," she said, as she

decided that she wouldn't go straight back to the office. Turning her glass over, she pushed it forward.

Slowly, he poured a vodka for her, but perhaps thinking better of it, chose not to pour one for himself and set the bottle back down on the table. "Walk me through this," he said.

Tossing back the shot, Ryan took another look around the room and then leaned forward. "As you know, Matterhorn was recruited *and* run by Carlton."

Kopec nodded. "That's how he explained it."

"Only a handful of people were ever aware of his existence," she continued. "The Russians thought Matterhorn was spying for them, and he was. But in addition to legitimate intelligence, he was also feeding them a lot of misinformation as well, specifically about NATO."

"Which is precisely why we want him. To keep the Russians off balance."

"I understand, but there's one problem. Carlton never revealed his identity."

"What?"

"Never. Not to anyone. It was one of his most closely guarded secrets."

"Then we need to go talk to him."

She shook her head. "I've tried. Over and over again. That part of his mind isn't coming back. It's a secret he'll take to his grave. Unless . . ." Her voice trailed off.

"*Unless* what?" Kopec asked.

"Unless we can piece the identity together through his personal papers. He kept journals, much of the material coded. We've made a little progress, but a lot of it is slow going. We have to cross-reference where he said he was and what he was doing with classified accounts in the CIA archives. It's like trying to put together a puzzle in the dark."

Tapping the top of her tiny glass, she gestured for him to refill it. Once he had, she sipped it and began to spill her guts. "You have no idea how frustrating all of this has been. If I had known what I was walking into, I don't know if I ever would have agreed to take this job.

"Every time I turn around, there's another hole in the dike that needs plugging, but only Reed Carlton's fingers fit and he can't remember where to put them. I don't know what I'm going to do."

Kopec didn't know how to respond. He couldn't be sure if it was the alcohol talking, or if Ryan was simply unburdening herself to a trusted colleague. Either way, what she was revealing about the disarray in her organization was quite troublesome.

He listened intently and slowly began to steer their conversation back to Matterhorn. "Realistically, how soon do you think you might have the identity?"

She stopped, mid-sip in her vodka, and pondered his question. "It could be a day, a week, or a month. Who knows? There's also the problem that, even if we could come to some sort of an agreement about Matterhorn, Carlton is unable to introduce a new handler and orchestrate a handoff."

As far as Kopec was concerned, that was the least of their worries. Just knowing whom the asset was would be a huge step forward. "Let me ask you something," he said, shifting gears. "Do you know why Carlton selected the codename *Matterhorn*? Was it significant somehow? Connected?"

Finishing the shot, she returned the glass to the table and shook her head. "When it comes to Reed Carlton, I don't have the slightest clue. I can't even begin to think the way that he does—even on his worst day. He was always ten steps ahead of everybody."

"That he was," agreed the Pole as he started to pour her another drink.

Ryan, though, politely waved him off and turned over her glass.

"I've already had too much. I apologize."

"Don't apologize. You've got a lot on your plate," he said.

Looking down, she realized that she hadn't even touched her caviar. Assembling a blini, she directed their conversation back to the upgrade kits. "If I gave you my word that you can have Matterhorn—if and when I identify him—would you be willing to push into Belarus for me?"

"For *you*? Or for the United States?"

"For me," she replied.

Kopec thought about her offer for several moments. Looking at her, he finally said, "For you *and* for five hundred thousand dollars, I'd be willing to take the risk of pushing into Belarus. But understand something, Lydia. I'm trusting you. Don't make me regret that trust. That would be a very foolish thing to do. Believe me."

CHAPTER 26

The wrecking yard was attached to an auto body shop in a warehouse district on the other side of Visby. Harvath had already texted his team to give them an update. Pulling up to the gate, Chief Inspector Nyström removed a set of keys from his pocket and exited his vehicle.

After unlocking the chain and throwing the gates open, he returned to the car.

"You've got your own key?" Harvath asked.

"Small island," Nyström replied, putting the car in gear and driving forward. "This is my uncle's business. When I work nights, I often drop by to make sure everything is okay."

Circling around to the back, they parked and got out. Nyström popped his trunk and removed a rather mediocre flashlight. "We'll probably need this," he said, clicking it on.

Harvath slid his hand into his coat pocket and withdrew his tactical flashlight. When he depressed the tail cap, it produced a quick, intense strobe. "Mine's better."

"Americans," the Chief Inspector sighed, as he led Harvath to the back of the lot.

When they arrived at the southwest corner, Nyström shone his flashlight across the wreckage of Lars Lund's vehicle.

It was a ten-year-old white Volkswagen Passat. The Chief Inspector had not been exaggerating. The damage was quite extensive. Seeing the state of the car for himself, Harvath could understand why the accident had resulted in a fatality. The question, though, was what had caused it.

Circling the vehicle, Harvath examined every square inch under his flashlight. He stopped at the left rear quarter panel.

It was in bad shape, just like the rest of the vehicle, but there was something else. It was a scratch, about three inches long, but in a completely different color from the rest of the car. It looked like some shade of olive, almost a military-style green.

Not wanting to draw Nyström's attention, he moved on. When he got to the other side of the car, he asked, "Did the vehicle crash through any guard rails?"

The Chief Inspector shook his head. "It was open countryside."

"No livestock or property fencing?"

"No. Only rocks, and trees, and grass. Why? Did you find something?"

Harvath shook his head. "Just trying to wrap my head around all the damage."

Continuing his investigation, he proceeded slowly around the Volkswagen until he was done. Nothing, though, jumped out to him other than the olive-colored scratch.

"I'm done," he said. "Thank you."

"Okay, then," replied Nyström. "I'll give you a ride back."

Walking back to the entrance, Harvath waited as the Chief Inspector reversed his car out, and then closed and locked the gates for him.

Sliding back into the front passenger seat, he shut his door and they headed for the airport.

"Do you have any idea where Mr. Lund was staying?" Nyström asked. "There was no hotel keycard among his possessions. Could he have been staying at the garrison without telling them the true purpose of his visit?"

"It's possible," Harvath lied. The man in the hat was supposed to have arranged a safe house for all of them—someplace where they could interrogate their person of interest without being disturbed.

Allegedly, the man in the hat also had their subject under passive surveillance. Cameras had been set up to monitor his coming and going. When Lund had hinted that he might take a more active role and start following him, to see where the subject went and whom he met with, Harvath had tried to dissuade him. You couldn't do surveillance, at least not effectively, with just one person. It was too dangerous.

Now the man in the hat was dead. After having looked the Passat over, Harvath was growing more convinced that Lund's death hadn't been an accident. Somewhere along the way, Lars Lund had screwed up and it had cost him his life.

"How about you?" the Chief Inspector asked.

Harvath, who had been processing all of the information, hadn't caught the question. "I'm sorry. What was that?"

"Did Mr. Lund make arrangements for you?"

"He was going to set something up, but I don't know where."

"I'll have an officer reach out to the different hotels; perhaps we can find where he was staying."

Harvath nodded.

"Will you be staying or returning to Brussels?"

"I think we'll be staying, at least until SHAPE decides what it wants to do."

"Of course. If, in the meantime, you need any help finding rooms," said Nyström, "let me know. I'm sure we can assist you."

"Thank you."

Fishing a business card from his pocket, the Chief Inspector handed it to Harvath. "My cell phone number is on the back. If anything comes to mind that you think might be useful in our investigation, please call me. Day or night."

Harvath took the card and tucked it inside his jacket. He'd been toying with revealing the name of their subject. With Lund deceased, he was at a literal dead end. He didn't know where to find him. He decided to take the police officer into his confidence.

"There may be something," he offered.

Nyström kept his eyes on the road, but even in the dark of the car, it was obvious that his interest had been piqued. "What is it?"

"I assume you have heard about the attacks on the three NATO diplomats?"

"Yes. Most terrible."

"And the situation in Norway?"

"Yes," the Chief Inspector repeated. "The same group was allegedly involved there as well. The People's Revolutionary Front. They had planned to sabotage military equipment, correct?"

"Exactly," said Harvath.

"Is there some sort of connection to Mr. Lund or to Gotland?"

"We don't know," Harvath lied, again. "But as you can imagine, in light of these attacks, NATO has adopted a much higher security posture. Part of our assignment here was to do a security assessment."

"What does that entail?"

"Pretty basic stuff, really. Is Gotland safe for NATO personnel? Are there any anti-NATO elements here who may be connected to the People's Revolutionary Front, et cetera."

"As far as the police are concerned, we are not aware of any anti-NATO groups here on the island. I'm sure people have opinions, but organized resistance? No. Back on the mainland might be a different situation, especially in and around Stockholm, but not here."

"That's good to know," replied Harvath. "There is, though, one person we have interest in."

"On Gotland?"

"Yes."

"Who is it?"

"His name is Staffan Sparrman. Are you familiar with him?"

The Chief Inspector pulled his car over to the side of the road and stopped. Turning to look at Harvath, he said, "I am going to give you one chance—that's all—to tell me what the hell is going on. If you don't, I'm going to place you and the rest of your people under arrest until we get all of this sorted out."

"Obviously, you're familiar with him," said Harvath.

"Of course I am," Nyström replied. "Staffan Sparrman is the son of Kerstin Sparrman, the Governor of Gotland."

CHAPTER 27

Based on the circumstances, Harvath was forced to unpack a lot more information for Nyström than he had intended. But to his credit, the Chief Inspector listened well, asked intelligent questions, and was forthright with information.

Staffan Sparrman was in his late twenties and was known to have flirted with socialism while at university in Uppsala and for a short time afterward. This being Sweden, though, that didn't mean much. Sweden was known as an extremely liberal country. And by all accounts, Sparrman had drifted away from politics.

In fact, the man had become so apolitical that he even refused to work on his mother's campaign for Governor. It was quite the scuttlebutt at the time and resulted in continuing tension between them.

Sparrman, instead, occupied himself with the management of the family farm left by his maternal grandparents. His father, who divorced his mother when he was a teen, lived back on the mainland. They did not have a very good relationship either.

As if to add emphasis to his certitude that Sparrman had abandoned any affinity for socialism or communism, Nyström pointed to the fact that the young man even imported cheap farm labor from Eastern Europe, rather than hire—and pay—local Swedes.

With each point he made, the Chief Inspector was only convincing Harvath that he had the right guy. Sparrman fit the profile of a Russian espionage recruit to a T.

Yet, with all that Nyström had shared with him, there was one piece of information that he wouldn't give up— where Harvath could find Staffan Sparrman.

"I think it would be better if I go out and speak to him alone," said the Chief Inspector.

"And tell him what? That some American just landed and he's got a bunch of questions?"

"I'll be a bit more subtle than that."

Harvath didn't doubt it, but by the same token he didn't like the idea of Nyström tipping his hand. "Why don't we sit on this for a couple of days? Let my team surveil him while I gather some more information. SHAPE may want to involve the local garrison commander after all. There's no rush here."

The Chief Inspector shook his head. "I have a fatal car crash involving a member of the Swedish armed forces. I have a NATO representative telling me a member of the Gotland community is a person of interest, possibly connected somehow to a string of attacks on NATO diplomats, as well as members of Norwegian law enforcement and the Norwegian military. And oh, by the way, the person of interest is the son of the island's Governor.

"I can't help but move this forward. If I delay my investigation, it might look like I was giving Sparrman special treatment just because of who his mother is. I could lose my job over something like that."

The man was in a tough spot, Harvath understood that, but there had to be some sort of an accommodation they could come to. "You have to do something, I agree.

But does it have to be direct confrontation? Couldn't you open up a separate investigation and place him under surveillance for a couple of days? Technically, that wouldn't be a delay. You'd be gathering evidence and would be able to document everything."

Nyström thought about that. "Technically, I suppose you are correct. There's no evidence connecting Sparrman to the car accident. Your claim that he's a person of interest in the anti-NATO attacks is new information, which, if we choose to pursue it, would constitute a new and separate investigation."

"There you go," said Harvath.

"But there's just one thing," said the Chief Inspector. "I report to a chain of command. We also have laws in Sweden regarding surveillance that must be followed."

"Meaning?"

"Meaning I can't do all of this in a bubble, by myself. I have to get permission."

Harvath had been around law enforcement long enough to know that there were plenty of things that cops did without permission. He doubted it was any different in Sweden. "Listen," he said, "I understand the position you're in, but think about this. What if there is a Russian network here and Sparrman is the only link we have to it? If you go in and start asking him questions, who knows what could happen? He could run. Or, worse still, he could do what he's supposed to do and report your visit to his handler. At that point, his handler will have a decision to make—pull Sparrman out, kill Sparrman, or kill you."

Nyström grinned. "Are you trying to scare me?"

"I'm telling you the truth. And you should be scared. The Russians are brutal. Killing a police officer would be nothing for them."

"How do we know they didn't kill Lund and make it look like an accident?"

"That's precisely it," said Harvath. "We don't know. That's why you can't go paying Staffan Sparrman any visits. Beyond what I've told you, you don't have cause. If he's half as smart as I think he is, his internal alarm bells are going to start going off if you show up asking questions for no apparent reason.

"I'm not trying to tell you how to do your job, but I am asking you, cop-to-cop, to not prevent me from doing mine. If Sparrman *is* working for the Russians, and if he *is* connected to these anti-NATO attacks, we can use him to climb the ladder and dismantle the entire network. But first, we need to find out what he's up to."

Having laid out his case, Harvath took a breath and settled back into his seat. The ball was in the Chief Inspector's court now.

"Building a proper case," said Nyström, "takes time. How much time would you need to carry out your assignment?"

"That depends."

"On what?"

"Where the starting line is. I could move a lot faster if I knew where to find Staffan Sparrman."

"And if you knew where Sparrman was, how much time would you need?"

"Forty-eight hours. Tops."

Reaching across Harvath, the Chief Inspector opened his glove compartment and pulled out a pen and a pad of paper. He then drew a map of the island and identified the Sparrman farm.

Tearing the sheet from the notebook, he handed it to him. "Forty-eight hours," said Nyström. "That's as much as I can give you. Then I take over."

• • •

Across town, one of the two patrol officers who had met Harvath's plane at Visby Airport used a side door to enter the hospital. Avoiding the intake desk at the emergency room, he made his way to a stairwell and headed down to the basement.

There, he walked past the morgue to the hospital security office. The door was unlocked, and opening it, he stepped inside.

Sitting in front of a bank of monitors, glued to his iPhone, was the sole security guard in the office.

Looking up and seeing his visitor, he immediately pocketed his phone and stood, almost at attention. "Officer Johansson," he said. "Good evening."

"Good evening, Lucas," the officer replied. "Quiet night?"

"So far," the young man stated.

"I can see that. Are you being paid to monitor your Instagram account or the hospital's closed-circuit cameras?"

Lucas hung his head. He had already failed the police entrance exam once. All he wanted to do was to become a cop. Now he had been caught shirking his professional responsibilities by an officer from the same department he wanted to join.

He was convinced he had blown any chance of being hired until Officer Johansson said, "Never mind. I need a favor."

"Certainly. What is it?"

Pulling a portable drive from his uniform pocket, the tall man handed it to the young security guard and said, "I need all your footage from the last hour."

"Why?" the guard asked, as he accepted the drive, found a cable, and attached it to his system. "Are you looking for someone?"

Obviously I'm looking for someone, thought Officer Johansson. *Goodness, this kid is a moron.* How he'd even been hired by the hospital was beyond him.

"I don't have a lot of time," Johansson said, ignoring his question.

"How is it out on the street tonight?" asked the guard as he tapped several keys on his keyboard and isolated the footage the policeman had requested.

"Can I trust you to keep this between us?" the officer replied, as the footage began to download.

"Yes, sir. Absolutely."

"We're hunting a jewel thief."

"A *jewel thief*? In Visby?" the eager security guard asked, as the download neared completion. "Did you think he came here? To the hospital?"

"What do you think?"

The young man paused for a moment, thinking, and then replied, "Of course! That's why you're here."

"You're going to make an excellent police officer one day, Lucas. You have a real nose for it. How much longer on the download?"

"Done!" the guard exclaimed, unplugging the device and handing it back to Officer Johansson.

"When's the next exam?" the cop asked.

"Two months."

"Are you ready?"

The guard grimaced.

"Keep studying," advised Johansson.

"I will sir."

"Good."

When the officer got to the door, he turned and addressed the young man one last time. "A patient's car was broken into in the parking lot tonight. Her bracelet was stolen. If you see or hear anything about our jewel thief, let us know."

And with that, Johansson left the security office and exited the hospital. He'd have to wait until his shift was over and he could establish a secure connection, but he had no doubt that his handler and Moscow were going to appreciate having video footage of the American.

CHAPTER 28

Oleg Tretyakov poured himself a glass of wine as he processed the recent spate of intelligence reports he had received. The first had been the most troubling. The cell on Gotland had been under surveillance. But as far as they knew, by only one person—an older man in his sixties.

Staffan Sparrman had noticed him multiple times—both in his white Volkswagen Passat, and on foot. When the man had been on foot, he was particularly conspicuous because of his distinctive Alpine hat.

The handler for the Gotland cell was one of Tretyakov's most trusted lieutenants. The strategic importance of the Swedish island had made it imperative that he put his best man in charge. Ivan Kuznetsov was that man.

Kuznetsov was brilliant, brutal, and beyond loyal. Had Tretyakov wanted, he could have also added the word "butcher" to describe him, as Kuznetsov had grown up in a family of butchers and had begun expertly butchering hogs at a young age.

His knowledge of butchery, his brutality in dealing with Russia's enemies, and his skill in using a knife had earned Kuznetsov the nickname "Kutznutzov."

His peasant upbringing, though, had always been a millstone around his thick neck. It had been a source of derision for others while he was in the military. He had no formal education to speak of, having left school in the fifth grade to work full-time for his family's business. But, as the Russian Army freed him from his village and allowed him to see more of the world, he had educated himself through books—anything at all he could get his hands on.

He liked books about politics, history, and art. Though he had never been there, he hoped one day to visit Florence and Rome—to walk in the footsteps of Machiavelli and Michelangelo. For now, though, he was confined to Gotland.

Kuznetsov was a deep-cover operative, part of the Russian *illegals* program. The term "illegal" referred to a Russian intelligence officer operating in a foreign country without official cover, such as an embassy employee or consular staff member.

He was the quintessential gray man—a person of average height and average looks who was easily forgettable—brown hair, brown eyes, nothing special. He didn't call attention to himself.

Putting his butchering skills to work, he had found employment at an animal-processing plant on the island. He was knowledgeable, arrived early, stayed late, and never complained. It didn't take him long to climb the ranks.

He enjoyed getting out and meeting the various farmers and ranchers, seeing their livestock, and even lending a helping hand during lambing season and other such times.

His papers identified him as a refugee from Kosovo named Dominik Gashi. And even though he wasn't a

Swede, he was appreciated and well-liked. As such, he spent a lot of social time with the farmers, ranchers, and other members of the community. That was how he had spotted and assessed Staffan Sparrman for potential recruitment.

With Tretyakov's permission, he had then slowly begun to develop Sparrman, building a deeper, more personal relationship with him. He began getting together with him on a one-on-one basis, sounding him out on different topics—one of which was politics.

By the time the recruitment phase rolled around, he had Sparrman fully on the hook. The key to exploiting him wasn't some weakness like gambling, drugs, or adultery, but rather it was ideological. He was a true believer in communism, but he had grown disillusioned with what he saw as a watered-down Communist Party in Sweden. Convinced that he couldn't make a difference, he had given up and put all of his attention into the family farm.

His greatest hope was that one day he could find a woman with whom he was ideologically aligned. Perhaps, if things worked out, they could get married and raise a family. Sparrman was still young, and Kuznetsov had used this longing to his advantage.

The Russian had arranged to have an attractive GRU asset, who specialized in honey traps, vacation on the island. All he had to do was create a scenario where the two would cross paths, and he let the GRU asset handle the rest.

It was quite a steamy affair, and like most vacation flings, it eventually had to come to an end. But when the asset returned to Russia, she kept in touch with Sparrman via text messages, emails, and the occasional Skype video call. With as light a touch as possible, she encouraged him not to give up on the communist cause and built him up to believe he could do great things. Kuznetsov then handled the rest.

Sparrman was his entry point into mainstream Gotland culture, and Kuznetsov built his network of assets and spies from there. Coming from a political family, Sparrman seemed to know where everyone on the island stood. Having grown up with all of them, he also knew what their weaknesses were and where they were the most vulnerable for recruitment.

The fact that Kuznetsov could safely use the family farm of the Governor of Gotland as his base of operations was an incredible coup. Of course, it helped that Kerstin Sparrman had an apartment in Visby and preferred to live there rather than out on the farm, but nevertheless Kuznetsov—and by extension his superior, Oleg Tretyakov—had been widely heralded back at GRU headquarters for their ingenuity. Operating an intelligence network right under the nose of the most important official on Gotland was the stuff of legend.

For his part, Kuznetsov didn't see it as the stuff of legend. It just made good sense. The Sparrman farm was quite big. There were not only multiple places to have meetings undetected, but also countless places to hide caches of money, munitions, weapons, and assorted equipment.

But best of all, the farm allowed for the hiring of foreign laborers—big, strong men who under almost any other employment circumstances would have stood out on Gotland like sore thumbs. Tretyakov loved that he could create the Swedish cell and hide it in plain sight.

Sweden was undergoing a shortage in the labor market—particularly when it came to manual labor such as farm work. Visas to import workers from abroad were easy to come by.

A GRU intelligence officer working under official cover at the Russian Embassy in Stockholm had someone on his payroll in the Swedish Immigration Department. The immigration official was essentially a rubber stamp. All the GRU man from the embassy had to do was put the paperwork in front of him and he would sign off. No questions asked. Tretyakov had had no problem getting the men he needed into the country, over to Gotland, and to work on the Sparrman farm.

Kuznetsov not only had his own homegrown espionage network to gather intelligence, but he also had his own team of Russian Special Forces soldiers, known as Spetsnaz, lying in wait for when Moscow gave the order to launch the cell's mission against the local garrison. It couldn't have all come together in a more perfect fashion.

Which was why the man in the Alpine hat sniffing around the cell had caused such concern throughout the ranks.

Though he needed Tretyakov's permission, Kuznetsov had already decided what needed to be done. The man had to be eliminated.

The word back from Tretyakov, though, was that it had to look like an accident. He had also wanted it done quickly, plus he wanted the man's phone, laptop, and any other items of interest he might be in possession of. If they could uncover who he was and why he had been following Sparrman, that would be a valuable bonus.

Staging a vehicle accident was not as easy as it appeared in the movies. Even so, Kuznetsov and the Spetsnaz operatives had plenty of experience and were confident they could pull it off. They also had the perfect piece of bait—Sparrman. All they needed to do was pick the right location and spring their trap.

Catching the attention of the man in the Alpine hat had been easy. They had set up what appeared to be a clandestine rendezvous between Sparrman and another farmer in an easy-to-observe location.

The other farmer, who owed Sparrman some mundane paperwork, handed the documents over and Sparrman furtively tucked them into his jacket pocket. It didn't have to be anything more than that.

Sparrman withdrew a map of the island and had a brief discussion with the farmer about spring grazing. Circling a location on the map, he thanked the farmer, shook hands, and returning to his vehicle, drove away. The man in the Alpine hat followed in his white VW Passat.

Kuznetsov and his team stayed in touch with Sparrman the entire time via encrypted radios. Gradually, they had him increase his speed. As he did, the white Passat trailing behind him matched his pace.

The Spetsnaz operatives had prescreened the route and had chosen the best location for the accident to happen. What they hadn't counted on was another car coming by so soon afterward.

The accident itself had gone off perfectly—even better than they had planned.

Traveling with the headlights off, the man in the white VW was so focused on Sparrman in front of him that he never even noticed the Spetsnaz men come up on him from behind in a green Mercedes SUV.

By the time he realized they were there, they had moved into the opposite lane, as if to pass. Then, all of a sudden, they brought their vehicle slamming into his left rear quarter panel, causing him to swerve and lose control.

The white VW Passat shot off the road, rolled, and slammed into a tree with such force it sounded like an explosion.

They had been prepared to snap the man's neck, but it turned out not to be necessary. By the time they got to his vehicle, he was already dead.

Quickly, they patted down all of his pockets and went through the rest of his car—taking his cell phone and his laptop bag, complete with a Toshiba notebook.

Before they could make a second, more thorough pass, they heard a car coming. They had no choice but to flee the scene.

As they left, they reached out to Johansson, another local member of the network, to let him know that everything had gone according to plan. They told him to expect a call to go out from his dispatcher shortly.

Knowing where and when the accident would take place, Johansson had arranged to be in the area so that he could be the first law enforcement officer on the scene. In case the Spetsnaz operatives missed anything, which he highly doubted, he'd be able to take care of it.

When the passing motorists stopped to see what had happened, the call to the police followed less than a minute later. Immediately, the dispatcher was putting out the call for all available units to respond. Johansson radioed back his position and that he was en route. He had a good fifteen minutes at the scene before anyone else showed up. Not that he needed it. The Spetsnaz members had done a perfect job.

Back in Kaliningrad, Tretyakov had been pleased to get the good news. The man in the Alpine hat had been taken care of and the cell was still intact, ready to act. The man's phone and the laptop would be couriered by one of Kuznetsov's people to an agent in Stockholm.

From there, it would be placed in the Russian Embassy's diplomatic pouch and sent to Moscow where it could be fully examined.

In the meantime, Tretyakov had authorized another attack by the People's Revolutionary Front. He had decided not only to oblige his superiors by moving up the timetable, but also to up the carnage.

If tonight's operation was successful, it would be their most spectacular achievement yet.

CHAPTER 29

Figurati was one of the hottest restaurants in Rome. Located on the glamorous Piazza Navona, it was at the intersection of Italian politics and culture. Frequented by celebrities and politicians alike, Figurati was *the* place to be seen, especially on a Friday night.

The tables in the main dining room were booked months in advance. Only the most powerful and most famous could get a table on short notice, and sometimes not even then.

Contessa Chiara Di Vencenzo had a standing reservation. Every Friday at nine o'clock, the buxom and vivacious Neapolitan, who had married well and divorced even better, held court at a round table in the center of the dining room. Her guests varied wildly. They included authors, filmmakers, actors, models, painters, poets, dissidents, politicians, and titans of industry.

Hers was one of the top tables in Rome, and an invitation for Friday dinner with the Contessa meant you were seen as a very big, very important deal.

On Fridays, the paparazzi parked themselves outside on the sidewalk waiting to snap photos of those she had invited. The next morning, newspapers across the city and websites throughout Italy ran their pictures, as well as stories about who else had been seen at the restaurant that night.

For those who couldn't get a table in the dining room, there was always the slim chance they might find space in the bar. It was standing room only by seven o'clock, but worth it just to catch a glimpse of the rich and famous who came to dine. As long as you were well dressed, Figurati was happy to have your business.

On this particular Friday, Jacopo Romano was very well dressed. He had polished his shoes until they shone like mirrors. His new navy blue suit was perfectly pressed, his crisp white shirt heavily starched.

In his girlfriend's opinion, three days' growth of beard was the perfect length for his handsome face. His taut, olive skin set off the deep green eyes on either side of his perfectly proportioned Roman nose. He was the picture of Italian good looks.

In his left hand, he carried a large Prada shopping bag. Inside it was a box, elegantly wrapped in gift paper and tied with an enormous satin bow. Taped to the side of the box was a bright yellow envelope, presumably containing a greeting card of some sort.

Romano navigated his way through the crowd and patiently waited for twenty minutes before a barman took his order. The restaurant was filled with the sound of laughter, animated conversations, and the tinkling of glasses. Overhead, speakers in the ceiling pumped out an eclectic mix of jazz and bossa nova.

Romano paid for his Campari and soda with cash, then stepped away from the bar and faded back into the crowd.

At nine o'clock on the dot, a jolt of electricity surged through the restaurant as the first of the Contessa's guests showed up. It was a British actress, filming a movie in Italy, who was alleged to be having an affair with the current, married, Prime Minister.

She looked absolutely stunning and was followed by another woman, just as gorgeous—a model who had been tapped as the new face of Gucci. After they were shown to the table, two men arrived—an Italian soccer star and a young fashion designer who was said to have been taking Milan by storm.

The remaining guests passed through a meteor shower of camera flashes outside, and then ten minutes later, the Contessa arrived.

It took the flaxen-haired beauty half an hour to make it to her table. Every two feet she was being stopped by someone or other, kissing her on both cheeks, asking how her family was and where she planned to spend the summer. She was quite visibly in her element and loving every moment of it.

Making a full circuit of her table she doled out hugs and kisses on both cheeks to each one of her guests. Pleasantries were exchanged back and forth until she insisted everyone sit.

Bottles of champagne were brought to the table, glasses were raised, and toasts were made.

There was no need for menus to be passed around. That was not the kind of restaurant that Figurati was. What's more, the Contessa liked surprising her guests.

The only clarification necessary was whether anyone at the table had any food allergies. They had become prevalent these days. The Contessa actually found it quite astounding. Growing up, she hadn't known a single person with a food allergy.

According to a physician she knew, the best science could understand was that first-world medicine had beaten back so many ailments that without anything to fight, immune systems were now turning against themselves. She found it fascinating that food allergies didn't exist in the developing world.

Having informed the waiter that there were no food allergies at their table, the Contessa turned her attention to her guests. As was her custom, she went around the table, asking her guests to introduce themselves with their name, their occupation, and what famous person they would like to sleep with.

It was a randy opener, to be sure, but it helped break the ice and set the mood for the evening. If you weren't any fun, the Contessa didn't want to have anything to do with you. *Life's too short* had always been her motto.

Accompanying the Contessa was her longtime boyfriend, Giovanni Lorenzo. A retired diplomat, Lorenzo had served as Italy's Ambassador to the European Union, as well as Deputy Secretary of NATO. Currently, he was president of a little-known NGO called the NATO Defense College Foundation.

Established to further the goals of NATO, the foundation worked closely with the Rome-headquartered NATO Defense College.

The college had been the brainchild of Dwight D. Eisenhower, the first Supreme Allied Commander of Europe. The idea had been to create a university where both civilian and military members of NATO could pursue training, which would result in the strengthening and constant improvement of the North Atlantic Alliance.

Romano was pleased to see Lorenzo there. It had been a fifty-fifty shot. While the retired diplomat was a regular guest, he didn't attend every one of the Contessa's dinners. She was a good twenty years younger, had a lot more energy, and craved the limelight much more than he did.

Stepping across the threshold into the dining room, the handsome Italian moved to the side to allow others to pass. He set the shopping bag down on the floor next to him and pretended to scan the room for a group of dinner companions.

Inches away was a waiter's station. As his eyes moved from table to table, he saw people engaged in their own conversations, occasionally glancing at the Contessa and her guests, but not paying attention to anything else, much less to him.

Casually parting the fabric skirt of the waiter's station, Romano pushed the bag underneath, greeting card facing out, with the toe of his beautifully polished shoe.

With his package placed, he strolled out of the restaurant, stopping only at the front door to depress a button on the wireless key fob in his pocket.

He was more than a block away when the bomb detonated. Even then, the blast was so intense that it shattered all of the windows around him and knocked him to the ground.

Within hours, newscasters would be calling it the worst bombing in Italy since the Marxist terror attacks of the 1970s, and the People's Revolutionary Front would be known as the deadliest European terrorist organization since the Red Brigades and the Baader-Meinhof Gang.

CHAPTER 30

Harvath didn't like having to deceive Chief Inspector Nyström about his true purpose and identity. The man seemed like a good cop. Deception, though, was a necessary part of the job—especially now.

They were in Sweden, running a black operation without the knowledge of its government. They were supposed to have had the help of one of its most senior intelligence officers, but Lars Lund was now dead. They were 100 percent on their own.

Harvath deeply regretted Lund's passing, but he was used to operating in this position, often in much harsher environments. He had only forty-eight hours. They would have to make it work. He wasn't going back to Brussels empty-handed.

Dropping Harvath back at the airport, the Chief Inspector had offered to stick around to help make sure all of their arrangements were taken care of. Harvath had thanked him and reiterated that he'd call him if he needed help. That reminded the policeman that he hadn't gotten Harvath's cell phone number, which he promptly asked for, "Just in case anything pops up and I need to get in touch," he had said.

Harvath didn't want the Swedish police being able to track his movements, so he provided Nyström with a dummy number Nicholas had set up that would dump right into voicemail and ping Harvath's current phone number if any messages were left.

Writing down the number in his notebook, the Chief Inspector thanked him, the pair shook hands, and the cop drove off.

With his most pressing headache out of the way, Harvath turned to the others on his list.

Because the man in the hat had been in charge of providing the team with vehicles and a place to stay, they now had to scramble.

The rental car situation was less than optimal. The car choices were lousy, and he could rent one only under his false "Hallman" identity. As the driver of the second vehicle, Chase Palmer would have to use one of his false driver's identities as well.

Fully backstopped covers were very time consuming and expensive to create. They didn't grow on trees. Among the major advantages of working with the man in the hat were the top cover he could provide and the preservation of the team's anonymity. ID wouldn't have been required for anything. That was a good thing, especially in a covert operation.

In fact, it was Tradecraft 101—something the Old Man had repeatedly pounded into him. As an example of what *not* to do, Carlton loved to cite a horribly botched operation Langley had run in Italy about a decade earlier.

Two dozen CIA operatives had participated in an assignment to snatch a Muslim cleric off the streets of

Milan and render him for interrogation. Inexplicably, the operatives not only traveled under their own names, but also used their personal hotel rewards programs to rack up points, and ran all around Italy with their personal cell phones, leaving a trail of electronic bread crumbs.

The Italian government tried all of them in absentia for kidnapping, false imprisonment, and torture, resulting in unanimous guilty verdicts. The trial was followed by sentencing, in which massive fines and jail time were levied. None of them would ever again be able to travel to Europe without fear of arrest and imprisonment.

To call it amateur hour would be an insult to amateurs. The Old Man had been adamant that Harvath and everyone else at The Carlton Group hold themselves to a higher standard.

But even in the presence of best intentions, an immutable law of covert operations remained—if something could go wrong, it would.

Harvath had already witnessed Murphy's Law on full display in Norway. He didn't intend to let Murphy pop his ugly head up here. Though, if it did, no matter what got thrown at them, they would adapt and overcome. Failure was not an option.

With Harvath's and Chase's aliases each tied to a rental car, they used Sloane's alias to book their accommodations. The less anyone could connect the team's dots, the better.

That same mindset applied to where they'd be sleeping. The fewer people who saw them coming and going, the better.

As Gotland was a popular vacation destination, Staelin had looked beyond hotels, searching for off-season houses and apartments that might be for rent. Within five minutes online, he had found the perfect spot.

Once paperwork had been completed and their vehicles—a blue Kia Sedona minivan and a gray Toyota Camry sedan—had been brought around, they transferred over the gear from the plane and headed out of the airport toward the rental house.

The old country house sat on fifteen allegedly "quiet" acres twenty minutes outside town. They stopped along the way at a gas station minimart to load up on provisions. Harvath stayed outside to keep an eye on the vehicles.

While he waited, he banged out a text on his encrypted sat phone. He wanted to give Ryan a fuller picture of what was going on and how they were dealing with it. With his message sent, he shut down the phone and turned his attention to the cars.

Since leaving the airport, he had kept a close eye on their six o'clock. It hadn't seemed as if they were being followed. But in the age of GPS, a person didn't need to physically tail you in order to monitor where you were going.

"Fleet management" was a fancy term for GPS tracking and was standard operating procedure for all major car rental companies. He disabled the fleet management system in the minivan first and then the sedan. After, he did a full inspection of each vehicle to make sure no secondary devices had been added. He didn't find anything.

Ten minutes later, the team exited the minimart, each carrying multiple grocery bags. Barton, the SEAL, was carrying several cases of bottled water, with a case of sugar-free Red Bull stacked on top.

"Somebody also bought coffee, right?" asked Harvath.

"Two kinds," replied Chase, who was right behind him. "They even had a grinder inside. I got to do the beans myself."

"At a gas station?"

"Welcome to Sweden," he said with a grin.

Harvath was glad to see him so upbeat. The last time they had run an operation in Sweden, it hadn't gone well. Multiple operatives had died, and Chase, who had penetrated deep inside a sophisticated terror cell, had been lucky to make it out alive.

Like Sloane Ashby, Chase Palmer had the right mix of what it took. He was young, sharp, and highly successful in the field. He was also fearless and, like Sloane, fully understood the threats that were massing around the world. They had had access to weapons and training the likes of which he had never seen at their age. Harvath envied them both.

They also had plenty of time left on the clock. They could go kinetic for years, if not decades, to come. Harvath, though, was already pushing his limit.

He was closer to exiting his forties than entering. He had been masking the pain that came from a lifetime of beating the hell out of his body with anti-inflammatories and the occasional Vicodin. In between, his preferred method was taking the healing waters of Buffalo Trace, Knob Creek, or Hudson Bay.

But despite everything that had been thrown at him, he worked hard to stay fit.

His training regimen had been crafted by one of the top sports medicine physicians in the country. In addition to massive weight and cardio workouts, he did what every successful operative did—he cheated.

The SEALs referred to it as the "cocktail," while Delta called it "Hulk sauce." It was a combination of performance-enhancing compounds developed by a group in Florida that worked on training and rehabilitating professional athletes.

Harvath had been the first at The Carlton Group to try it, even though Lara had cautioned him against it. The results turned out to be undeniable.

He had packed on ten additional pounds of muscle and had cut fourteen seconds off his mile. Even so, he was smart enough to know that there might be a price to pay. In time, the injections could be found to cause this or that illness. Right now, though, whatever allowed him to remain in the field was all that mattered.

Smiling back at Chase, he said, "So besides coffee, did we get anything else healthy, or is it all junk food?"

The young operative glanced in his bags. "Let me see. Vegan beef jerky, frozen Greek yogurt, wheat-grass-flavored mineral water—with extra pulp, and the pièce de résistance—probiotic Oreos."

Harvath shook his head. "Sounds delicious. Let's get going. I want eyes on Sparrman's farm before sunrise."

CHAPTER 31

The Gotland operation had always been envisioned as a snatch-and-grab of Sparrman. That meant concealable weapons, not long guns. But Harvath being Harvath, he had insisted that they bring one along—just in case. The weapon in question was a LaRue Tactical 6.5 Grendel FDE rifle with a Schmidt & Bender 5-25x56 scope with an illuminated reticle. In the case, Harvath had included a Summit thermal weapon sight for nighttime operations. They were glad to have all of it.

Across the road and slightly uphill from the Sparrman farm was a forest. It was the perfect spot for a hide site, a place to dig in and have an overwatch position of the key buildings on the property. Staelin and Chase had offered to take the first shift.

After pulling the car well off the road, the two former Delta Force operatives powered up their night-vision goggles and doubled back on foot as Haney unpacked the team's drone.

It was pitch-dark, but the device was outfitted with an infrared camera. Harvath wanted to do a quick reconnaissance of the area to see if there was anything in particular they needed to be aware of.

Haney worked quickly. Within five minutes of re-moving the Storm Case from the car, he had the drone airborne.

The live stream could be fed to multiple devices. Harvath watched on a small tablet.

The technology was advancing so quickly, it seemed as if they were upgrading their equipment on a monthly basis. Not only was the resolution incredible, but the sound had also been attenuated to such a degree that certain drones were scary quiet. One could be hover-ing several feet above your head and you wouldn't even know it unless you looked up and saw it directly. While good for his line of work, the rapid advancement in this and several other technologies gave him pause. He could envision a not-too-distant future where humans stayed behind in a tactical operations center while machines did all the work in the field—including, maybe some-day, snatching human targets.

Shaking the thought off, he focused on the footage that Haney's drone was sending back. It started far out-side and worked its way in.

The Sparrman farm had multiple kinds of livestock, predominantly cattle, sheep, and pigs. There was a large poultry barn, and from what the drone could see, it ap-peared they had a healthy number of chickens as well.

In addition to the poultry barn, there were a multi-tude of outbuildings, including what appeared to be a dairy barn.

The large property was cross-fenced, with water sta-tions in several places for the animals, along with plenty of run-in sheds and strategically placed grain dispensers.

Just off the road they had driven in on was the main house. It was two stories tall and a stone's throw from an old wooden structure, which was probably the farm's original barn. Behind it was what looked like a small administrative building. Across from that was what had to be a bunkhouse.

Harvath was particularly interested in the vehicles parked outside, and he had Haney zoom in for inspections. Even using the drone's IR illuminator, there was only so much information he could gather.

Once the preliminary reconnaissance was complete, he had Haney recall the drone, pack it back up, and return everything to the van.

They checked in with Staelin and Palmer one last time to make sure they had everything they needed and then returned to the rental house.

When they entered, they expected everyone to be sleeping, but they weren't. They were all in front of the flat-screen TV in the living room.

On it were images of incredible devastation. First responders worked feverishly to put out a roaring blaze.

The on-screen graphics, as well as the commentary, were all in Swedish. "What's going on?" asked Harvath.

"There was a bombing in Rome," said Jasinski, having pulled up the information on her phone. "At least that's what some outlets are saying. It hasn't been confirmed yet."

"Where did it take place?"

"Some restaurant on the Piazza Navona."

Harvath had just been in Rome, where he had helped disrupt a horrific attack. It seemed that no matter how hard they worked, it wasn't enough.

This was why Sloane and Chase would have permanent job security and why he needed to develop Jasinski and a thousand more like her.

"Has anyone claimed responsibility yet?" he asked. He wanted to know if it was an organization like ISIS, which had specifically listed Rome as a prime target. Something told him, though, that ISIS hadn't done this.

Jasinski kept scrolling.

Sloane was on her phone, too, and said, "An Italian communist newspaper in Rome called *Il Manifesto* says it received a statement from the PRF within the last hour taking credit. They say the target of the bombing was a former Italian diplomat known to frequent the restaurant, named Giovanni Lorenzo."

Jasinski knew the name right away. "Lorenzo used to be Deputy Secretary for NATO."

"Is he still involved with the organization?" asked Harvath.

Sloane searched farther in the article until she found it. "He heads the NATO Defense College Foundation based in Rome."

Jasinski looked back up at the terrible images unfolding on TV. "A popular restaurant, on the Piazza Navona, on a Friday night. The list of dead and injured civilians is going to be staggering. All to get to a former diplomat who now runs an NGO. It makes no sense."

Harvath looked at her. "It's horrible, but it makes perfect sense. This is what no rules looks like. This is how you create chaos. The people in Italy are going to be up in arms. And it will spread. Portugal, Spain, Greece—those countries that already lost diplomats—will be next. Then the rest of Europe will begin to bubble over. But that's not the worst part."

"What do you mean?" she asked.

"You don't dial your operation down after an attack like this. You dial it up. If the 'PRF' didn't have the world's attention before, they do now. Their attacks are going to start getting worse."

CHAPTER 32

It was never a good thing to be unexpectedly summoned to the White House. It was even worse when you had been out drinking.

Lydia Ryan didn't need to defend her behavior to her former boss. He had worked with enough spies on both sides of the Iron Curtain (before and after its collapse) to know how much alcohol was part of the espionage business.

"We'll keep it informal," Bob McGee, Director of Central Intelligence, said. "I'll ask President Porter to see us in the Residence. In the meantime, start hitting the black coffee."

"You know that coffee doesn't counteract booze, right?"

"Do it," McGee instructed. "And leave your car where it is. Grab a taxi. I'll have another cup waiting for you when you get here. Use the East Executive Avenue Gate."

When she arrived, McGee was on the other side of security waiting. In one hand was a coffee and in the other was his briefcase. After hanging her badge around her neck, she joined him.

"How are you feeling?" he asked, as he handed her the coffee.

"I feel like I shouldn't be here."

"You'll be fine. Don't worry."

"This isn't professional."

"Relax, Lydia," he said. "Do you have any idea how many times advisors have been summoned to the White House after hours? Tons. They've had to leave dinner parties, birthday parties, you name it. You're not the first person to have set foot on the grounds after having had a couple of cocktails.

"Look at it this way. When you eventually write your memoir, this'll make for one hell of a chapter. All I ask is that you wait until I'm retired before you publish."

Ryan grinned. "Deal," she said as she fished a tin of Altoids from her purse and popped two into her mouth.

Together they entered via the East Wing and proceeded to the Residence. President Paul Porter was waiting for them on the second floor in the Treaty Room, just down the hall from the master bedroom.

The Treaty Room functioned as a less formal office for the President. Near the windows was a large, leather-topped rectangular desk stacked with briefing books. At the other end of the room a large television hung on the wall, tuned to a cable news channel, but with the sound muted.

A fireplace with a white marble mantel occupied the room's west wall. Above it hung an enormous gilded mirror.

Reflected in the mirror was the sitting area on the other side of the room—a pair of leather club chairs, a coffee table, and a very long couch. Hanging over the couch was a vibrant expressionistic oil painting of George Washington crossing the Delaware by American artist

Steve Penley. The pops of color and splatters of paint gave the room a much more modern feeling than was present in the rest of the White House.

As Ryan and McGee were shown into the room, President Porter stood up from behind his desk and walked over to greet them.

"Bob, Lydia," he said, shaking their hands. "Thank you for coming."

Porter was a lean, rugged outdoorsman with a perpetual tan. Glossy profile pieces often compared him to Teddy Roosevelt. He enjoyed entertaining heads of state at Camp David, where he took pride in showing off the hiking trails he had helped clear.

The President showed his two guests to the seating area, where he had them sit on the couch while he took one of the chairs.

He wasted no time getting to the point. "How sure are we that the Russians were behind the bombing tonight in Rome?"

"*Il Manifesto* is a small Italian newspaper, but ideologically aligned with what the People's Revolutionary Front claims to represent," said McGee. "If they're looking to gin up support for an anti-NATO movement, there are a lot of fellow travelers in *Il Manifesto*'s readership. It makes good sense to make the claim of responsibility there first."

"*First?*" said Porter. "Who else have they contacted?"

Removing a folder from his briefcase, McGee replied, "As of right now, *La Repubblica* and *La Stampa* newspapers, as well as RAI and Sky Italia Television."

"Where does the death toll stand?"

McGee flipped to another page. "The restaurant was very crowded. Right now they have more than thirty-five dead and more than a hundred injured."

"Do we know anything about the bomb?"

"Not yet, but the FBI has dispatched a team to help assist the Italians in their investigation."

"And this Giovanni Lorenzo?" asked Porter. "Have we confirmed yet if he was present during the attack or what his status is?"

"We believe so. One of the paparazzi outside filed photographs with his press agency of Lorenzo arriving shortly before the bomb went off."

The President took a deep breath, slowly exhaled, and then looked at Ryan. "Could we have prevented this?"

"No, sir," she said. "We had no idea, no advance warning that Lorenzo, or anyone from the NATO Defense College or the Foundation, was actively being targeted."

"Three diplomats have been murdered, then the Norway incident, and now Rome. Can you honestly sit there and tell me that we should still be quiet about this? That we shouldn't expose the Russians and bring holy hell down on them?"

"I don't think so, sir," she replied.

"Why not?"

"First, we don't have enough concrete evidence that we could release to the media. It would be our word against the Russians'. They would spin it as a wild conspiracy theory. Fake news. Perhaps even claim it is a plot by us to discredit them. As we discussed before, if we can't completely control the narrative, we don't want it out there."

"And, if I might add," injected McGee, "putting the story out there might not change anything. All we'd be doing is tipping our hand to Moscow. We should stick with Harvath's plan."

"It's turning into a bloodbath," stated the President. "We have to do something."

"We are doing something," Ryan reassured him. "We're actively targeting their propaganda apparatus, as well as the PRF itself. Director McGee is right. We need to stick to the plan."

"But can you assure me that it's working?"

"Yes. It's working."

Pointing at the coverage on his television, Porter replied, "Because that doesn't look like it's working to me."

"Mr. President," said McGee, "the Russians were always going to have a head start on us. We had no idea where or when the starting gun was going to go off. Now that it has, we're right on their heels."

Porter looked at Ryan. She was the one in charge of the ground operation. "Is that true?" he asked. "Are we *right on their heels*?"

No, it wasn't true and Ryan knew it. In fact, they had taken a huge step backward. Losing Lars Lund had been a terrible blow to their progress. Harvath was working in a ridiculously tight window, and it was all but impossible to make up the ground Lund had covered before the Swedish police stepped in and froze them out.

Nevertheless, she had to give him a chance, carve out a little breathing room that might allow him to make up that lost ground. If anyone could pull it off, it would be Harvath.

What was more, this wasn't the time for the President to be having second thoughts. Ryan abhorred the loss of life, too. She would have given everything to have prevented one drop of blood from being spilled. But the fact was, America and her allies weren't spilling the blood. The Russians were.

Coming out publicly wasn't the answer. McGee was absolutely right. They'd only be tipping their hand to the Russians. Moscow would very likely see it as a sign of weakness, which might even embolden them further. It was better for America to keep its cards to itself and push on. The challenge, though, was in convincing Porter to stay the course.

If not for the liquor in her bloodstream, Ryan might not have had the courage to say what she said next.

"Mr. President, with all due respect, you gave us this mission. You said, and I quote, 'No matter what the cost, prevent an Article 5.'" Drawing his attention to the TV, she said, "*This* is the cost, and it *is* terrible. Those are allies and innocents being maimed and killed. But it pales in comparison to what another world war would look like.

"You made the right decision. Now, please, trust us to do our jobs. I promise you, we can do this."

Porter knew she was right. They had to see this through. It didn't make it any easier, though, to watch it unfold. Nor did it ease his mind about what might come next.

Which brought him to the other item he wanted to discuss. Pausing, he said, "Let's talk about what we're going to do regarding Matterhorn."

CHAPTER 33

After a few hours' sleep, Harvath had come downstairs to relieve Haney and monitor radio traffic from the team out at the Sparrman property. So far, not a creature was stirring, though it being a farm, he expected activity to start pretty soon.

The country house they were staying in was an eclectic mix of old and new. The furniture was modern and brightly colored, while everything else looked as if it had been frozen sometime in the late 1800s. It smelled like lavender, and Harvath strongly suspected that the owner had placed sachets of it in hidden locations around the home.

He was sitting at the dining room table, killing time, with a mug of hot coffee and a book, when he heard Jasinski come downstairs.

"What are you doing up?" he asked.

"I kept tossing and turning. I can't stop thinking about what happened in Norway, and now Rome."

"I eventually turned the TV off. They just kept repeating the same images. Did you get any sleep at all?"

"A little. Not much," she replied.

"There's coffee in the kitchen."

Jasinski thanked him and joined him at the table a few minutes later with her own mug. "What are you reading?"

Harvath held the book up so she could see it. "*Writer, Sailor, Soldier, Spy* by Nicholas Reynolds."

"How is it?"

"It's fascinating—all about how Ernest Hemingway was a spy for both U.S. and Soviet Intelligence."

"He was?"

Harvath nodded. "Did you ever read Alexander Foote's *Handbook for Spies*?"

"No. Should I?"

"It covers some of the same material regarding Soviet spy networks, but it's a first-person account. I think it should be required reading for anyone in our business."

Jasinski looked at him over the rim of her mug. "So, you're a spy?"

"To be honest with you, Monika, I don't know exactly what I am."

She smiled. "I was always told that when someone says, 'to be honest with you,' it often means they're lying."

Harvath smiled back. "Not this time."

"If you're not a spook, what are you, then?"

It was a good question, and one that Harvath had been trying for a while to come up with an answer for. "I don't think there's a word for it. At least not one that covers all the aspects of the job."

"Well, there has to be a word better than *consultant*. Why don't you tell me about the person you work for? I understand he and Lars Lund and Carl Pedersen knew each other."

"They all go way back," said Harvath. "Cold War guys."

"What did your boss do?"

"He was an intelligence officer at the CIA. He helped create the Counter Terrorism Center. Brilliant man."

Finally, she was getting some answers. She decided to keep pushing. "And he now works at the Supreme Allied Command Transformation back in Norfolk?"

Harvath smiled. "No. SACT, and NATO more specifically, is our client. After retiring from the CIA, my boss took everything he had learned and set up his own business."

"Doing what?"

"I'm still trying to find a better word for it."

Jasinski rolled her eyes. "Try *contracting*."

Harvath shook his head. "That conjures up images of ex special operations personnel doing security details. We do more than that. A lot more."

"If you had a brochure," she asked, "what would it say?"

He thought about it for several moments and replied, "Hypothetically, it would say that we offer a suite of products, services, and turnkey solutions comparable to the CIA, but without all the bureaucracy."

"*How* comparable?"

"Extremely."

She couldn't believe it. "You've privatized the espionage business."

"Some things work better away from all the red tape."

"But what about accountability? Some semblance of oversight?"

"We answer to the client."

"What does that even mean?" she asked.

"It means we've been given a certain amount of flexibility in getting our job done."

"We're back to *creativity* and tossing out the rulebook, aren't we?"

"My boss likes to say that in every operation there's above the line and below the line," he replied. "Above the line is what you do by the book. Below the line is how you get the job done. We do what we need to do to get the job done."

"Is that what you plan to do here? With Sparrman?"

"We're going to work our way up the food chain. First we'll start with Sparrman. Then we'll go after the person above him. And so on and so on."

"And what if Sparrman doesn't want to give up the person above him?" she asked.

"He will."

"How can you be so sure of yourself?"

Harvath smiled again. "Experience."

"This isn't a fact-finding assignment. You're going to kidnap him, aren't you? Just like that GRU agent you snatched in Berlin."

"You don't have to come along."

"Look around you," she said, holding out her arms. "I'm already here."

"So are the Russians, Monika."

He was right. She couldn't argue with that. Taking a sip of her coffee, she looked away. She now understood they were not there to confirm suspicions. They had already decided that Sparrman was working with the Russians.

"You know I read your file," he continued.

It seemed to her an odd thing to say. "And?" she asked.

"And I know you hate the Russians every bit as much as I do."

"You read my file and you think you know me?" He had touched a raw nerve and pissed her off. "You don't know anything about me."

"I know you work in the terrorism intelligence cell, but have been instrumental in uncovering multiple Russian spies at SHAPE. That doesn't happen by accident.

That happens because you want to stick it to them. Because you want to cause them as much pain as possible. You've got a score to settle."

"You don't know what you're talking about."

But he did know what he was talking about. And he could see it written all over her face.

They sat without speaking for several minutes, before she finally broke the silence. "They killed him," she said. "It was the Russians. I don't care what anyone else says."

CHAPTER 34

Her eyes were moist as she fought to keep her emotions in check. It was incredibly painful and difficult to discuss.

Harvath didn't push. Monika was the one who had to decide if she wanted to go into detail. This was completely up to her.

"In April and May of 1940, the Soviet Union committed a series of mass executions of Polish military officers, politicians, and intellectuals. Among the so-called intellectuals were police officers, lawyers, priests, doctors, bakers, and schoolteachers. In all, twenty-two thousand were executed and their bodies were dumped in mass graves in the Katyn Forest outside Smolensk, Russia.

"The murders were carried out by the precursor to the KGB—the Soviet secret police known as the NKVD. It was done with Stalin's full knowledge and support.

"For years, the Russians lied and dissembled about their involvement. They first blamed the Nazis. Then after the fall of communism, they blamed the no-longer-existent Soviet Union. Finally, they stopped discussing it altogether, saying that because the perpetrators were all dead, there was no point. They refused to fully accept the blame, much less discuss reparations.

"As far as the Polish people were concerned, it should

have been classified as a war crime or genocide. Instead, the Soviet-era cover-up was simply swept under the rug and largely ignored. Poland, though, kept pushing.

"Because it refused to give up, Poland forced Russia to finally and officially accept its role. Of course, in its proclamation the Russian Duma blamed Stalin and a collection of party officials, but it was at long last recognition of the evil that had been done.

"That was eight years ago—the seventieth anniversary of the massacre. As a gesture of what was believed to be goodwill, Russia agreed to allow a party of Polish dignitaries to visit the site of the massacre and pay their respects. It was supposed to have served as a commemoration ceremony—a closing of a very painful wound.

"What no one knew, at least not in Poland, was how much deeper and more painful that wound was about to be made."

Jasinski took a moment and several deep breaths in order to maintain her composure. The worst part, for her, was what came next.

"On April 10, 2010, eighty-nine passengers and seven crew members boarded a Polish Air Force Tupolev TU-154 jet in Warsaw for the flight to Smolensk. On board were the President of Poland and his wife, the last surviving President of Poland in Exile during the Soviet occupation, the Chief of the General Staff, as well as the Commanders of the Polish Army, the Polish Navy, the Polish Air Force, and the Polish Special Forces, the President of the National Bank of Poland, eighteen members of Parliament, the Deputy Minister for National Defense, the Deputy Minister for Foreign Affairs, prominent clergy, and several relatives of victims of the Katyn massacre."

Once again, she breathed deeply. Her eyes were

damp with tears as she said, "In addition to other dignitaries, there were a handful of key aides along to make sure the trip went smoothly. One of them was my husband, Julian.

"According to the Russian reports, the aircraft tried to land in a rapidly deteriorating weather situation. There was a dense fog, which reduced visibility to less than five hundred meters. Allegedly, the plane came in dangerously low, its left wing striking a birch tree, which caused the plane to roll and crash into the woods near the airport, killing everyone on board.

"Despite their claims that it was just an accident, the Russians stonewalled the investigation at every turn, refusing to turn over the flight recorders, refusing access to the site, and refusing to produce key pieces of the wreckage.

"Only through incredible international pressure did Russia finally begin to cooperate. By then, a large portion of the Polish people believed that Russia was complicit in the crash—that it had been a massive political assassination, a decapitation strike.

"The Polish government that came to power in the aftermath of the crash was much more favorable to Russia than its predecessor. That fact is undeniable, and further supports the theory that the Russians caused the crash.

"Many people in Poland would rather close the book on the crash, to not pick at the scab, as it were. To this day, it is still a very hotly contested subject in Poland.

"That said, three years ago a different government came to power—one that does not hold Russia in such high regard. The new government decided to reopen the investigation and has gone so far as to exhume the remains of the deceased President.

"From what I have been told, traces of explosives were found on the plane's left wing. There are some very powerful people who believe this was absolutely a plot by the Russians to weaken and destabilize Poland."

Harvath knew the conspiracy theories were not popular in Poland and that polling ran two to one against its being anything but a crash in bad weather due to pilot error. In fact, the unit the pilots had come from had been disbanded for how poorly its members were trained, and several senior level officers had been forced to resign.

He also understood people wanted answers, especially for such a terrible, terrible tragedy. Having done presidential protection with the Secret Service, he couldn't for the life of him understand why the Poles had packed so many extremely important, high-level government figures onto one plane. The protocol had been changed since, but it was just plain foolish from a continuity-of-government perspective.

There was nothing Harvath could say other than "I'm so sorry."

"Thank you," she replied.

Even if the Russians hadn't been involved in crashing the plane and it had been an accident, they had handled the aftermath in such an atrocious fashion that he couldn't blame her for hating them and letting that hate creep into blame for the entire thing.

There was also the possibility, no matter how remote, that the Russians *had* been involved in bringing the aircraft down. It wouldn't have been the first time, and sadly, it likely wouldn't be the last.

Taking a sip of her coffee, Monika looked away from him and out the window. "As terrible as it was," she continued. "There was one more wound I was forced to suffer."

Harvath had already known about her husband and the crash, but that was pretty much the extent of it. He waited for her to continue.

"I was pregnant," she said. "We hadn't told anyone yet. Julian and I were trying to decide what we were going to do. We had talked about my leaving the Army.

"In the end, it didn't matter. In addition to losing my husband, I miscarried and also lost my baby."

Harvath felt terrible for her. "Monika, I am so sorry. No one should have to go through that."

"Apparently, I did."

How to respond? Harvath wasn't exactly skillful at talking about his own feelings, much less somebody else's. The one thing he knew, though, was that if he wasn't careful, he could very likely make things worse. He decided not to say anything, and they sat there for several more minutes, as they had in the beginning, in silence.

He watched her, turned away from him and looking out the window. He couldn't even begin to fathom what she was feeling.

It made him realize, though, how fortunate he was to have someone back home waiting for him. It also made him wonder if he hadn't been taking Lara for granted.

The Old Man, before he really began slipping away, had pushed him to do the right thing and marry her. He had even gone so far as to call Harvath a "dope" for not already having done so. He said it would serve him right if another man came along and swept her off her feet. And that it would be doubly poetic if it happened while Harvath was on one of his many trips abroad.

The Old Man probably had a point. In fact, if Harvath was honest with himself, there was no "probably" about it. Harvath needed to figure out what he wanted, and then act on it.

He was about to grab another cup of coffee when his radio crackled to life. It was Staelin. "We've got activity."

Harvath wasn't surprised. It would be daylight in an hour. There were countless things that needed to be done on a farm every morning. "What do you see?" he asked.

"The farmhands are jogging."

"*Jogging?*"

"Yes," said Staelin. "In formation. *Military* formation."

CHAPTER 35

Harvath would have liked to have seen it for himself, but he never would have gotten there in time. Instead, he had Staelin describe, in detail, what was taking place.

Apparently, eight rather fit men had assembled outside, two abreast, and had run off in a column. Normally when runners go out in a group, it's casual and they run in a pack. To run in formation was unusual. It suggested that structure and discipline were being imposed.

Harvath's mind went back to what Nicholas had said about placing a deep-cover team of Spetsnaz operatives on the island. He also remembered what Nyström had said about Sparrman hiring from Eastern Europe. While the Swedes were excellent in English, he doubted they could tell a Russian from a Romanian or a Moldovan. If the GRU had a willing local, a farm would be a perfect place to hide a team of Special Forces soldiers.

Harvath told him to keep an eye on everything and that he'd be sending in Ashby and Barton soon to relieve them.

Signing off, he began formulating a plan. Eight potential Spetsnaz troops was not a fight he wanted to have. If they came out of the GRU's unit, they were battle-tested and had seen plenty of action—most recently in places like Syria and Ukraine, if not as far back as Chechnya and Georgia.

Taking Sparrman at the farm might be too dangerous. Harvath and his team might have to snatch him on the fly, while he was in transit. That posed a whole other set of problems.

If Sparrman had been involved in Lars Lund's accident, which Harvath had a pretty good feeling he was, then the man might be a lot more switched on than usual, paying close attention to whether he was under surveillance.

Harvath would need to identify the best possible location, as well as the best possible circumstances under which to grab him—all with having little to no surveillance on him.

This, of course, presupposed that Sparrman even left the farm at all. If he didn't, if he was under the weather or was just some sort of recluse, Harvath was going to need to come up with a plan to go in and yank him out.

And no matter which route he took, Harvath would have to make his move before the window closed and Nyström set up his own surveillance and actively took over the case. He had only thirty-six hours left.

But the more Harvath studied the situation, the more problems he saw staring back at him. He wasn't exactly being pummeled by the good idea fairy. It was going to be a long day.

Surveillance, like a lot of the work performed in the intelligence game, involved long periods of extreme boredom. The Sparrman farm assignment was a textbook case.

With the sunrise, Ashby and Barton had been able to provide Harvath with the makes, models, and colors of the vehicles parked at the entrance of the property. None were any shade of olive.

Other than that, no useful intelligence was produced. Nobody visited the farm. Nobody left the farm.

By late afternoon, Harvath and Haney were debating the risks of doing another, more aggressive drone flight. Harvath had already begun fleshing out an assault on the farm and needed more information to help plan their approach. They decided to wait until dark and then go out to check on the surveillance team.

When the time came, they filled a thermos they had found in the kitchen with hot coffee and headed out to the minivan. The Camry was with the surveillance team in case Sparrman left the property and offered an opportunity to be followed.

They all knew what Sparrman looked like. A Gotland newspaper had done an article about the farm two years ago and had run his picture with it. Harvath had made sure that everyone downloaded a copy to their phone.

There had been sporadic sightings of him throughout the day. His shock of almost orange hair was unmistakable. Sloane had started calling him the "Ginja Ninja."

"Tomorrow's Sunday," mused Haney, as he turned left onto the main road. "What are the chances the guy hops in his car to go meet up with his mom for church?"

"Church. Brunch. Paddle boarding. All we would need is an opening," answered Harvath. "But our forty-eight hours expires tomorrow night."

"Do you think that Nyström guy is going to start right up? Maybe he'll wait until Monday."

"And if he doesn't?"

"Good point," replied Haney. He, like Harvath, knew

that as soon as the police took over, it would be extremely difficult to grab Sparrman.

Tonight was going to have to be the night. Harvath had already resigned himself to it. He had also, along with the rest of the team, resigned himself to the fact that the men who had been seen that morning going on their group run were indeed Spetsnaz operatives.

The thorniest issue for Harvath was how to get everyone in and out without raising the alarm.

Sparrman occupied the main house by himself, but had two very large dogs. From what Ashby and Barton had seen, they looked like Great Pyrenees. As soon as anyone got near the house, they were going to start barking. If that happened, the element of surprise would be lost.

Back when Harvath and Nicholas had been on opposite sides, Harvath had figured out how to get around the two guard dogs. He didn't like punishing animals. They were only doing their job. Still, they had to be dealt with. As soon as he and Haney had checked in with the surveillance team and had completed their drone flight, they'd drive into town to get what he needed.

CHAPTER 36

Harvath and Haney dropped off the thermos of coffee and took over surveillance so Ashby and Barton could have a ten-minute break. Harvath also wanted a better look at the front of the farm.

As the two men held down the hide site, Harvath rattled off a specific list of things Haney should make sure to capture when he flew the drone overhead. He was trying to cover every possible eventuality, and this was likely going to be one of their last looks before they breached the property on foot.

When Ashby and Barton returned, they all traded places and Harvath and Haney returned to the minivan. Five minutes later, the drone was airborne and Harvath was watching a live feed via the tablet again.

In addition to primary and contingent means of entering and leaving the farm, Harvath was interested in several possible areas in which to create a diversion.

From takeoff to touchdown, the drone had been up for a little over twenty minutes. Satisfied that he had seen what he needed to, they packed up and headed for town.

First on his list was the pharmacy. Having checked it out online, he knew they would only be open for another hour. The grocery store would be open much later, and even if they somehow missed it, there was always the gas station minimart.

He had just entered the store and had been directed by a clerk to what he needed when his phone rang. It was Jasinski. She had agreed to monitor the radio while he and Haney were out of range.

"Sparrman is on the move," she said when Harvath accepted the call.

"Alone?" he asked, taking his items to the front of the store so he could pay for them.

"No. There are at least two other people in the car with him. Ashby is going to stay and watch the property. Barton will follow and see where they're going."

"Negative. I want it to be Sloane. A woman will draw less attention if they park and she has to get out and follow on foot. Have her call me as soon as she's on the road."

"Understood. I'll relay your instructions."

Disconnecting the call, Harvath paid for his items and quickly exited the store. Haney was outside with the minivan.

"Sparrman's on the move," Harvath informed him.

"Who's in the follow car?"

"Sloane."

Both men hopped back in the minivan and Haney asked, "Where to?"

"Start heading toward the farm. As soon as Sloane calls, we'll have more information and can adjust our course."

"Roger that."

Pulling out into traffic, Haney headed back the way they had come. Moments later, Harvath's cell phone rang. It was Sloane. He put her on speaker so that Haney could hear her, too.

"Okay, Sloane," said Harvath. "What do you have?"

"He's driving the red, late model Volkswagen Golf headed north-northwest on Route 143. Two passengers are with him. I'm guessing Spetsnaz."

"Stay on him, but don't get too close."

"So getting right up on his ass is a bad idea?" she snarked. "If only I knew what I was doing."

"You know what I mean," Harvath replied. "I want everybody to stay cool. This may be the opportunity we've been looking for."

"Roger that."

"What should we do about the rest of the team?" Haney asked.

"Let's spin them up," said Harvath, gesturing for Haney's cell phone. "Once we know what the destination is, we can decide who goes back to pick everyone else up."

Haney handed over his phone and Harvath used it to call Jasinski. He told her what they knew so far and asked her to relay everything to Palmer and Staelin.

"What about Barton?" she asked.

"Same thing," he replied.

Disconnecting the call, he asked Sloane for an update.

"No change. Still headed toward Visby on 143. Looks like we're about twenty klicks out."

Harvath decided to disengage. Looking at Haney, he said, "Pull over."

Haney did as instructed.

Then, addressing Sloane, he said, "Sloane, we've pulled over. It's Saturday night and I think—"

He was interrupted by Jasinski calling back on Haney's phone. "Hold on," he said to Sloane as he activated the other call. "What's up?"

"According to Barton, two additional vehicles just left the farm. The first, a blue Jeep Wrangler, is carrying four of our Spetsnaz friends. The other vehicle is a silver Fiat Bravo carrying the remaining two."

"Good copy," said Harvath, as he disconnected the call and turned his attention back to Sloane. "As I was saying, it's Saturday night and it looks like the farmhands are all riding into town. Watch your six. Two more vehicles just left. Blue Jeep Wrangler and a silver Fiat Bravo."

"Blue Jeep Wrangler. Silver Fiat Bravo," Sloane repeated. "Good copy."

Looking at Haney, Harvath said, "If they remain on course, they'll drive right past us. Let's get on the other side of the street so we can pull out behind them once the last of the vehicles drives past."

"Roger that," Haney said, pulling back out into the street and looking for a place to turn around.

Once he had, Harvath saw a parking spot up ahead and told him to grab it. It was right in front of a trendy women's clothing boutique.

Pulling a pen from his jacket pocket, he asked Sloane what her sizes were.

"What for?" she asked.

"Because you're going to need to look the part."

"What part?"

"Don't worry, just give me your sizes," he said, getting out of the minivan.

As he did, he handed Haney his phone back, instructed him to put the same question to Jasinski, and have her text back the information.

He needed to move fast. At best, the vehicles were fifteen minutes outside of town.

CHAPTER 37

You've got to be kidding me," said Sloane, who had parked and was now in back of the minivan. "What did you do? Pop into a Whores-R-Us and ask for the sluttiest stuff they had in my size?"

"It's a little black dress," Harvath replied. "Don't be so melodramatic."

"You got the *little* part right. But this isn't a dress. It's a cocktail napkin with straps."

"You're going to look great."

Sloane gave him the finger and then, turning it upside down, signaled him to face the other direction. Politely, he obliged her.

He had made it out of the boutique with only moments to spare. After he had tossed the bags in the minivan, it was less than a minute before Sparrman drove past, with Sloane several car lengths behind. Behind her were the other two vehicles filled with Spetsnaz operatives. As they passed, Harvath could see that's what they were. They were hard, switched-on fighters.

Harvath had consumed enough alcohol with enough operators to know that they didn't become any less aggressive when they were out drinking. Some became even more so. He hoped, though, that after a few rounds, they'd loosen up; relax a little. All he needed was a sliver of daylight, for the figurative door to be opened just a crack, and he would exploit the hell out of it.

"Okay. You can turn back around," Sloane said.

The dress looked amazing—as if it had been designed just for her. "Not bad."

"Fuck you, *not bad*. I'm sure I look fantastic," she replied from the backseat of the minivan.

They had driven into Visby's walled Old Town and watched as Sparrman and his crew parked their vehicles and entered an Irish-themed sports bar and restaurant called O'Learys. It was a chain, with outlets all across Sweden.

The entrance was via a large patio, which had a retractable roof and was dotted with seating areas and portable gas heaters. Inside was a long bar with additional chairs and tables. Televisions were mounted everywhere. Even on the patio, customers could catch a range of matches happening around the world—all of which appeared to be either rugby or soccer.

Haney had taken up a position across the street to keep an eye on O'Learys, while Harvath had parked the minivan around the corner and linked up with Sloane.

"I bet at least half the women in there are going to be wearing jeans," she complained.

"Then that's just going to make your job all the easier," he replied.

"Next time you tell me to pack a bag, I'm going to make sure I pack my *own* dress. *And* shoes."

Pulling out a shoebox from the shopping bag he had handed her, she removed the lid and looked inside. "Hooker heels?" she asked, holding up one of the shoes so he could see its tall, Lucite heel. "You really did go to Whores-R-Us. You couldn't have bought me a nice pair of thigh-high boots?"

"They didn't have any in your size."

"How am I supposed to operate in these?"

"You'll figure it out," he said. "Besides, the only *operating* you're supposed to be doing is capturing Sparrman's attention."

"How about you come in with me, and I give you a full-on ass-kicking for this costume? Think that might get his attention?"

Harvath grinned. "Probably, but not in the way we'd like."

"Consider yourself lucky then, because it wouldn't have been pretty. I mean, *I* would have been pretty, but *you* would have ended up curled in a ball and crying on the floor of the ladies' room."

Drawing an oval around his face with his index finger, he encouraged her to put her makeup on.

Turning the bag upside down and dumping the remaining items on the seat, she looked at everything and said, "Don't ever go clothes or makeup shopping for Lara. Stick to jewelry, okay? Because you are beyond hopeless."

He shook his head.

Opening a metal tube, she extended a bright lipstick called Dynamite Red. "Subtle. Can't wait to see the eye shadow."

The eye shadow, as it turned out, was not half bad. The lipstick, too, looked great on her.

Finishing up her makeup, she did her hair, and then asked Harvath, "How do I look?"

"Terrific," he replied, and he meant it. As a rule, he ignored her looks and focused on her brains and her skills—which were also formidable. The truth was, though, that she was hot. And the way she was put together now, she was super hot. "Dressed to kill."

"Or at least *capture*, right?"

Harvath laughed. "Correct. Let's roll."

Opening the door, he waited for her to slip her heels on and then helped her out. "Don't rush anything, okay? Take your time. Play hard to get. The more he drinks, the better off we'll be."

"Trust me," she replied. "I know what I'm doing."

Of course she did, but Harvath was a detail guy. He needed to make sure she understood how he wanted the operation to unfold. That said, he knew that the minute she walked into that bar, anything could happen.

"Just be careful," he said. "Don't take any unnecessary risks. I'll be close by if you need me."

Holding out her hand, she waited for him to count off a stack of currency. Once he had, she grabbed her cell phone and headed for O'Learys. She really did look fantastic.

"You'd better not be looking at my ass," she warned, without turning around.

Harvath laughed and watched until she disappeared around the corner. Moments later, Haney came and joined him.

"She's inside," he stated. "Am I good to go?"

Harvath nodded and handed him the keys to the minivan. "Get back here as soon as you can. Jasinski's bag is on the backseat."

"Got it," said Haney. Sliding into the driver's seat, he fired up the minivan, put it in gear, and headed back to the rental house.

Harvath decided to go check out the three vehicles Sparrman and his crew had driven into town from the farm. They were parked about a half block up and he began walking.

He had only made it a quarter of the way when he

saw a marked police car coming down the cobbled street, and he ducked into an archway.

The vehicle was moving slowly, almost purposefully. He couldn't tell if the cop was looking for something specific, or if he was just making his rounds. Receding further into the darkness, Harvath pressed himself up flat against the wall.

As the car neared, Harvath recognized the officer. He was one of the two uniformed cops who had met the plane last night—the taller one. Harvath paused for a moment, trying to recall the man's name. Then it came to him—*Johansson*.

Visby was a small town. Maybe Johansson was just on patrol and they had ended up in the same place at the same time. That wouldn't have been so unusual. Harvath was tempted to write it off as a coincidence.

By the same token, he had made it a rule not to believe in coincidences. That rule had saved his life more times than he could remember.

Once the officer had rolled past, Harvath looked out from the archway and then stepped back onto the street. He had a bad feeling about it and decided to take Johansson's presence as an ominous sign.

CHAPTER 38

The only person Artur Kopec could trust with more than one hundred thousand dollars in cash was Tomasz Wójcik.

Wójcik had made a fortune in bribes and kickbacks while head of Poland's Central Anticorruption Bureau, or CBA. If not for Kopec, he probably would have gotten away with it. Wójcik was absolutely amazing when it came to offshore banking and laundering money.

What had tripped him up was a singular piece of misfortune. He had employed someone who was already an intelligence asset on Kopec's payroll. When the asset informed Kopec of who Wójcik was and what he wanted, Kopec encouraged him to take the illicit job and further the relationship. Once Wójcik had fully implicated himself, Kopec had sprung.

He had given the corrupt official two choices—he could be prosecuted and go to jail, or he could come to work for Kopec. The man had chosen wisely. He had gone to work for Kopec.

It was a mutually beneficial relationship. Considering the side jobs Kopec took from time to time, like the one he was on for the Americans right now, a man like Wójcik was good to have on the payroll.

Now, a leather Gurkha messenger bag slung from his shoulder, Wójcik made his way through Gorky Park—the oldest park in the city—named after the Soviet-era writer known as Maxim Gorky.

Wójcik's psoriasis was flaring up. Even though he had slathered his body with ointment before leaving the hotel, the flaky patches of red skin had returned. They were inflamed and itched terribly.

Though it was the stress, he blamed the weather. He hated it in Europe. He would have much preferred retiring to the Caribbean, or maybe the Florida Keys, but Kopec had forbidden it. Vacations? No problem. Permanent residency outside Poland? No way.

The Polish intelligence officer lorded his power over him. Wójcik's life was not his own—at least not to the degree any free person would have desired. Though he lived comfortably in Warsaw, he lived as an indentured servant. Kopec could pull his passport at any time. Even more troublesome, he could turn him over to the authorities.

Wójcik tried to keep that in mind and to find the bright side. His wife of forty-seven years had died the winter before. He had been by her side when she passed, rather than rotting away in a Polish prison cell. He saw his children and grandchildren on a regular basis. He came and went, within reason, as he pleased. It was a prison of sorts, but it could have been much worse.

He thought about that as he strolled through the park toward the planetarium on the other side of the fifty-six-meter-high Ferris wheel.

It was a Saturday night and the park was quite lively—packed with families and lots of young people. He could hear music and laughter all around.

Kopec had sent him as a courier, his leather bag filled with American currency. He was to meet with his counterpart from Belarus, Pavel Kushner.

Kushner had been chairperson of the Central Department for Combatting Organized Crime and Corruption at the Belarusian Ministry of Internal Affairs.

The pair had met, quite by accident, via a shared private banker in Switzerland. Certain financial synergies quickly became apparent. Within months, they had discovered a very profitable way to exploit the border between Poland and Belarus.

That exploitation was why Wójcik had been sent to see his old friend and business partner.

At the third bench before the observatory, Wójcik took a seat and unslung the messenger bag.

Setting it next to him, he slid his hand beneath his coat and scratched at the painfully dry skin of his upper left arm and shoulder.

Unfortunately, it didn't bring him much relief and might have only made it worse.

Fishing a flask from his interior coat pocket, he looked around to make sure he wasn't being watched, unscrewed the cap, and took a long pull of a spiced Polish liqueur known as *kardamonka*.

Down the esplanade, he could see Kushner, slightly bent, and in his trademark black trench coat, walking in his direction. Wójcik returned the flask to its hiding place and stood to greet him.

The two men embraced each other and then sat down.

"I'm sorry to take you away from your weekend," said Wójcik. "Thank you for coming back into town to see me."

"Our dacha is only an hour away," replied Kushner. "Besides, you said it was important. And worth my while."

Wójcik nodded at the Gurkha. "The money and the photos are inside."

Unzipping the briefcase, Kushner looked inside. "I don't know much about missile technology," he said. "But if your missing upgrade kits came into Belarus, there's only a handful of people who can move them. I know someone I can ask."

"How long do you think it will take?"

"Give me a couple of days. Where are you staying?"

"The Crowne Plaza."

Kushner shrugged. "A little too brightly lit for me. But it's okay, I suppose. Would you like for me to arrange a girl for you?"

"No," said Wójcik. "That isn't necessary."

"Of course it is necessary. You're still a man, aren't you?"

"I am an *old* man."

"So am I, but it doesn't stop me. There is an oyster bar not far from the hotel. I can get you a table. It will help you put some lead in your pencil. Or I have the blue pills if you need them. Wiagra," the Belarusian said, mispronouncing the name.

"Viagra," his friend corrected.

"That's what I said."

Wójcik smiled. "No girls. No oysters. No Viagra. Thank you."

"In other words, no fun."

All the Pole wanted to do was get back to his room and reapply his lotion, but that kind of personal information wasn't something he felt prepared to share. Rising from the bench, he left the Gurkha and said, "It was good seeing you again. I am sorry for interrupting your weekend."

"It's always a pleasure to reconnect with an old friend," Kushner replied. "If you change your mind about anything, no matter what you need, call me."

"I will," said Wójcik. "Thank you. And please remember, this is a rush job."

"Of course," said the Belarusian. "I'll handle it. Don't worry."

Smiling, the Pole shook his friend's hand and, turning, walked out of the park.

As he made his way back to the hotel, he never even noticed that he was being followed.

CHAPTER 39

S loane lingered at the hostess stand long enough for everyone inside to get a good eyeful. If Harvath had had any doubts about her talents, seeing the very discreet yet seductive way she handled herself would have put all of them to rest.

After acting like a chatty American, and having explained how she was working in Stockholm and had come over on the ferry for a fun weekend on Gotland, she was shown to a table by the hostess. She promised to be on the lookout for Sloane's "friend" and would bring her over as soon as she arrived.

A few minutes later, a waitress arrived to take her order. O'Learys specialized in American-style bar food—things like burgers, wings, nachos, and Jalapeño poppers.

She and the team had been on the road for over a month. A taste of home, even though she was on the job, would be a real treat.

After ordering a Red Bull and a plate of wings, she settled back in her chair and took a look around.

Sparrman and his crew had all seen her come in. She had seen them, too, though she hadn't let them know it.

Even now, their eyes were still all over her. Pulling out her phone, she texted Chase to see how much longer they would be. Haney hadn't gotten there yet. Based on his estimate, they were at least ten minutes away.

Starting a new text, she gave Harvath a SITREP from inside to let him know how things were going. Glancing up at Sparrman and the Russians, she saw that their attention had shifted to one of the TVs, where a new soccer match was about to begin. The matchup appeared to be between Russia and the Czech Republic.

Apparently, they were big fans of the sport, which she hoped would work to her advantage. If the game went well and they were enjoying themselves, it might provide her with the perfect opportunity.

She knew plenty of women who would have said no to an operation like this. They would have been offended even at the thought of being used as "bait." Sloane, though, didn't have a problem with it. She wasn't being asked to be part of a honey trap. Harvath had never asked her to do something like that, nor would he ever. He knew, without even asking, what her answer would be.

He also knew why she was so determined to do this kind of work. Despite her parents' willingness, and ability, Sloane had paid her own way through college via the ROTC program. She had attended Northwestern University, where she studied math and chemistry.

She had grown up in an affluent household and had been a competitive figure skater through high school. Once she got to college, she had switched over to snowboarding, where she became not only more competitive, but happier. Where she hadn't been happy, though, was after college when she entered the Army.

The only reason she had agreed to sign up was that she was promised combat. She didn't believe in taking money for school and not paying it back as fully as she could.

She did two tours in Afghanistan, during which she killed more enemy combatants than all of the other female soldiers combined. When word of her prowess leaked, a popular women's magazine back in the States did an unauthorized profile of her. As soon as Al Qaeda and the Taliban discovered it, they placed a bounty on her head and the Pentagon pulled her from combat.

She ended up working with the all-female Delta Force unit known as the Athena Project, but as a trainer, not an operative. While she was proud to be part of such a prestigious program, it continually pissed her off to see those women being sent out on assignments as she remained behind at Fort Bragg.

When Reed Carlton had offered her the opportunity to join his company and do all of the things she longed to do, she had jumped at the chance. In hiring her, he was putting into effect the same modus operandi Athena was—take highly intelligent, highly accomplished, highly attractive female athletes, give them the same training as the men, and set them loose in the field.

Women like Sloane were so successful not only because they were good at what they did, but also because their beauty negated them as a threat. The simple fact was that when most men saw a good-looking woman, the blood flow to their brains got diverted to south of their belt buckles.

Her looks were an asset and she had no problem leveraging them. She could only do that, though, because she knew Carlton and Harvath valued her for everything else she brought to the party.

The waitress returned with her Red Bull, and while Sloane waited for her appetizer, she scrolled through a series of news feeds on her phone. As part of operational security, the team wasn't allowed to check their social media accounts while they were on assignments.

It was smart policy, which was Harvath in a nutshell. He was constantly hammering home the importance of good tradecraft.

She also knew that good tradecraft could be the difference between life and death. Having been a hitter for so long, Harvath had plenty of those lessons to share.

He knew his stuff. More important, he wasn't half bad at teaching others. He had helped her to become an even better operator. And for that, she was grateful.

Looking up, she saw the waitress arriving with her wings. She was almost done with them when Jasinski arrived.

"Nice boots," said Sloane, as the hostess showed Jasinski to the table. They were black and came up almost thigh-high. Her dress was incredibly form-fitting and left nothing at all to the imagination.

"I think Harvath enjoyed picking out our outfits," Jasinski replied.

"No question. You look great, though."

"Thank you. You, too. What are you drinking?"

Sloane held up her glass. "Red Bull."

"I'll have one as well, please," she said to the waitress, who had just arrived at the table. "How are the nachos?"

"Excellent," the waitress answered.

"And some nachos, then, please."

When the waitress had walked away, Jasinski looked over at the bar and said, "So that's them?"

Sloane nodded.

The Russians were a rough-looking bunch. They stood out like sore thumbs. Sparrman, even with his red hair, resembled every other local in the place.

Alpha dogs had a way of recognizing other alpha dogs, and Harvath had worried that if any of his male team members locked eyes with any of the Spetsnaz soldiers, they would have known something was up and that would have been the end of it. Harvath wanted to maintain the element of surprise for as long as he could. That was why Sloane and Jasinski had been sent in on their own.

Returning her attention to the table, Jasinski said, "This is your show. I'm here to back you up, but only if you need me. We can get started whenever you're ready."

"We've already started," Sloane replied, as she glanced over and caught Sparrman looking at her. "And I will need you, but let's wait for your food first. Then we can kick this thing into gear."

Jasinski admired the woman's cool and her confidence. She seemed not only ready, but also eager for what was about to happen.

CHAPTER 40

Sloane knew exactly what she was doing. Dressed in the clothing Harvath had bought her, she was already fishing with dynamite, but clothing was only part of a successful seduction. It was a dance, a series of almost imperceptible cues—of motions, glances, and expressions.

She did her best to ignore Sparrman, only allowing him to catch her looking at him when she wanted to be caught. That was part of the game as well.

She spent most of her time focused on Jasinski, who acted as her eyes, telling her what was going on at the bar and if her target was looking at them.

Jasinski knew the game and was an exceptional wingman. She knew how to dial her energy up, smile, and laugh. They were competing with the soccer match. It was important that they be more fun, and more enticing. Soon enough, they had their answer.

Sparrman left the bar, walked over to their table, and asked the two ladies where they were from.

Harvath had already worked out the cover story with both of them. They gave the Swede the short version, after which he asked if he could sit down at their table and buy them both a drink. Jasinski said yes, even though it was obvious that he was speaking to Sloane.

Sparrman took a seat and called the waitress over. He ordered another beer for himself and asked the ladies what they wanted. They ordered Amstel Lights. There was no telling how long they would be drinking. The lower the alcohol content of what they were consuming, the better.

Sloane elaborated on their cover story, going into more detail about where they were from, and what they were doing in Sweden.

When she asked Sparrman what he did for a living, he told her he owned one of the biggest ranches on the island. She said she didn't believe him and asked to see his hands. When he showed her, she lightly traced the lines and calluses with one of her fingers. If the man wasn't hot already, his temperature was definitely beginning to climb. And, she had learned something about him, something he hadn't said.

They finished their beers and Sparrman bought another round. They continued to laugh and make small talk.

When the third round came, Jasinski excused herself to use the ladies' room. While there, she texted Harvath a SITREP. Everything was going well, but Sparrman seemed content to just sit with a pretty woman, drink beer, and glance up at the TV whenever he heard his colleagues at the bar cheer or let out a collective groan.

Harvath texted back that Jasinski needed to get Sloane to dial up the heat. Jasinski refused, telling him that Sloane was doing a great job and that he would just need to be patient.

After leaving the ladies' room, she stopped by the bar to break a large bill so she could have money for the jukebox. One of the Russians was ogling her and so she asked him, in English, if there were any songs he wanted to hear.

The question seemed to have taken him by surprise. She could almost hear the gears grinding away in his head. The man's response finally came in a thick, unquestionably Russian accent. "Bruce Springsteen," he said.

"The Boss," Jasinski replied, with a smile.

"Yes. The Boss."

"I'll see if they have him," she said, as she accepted her change from the barman. Noticing the ink on the man's arm, she added, "Nice tattoo," before leaving the bar and walking over to the jukebox.

Springsteen, she thought to herself as she walked. Interesting choice, especially for a Russian, but that was the power of American culture.

There were only a handful of Springsteen songs she actually enjoyed, and she was glad to see they had at least one of them. Inserting a bill into the machine, she made her selections.

As she walked back to her table, the horns from "Tenth Avenue Freeze-Out" began playing. It was obvious by the look on the Russian's face that he'd never heard it before. She flashed him the thumbs-up. Confused, he flashed a thumbs-up back.

Laughing, Jasinski sat back down.

"What's so funny?" Sparrman asked.

"That guy at the bar," she replied, nodding toward the Russian.

"What about him?"

"I asked what kind of music I should play. He said *Springsteen*. I don't think he knows this one. Maybe I should have played 'Born in the USA.'"

"His name is Nikolai. You should go back to talk to

him," Sparrman suggested, obviously trying to get rid of her.

Jasinski looked over at the Russian. "I don't know. He's not much of a conversationalist and is even a little scary, to be honest. He's got a tattoo, of a scorpion, on the inside of his arm."

"No. He's very kind. He's in charge of the animals on the farm."

"You have animals? What kind?"

"Go ask Nikolai."

"Oh, I get it," Jasinski replied. "You two want to be alone. Not a problem. I'll be at the bar with Nikolai, I guess."

"Thank you," said Sparrman, who was enthralled with Sloane and not even looking at Jasinski. "Have him buy you a beer. Tell him I said so."

"I'll do that," she said, standing up and stepping away from the table. She hoped that Sloane had understood her message. Sparrman's farmhands were definitely Spetsnaz. The scorpion was a popular tattoo in a lot of their units.

Just as Monika had noticed the tattoo, Sloane had noticed that Sparrman had stains on his fingertips. As his leg bounced up and down under the table, she could tell he was jonesing.

"How long ago did you quit?" she asked.

"Quit?"

"Smoking."

"How did you know?"

Sloane smiled coyly, "I can read your mind."

"I'm in big trouble then," Sparrman said with a grin.

"We'll see about that. In the meantime, answer my question. How long has it been?"

"I quit a week ago. Very few Swedes actually smoke,

maybe 10 percent of the country. That's it. My mother, though, hates that I'm part of that 10 percent. I don't much care what she thinks, but whenever I see her, she bothers me about it. I thought it would be cool, the next time I see her, to be able to say I had quit."

Sloane continued to play coy. "You may have quit a week ago, but have you been a good boy? Or have you *cheated*?" She drew out the word "cheated" as if she was asking him if he had been sexually mischievous.

Sparrman's grin broadened. "I may have cheated once or twice."

"I have a secret," she said, beckoning him closer. She playfully bit her bottom lip, as if she had been bad herself and was contemplating whether to confess. And then she did. "I quit two years ago and I *still* cheat."

"You do?"

"I do."

"When," asked Sparrman, leaning in more closely and trying desperately to be suave, "have you cheated?"

"There's really only two occasions when it happens. When I'm drinking," she replied, running her finger around the lip of her beer bottle, "or if I've had really good sex."

Though Sparrman tried to hide it, she could see his Adam's apple move in a quiet gulp. Not only had she hooked him, but he had swallowed the lure. It was time to reel him in.

"You know what I would love right now?" she asked.

In his mind, the Swede was saying, *Please say sex*. What came out of his mouth, though, was. "I don't know. What would you love?"

"To share just one cigarette. You and me. The way I look at it, it wouldn't really be cheating. Not if we shared it. Does that sound like fun?"

Sparrman wasn't an idiot. His mother be damned. He was going to have a cigarette with this woman. He could get back on the wagon tomorrow. "It sounds delicious."

"Wonderful. Do you have any?"

"No, but I'll be right back. Don't move," he said.

Getting up from the table, he quickly crossed to the bar and interrupted Jasinski and Nikolai, asking the muscular Russian for a cigarette.

The Spetsnaz operative must have known his colleague had been trying to quit smoking, because he rolled his eyes and made a half-hearted attempt at dissuading him. But as he really didn't care what happened to Sparrman, he removed a pack from his coat pocket and handed it to him along with a cheap plastic orange disposable lighter.

"Thank you," said Sparrman, as he tapped out a lone cigarette and handed the pack back.

"Take the whole thing," Nikolai insisted in his heavy accent.

"I only need one."

"You never know," the Russian said with a conspiratorial wink. "Misha has two packs with him. Do not worry."

"Thank you," Sparrman said, clapping his hand on the soldier's shoulder and then returning to Sloane.

"Ready?" he asked her, smiling, as he held up the cigarettes.

Glancing past him, she saw Jasinski at the bar. Their eyes briefly met, but in that split second, the Polish intelligence officer nodded. *Game on.*

CHAPTER 41

S weden had some of the most restrictive smoking
laws in the EU. Not only was it illegal to smoke
in bars and restaurants, you also couldn't smoke
immediately outside them. Smokers in the Scandinavian country ranked just below lepers.

Not that Sloane minded. She had never been a
smoker in her life. Seeing Sparrman's nicotine-stained
fingers had been a gift. Pay attention to everything—
another of Harvath's rules of tradecraft.

She had worried that only the promise of a blow-
job could have dislodged Sparrman from the premises.
Fortunately enough, there was a craving stronger than
sex, stronger even than cocaine. Smoking was one of
the hardest habits to kick. And once a smoker, always a
smoker. It only took the right combination of circumstances to relapse.

In this case all it took was booze, a little T&A, and
probably the stress of Lars Lund's surveillance and sub-
sequent murder. That is, if Harvath was correct, and it
hadn't been an accident. Like her boss, Sloane had been
taught not to believe in coincidences either.

As she and Sparrman left the restaurant and crossed
the patio, she only had one lingering concern. *How
would Jasinski get out?*

They hadn't had enough time to cover every eventuality. She had to trust that she'd come up with something.

Right now, Sloane needed to focus on getting Sparrman into the minivan and getting the hell out of town without his Spetsnaz pals noticing. It was a very dangerous proposition and probably much easier said than done.

The moment they hit the pavement, the Swede's hands were all over her. It started with one on her hip. When she didn't object, it quickly moved to her ass.

Though this was part of the job, she made a mental note to make sure to squeeze some sort of pain and suffering out of Harvath for it.

Smiling, she gently brushed his hand aside and began moving away from the entrance, toward the minivan that she knew would be idling at the end of the block.

Sparrman cooperated for a moment. Then he stopped and pressed her up against the wall, kissing her neck.

Gathering up the front of his shirt in her fist, she brought him close enough to deliver a vicious head butt, but instead, gave him a peck on the cheek.

"Slowly," she cooed. "What's your rush? Let's go have our cigarette first."

Smiling brightly once more, she gestured for them and Sparrman handed the pack over.

As if she'd stolen the ball and was heading for the goal, she squealed and ran as best she could, in heels, down the sidewalk.

Enjoying the game, Sparrman followed, growling and closing in on her with each step.

At the end of the block, she ducked around the corner, out of his sight. Sparrman wasn't deterred.

As she disappeared, he chased right after her, chanting, "Here, kitty, kitty, kitty."

Coming around the corner, his chants instantly stopped.

"Hi there," said Harvath, as the Swede came to a screeching halt right in front of him. Haney had brought back Chase and Staelin, who were standing next to Scot. Sloane was behind them.

"What the hell is this?" Sparrman demanded. "Who are you?"

"The tooth fairy," Harvath replied.

Stepping forward, Chase deployed his Taser and let the Swede ride the lightning. Instantly the man's muscles seized and he fell to the ground. Harvath then gave the *Go* command and everyone sprang into action.

While Haney backed the minivan up to their position, Staelin Flex-Cuffed Sparrman, put a piece of duct tape over his mouth, and pulled a hood down over his head.

They had debated disabling the Spetsnaz vehicles, possibly by slashing their tires, but decided instead to make it look as if Sparrman had simply left with a woman he had met in the bar. If they went to the police, that was all they would be able to report.

Patting him down, Sloane found his car keys and headed off to where she had watched him park.

Harvath helped Staelin get Sparrman into the minivan and then told him and Haney to get back to the rental house. He and Chase would keep the Camry and join them as soon as they could. First, they had to make sure that Jasinski got out of O'Learys.

As Haney and Staelin took off with their prisoner, Harvath pulled out his phone and texted a prearranged one-word code to Jasinski: *Bootsy*.

· · ·

Back inside O'Learys, Jasinski looked down at her phone, which was sitting atop the bar. Harvath's text had just come in. It was time to execute her exit plan.

She had begun looking for ways out the moment she had walked in. It was one of the reasons she had gone to the ladies' room. Its windows, though, opened onto a small courtyard, framed by the medieval city wall. Without climbing equipment there was no way she was going to be able to get up and over it. It was too tall.

If they'd had time to prepare, perhaps she could have hidden a length of rope and a pair of athletic shoes, but they'd had to do this on the fly. As she had been trained in the Army, she needed to adapt and overcome. *Think*, she had told herself. *What other ways are there out of here?*

Nikolai was interested in his soccer game, but he was also interested in her. If she got up from her stool, he would want to know where she was going. And despite appearing a bit brutish, he didn't come off as unintelligent.

The Russian was paying attention to his surroundings—watching who came and went. Jasinski had a pretty good feeling he had been keeping a mental clock on how long Sparrman had been gone as well. If he saw her walk out the front door, he was going to be very suspicious. He might even follow her. That couldn't be allowed to happen.

The kitchen was her best shot. From what she could tell, it had a back door of some sort that opened onto a gangway that, she hoped, led to the street. The only problem was that the kitchen could be seen from where they were sitting at the bar. If Nikolai, or any of his comrades, saw her walk in there, they'd immediately suspect something was off.

The key was to do it without their seeing anything. She needed a quick diversion. It only had to last long enough to get her into and through the kitchen. On her last trip to the ladies' room, she had seen just the thing.

Swallowing what was left of her beer, she playfully teased Nikolai with the empty bottle. "Buy me another?" she asked, pretending to be a little more buzzed than she was.

In the Russian's estimation, the beers were very expensive. *Too* expensive. Nevertheless, if he ended up getting laid, the investment would be worth it. The woman was attractive and had put her hand on his arm several times, which was a good sign. She also didn't talk too much. She seemed content to let him watch the game and talk with his buddies. She was almost too good to be true. Signaling the barman, he gestured to bring the woman another round. If he didn't end up sleeping with her, he could always insist Sparrman pay him back.

"Will you excuse me, please?" Jasinski said, as she slid off her stool.

"Where are you going?" the Russian asked, one eye on the match.

"To the little girls' room."

The man looked at her, puzzled.

"The toilet," she explained.

"Oh," said Nikolai, embarrassed, returning his attention to the TV. "Okay."

Picking up her phone, she headed for the ladies' room.

Once inside, she made sure she was alone, and then unscrewed the pump for one of the soap dispensers. Removing the spring, she screwed the pump head back on and then uncoiled the piece of wire.

Pulling up Harvath's message on her phone, she texted him back: *Outside in 90 seconds.*

Good copy, Harvath replied. *We'll be waiting.*

Stepping out of the ladies' room, she approached the breaker box, opened the cover, and threw the breakers. Instantly, the restaurant was plunged into darkness. All the TVs cut out, as did the music.

Shutting the box, she threaded the piece of wire from the soap dispenser through the area meant for a lock and twisted it as quickly and as tightly as she could. It wouldn't prevent someone from opening it, but it would slow them down.

Leaving the circuit breaker, she moved as fast as she could in the darkness to the kitchen.

Gotland was an island, and as with most islands in Europe, its inhabitants were used to suffering power outages. As a wave of annoyed groans rolled across the establishment, the staff hunted for flashlights while customers activated the lights on their phones. Jasinski made it into the kitchen right before a beam swept over her.

Taking out her own phone, she activated the flashlight and used it to light her way to the side exit. She was moving with such purpose that no one in the kitchen bothered to question who she was or what she was doing.

Pushing through the door, she ended up in a narrow gangway between O'Learys and the building next door. Seeing the gate at the end, she ran for it.

She was only steps away when her eyes zeroed in on the chain and padlock. She'd seen enough security theater in her lifetime not to assume it was locked. Besides, if the restaurant caught fire, the gangway would be a death trap.

Getting to the gate, she gave the chain a tug. It was definitely locked. *Shit.*

The gray Camry had just pulled near the entrance. She could see its taillights. Pulling out her phone, she called Harvath.

"Back up ten feet," she told him when he answered. "I'm in the gangway, but the gate is locked."

"Can you climb over it?" he asked, as he relayed the instructions to Chase to back up.

The gate area was covered by a metal roof. It was likely meant to serve as a space where deliveries could be made and inventoried without the threat of the elements. Jasinski examined the space, but wasn't hopeful.

The gate came up nearly to the underside of the roof. There wasn't enough room to squeeze in between. There wasn't enough room to go under it either. *Think*, she challenged herself once again.

The only thing in the gangway besides her and the locked gate were stacks of plastic crates used to haul beer bottles. They were her only hope of getting out.

She was halfway through stacking them when Harvath materialized and began yanking on the gate. It didn't budge for him either.

"Hurry," he said, as he disappeared from view.

Hurry? she repeated to herself. *Did it look to him like she was taking her time?*

Starting with the highest column—the one that would allow her to hop onto the roof—she stacked the crates in descending columns, forming a makeshift staircase.

It didn't have to be pretty, and it wasn't. It only had to work. Fortunately, many of the crates were already stacked up against the wall. All she had to do was drag them out and get them into place.

With the last one set, she began her rickety climb. But

no sooner had she begun than there was an angry voice from behind her in the gangway.

"Stop!" it demanded. The voice belonged to Nikolai.

When the lights went out, he must have come looking for her, and now he had found her, trying to escape. Running down the gangway, he charged toward her, shouting and cursing in Russian.

She tried to move faster, but the crates were unstable and wobbled on the uneven cobblestones of the alley. The quicker she moved, the more unbalanced everything became.

The Russian had reached her staircase now and was kicking and ripping away the crates like a madman.

He reached for the last stack of them a fraction of a second before she leaped onto the roof. Jasinski knew she was going down before gravity had even taken hold of her.

But before she could fall, she felt something grab her arm. Looking up, she saw Harvath, who had climbed onto the roof from the street.

"Give me your other hand," he said.

Reaching toward him, she did, and he pulled her the rest of the way up.

"We've got to move," he said, pointing to the other side of the roof and the sidewalk below it. "Hurry up and jump."

Jasinski moved as quickly as she could to the opposite edge, lay down on her stomach, hung her legs over, and dropped to the pavement.

Looking through the gate, she could see that Nikolai had already run back inside. He would be on the sidewalk in seconds.

"Get in the car," Harvath ordered as he jumped down. "I'll catch up with you."

She did as he instructed and her door wasn't even closed before Chase peeled out. Out the rear window, she could see Harvath running up the street in the opposite direction.

"Where's he going?" she asked, as Chase pulled a hard right turn.

"He changed his mind. He's disabling their vehicles. We're picking him up at the next corner."

Accelerating up the street, Chase barely tapped the brakes to take the next turn.

When they got to their rendezvous point, they could see Harvath running toward them, with the Russians in hot pursuit.

"Reach behind you and open the rear passenger door," said Chase.

Unbuckling her seat belt, she leaned back and threw the door wide open. Seconds later, Harvath leaped in.

"Go! Go! Go!" he commanded, slamming his door shut.

Lying on the backseat, he focused on catching his breath as Chase punched the accelerator and got them the hell out of town.

CHAPTER 42

The Rome bombing, despite his concern about moving it up, had gone off perfectly. It was exactly what his superiors back in Moscow had needed to see. It had also garnered wall-to-wall media attention.

The fuse had been lit. Tretyakov could stop right now and everything would probably take care of itself. But that would be leaving too much to chance. He didn't believe in trusting things to chance—especially for something this important. There were still many more things to be done.

Chief among them was getting to the bottom of what NATO knew, and what their level of preparedness was. Because the haystack fell partially within his jurisdiction, he was one of several people charged with finding those needles.

Any intelligence operatives who delivered intel to Moscow that proved helpful for its Baltic invasion would be able to write their own tickets. They would not only receive rank advancement and state acknowledgement, but they would also be positioned to reap incredible financial benefits. Just as the punishment for failure could be extreme, so could the rewards for success. Sometimes, as much as he hated to admit it, the underpinnings of capitalism made sense.

What didn't make sense, though, was who the American on the CCTV footage from Visby Hospital was. That was needle number one.

Ivan Kuznetsov had received the footage from one of his assets on Gotland, a police officer named Johansson. The American had identified himself as "Stephen Hall" and had NATO credentials. But based on all of its NATO sources, Russia couldn't find anything on him. For all intents and purposes, Stephen Hall didn't exist. Tretyakov was certain the man was an intelligence operative, likely CIA or possibly DIA.

He forwarded the footage to Moscow, where they ran it through all sorts of analysis and facial recognition programs. They thought they had a partial match with a piece of Al Jazeera footage from a few years back. An American soldier had been caught on tape beating a local man in a Middle Eastern market, but the comparison was inconclusive.

Other than that, they had come up empty. The guy was a ghost. That only further served to convince Tretyakov that he was dealing with an intelligence professional—probably one who was very highly skilled.

Flying a team into Gotland on a private jet was a big deal. NATO had money to burn, but not for run-of-the-mill personnel conducting site surveys for alleged training exercises. The local police might have bought a cover story like that, but not Tretyakov.

The fact that the people on the plane were there to meet a Swedish intelligence operative, the same man who had Staffan Sparrman under surveillance, concerned Tretyakov—and rightly so.

Even though the man's death had looked like an accident, Tretyakov was now worried that they had been too rash. The Gotland cell was too valuable to lose—especially right now.

Kuznetsov, though, had told Tretyakov not to worry. According to Johansson, the local Chief Inspector hadn't suspected anything.

The worst thing that they could do at this point was to change their routines or to start acting suspiciously. The beauty of the Gotland cell was that it wasn't trying to hide. It was operating right in the open for everyone to see.

Tretyakov supposed he was right, but he didn't like it. What bothered him was not knowing what his opponents knew. If they had anything of substance, they would have rolled the entire cell up by now. Putting it under surveillance seemed to suggest that they were still gathering information.

Tretyakov was willing to go along with Kuznetsov and let it ride, for the time being. He didn't want to be the one to tell Moscow that they needed to shut the Gotland cell down. There was too much riding on them.

The second needle he had to deal with was the alleged Gryphon missile upgrade kits. He used the term "alleged" because like "Stephen Hall," none of his NATO sources knew anything about the missiles, other than the fact that they were supposed to have been destroyed. By all accounts, there were no Gryphons in NATO's inventory. But did that mean they didn't exist?

Tretyakov didn't trust the Americans, not one bit. Therefore, he was willing to entertain the idea that they secretly, and in violation of the treaty, had either left in place or removed, and later smuggled back in, land-based cruise missiles in Europe. His issue, though, was that the level of secrecy that would be required for something like this was almost outside NATO's capability.

America and its allies had always been obsessed with following the rule of law and the terms of their treaties. To take such a gamble was so far outside their comfort zone that the missing upgrade kits had started to feel like disinformation to him. Yet Russia's GRU and FSB had both received solid, separately sourced reporting on it.

That's what really had made it difficult. If the corroborative reporting hadn't been there, it would have been much easier to brush the entire idea aside. But they couldn't ignore what had come in—including the report from the United Nations in New York City. The behavior of the American and Baltic Ambassadors had all but verified the theft of the missile kits.

Based on his sources, the search had moved from Poland into Belarus—Minsk to be exact. The presence, or lack thereof, of the Gryphon missiles in the Baltics was a top-level concern for Moscow. They wanted proof, either way, and they wanted it ASAP.

Tretyakov had activated a team in Minsk to observe the progress there, and had also been shaking down every contact he had in Lithuania, Latvia, and Estonia. The road mobile launchers used for the missiles were not vehicles that were easy to hide, nor were rumors of their existence. Somebody, somewhere, had to know something.

In the meantime, Moscow continued to tighten the screws on him. They not only wanted answers, but they were also anxious to finish prepping the battlefield so that they could launch their invasion.

They wanted him to capitalize on the success of Rome. More than that, they wanted him to improve upon it. They were focused on civilian casualties. Civilian deaths captured the media's attention. Once you had the media's attention, the public's followed, like a dog on a leash.

The question was how he would follow up on the Rome bombing. That attack had been perfect. It had also been unique, on many levels. Replicating it wouldn't be easy.

But if easy was what had been needed, there were many untold numbers Moscow could have called. He occupied the position he did because he delivered what others couldn't. He delivered the impossible.

And, as he cleared his mind and decided which attack would come next, he realized there was no better word for it than *impossible*.

CHAPTER 43

Harvath took a good, hard look at Staffan Sparrman. Haney and Staelin had him tied to a chair in an equipment shed on the edge of the rental property. It smelled like gasoline and rotten wood. They had stripped him down to his soiled white underwear. His hood was still on.

The cold had gotten to him. He had only been in the shed for a while, but he was shivering.

There was a tarp in the corner. Harvath gathered it up and draped it over his shoulders.

"Staffan, listen to my voice," he said. "The worst of this can already be behind you. It is your decision. If you cooperate with me, you will be home, in your own bed, before the night is over. Do you understand me?"

Harvath watched as the man slowly nodded.

"That's good. Now, before we get started, I want you to know the ground rules. Only a few kilometers from here, we also have your mother, the Governor, in custody."

It was a lie, of course, but Sparrman didn't know that. All he knew was that he had been taken captive. Why wouldn't the same people have been able to do the same to his mother? This was Gotland. She didn't have police protection. There was no need.

Harvath watched as Sparrman's body tensed. As Harvath had suspected, despite the man's difficult relationship with his mother, he still cared for her.

"If you answer my questions truthfully," he continued, "no harm will come to her. Do you understand? If so, nod."

Again, the man slowly nodded.

"Good. Here's the flip side. If you lie to me, or if I suspect you are lying to me, whatever pain I make you feel, your mother is also going to feel. Is that clear? If so, nod."

Even more slowly this time, the man nodded.

"Good," said Harvath. "Let's give this a try. We'll start with something easy. You have Russian Special Forces soldiers working on your farm."

Instantly, the man shook his head.

Harvath drove the open metal contacts of Chase's Taser into Sparrman's ribs and depressed the trigger.

Sparrman's body went rigid as he cried out and wet himself again, the urine running down his left leg and onto the floor.

Harvath pulled the Taser back and gave the man a chance to regain his composure.

"Did you see what happened in Rome, Staffan?"

The man's head lolled from side to side. There was a fog detainees could slip into. It was the brain disconnecting from the trauma being inflicted on the body. In essence, it was a psychological safe space. Harvath was having none of it.

Drawing his open hand back, he brought it slicing down and slapped Sparrman hard, on the side of his head.

With the duct tape still over his mouth, there was only so much noise he could make.

Raising the radio to his mouth, Harvath said, "Taser the Governor."

Immediately, Sparrman attempted to cry out and shook his head from side to side.

Moments later, a distant woman's scream came back across the radio. Hearing it, Sparrman slumped.

"Are there Russians working on your farm?" Harvath asked.

This time, the man answered with the truth. He nodded.

"Are they Spetsnaz?"

Again, Sparrman nodded.

"Who's in charge?"

It was the first time he had asked something other than a yes or no question. With the tape over his mouth, Sparrman wouldn't be able to answer.

Reaching under the hood, Harvath found the duct tape and tore it off. It was painful and the Swede flinched.

"Who?" Harvath repeated.

"Help!" Sparrman screamed in Swedish. "Someone, please! Help me! Help!"

Balling his hand into a fist, Harvath drew it back and hit him so hard in the side of his head that it knocked him, and his chair, over onto the floor.

With the man on the floor, stunned, or maybe even unconscious, Harvath took a moment to examine his hand. No matter how careful he was, hitting someone that hard always hurt like hell.

Why didn't they ever just cooperate? he wondered. *Why did they always resist? What was the point?* Until they told him what he wanted to know, there was no escape, no getting out. He was in charge. But how bad things would get was totally up to them. Yet they still fought.

That was fine. Eventually, they all broke. *All of them.*

Pulling the chair back upright, he gave Sparrman a few light slaps through the hood to bring him back around.

"Can you hear me, Mr. Sparrman?" he asked.

Beneath the hood, the man nodded.

Holding up his radio, Harvath said, "Good. Now listen to what is about to happen to your mother."

With that, there were a series of what sounded like distant slaps followed by more of the same woman's screams. Though they were allegedly happening kilometers away, Sparrman winced and felt each one personally. Sloane was doing a very convincing acting job.

Setting the radio down, Harvath looked at his prisoner. The tarp he had kindly draped across his shoulders lay on the floor. He was bleeding from beneath his hood. If Harvath had to guess, it was from his mouth or his nose—maybe his ear as well. He was shaking again from the cold. He was in bad shape.

"How much more will you put your poor mother through, Staffan?" he asked.

The man didn't seem ready to answer. That was fine by Harvath. Inside the shed was a large plastic bucket. Crossing over to it, he picked it up and brought it back over to where Sparrman was seated.

Lifting the man's feet, he placed them inside the bucket. Then he walked over to the corner and retrieved a large gas can.

Bringing it back over, he unscrewed the cap, and held it under Sparrman's nose for several seconds. After affixing the spout, he began to pour, sloshing plenty of it over the Swede's legs and thighs.

Some even splashed against the man's private parts. It stung like hell, and that's when Sparrman began screaming.

CHAPTER 44

Are you going to cooperate with me?" Harvath asked. "Because if this is just another game, I promise you I will not be happy."

"I will cooperate," the man shouted from beneath his hood. "Please. It burns."

Harvath yanked off his hood. "The sooner you tell me what I want to know, the sooner you can get cleaned up. Who is in charge of the Russians on your farm?"

"His name is Dominik Gashi," replied Sparrman.

Harvath studied him, watching for any of the tics or subtle facial cues that might indicate that he was lying. "And who is Gashi?"

"Will you let my mother go?"

"It depends on what you tell me. Who is Dominik Gashi?"

"He works at an animal-processing plant here on the island. It's called FörsPak."

"What was your involvement in the death of Lars Lund?"

"Nothing," the man insisted. "He was following me, so I told Dominik. He said he and the Russians would take care of it."

"Why would you report something like that to Dominik?"

Sparrman didn't answer.

Harvath held up the Taser. "Listen to me, Staffan. You're sitting in gas, literally up to your balls. In addition to a shitload of electricity, this Taser produces a real beefy spark—nineteen sparks per second, to be exact. What do you think might happen if I have to Tase you again?"

The Swede looked at the device and then down at his underwear, his legs, and finally his feet, submerged in the bucket of gasoline.

"I report to Dominik as well," he admitted. "We all do. He is in charge of everything."

"Define *everything*."

"He controls the Russians. They only work on my farm as a cover. I assume they are soldiers of some sort. Then there are the rest of us. Local Swedes, sympathetic to the cause."

"What cause?" asked Harvath.

"The Russian cause."

"Communism?"

Sparrman didn't answer. He didn't have to. Harvath knew that was exactly what he meant.

"How many Russians are on your farm?"

"Eight," said the Swede.

"Any non-Russians?"

The man shook his head.

"How many locals, sympathetic to your cause or otherwise, are part of your cell?"

"Six," replied Sparrman.

"I'm going to want their names, occupations, and where they live."

"Promise me you will let my mother go. I will give you whatever information you want."

"This isn't a negotiation, Staffan," Harvath reminded

him. "Every single thing that happens to you is completely within your control. If you cooperate, everything will be fine. If you don't, then you'll see what happens. That's the last time I'm telling you."

Tucking his Taser in his back pocket, he pulled out his phone, activated the voice memo feature, and, holding it up, said, "Now, let's have those names."

Sparrman rattled them off. "Marcus Larsson. He works for one of the Gotland radio stations and lives in Visby. Henrik Erickson is an auto mechanic. He lives and works in Hemse. Ove Ekström lives in Tofta and is unemployed. Ronnie Linderoth is a handyman and lives in Klintehamn. Hasse Lustig works on the ferry and lives outside Visby. And then there's Magnus Johansson—"

"Police officer," a voice interrupted from the doorway of the shed. "I also live just outside Visby."

Harvath spun. Standing there, with his service weapon drawn, was Johansson—the same cop Harvath had seen driving past in Old Town earlier that night.

"Drop the phone," the officer ordered. "Hands in the air. Keep them where I can see them."

Harvath, who had been in the shed alone with Sparrman, did as he was instructed. "How did you know we were here?"

"The car rental agency gave me descriptions of your vehicles," he replied. "Someone thought they had been seen near the Sparrman farm, but we couldn't confirm that. Tonight, though, I saw your Camry parked in Visby.

"I placed one of these inside the wheel well," he said, holding up a small, inexpensive GPS device. "When Staffan disappeared from O'Learys, Nikolai called Dominik and Dominik called me. This was the first place I came. When I heard him cry out for help, I knew I had done the right thing."

And he probably alerted everyone else in the cell that he was coming, thought Harvath. *At least the Spetsnaz team, with their vehicles disabled, won't be able to back him up anytime soon.*

That didn't change the fact, though, that Johansson had the gun and thereby, the upper hand. Harvath had to think of something, quick.

Sparrman was blabbering at his comrade in Swedish, probably telling him he wanted to be untied so he could rinse all the gasoline off his man parts.

Johansson said something back and then looked at Harvath. "Turn around, slowly, and face away from me," he ordered.

Harvath obeyed.

"Now place your hands behind your head and get down on your knees."

Harvath didn't like the "get down on your knees" part. The cop was either going to cuff him or put a bullet in the back of his head.

"Do it," Johansson ordered.

Clasping his hands behind his head, slowly Harvath lowered himself to his knees.

He heard something being scuffed out of a leather case, and then the rapid, unmistakable click-click-click of handcuffs being prepared.

But then, suddenly, as if Johansson had changed his mind, there was the sound of a pistol hammer being cocked.

Johansson, though, carried a Glock. And Glocks didn't have external hammers.

CHAPTER 45

"Very, very slowly," said Jasinski, who was holding one of the team's Sig Sauer pistols. "I want you to holster your weapon. Do it now."

Johansson did as she instructed.

"Lock it closed and snap the retention strap."

He did that as well.

"Now drop the handcuffs, kick them back toward me, and place your hands on the back of your head."

Once the police officer had complied, she told Harvath he could stand up.

"Nice to see you," he said to her. "Just out for a walk?"

"You're welcome," she replied.

"For what?"

"Saving your life."

"I guess that makes us even," he said with a smile. Approaching Johansson, he got right in the man's face and said, "There's only one thing I hate more than the Russians."

"Really?" the man foolishly replied. "What's that?"

"A dirty cop," said Harvath, driving his knee into the officer's groin.

As the air rushed from his lungs, he dropped to the ground, doubled over in pain. Harvath then punched him behind his right ear, laying him the rest of the way out.

Collecting the handcuffs from Jasinski, he cuffed Johansson and used an outdoor extension cord to bind his ankles and hog-tie him.

"Check his phone," said Harvath as he removed the man's duty belt and cast it off to the side. "I want to know everyone he has called or texted over the last two hours."

Patting him down, she found Johansson's iPhone in his coat pocket. "It's locked," she said.

Grabbing the man's right index finger, Harvath bent it back so far and so fast it almost snapped. "Here," he said, as the man cried out in pain. "Try this."

She placed his finger on the sensor pad and the phone unlocked. "I'm in," she said.

Scrolling through the call logs, she could see that he had talked with someone named Dominik twice in the last hour. The most recent call was ten minutes ago. She shared the information with Harvath.

"What should we do?" she asked.

Harvath duct-taped both men's mouths and replaced Sparrman's hood. Picking up the radio, he hailed Haney via his call sign and told him that they had received a visitor and to get down to the shed with an extra hood on the double. Then he motioned for Jasinski to follow him outside.

Once they were out of earshot, he said, "We're going to have to pack up. We can't stay here. It's not safe."

"What are you talking about?"

"Johansson probably didn't give this location to his dispatcher, but I'll bet he gave it to the cell leader."

"Is that the one from Johansson's phone?" she asked. "Dominik?"

"According to Sparrman, his full name is Dominik Gashi. Probably an alias."

"GRU?"

"That'd be my guess," said Harvath.

"So what do you want to do?"

"I want to get the hell out of Sweden, but first I want to get my hands on this Dominik character."

"How are we going to do that?"

"We're going to have to ask for help," he replied.

"From who?"

"The local police."

When Harvath rolled up to the wrecking yard in a Swedish police car, Chief Inspector Nyström's first instinct had been to draw his pistol. He didn't, deciding instead to honor his promise to hear the American out.

Opening the gate, he allowed the car to pass through and then closed and locked it behind him.

"Where's my officer?" Nyström asked once Harvath had stopped and gotten out.

"He's safe."

"That was going to be my second question. This is Johansson's vehicle. Where is he?"

"He's not far," said Harvath.

"What's this all about?"

"I think Johansson should tell you."

The moment Harvath's hand went inside his coat, the Chief Inspector went for his gun.

"Easy," cautioned Harvath, showing him the phone. "Everything's okay."

"Keep your hands where I can see them," Nyström ordered, uncomfortable with all of the subterfuge.

"Chief Inspector, you've got a very dangerous cell of Russian operatives here on Gotland. The cell includes a contingent of Russian Special Forces soldiers. Of the six Swedish nationals who are members of the cell, your officer, Magnus Johansson, is one."

Nyström wasn't quite sure how to respond. "Johansson? He's an exemplary officer. You had better have some very strong evidence."

"I do," said Harvath as he played back a portion of the audio from the equipment shed.

The Chief Inspector listened in disbelief. He wanted to say that it wasn't Johansson; that it couldn't be, but the voice on the recording was unmistakable. It was Johansson, and he had incriminated himself by admitting to the unthinkable.

"I'm sure you recognize his voice," said Harvath.

Nyström nodded. "Yes, that's him. Where is he?"

Harvath walked back to the squad car and popped the trunk. Coming to join him, the Chief Inspector looked inside. There, still hog-tied and hooded, was Johansson in his uniform. Harvath pulled the hood from his head so Nyström could be certain.

Reaching up, the Chief Inspector took hold of the lid and slammed it shut. "What is it you want?"

He was angry, and understandably so. Harvath needed to be very careful about how he threaded this needle.

"First and foremost, I believe I want the same thing you do."

"Which is what?"

"For the Russians not to invade Gotland," said Harvath. "For them not to invade anywhere. For them to be contained."

"But that is not my job. That's the job of the Swedish military, the government."

"Have you seen their plan to protect Gotland?"

"No," said Nyström. "I have only heard about it."

"I've actually seen it," said Harvath. "In fact, the entire American military has seen it and we have been begging Sweden to change it. Their plan is to wait for help, to wait for NATO to come and liberate Gotland."

"I have always heard they would bring in more troops from the mainland."

"How?"

"I don't know, by boat I guess, or by air."

"Russian submarines and Russian fighter jets will make sure those troops never arrive," Harvath remarked. "This island is too important to them. If it's worth invading, which it very much is to them, then it's worth defending. I guarantee you, Sweden will only risk so much to take it back. They will decide it is better to wait for help.

"And during that time, what do you think will happen? What will happen to you and your fellow police officers? What will happen to the people of Gotland, to the business owners like your uncle? What will happen to them if they do not comply with the Russian occupiers?"

The Chief Inspector didn't need to think about what would happen. He already knew. European history was all too clear on that subject. Sweden had dodged the horrors of Nazi attack and occupation, but only because it had declared itself neutral and had helped feed the Third Reich's war machine by supplying it with much-needed iron ore, steel, and machine parts. It was an inconvenient truth if ever there was one.

"I still don't understand what you want from me," said Nyström.

"I want you to help me get Dominik Gashi—the cell leader."

"I can't do that."

"What are you talking about?" Harvath replied. "You took an oath to protect this island."

"I took an *oath* to uphold the law."

Harvath shook his head.

"This needs to be brought to the attention of the garrison commander," Nyström continued. "This is a national security matter."

"It's bigger than that," said Harvath. "It's an *international* security matter. Do you know what happens if the military or the government gets involved? Dominik Gashi gets arrested. Then, he gets a lawyer. And at some point way in the future, he gets a trial. In the meantime, you saw what happened in Rome last night?"

"The bombing? Yes, it was terrible."

"Well, that's what Europe gets—attack after attack. Maybe even some right here in Sweden.

"I think you're exaggerating," said the Chief Inspector.

"I wish I was," Harvath replied. "The fact is, the only link we have is Gashi."

"How am I supposed to believe you? You lied to me. You told me you were here to meet Lars Lund to plan a pending military exercise."

"Yeah, the most important exercise of all—the rescue of Gotland. That's why I'm here. And no, I didn't lie to you. As part of my assignment, I was supposed to figure out how to prevent a rescue from even being necessary. That's why I was looking for Staffan Sparrman. If we could locate and identify the Russian cell, our job was to break it up.

"Then we were to take whatever we had learned and climb the ladder, go after the people on the next level. My job is to prevent a war. We're trying to stop the Russians before they can launch any invasion. But make no mistake, they're coming for Gotland.

"Now, maybe the Swedish military can repel their attack. I don't know. Maybe Gotland can hold out until NATO comes to its rescue. But no matter what, people on your island, people you have sworn to protect, are going to die. I don't want that to happen. I know you don't want that to happen. And it doesn't have to happen—*if* we can get to Dominik Gashi."

The Chief Inspector put his fingers beneath his glasses and pinched the bridge of his nose. He then walked away from the patrol car in order to think.

Harvath watched as the man, torn, paced slowly up and down in the wrecking yard.

There were only two potential outcomes. Either Nyström was going to help, or he wasn't. Harvath hoped he chose Option A, because if the man chose Option B, it was going to get very bad, very quickly.

Leaning against the car, Harvath watched as his breath turned to steam and rose into the night air. His Sig Sauer was tucked in his jeans at the small of his back, and the Taser—with a brand-new cartridge—was in his left coat pocket.

Finally, the Chief Inspector came back over. "If I help you," he said, "I want the information about every single person in that cell, *especially* the locals."

"Done," said Harvath.

"And," Nyström added, "whatever it is you need, it can't appear to have any official police sanction, and it absolutely cannot appear to have come from me."

Harvath understood the man's position, but his conditions were going to be a lot easier said than done—especially with what Harvath had in mind.

CHAPTER 46

The FörsPak processing plant was a half hour north of Visby and just inland from the coast. Its owner had been born and raised on the island. He had spent his entire life there, except for a two-year period while serving in the Swedish military.

What had intrigued Harvath the most about him, though, was that a quick scan of Facebook revealed him to be a member of the Gotland Runners Club. Not only did Nyström know Martin Ingesson, but they were also friends. It was, the Chief Inspector admitted again, "a small island."

Trying to hew as close to Nyström's conditions as possible, Harvath had suggested that the Chief Inspector characterize their middle-of-the-night visit to Ingesson as personal. "Friends don't wake friends up in the middle of the night," was the man's response.

When they arrived at his home, the lights were on and Ingesson was up waiting for them. Hearing the car pull into the drive, he met them at the front door.

Martin Ingesson looked like a Viking. He was at least six-foot-four with blue eyes, blond hair, and a big blond beard. His chest and arms were twice the size of Harvath's. The man could have passed for a competitor in the World's Strongest Man contest. It wouldn't have surprised Harvath in the least if he spent his lunch breaks dragging truck tires around a parking lot.

Ingesson invited them inside and led them back to the kitchen where he already had coffee ready. It was a modest home, paneled in blond wood, with ceramic masonry stoves in several of the rooms they passed. The hallway was lined with family photos.

Nyström made the introductions and they kept their voices low so as not to wake Ingesson's wife and children.

"Anders tells me you're with NATO?" the big man asked.

Harvath nodded. "And he tells me you were in the military. Which branch?"

"Army. K4."

"Noorland's Dragoons," Harvath said, respectfully.

Ingesson was impressed. "You know it?"

He did. They were Sweden's crack Ranger battalion— expert light infantry trained to carry out missions behind enemy lines.

"I started out with SEAL Team Two," said Harvath. "We cross-trained with K4 in Lapland. Up until that point, I had thought Alaska was the coldest place on earth."

The big man grinned. "SEALs are excellent warriors. But I think the cold water eventually breaks you. That's why you retire to places like Florida and Texas."

Harvath laughed. "In addition to nice weather, those states also have no income tax, are good places to raise a family, and don't mind if you own guns."

"Fair points," Ingesson conceded, as he poured coffee and pushed a plate of pastries forward. "So, what are we all doing in my kitchen?"

Nyström had made the introduction. That was as far as he was prepared to go. "I'm going to take my coffee into the living room."

Harvath waited until he was gone and then began speaking to his host. "I wanted to talk with you about one of your employees."

"Which one?"

"Dominik Gashi."

"He's one of my best employees. What about him?"

"How well do you know him?" Harvath asked.

"He's smart. He works hard. And he's always on time. What else should I know about him?" asked Ingesson.

"What about his background?"

The big man thought for a moment. "From what I understand, he's from a small village in Kosovo. His family, most of whom are dead, were in the butchery business. That's about all I know."

"Have you ever met any of them?"

"No, I have not."

"Have you ever heard him speak Albanian or Serbian?" asked Harvath.

"No."

"Have you ever seen him reading any books, magazines, or anything else in Albanian or Serbian?"

Ingesson shook his head.

"Have you ever heard him speaking Russian?" Harvath asked.

"Is that what this is all about? You think Gashi is Russian? Not Kosovar?"

"Yes. In fact, we think he's GRU."

Ingesson's eyes almost popped out of his head. "Russian military intelligence? Gashi? That's impossible."

"Why?"

"It just doesn't fit."

"Really?" replied Harvath. "You were K4. You were trained to conduct reconnaissance and sabotage behind enemy lines. If you were Russia, and you were going to place a deep-cover operative on Gotland, exactly what type of person would you choose?"

"Probably a man just like Dominik Gashi," he finally admitted after several moments of thought. "I'd take advantage of Sweden's soft spot for immigrants, especially from conflict-torn countries. And I'd place him in an industry few people want to know anything about, much less be part of, like animal processing."

"There you go," said Harvath.

"Of all people, I should have seen it."

"If there was nothing suspicious about him, there's no reason you should have suspected anything."

"So you think he's here as part of some GRU operation. To do what?"

"We think he's running a cell responsible for gathering intelligence and conducting sabotage, in advance of a Russian invasion."

Again, the big man shook his very big head. "I knew it."

"You knew what?"

"I always suspected the Russians had operatives here. It just makes sense. Strategically, they need Gotland. Nobody, though, has ever been able to catch them."

"Well, they're here," said Harvath. "And part of the cell includes a contingent of Spetsnaz soldiers."

"I'm not surprised," he replied. "That's exactly the kind of thing K4 would do. But if you know all this, why hasn't Anders arrested them?"

"That's why I came to see you," said Harvath. "How do I put this appropriately? The way some of the intelligence was gathered makes it difficult for the Chief Inspector to use in court."

Ingesson nodded knowingly. "I am assuming, based on how it was gathered, that it would be difficult for any Swedish authorities to use this intelligence as well."

"Correct. That's one of the reasons I was brought in. My team and I allow Sweden to keep its hands clean."

"I think Americans call it *plausible deniability*."

"Correct again," replied Harvath.

"What do you wish to do with Dominik Gashi?"

"We just want to talk with him."

Ingesson laughed and repeated the word "talk," with air quotes.

"He may not want to talk with us," said Harvath, "but he doesn't have a choice. We believe he is part of an overall operation to weaken NATO and prepare the battlefield for an ultimate Russian invasion of the Baltic States."

"Which is why they would need Gotland. To control the Baltic Sea."

"Exactly," Harvath stated, relieved to be speaking with someone who understood the big picture. "America doesn't want to go to war and we're certain that Sweden doesn't want to either. In our opinion, all that matters—"

"Is stopping the Russians—no matter what it takes."

Harvath nodded. "That is our position."

"It is the right position," replied Ingesson. "What can I do to help you?"

"Do you have a picture of Gashi?"

"Sure. I can pull his file from the company server. What else?"

"I have spoken with two of his associates, neither of whom has ever been to his home. Can you give me some idea of where he lives?"

"I can do better than that," the big man replied. "I'll take you right to him."

CHAPTER 47

Gashi lived in a crappy, run-down cabin on a poorly maintained piece of land in the middle of nowhere. Ingesson knew it because he had driven the man home after he'd had too much to drink at the company Christmas party.

Gashi allegedly augmented his income from the processing plant by acting as a caretaker. He worked for several mainland homeowners who rented out their beach houses to the tourists who flocked to Gotland in the summer.

Off-season, he simply dropped by once a week to make sure pipes hadn't frozen and nothing had been stolen.

It was easy money. What he did with it, though, was anyone's guess. He definitely wasn't putting it into where he lived.

Haney assembled the drone and got it up overhead. Harvath told him to take his time. He definitely didn't want a repeat of Norway.

Slowly, Haney conducted a reconnaissance of the property. In addition to the cabin, there was a detached garage, a woodshed, and an old, decrepit outhouse.

Harvath, as usual, stood next to him, watching the feed on the tablet.

"Looks pretty quiet," said Haney.

"I know," Harvath replied. "That's what bothers me."

"Maybe the guy's just inside sleeping."

Harvath knew there wasn't a chance in hell that was so. Johansson had already admitted that Nikolai had called Gashi, filling him in on everything that had happened at O'Learys, and that Gashi had then called him. There was no way that Gashi would just roll over and go to bed at that point. He'd want to know what Johansson had uncovered. And when Johansson failed to report back in, Gashi would be forced to assume the worst.

If Gashi *was* inside that cabin, he'd probably be sitting behind the front door with a shotgun, ready to blast the first person who showed up. More than likely, he had already taken off. But to where? Unless he had a boat or a plane, there wasn't much he could do besides go to ground. Harvath decided he needed to see the cabin for himself.

Looking at Sloane, he said, "You're with me. Haney stays on the drone. Staelin and Palmer will come in via the woods to the south. Barton's had the longest day of all of us. He'll watch the vehicles. Jasinski, you can stay with Barton, or come with us. It's your call."

Jasinski hadn't expected to be in a position where she had to decide whether to opt in or opt out. "I'm in. I'll go with you."

"Okay," said Harvath, pleased with her answer. "You're with us." Then, addressing the team, he said, "Everyone should *absolutely* be expecting booby-traps. Is that clear?"

"Roger that," they all replied.

Ingesson had wanted to be part of the raid. He had even volunteered to carry his own weapon, a short-barreled tactical rifle he kept, in violation of Swedish law. By the looks of him, he was no stranger to dodging bullets and kicking serious ass, but Harvath had politely said *no*.

The former K4 Army Ranger was too valuable a find. A pro-Western local, with elite military training, skilled at surviving behind enemy lines, was something Harvath would rather keep as a future asset, already in place.

Fortunately, in short, as formidable as he was, they didn't need him. Harvath's team was more than well-equipped to handle this.

Taking the lead, Harvath cut across the adjacent property and approached the cabin from the east with Ashby and Jasinski tight behind him.

They moved as one unit, each covering their respective pieces of the pie, weapons up and ready to engage. They were carrying a new close-quarters weapon called the Sig "Rattler," a compact tactical rifle in the .300 Blackout caliber. Theirs had collapsible stocks and were outfitted with suppressors. They were super smooth and returned almost zero recoil.

Two hundred meters out from the target, Harvath slowed down. They needed to be very careful now. As good as their goggles were, any trip wires would be basically invisible.

Step by careful step, they moved forward. Every tree, every rock, every pile of leaves might hide a Claymore-style antipersonnel device.

Coming up from the south, Palmer and Staelin exhibited the same degree of caution. There was every reason to believe that this cabin would be as well protected as the one in Norway.

In addition to trip wires, Harvath was also concerned about land mines with pressure plates. Via a submarine a few miles off the coast, it would have been nothing for Russian commando teams to get all sorts of equipment onto Gotland. Harvath wasn't taking anything for granted.

As they neared the cabin, he had his team find cover and then called for Haney to bring the drone in for an extreme close-up.

Harvath didn't have the tablet with him, so he had to go by the play-by-play coming in over his earpiece from Haney.

"Garage windows impenetrable to camera. Possibly painted, or just really dirty. Moving on to woodshed."

Several seconds later, Harvath said, "Woodshed appears to be clear. Three, maybe four cords. Nothing else visible."

"No clear angles on outhouse interior. Proceed with caution in regard to all structures."

Harvath waved his team forward. The first building they came upon when accessing the property was the garage. Its windows had been painted black. He tried the main door. It had been locked. Pulling out a short crowbar affixed to his pack, he went to work.

Seconds later there was a snap, along with the sound of a piece of metal skittering into the garage. The door was open. Lifting it, Harvath looked inside.

In the center of the small space was a vehicle covered by a tarp. Approaching it, Harvath flipped back a corner of the canvas.

Underneath was a 1990 Mercedes Benz 250-GD SUV. Flipping up his goggles, he pulled out his flashlight and turned on the low beam. The vehicle's color was olive—an exact match for the mark he had found on Lars Lund's Volkswagen.

Pulling the cover the rest of the way off, he walked

around the front of the vehicle and found damage along the right front quarter panel. This was the car that had been used to kill Lars. He was certain of it.

Turning off his light, he flipped his goggles back down and allowed his eyes to readjust. Then he checked out the woodshed and the outhouse. They were both clear.

He asked Haney to do a final flyby and search the windows of the cabin. He, Ashby, and Jasinski took cover positions while he did.

It took several minutes for him to scan each of the tiny openings and what lay inside. Finally, he reported, "No heat signatures and no movement from inside."

This only made Harvath more nervous. Had Dominik Gashi been inside, there was the hope that the cabin hadn't been wired to explode. The Russians weren't big on suicide. They might drink themselves to death, but that was seen as a virtue, religiously committed to over a significant period of time. Booby-traps were something else entirely.

An empty house, previously inhabited by an assumed GRU intelligence officer, now believed to be on the run, could only be bad news. There were dozens of ways that it could be wired to explode.

A device could be affixed to the door and detonate on entry. It could be rigged to a specific floorboard and explode once an unlucky member of the entry team put weight on it. It could be attached to a closet door or a dresser drawer, just waiting for some poor bastard to open it. The options were both endless and terrifying.

Harvath was aware of them all and he took the lead, starting with the front door.

After checking, as best he could, to make sure it wasn't wired, he pushed it open with the toe of his boot and stepped back.

Nothing happened.

Relieved, Harvath slowly crept inside.

The structure was built around a rough stone fire-place, big enough to walk into. Horns and antlers were nailed to the walls. There was a variety of dead animals, in various stages of taxidermy, scattered throughout the space. A rough-hewn railing blocked off an elevated sleeping area above. The entire place smelled like mold.

Harvath scanned his weapon from left to right as he and his team made entry.

"Clear!" he heard Ashby eventually yell.

Jasinski responded in kind. "Clear!"

Reluctantly, Harvath added his assessment. "Clear!" Dominik Gashi was not here.

Rapidly, they searched chests and wardrobes, under the couch, and inside the tiny bathroom. There was no sign of the man.

There was, though, a sign that he had recently been there. Seeing a bright blue kettle sitting on the stove, Harvath reached out and placed his hand above it. It was still warm. Gashi had been here, and not that long ago.

He gestured Ashby and Jasinski over to show them what he had found. Each of them touched the kettle, and then, nodding, they fanned out and conducted a re-newed search.

"Friendlies," Palmer said over the radio as he and Staelin arrived at the front door.

Knocking twice, they waited for a response, and when Ashby gave the all clear, they entered.

Looking up from her search, she pointed at the kettle on the stove, indicated it was still warm, and then went back to what she was doing.

"I think I've got something," Harvath said from up-stairs in the sleeping loft.

Inside a small cubby he had found a key rack. On it was an assortment of keys, each with a brightly colored plastic tag. Inside each tag was a piece of paper with what looked like an address. One of the pegs was empty.

Explaining what he had found, Harvath slung his Rattler and went back to his search. He was looking for any information about Dominik Gashi and what he was doing on Gotland.

Minutes later, as Staelin was scanning the man's bookshelves, it was Chase who called out, "I may have something."

Harvath came to the railing. "What is it?"

"It looks like a ledger."

"What kind of ledger?"

"A property ledger. There's a chart here with multiple addresses. Then there are dates last visited, status, repairs needed, that kind of thing."

"Read out the addresses," said Harvath as he went back, pulled the keys off the rack, and lined them up on the bed.

As Chase read off the addressees, he discarded the corresponding sets of keys. At the very end, he was able to identify the property to which the matching set belonged.

Pulling out his cell phone, he looked it up on his mapping app and then called Nyström.

"Yes," the Chief Inspector said. "I know it. There are a lot of houses on that stretch of beach. Some are quite close together. But at this time of year, it's normally quiet. Those are almost entirely summer cottages."

Harvath, convinced that he knew where Dominik Gashi had gone to ground, asked Nyström for a favor— a big one.

"I don't think I can do that," the Swedish police officer answered.

"We don't have a choice," replied Harvath. "Beyond the public safety concern, if you don't, everything we have done up to this point is worthless. And we also will have handed the Russians a huge leg up."

Nyström, as was his custom, took several moments to consider what Harvath was asking of him. Each of the American's requests seemed to be more involved and more dangerous than the last.

Finally, the Chief Inspector said, "I'll do it, but only on one condition."

Harvath wasn't a fan of conditions, but he also wasn't in a position to say no, especially not now. "What is it?"

"After this, it's over. All of it. You and your team get on your plane and are gone. Before sunrise."

Harvath had no idea if he'd be able to live up to that kind of promise or not. There was no way he was leaving Gotland without Gashi in tow, but he needed to humor Nyström. In an attempt to prolong the Chief Inspector's cooperation, Harvath agreed. "We'll be gone by sunrise. You can count on it."

"I'll try to pull together what you asked for," the man replied. "Meet me in a half hour."

Harvath hung up the phone and immediately began forming Plans B, C, and D. He had very little faith that what they were about to attempt was actually going to work.

CHAPTER 48

As far as beach houses went, the tiny rental near the village of Nyhamn was not at all what Harvath had expected.

When the sun was up, it probably had a million-dollar view of the ocean. But in the dark, it resembled a double-wide trailer with a long, covered porch and a smattering of cheap outdoor furniture.

By the time Chief Inspector Nyström got to the rendezvous location, Haney had already done multiple drone passes over the target.

"What is the situation?" Nyström said as he climbed out of Johansson's squad car, dressed in a patrolman's uniform.

"All quiet," Haney replied. "No movement inside."

"Where are your people?"

Using a still from the drone, Harvath marked the locations on his tablet and then asked, "Were you able to get what I asked for?"

Nyström tilted his head toward the backseat of the cruiser.

Harvath opened the door and removed a duffel bag. Dropping it on the lid of the trunk, he unzipped it and inventoried the contents. There was a regulation police uniform, boots, duty belt, cap, and jacket. There was also body armor.

"Were you able to get the other item?"

He nodded and knocked on the side of the trunk.

Harvath cleared his gear off the lid and opened it. He ignored Johansson, who was still lying inside, and grabbed the plastic case.

The Chief Inspector still hadn't decided what to do with Johansson. Fortunately, Johansson was off-duty when Harvath caught him. Neither he nor his patrol car, which was a take-home vehicle, would be missed until tomorrow night.

Closing the lid, Harvath put the case on the trunk and opened it up. Inside was a tear gas launcher with several canisters.

"I am hoping we don't need that," said Nyström.

"Me too," replied Harvath. Latching the case, he handed it to Haney and told him, "Get this to Sloane and then hustle back."

The Marine accepted the case and struck off into the pines on the side of the road, disappearing into a gathering mist.

"What do we know about the nearby houses?" the Chief Inspector asked.

Picking up his tablet from where he had laid it on the roof of the patrol vehicle, Harvath pulled up another photo. "There are four of them. As far as we can tell, they're all empty. But, if we did have to go hot and a round over-penetrated and exited our target house, there's a possibility it could enter any one of them."

"Based on your conversation with Martin Ingesson, I overheard that you were a Navy SEAL?"

Harvath nodded.

"I assume you were taught to control your rounds?"

"It's not my rounds I'm worried about," he replied. "Dominik Gashi, or whatever his real name is, may have Sparrman's Spetsnaz operatives in there. It doesn't take much to get those boys into a gunfight. And when they're triggered, they don't give a damn where their rounds go."

Nyström took one of his long, pregnant pauses as he tried to figure out the best course forward. "How do you know the other houses aren't occupied?"

"No lights on inside, no cars outside. We looked through the windows using IR and thermal."

"There's no cars outside the target house either."

"True, but that could be for several reasons. At the cabin Ingesson sent us to, we found an olive Mercedes SUV, under a tarp. If you reexamine Lars Lund's vehicle back at the wrecking yard, you should see damage to the left rear quarter panel that contains traces of the same paint."

"So you *did* notice something when you examined the car."

"I notice lots of things," said Harvath. "It's part of my job. It wasn't worth mentioning at the time. Now it is."

"Fair enough. What other reasons might there not be any cars near the target house?"

"The house may have been a fallback location for Gashi and the Spetsnaz. If they're hiding here, they wouldn't want to give their presence away.

"I disabled their two vehicles in Visby. If they got them working again, maybe they drove here and hid them. They also could have Ubered to a location nearby and hiked the rest of the way in. Same with Gashi."

It made sense to Nyström, and he nodded. "Before we do anything, I have to check the nearby houses."

"I just told you they're empty."

The Chief Inspector held up his hand. "And I'm the one who might have to answer to a police review board at some point. Change clothes. While you do, I'll check the houses for myself."

Reluctantly, Harvath agreed. He waited for Haney to reappear and then sent the two men off together.

Opening the trunk of the car, he removed Johansson's hood and peeled the duct tape from his mouth.

"Are you thirsty?" he asked.

The man nodded.

Nyström had some water bottles in a crate in the trunk. Grabbing the corrupt cop by his tunic, Harvath lifted him into a kneeling position. Then, opening one of the bottles, he tilted it so that he could drink. Once Johansson had had enough, Harvath screwed the cap back on the bottle and set it back down in the crate with the others.

"Thank you," said Johansson. "May I urinate?"

There was a time in Harvath's past where he probably would have vented his anger at the corrupt cop by slamming the lid down on the man's head. Instead, he looked down at him and said, "Be my guest."

As he began to object, Harvath tore off a new piece of duct tape, slapped it across his mouth, and put the hood back over his head.

Closing the lid, he picked up the duffel bag, dropped it on the trunk, and began to gear up.

By the time Nyström and Haney returned, Harvath looked like a model Swedish policeman.

The uniform fit so well, he could have been posing for officer of the month, or the much maligned, yet extremely popular Swedish policeman's calendar.

"Put your coat on," ordered Nyström. Then pointing at Harvath's Rattler, added, "Sidearm only. In its holster.

Nice and easy. We're just two cops responding to a suspicious activity call."

Harvath appreciated the man's attention to detail, but he hadn't intended to bring the Rattler. No need to tip Dominik Gashi that anything was out of the ordinary.

Haney did a final team radio check, and then flashed a thumbs-up. They were all ready to go.

Harvath looked at the Chief Inspector and said, "Just two cops, responding to a suspicious activity call. A casual knock and talk."

CHAPTER 49

I n their patrol uniforms, they both got into the patrol vehicle and headed down the narrow beach road toward the house.

A light fog had begun to gather. Nyström was on edge. Harvath could see it by how tightly he gripped the steering wheel.

"Everything's going to be okay," said Harvath.

"Have you done this a lot?"

"Use the police as a ruse in order to capture a bad guy?"

The Chief Inspector nodded.

"I have, actually."

"Where?"

Harvath thought for a moment. "The last time was in Germany. Similar to this. We had an actual Bundespolizei officer, in uniform, as another member of my team posed as a plainclothes detective from the Kriminalpolizei."

"I assume it worked, or we wouldn't be doing this, right?"

"It worked perfectly. The target was also a Russian. They treat the police in their own country with disdain, but when operating abroad, especially illegally, they're highly deferential to law enforcement.

"That's why I like this approach. It's safer. They don't want any trouble, so they go along with what a uniformed officer asks. By the time they realize what's happening, it's too late. You have them."

"And what happened to that Russian?" asked Nyström.

"To be honest," replied Harvath, "I don't know. It was only my job to pick him up."

"Who hired you for the job?"

Harvath smiled. "I can't remember."

"I see," said the Chief Inspector, relaxing a little bit. "I imagine memory loss happens a lot in your business."

"I wouldn't know. I keep forgetting."

Nyström grinned. He was fairly certain that the American was much more than just a NATO liaison.

As they neared the house, the Chief Inspector said, "Don't talk. Just follow my lead."

Harvath nodded. "Don't worry. My Swedish isn't that good. That's why I have you along. I plan to let you do all the talking."

"Good. We'll start off with an inspection of the perimeter. You still have your flashlight? The one that's brighter than mine?"

He pulled it from his pocket and gave a quick flash against the palm of his hand.

"Okay, then," said Nyström, pulling up near the house. "Here we are."

Reaching behind, he withdrew a handheld spotlight, plugged it into the cigarette lighter, and handed it to Harvath. "Roll down your window and sweep the light slowly across the house and around the perimeter."

Harvath did as the Chief Inspector had asked. When it was complete, he turned off the light, rolled up his window, and handed it back. "What now?"

"Now," he said, lifting the microphone of his police radio to his mouth and pretending to toggle the Talk button, "we call it in, and then we exit the vehicle."

Harvath followed his lead and exited the vehicle. They both got their flashlights out and began sweeping the area with their beams. Then, slowly, they walked a complete circle around the house. Though he couldn't see his team set back in the trees, Harvath knew they were there.

Curtains were drawn across most of the windows. Where they could, they peered inside. Either house-keeping had never come after the last set of guests, or there were several people inside who had quickly scrambled for cover. There were coffee cups and dirty dishes visible in the kitchen.

Nyström rattled the back door, to see if it was unlocked, and then kept moving. Eventually, they made it back around to the front of the structure.

Walking up the front steps, the Chief Inspector approached the front door and gave a loud "police" knock.

He allowed a few moments for a response, and when no one came to the door, he knocked again, even louder this time. He knew there were people inside and he was making it quite obvious.

Suddenly, they heard noises as someone made his way to the door. In a move so subtle that Nyström didn't even see it, Harvath unfastened the safety mechanism on his holster. Fortunately, the Swedish police also carried the Sig Sauer, so he had been able to bring his own sidearm along.

He stood half a step back, just behind the Chief Inspector's right side. He had wanted to be up front, but it was out of the question. Nyström had to take point, as the encounter had to be done in Swedish.

Having dated several Swedish flight attendants, Harvath spoke a little of the language, but his vocabulary was composed of relatively useless words—pickup lines, a few naughty sentences, drinking songs, and some tourist phrases he had used when he'd previously been over to visit. And, of course, it was all built upon the foundation of the first thing anyone learns in a foreign language—swear words.

All of it was useless as the door opened and Nyström leaned in to engage.

The first thing the man did was something Harvath had watched seasoned American cops do. The moment the door opened, he stuck the toe of his boot inside so that it couldn't be closed.

As soon as Harvath saw him, he knew that they had their man. Gashi's Swedish was terrible, and he asked the police officer if he spoke English. As he had done with Harvath upon their first meeting, the Chief Inspector instantly transitioned over.

"Good evening," he said. "Just a routine check. A neighbor called in a report of suspicious activity."

Gashi looked around, trying to ascertain which neighbor it might have been, then flicked his eyes toward Harvath. "I haven't seen anything," he said,

"Are you the owner of this house?"

"No, I am the caretaker."

"Are you alone inside?"

"I'm sorry," Gashi replied. "What exactly is it that you are looking for?"

"We're just here taking a look and making sure everything is okay," Nyström reassured him. "It's quite late. Are you living in this house?"

"Me? No. I have a full-time job at FörsPak. I do my caretaking on the side—at night and on weekends."

"May I see some identification, please?"

"Of course," the man replied, flicking his eyes toward Harvath again.

If Harvath didn't know any better, he would have sworn that the man had recognized him from somewhere. But that was impossible.

What Harvath couldn't know was that Gashi recognized him from the CCTV footage that Johansson had pulled from Visby Hospital.

Regardless, Harvath's "Spidey sense" was officially tingling. Transitioning the flashlight to his left hand, he let his right hand drop and hover just above his holster.

Keep an eye on his hands, he thought as Dominik Gashi reached back as if to retrieve his wallet.

Instead, the man pulled out something that looked like a Victorian surgical instrument. It was long and highly polished, catching what little light there was in the fog.

Gashi slashed in a downward motion with amazing speed. His target—Chief Inspector Nyström.

Upon seeing the blade, Harvath reacted. He drove his left shoulder into Nyström, trying to knock him out of the weapon's path.

At the same time, he double-punched the tail cap of his flashlight, triggering an eruption of strobe lights. He tilted the beam as best he could, hoping to catch Gashi in the face to blind him, as he drew his pistol.

He fired twice at the man's left knee and then two more times into his left shoulder. He wanted him incapacitated, not dead.

The Russian dropped the knife and it clattered to the ground as he stumbled backward. Stepping in, Harvath kicked it aside and shoved Nyström fully out of the way.

Holstering his pistol, he quickly patted Gashi down

to make sure he didn't have any more weapons. Then, grabbing him by the collar, he yanked him away from the house and back toward the patrol car.

The Chief Inspector was slow to follow.

When Harvath looked back, he could see that the Swede was badly injured. He was bleeding profusely from his left arm and part of his chest.

He had raised his arm to shield himself from Gashi's knife, which had cut right through the chunky plastic strap of his digital watch, and deep into his forearm, and had kept going across part of his chest—above where his vest was. The weapon was incredibly sharp, having cut through his jacket and the uniform beneath before slicing through his flesh, revealing bone.

Dumping Gashi behind the patrol vehicle, Harvath buffaloed him with the butt of his Sig Sauer and gave the signal for his team to move in.

Just as they began to appear from the trees Gashi's own team appeared in the windows and the doorway of the house, and opened fire.

CHAPTER 50

Nyström, despite his injuries, found a reservoir of strength and summoned an incredible burst of speed.

As he caught up with Harvath behind the patrol vehicle, his pistol was already out and he was putting rounds on the house.

"Where's your med kit?" Harvath yelled as he slammed a fresh magazine into his Sig and returned fire at the Spetsnaz soldiers.

"I'll be okay."

Nyström was bleeding a lot and starting to look weak. He clearly needed medical attention, and soon. But before that could happen, they needed to neutralize the threat inside the house.

Hailing Sloane over his radio, Harvath said, "Hit them with the gas!"

Seconds later, the first tear gas canister sailed out of the launcher, crashed through one of the windows, and began aerosolizing.

Quickly, Sloane worked her way through the trees and pumped three more rounds into different parts of the house.

Harvath had made the rules of engagement crystal clear. Whoever stepped outside holding a weapon was a legitimate target.

With tear gas filling the structure, Harvath secured Gashi with Flex-Cuffs and then searched for the medical bag in the patrol car.

Finding it, he returned to Nyström.

The Chief Inspector was leaning against the left front tire, trying to use the engine block as cover. Laying the bag on the ground next to him, Harvath tore it open and removed what he needed to tend to the injured man.

Around them, gunfire crackled as his team returned fire and put rounds on the beach house. Windows shattered and shards of glass went flying as pieces of wood splintered in all directions.

Using a pair of shears to cut away the clothing, Harvath examined Nyström's wound. He was bleeding badly, but the wound wasn't spurting. Applying a tourniquet could mean the loss of his arm.

He ripped open packages of bandages and used an Israeli battle dressing to stanch the bleeding. It was all he could do for the moment.

Taking the cop's empty sidearm, he ejected the spent magazine, flicked it aside, and inserted a new one. "You're topped up," he said as he depressed the slide release and handed the weapon back to the Chief Inspector.

Popping up over the hood, Harvath focused on the front door. When two Spetsnaz operatives emerged, choking on tear gas, but with weapons still in their hands, he and his team let their rounds fly. Both men dropped dead right there on the doorstep.

From the rear of the house came the sound of more gunfire. Harvath knew that meant additional Spetsnaz operatives were likely trying to escape via the back door.

Three more Russian soldiers appeared at the front door, stumbling over the bodies of their dead comrades, but with their hands held high.

Unlike his lousy Swedish, Harvath actually spoke some passable Russian, and he yelled out a series of commands, which the remaining men obeyed. He warned them to stay facedown on the ground, and said that if they did not, they would be shot.

With the three Spetsnaz lying in the dirt, plus the two dead at the door, that made five. He radioed Sloane, who told him that they'd killed three more who had come running out the back with their guns blazing. That brought the total to eight—the same number of men that had been seen running at the Sparrman farm.

Harvath glanced down at Nyström. He was bleeding through the thick bandages. They couldn't wait any longer. Harvath had to get him to a hospital.

Though it had taken multiple rounds, the police vehicle was still functional. Haney helped load the Chief Inspector into the passenger seat.

He left the medical kit so that Staelin could tend to Gashi. And, after a brief rundown of what he wanted everyone to do, Harvath lit up the light bar and raced for the hospital in Visby.

In a police car, in the early Sunday morning hours before dawn, with no one on the roads and no fear of being pulled over, Harvath should have been able to make the half-hour trip to Visby in fifteen minutes. The fog, though, had gotten worse, and he was forced to drive more slowly than he would have liked.

On the flip side, it might have been for the best, as the fog provided them with a modicum of concealment. A bullet-ridden police car, driven by an officer no one on the island recognized, would have raised a lot of alarms.

As absolutely messed up as everything had been, they still had managed to keep most of the operation "quiet."

Harvath kept Nyström engaged by talking to him and asking lots of questions. They made it to the hospital in just over twenty minutes, which meant that—for the conditions—Harvath had still been driving way too fast.

Skidding up to the Emergency Room entrance, Harvath saw the redheaded nurse at the desk inside and waved for her to come out and help.

Exiting the vehicle, he came around to the side and opened the passenger door for Nyström.

"We made it," said Harvath. "You're going to be okay."

"Thank you," the Chief Inspector replied. His voice was weak, his eyes a little glassy.

As the nurse came running out, pushing a wheelchair, she already had two doctors in tow behind her.

"Knife wound. Left arm and left side of the torso," Harvath said to them. "He has lost a lot of blood."

They positioned the wheelchair next to the vehicle, carefully lifted the policeman out, and transitioned him over.

The nurse recognized Harvath from earlier, but Nyström hadn't bothered introducing him. Now he was back, wearing a Swedish police uniform, and speaking in American-accented English, not Swedish. She didn't really know what to make of it.

"He's a good man," said Harvath, interrupting her thoughts. "Take care of him."

As the doctors rushed the Chief Inspector inside, she nodded and then turned to follow them.

At the doorway, she turned back around, but the American had already gotten back into the patrol vehicle and had disappeared into the mist.

CHAPTER 51

The team met back at the wrecking yard. After the rental house had been compromised, Nyström had agreed to let Harvath and his people use the office there as a secure location until they left Gotland. Neither his uncle nor any employees would show up there until Monday morning.

Harvath had a lot of loose ends to tie up. What's more, he was only going to get one shot. If he screwed up, he wouldn't be able to come back and fix them later. It would be too late. He needed to think. In fact, what he really needed was coffee.

Hopping into the Camry, Chase left the yard and drove back to the gas station minimart—one of the few twenty-four-hour places on Gotland—and returned with supplies. They had left the rental house so quickly that no one had packed up the kitchen.

With a cup of hot coffee in his hand, Harvath sat at a battered worktable jotting down notes.

Under the heading of "Absolutely Unbelievable" was the fact that Johansson had survived the shootout. Multiple rounds had pierced the trunk of the police cruiser, but not a single one had touched him. God must have intended for the corrupt cop to a do a very lengthy prison sentence.

Then, in his own category, was Sparrman. He had been trussed up with Flex-Cuffs, hooded, gagged, and left in the minivan up the road from the beach house. At some point, very soon, his mother was going to start looking into what had happened to him.

On top of the treasonous twosome, there were the three surviving Spetsnaz soldiers—also bound, hooded, and gagged at the wrecking yard.

Harvath hadn't decided what to do with any of them yet. Right now, the only captive whom Harvath cared anything about was Dominik Gashi. Gashi was the key to the next level.

Fortunately, Harvath's shots had been well-placed and none of Gashi's injuries was life-threatening. The wounds probably hurt like hell, which was okay, but more important, the Russian would survive. Staelin had done an excellent job of patching him up.

It was likely that Gashi would need surgery to remove the bullets from his left knee and shoulder, but that was so far down Harvath's list that he couldn't have been bothered to care. Hell, where Gashi was ultimately headed, he didn't have a lot of need for healthy knees and shoulders.

Harvath was more concerned with making sure Nyström was covered. Carl Pedersen had already reached out to a colleague at MUST. He replied that, though Harvath's operation hadn't been officially sanctioned, if it truly had disrupted a Russian cell intent on promoting a Russian invasion of Gotland, they could handle the cleanup.

He had also said that if the Russians had been involved in killing Lars Lund, and if Harvath had exacted revenge, the Swedish government would probably give him a medal. If not, MUST definitely would.

Of course, MUST would need all the evidence, as

well as the names of those involved—especially the Swedish nationals collaborating with the Russians.

Harvath didn't have a problem with MUST having any of the information. They would do the right thing with it. His biggest concern was making sure that Nyström was properly recognized and not thrown under the bus for his involvement. From what Pedersen had told him, MUST was going to make sure Nyström came out on top.

They were already launching a team from Stockholm to come over and deal with the beach house, the dead Spetsnaz operatives, and the prisoners. All the prisoners, that was, except for one. Harvath and the team were taking Gashi back with them.

The MUST team would also be arranging to bring back Lars Lund's body. There was talk of a search for Russian weapons caches on the island, which probably would take place after MUST interrogators were able to spend some time with the surviving Spetsnaz operatives.

From there, they would concoct a narrative and decide how the story would play out. Harvath, though, would already be off of Gotland and on to the next chapter—all within the promised forty-eight hours.

How quickly that next chapter would be written was now the biggest question. Dominik Gashi had not proven to be very cooperative.

Harvath's standard operating procedure with injured detainees was that they were not to be given any pain medications if they refused to play ball. Gashi was refusing to play ball.

Harvath had seen his kind before. He was a hard, seasoned Russian operative. It wouldn't be easy breaking him. In fact, it would take a lot of work. So Harvath had decided to bring in a specialist to speed things up. He would be flying into Brussels later that day. All they had to do was to make sure Gashi remained stable until the man got there. Harvath felt confident that they could do that.

What he wasn't so confident about was taking off. According to the pilots, the fog didn't look as if it was going to lift any time soon. In fact, it was forecast to get worse.

That opened up a whole new bunch of problems for the team. The longer they stayed in Sweden, the greater their chances of getting rolled up by the local authorities. Just because a MUST team was coming over to sanitize everything didn't mean they'd go to bat for the Americans. Truth be told, they were counting on Harvath and his team to be long gone before they got there. That was what Harvath wanted, too.

Their only option was to get to the airport, board the jet, and hope to get a break in the weather that might allow them to take off. Harvath had already contacted the pilots and told them to begin their preflight checks. He wanted to be wheels-up at the very first opportunity.

As they began to make ready at the wrecking yard, Jasinski pulled him aside. She was understandably nervous, especially considering how she had lost her husband. "Are you sure about this?" she asked. "Can we fly in this weather?"

"Our pilots are exceptional. If they say we can do it, we can do it."

"And if not?"

"Then we wait," said Harvath. "We're not going to take any unnecessary risks. Trust me."

Jasinski wanted to trust him, but she didn't believe for a second that if it were a fifty-fifty shot, that he wouldn't push the crew to get the plane off the ground and up into the air. Though she was nervous, she tried to put her fear aside and focus on the task at hand.

The MUST team had transmitted instructions on how they wanted the prisoners secured. On Nyström's behalf, they would reach out to his uncle and confirm that no one was coming in before Monday morning. It would be disastrous if an employee showed up and called the cops, or even worse, let the prisoners go.

They took pictures and created dossiers on each one, so that the MUST team would know who they were dealing with when they arrived. Then, after giving the men some water and a chance to relieve themselves, they secured them in a storage room, threw a tarp over the damaged police cruiser, and headed for the airport.

Harvath broke his rule about pain medication and decided to sedate Gashi. It would make him more compliant and less likely to cause a scene at the airport.

Pulling the minivan right up to the jet's airstairs, Staelin and Haney lifted the man out of the back and carried him on board. The fog was so murky, they were confident that no one had seen anything.

Loading up the rest of their gear, they all climbed aboard, and the plane taxied out to the runway. There it sat, waiting for the fog to lift.

This was always the part that gave Harvath the most concern. Being at the mercy of a control tower produced a certain amount of anxiety in him. You could do everything right, but if the police or some other actor came and yanked you off the plane before takeoff, that was it. It was over.

The pilots were already well aware of how he felt. Though he didn't let Jasinski overhear, he had told them that the moment they saw an opportunity, they were to take it. He wanted to get out of Sweden as soon as possible. The minutes were ticking away.

"Can I ask you something?" he said, bringing up a topic that had been on his mind all night.

"Sure," Monika replied. "What is it?"

"When Johansson had me in the equipment shed, how did you know I was in trouble?"

"I didn't. Not really. I just had a feeling."

"And that's why you had the gun?" he asked.

She shrugged. "Call it a sixth sense. Call it luck. I don't really know. I just had a feeling something wasn't right. Maybe I heard him pull up at the property. Maybe because you saved my life, we're connected somehow."

"Maybe," Harvath replied, closing his eyes and trying to relax.

They sat quietly on the tarmac for almost an hour before a chime rang through the cabin. It was followed by the engines winding up. Finally, the fog had partially lifted and the pilots were going to make a go of it.

Harvath watched Jasinski as she snuck a worried glance out her window and then tightened her seat belt.

Moments later the massive engines roared to life and the jet went screaming down the runway. Airport buildings were barely visible as they went racing past.

The plane lifted off the ground and soared up and into the foggy night sky. They had done it.

With altitude, the air began to clear. Banking out over the Baltic Sea, the pilots pointed the plane south and headed for Brussels.

Harvath closed his eyes, but as the stress of escaping Sweden began to recede, a new pressure replaced it.

Would they be in time to stop the next attack?

CHAPTER 52

Turkey was at the political crossroads of West and East. It was not only a NATO member, but also had the second-largest army within the organization.

Positioned on Syria's northernmost border, Turkey had been unhappy with the "solutions" America was pushing in the country. In particular, it didn't like at all the idea of a thirty-thousand-member "border force" composed of Kurdish fighters, whom Ankara saw as terrorists.

For its part, America had been concerned about how Turkey was drifting ever closer to authoritarianism. An attempted coup two years earlier had given the current nationalist President an excuse to consolidate power and conduct a purge, jailing many of his opponents—including teachers and intellectuals. Anyone who had spoken out about him had been imprisoned.

He had been particularly ruthless in regard to the military, firing any officers he felt were too pro-West. Hundreds of military envoys to NATO were recalled. Many fled rather than be thrown in jail. Those who replaced them mirrored the President's thinking when it came to a collective dislike of NATO.

It wouldn't take much to collapse Turkey's relationship with NATO, leading to its withdrawal. That was why Oleg Tretyakov had decided to launch his Istanbul attack next.

Inflaming the Turks would not only drive a deeper wedge between them and the West, but would also drive them deeper into the arms of Russia.

The Russian President had been involved in a major charm offensive with the Turkish President. By all accounts, it had been working. *Spectacularly so*.

Turkey had invested tens of millions of dollars in multiple Russian air-defense systems. The purchase sent shockwaves through NATO, as the Russian system was incompatible with their systems. What's more, Turkey would have to import Russians to run the new systems and, worst of all, would likely be sharing highly classified information about the NATO air-defense systems with their Russian counterparts. It was a very, very bad development. Turkey was an anti-NATO tinderbox— all it needed was the correct spark.

The best part for Tretyakov's plan was that Turkish nationals with deep anti-NATO sentiments were not difficult to find. In fact, there had been an abundance of them. The greatest challenge was to find competent cell members with the right skills. The bombs Tretyakov wanted were difficult to build. They were even more difficult to transport and conceal. But *difficult* did not mean impossible.

His GRU team had successfully recruited a handful of highly qualified young Turkish men. With degrees in chemistry, physics, and electronics, they took to the technological aspects of the job quite easily.

Tretyakov's biggest fear was that when it came time to plant the bombs, the young men would have crises of conscience, and would back out, unwilling to expose civilians to death and dismemberment. That was why the cell leader position had been such an integral component.

The man chosen was a Russian patriot of incomparable magnetism. He could have even the most hard-hearted cynic eating out of his hand and committed to his cause in an afternoon.

The young men had no clue that they were being manipulated by a foreign actor. They believed NATO was a blight on their country and that this attack would drive NATO out. By driving it out, the President of Turkey would then be unshackled. He would be free to create a perfect society for the Turkish people.

It was pure propaganda, of course, but it was a message that resonated with the young men. One which they wanted and needed to hear. It was much easier to blame Turkey's problems on NATO rather than on the Turks themselves.

So, in a small house in an Istanbul slum, the materials for the bombs were collected and the bombs assembled.

The work was nerve-wracking, requiring painstaking attention to detail. The hours were long and the home was stifling. The men were forbidden to speak with friends or family members, especially toward the end, lest they give the plot away. In fact, they weren't even aware of the final target until the last minute.

In order to protect the operation, the bombers had been required to conduct surveillance on multiple locations. There was a list of things the cell leader had instructed them to look for and to study.

When they returned from reconnaissance missions, he would quiz them for hours, testing how thorough they had been in their observations. Sometimes, he would even follow and surveil them himself—using his observations to further critique their performance. This had the added benefit of letting the men know that they were constantly being watched. Fear, in its many forms—even fear of failure—was a powerful motivator, and the Russians were experts in wielding it with surgical precision.

On the day the attack was to take place, the cell leader gathered the men together and finally revealed their target.

The Sirkeci railway station, once the terminus for the famed Orient Express, would be jammed with travelers returning to the city after a long weekend. Looking at a floor plan of the terminal, the cell leader discussed the best locations to plant their devices in order to maximize the damage.

As they went over the details of the operation, the cell leader studied them—their body language, facial expressions, tones of voice, and what they said. He searched for any indication that even one of them was having second thoughts. There was no such indication. The operation was a go.

Carefully, they went through their final checks and packaged the devices. Most went into suitcases. Some went into backpacks.

Their target was the Marmaray subway platform beneath the train station, where the density of travelers would be the greatest.

At the appointed time, the men headed out in their separate directions. They would all be converging on the platform at the same time, but by different means—some via connecting trains, others on foot.

Oleg Tretyakov had wanted redundancy. If one of the bombers was delayed or captured, or his device failed to detonate, he wanted to make sure that there were multiple backups.

Each of the bombers had also been given deceptive pocket litter. If any of them were discovered by police and searched, evidence on their person would suggest a completely different target. This would put police into overdrive, and fritter away their resources as they rushed to a completely incorrect location, hoping to prevent any other bombers from striking.

At one point, Tretyakov had contemplated creating a cadre of red herrings—a separate cell of useful idiots meant to get captured and completely cut off from the real bombers. He had abandoned the idea, though, as being too complex, and actually more likely to fail. There was also the very real prospect that even providing false clues could cause the entire city to go on high alert. Simple was better. So the members of the lone cell had been dispatched.

According to the plan, they would all converge at 4:58 p.m. Based on their traffic analysis, that gave them enough time to get in place, plant their devices, and leave just as they detonated.

Using the example of the train bombings in London and Madrid, the cell leader had taught them the importance of tradecraft, and what exactly to do, and not to do. They had practiced over and over again until everything was second nature. When word had come from Tretyakov that it was time to execute, the cell leader had every confidence his men were ready to go.

At two minutes before five o'clock, the polished, brightly lit subway system was packed. Men, women, and children were returning home from spending an afternoon or the weekend outside the city. It was an unusually pleasant day along the Bosporus. There had been plenty of sun and above-average temperatures.

Now, as the travellers trudged back to Istanbul, many

carrying suitcases, backpacks, or messenger-style bags, their thoughts were on tomorrow and the start of the workweek. Very few were paying attention to what was going on around them.

Even fewer noticed the suitcases and backpacks that had been left along the crowded platform, or inside the packed train cars.

As the bombs detonated, they tore through everything—flesh, bone, steel, tile, and concrete.

Aboveground, buildings shook violently. Some thought it was an earthquake. Not until smoke began to billow out of the subway entrance did people begin to realize the horror of what had just happened.

CHAPTER 53

It was Sunday and the U.S. Mission to the United Nations was quiet. The offices were located in a building at First Avenue and Forty-fifth Street right across from the main UN building, which ran along the East River.

Ambassador Rebecca Strum received the three Baltic States Ambassadors in her private conference room. Her staff had catered a light brunch. Arrayed along the credenza was an assortment of pastries, meats, cheeses, fresh fruit, and quiche. There were also two large carafes of coffee—one regular, one decaf.

As the Ambassadors prepared their plates, they made small talk. Normally, this kind of talk was about the weather, what plays or exhibits they might have taken in over the weekend, or what new restaurants they had visited. This weekend, though, hadn't been normal.

The Ambassadors had been in their respective offices working, practically around the clock. On Friday, Lithuania, Latvia, and Estonia had come under a variety of cyberattacks—more than the normal probes they were all used to. As the weekend had progressed, the efforts against their governments had escalated. The situation was so concerning that by Sunday morning they had requested an urgent meeting with the U.S. Ambassador.

Strum had her assistant usher all the aides out of the conference room and then closed the heavy wooden doors behind them. She wanted this conversation to be absolutely private.

An hour earlier a countersurveillance team had completed its sweep of the office and had deemed it clean. Picking up a special remote, she pressed a button that closed the heavy draperies, followed by another button, which activated the room's countermeasures. Cell phones had been left outside the room as well. They were now secure and could chat at will.

Pouring coffee, they chose seats at the conference table and sat down. The Estonian Ambassador started things off. "Starting Friday, we saw a surge in attacks against our banking and health-care industries. We have several hospitals that have been locked out of their electronic medical records systems and an entire portion of southern Estonia where ATMs went offline."

"The situation in Lithuania is similar," said its Ambassador. "Though the focus has been on our energy resources. Rolling blackouts have been occurring in our major cities and multiple natural gas plants have been taken offline."

The Latvian Ambassador spoke last. "While our cybersecurity experts have seen probes in all of these areas—especially in regard to newspapers and the websites of our political parties—our issue is less cyberwarfare and more information warfare. Friday afternoon, embarrassing information—I believe the Russians call it *kompromat*—was released about our President and an alleged affair from two years ago, with a member of Parliament. There was video, obviously shot in some hotel room, as well as still photos. The leakers are promising to release more tonight.

"Needless to say, this has been very damaging to their respective political parties, but it has also raised questions about the legitimacy of his election, as the woman resigned after it was learned her brother-in-law had been involved in vote tampering. That stain has now spread to our President."

"I see," mused Strum. "Is there any indication, other than the affair, that your President has done anything untoward?"

The Latvian Ambassador shook his head. "Not that I know of, but ever since the story broke, Riga has been in damage-control mode. They are very nervous, and the suggestion that there's more to come is only fueling the scandal. If our election is seen as illegitimate, there will be a true crisis of confidence. The government is worried about the real possibility of street protests, maybe even violence."

"In addition to a potential health crisis, with doctors and nurses locked out of medical records, we're also concerned about a bank run," the Estonian Ambassador said. "After Russia's massive cyberattack in 2007 we promised our citizens that we would do everything we could to make sure it never happened again. If Russia keeps this up, we will also have a crisis of confidence."

Strum remembered the 2007 attack on Estonia. It had lasted for three weeks and had been absolutely unprecedented.

It had centered on one of her favorite towns in Europe, Tallinn. Situated on the Gulf of Finland, fifty miles south of Helsinki, it was Estonia's capital and largest city.

In Tallinn's center had stood a bronze war memorial

commemorating the Soviet war dead who had helped liberate the city from the Nazis.

Tired of a Soviet military monument in downtown Tallinn, and feeling it would be more appropriate in a cemetery, Estonia relocated the bronze statue, as well as the human remains underneath, to the Tallinn Military Cemetery.

The Russians had gone apoplectic. It made no difference to them that Estonia was a free and sovereign nation, and could choose what it wanted to do. Relocating the statue had been considered an incredible insult to Russia, and so they had decided to make Estonia pay.

The attacks came in waves, targeting anything and everything Estonia had connected to the Internet.

Though Estonia was careful not to make the situation worse by directly accusing Russia, quietly NATO had flown in highly specialized cyberteams to pinpoint the identity and location of the hackers, as well as to help Estonia beef up its cyberdefenses.

The fact that such an attack was possible, and on such a major scale, had been a terrifying wake-up call to the West in general and NATO in particular.

Now it was happening again, but on a much more precisely targeted basis. The Russians knew where to strike to cause maximum damage, and that's exactly what they were doing.

"Is it the opinion of the United States," asked the Latvian Ambassador, "that the time has come for us to mobilize our armed forces? Is this the precursor to the attack that we were warned about?"

"Lithuania asks the same question," said its Ambassador.

"And Estonia," added its Ambassador.

Strum knew that it was important to project calm and

confidence. "While we share your concern, we think any change in your military posture would be premature at this time—and might even be seen as antagonistic. You don't want to give the Russians an excuse to match your moves by massing troops and material on your respective borders."

"Isn't that what they're already doing?" asked the Lithuanian Ambassador. "Their claim of an unscheduled military training exercise is nothing more than a fig leaf."

"We do share that concern as well," said Strum. "And again, I need to stress that we are asking you not to change your postures. Let's not give the Russians any more help than we have to."

"Then in the meantime, what do you propose we do?" asked the Estonian.

"Keep the lines of communication open," she replied. "We are working on something we think may be helpful in this area."

"A solution?" asked the Latvian.

Strum tilted her head from side to side, weighing the correct wording. "Something more akin to *leverage*."

"When will we have this leverage?"

"We are working on it now. I hope to have something for you very soon."

"On behalf not just of our nations, but of the entire NATO alliance," said the Lithuanian Ambassador, "I must ask you to please hurry. I fear we are rapidly running out of time."

CHAPTER 54

After returning to their compound near SHAPE, Harvath and his team unpacked their gear, cleaned their weapons, and then placed everything where it belonged.

While the team caught up on a few hours of sleep, Morrison and Gage took turns watching over their prisoner.

Dominik Gashi was being kept in a storage room in the basement of the main building. It had been just big enough to get a small bed into.

Harvath had come around before hitting the sack and had checked the dressings. Staelin had put Gashi on an IV and had begun to administer antibiotics, just in case. Bullet wounds were infection magnets.

Satisfied that everything was well in hand, Harvath had gone back across to the guesthouse, dropped into bed, and fallen right asleep.

He awoke several hours later to Nicholas's dog, Argos, licking his hand. Opening his eyes, he saw the little man standing in his doorway. "What's up?" Harvath asked.

"You told me to wake you when the plane from Malta was inbound."

"How far out are they?"

"Touchdown in forty-five minutes."

"Roger that," said Harvath, rubbing the stubble on his face and throwing the blankets back. "Thank you."

"You're welcome," Nicholas replied. "I've got coffee and a late lunch in the kitchen if you're interested."

Harvath was definitely interested, but first he needed to grab a quick shower.

Standing under the hot spray, he let the water beat on his body. He ached in places he didn't even know he had. Getting older sucked, but it beat the alternative.

Five minutes later, he threw the temperature selector all the way to cold and measured how long he could stand it. He managed a good thirty seconds before he decided he'd had enough and turned it off.

Though he didn't fully agree with the K4 operative, Ingesson had a point about SEALs and cold. At some point, you just have had enough.

Harvath imagined a lot of things could have that effect—even field work. He wasn't ready to concede that point. Not yet at least.

After drying off, he wrapped the towel around his waist and stood at the sink as he lathered up his face and began to shave.

The face staring back at him as he looked in the mirror was the same face that it had always been. And while it may have aged a little, in his mind he was frozen in time at right around twenty-four years old.

There were, of course, at least a good two decades between that fantasy and reality. However, this was who he was. This was what he knew how to do. And despite his preference to operate alone, he had been reminded that he still worked well with a team. He was also pretty good at leading one.

But did that mean he was ready to take over for the Old Man? Rinsing off his razor, he took another look at himself in the mirror.

The idea that he could ever fill the shoes of someone like Reed Carlton was absolutely crazy to him. It was one of the biggest reasons he had said *no* when the Old Man asked him to become Director of The Carlton Group. He was not only afraid of failing at it, he was also afraid of taking on the additional responsibility, only to let Carlton down. That would probably be the most difficult thing to deal with—his disappointment.

Of course, simply saying no to the position had disappointed the Old Man, but on the scale of letdowns, Harvath figured it was a lot better than his taking over the entire organization only to screw it all up. The Old Man had invested too much of his time, money, and energy into it.

For some strange reason, that hadn't seemed to bother Carlton. "If it goes, it goes," he had said, like some Stoic philosopher. "But I don't think you're capable of screwing it up. At least not *that* badly," he had added with one of his wry smiles.

Carlton had a certain confidence in him that Harvath didn't have in himself, at least not in that way. Harvath was supremely confident in everything that he did. It was the absolute unknown of running an organization like The Carlton Group that he had found so daunting. He wasn't sure he would have confidence in others.

But the one big plus, the biggest plus actually, would be being home—if he chose and she agreed—with Lara. That was something that held a lot of appeal for him. With Lara and her son, Marco, he could finally put down roots and have the family he had always said he wanted.

But for a guy who told himself that was what he wanted, he really *was* spending a lot of time in the field.

In a way, he was sowing his operational oats. Some of the jobs had just been too good to turn down. Some had been so difficult and so dangerous that he didn't feel right giving them to anyone else. It was also a great way to avoid taking that next step at home.

That mindset was going to have to change. He couldn't keep taking all the most challenging assignments. Even if he was that twenty-four-year-old he saw staring back in the mirror at him, eventually he would break. Nobody could keep going at the pace he was on. It didn't matter how improved he felt his body to be. He was using injections to stay in the game.

And while the game was one of skill, it also involved a large degree of luck. At some point the odds caught up to you. And when that happened, all the luck in the world wouldn't be enough to save you.

For now, he prayed the odds would remain in his favor—just until he could complete this assignment and get his team safely back home. Then, he'd have to finally take a good, long look at everything else and decide what he wanted to do.

Splashing cold water on his face, he quickly brushed his teeth, got dressed, and headed to the kitchen.

It smelled as if Nicholas had grilled sausages. He was about to ask, when he noticed the little man paying rapt attention to one of the television monitors.

There were pictures of fire and billowing columns of black smoke. First responders were carrying injured people out into the street.

"What is it?" Harvath asked. "What happened?"

"Istanbul," he replied. "Multiple bombs at a subway station."

Turkey had a lot of political problems, but something told him that might not be what this was about.

If this was the Russians, they had picked a perfect target to hit with an anti-NATO PRF strike. No other member of the alliance was more precariously perched. Turkey had one foot out the door already, and Harvath chastised himself for not seeing this coming. It made excellent sense.

It also scared the hell out of him. The death count was going to be enormous. If this was what they had chosen to follow Rome with, what else did they have up their sleeve?

"Looks like a lot of women and children, too," Nicholas added. "Families. The Turkish government is going to go ballistic."

As they should, thought Harvath. "How long ago did this happen?"

"Within the last half hour."

He had known better than to think that nothing could knock the Rome bombing out of the news cycle. The devastation from both attacks would now be run in split screen on news stations around the world.

Watching the carnage only recommitted him to his purpose. Every fiber in his being wanted to walk across the motor court to take a pair of red-hot tongs to Dominik Gashi. He knew that would be the wrong move.

Gashi, like everyone else, would eventually break. As a GRU operative, though, which Harvath highly suspected he was, he would dribble out enough false intelligence to keep them chasing their tails for weeks, if not months. They didn't have that kind of time.

It was better to leave it to a professional, someone more skilled in the science of interrogation than he. Blunt force would only get them so far.

The Carlton Group's specialist was landing shortly and would quickly extract the most reliable intel Gashi had. Harvath's anger, for the time being, would have to be put on hold.

Plating a couple of sausages, he also poured a cup of coffee and sat down at the table. "Can we turn that off?" he asked as he began eating. It wasn't that he couldn't stomach it, it was that he needed a break from all of it for five minutes.

Nicholas obliged him and powered down the monitor. "I heard from Ryan," he said, changing the subject.

Harvath had meant to call her, but had been so tired when they got back in that he had sent her an email instead. "What did she want?"

"She said the U.S. Ambassador to the UN had an emergency meeting with the Ambassadors for Lithuania, Latvia, and Estonia this morning. They all came under a variety of cyberattacks on Friday. The attacks have grown much worse over the weekend."

"That means the Russians are getting ready to invade. We don't have much time."

The little man nodded. "Lydia wants a bow around my operation ASAP."

Nicholas had not only come up with an amazing hack, but with Harvath's help, had also created a tiny spy network of his own.

There was something poetic about using a man known as the Troll to disrupt the Troll *Factory*. His plan was to expose all of the Russians engaged in cyberoperations against the Baltics—real names and photos, as well as every fake website and social media account attached to them. It would be the ultimate cyber takedown.

"When do you think you'll have everything?" asked Harvath.

"My guy in St. Petersburg should have the last of it out tonight."

It had been a brilliant plan, but a huge undertaking. And it had cost a fortune. Nicholas and Ryan had gone round and round on the expense.

Also, no matter how well he performed, there was a lingering distrust based on his past unsavory deeds. He had made the CIA and the NSA look foolish on more than one occasion.

Harvath also suspected that the Old Man might have put a bug in Ryan's ear about Nicholas. Not that she needed him to tell her anything about the little man's history. She had already been well aware of him while she was at the Agency.

It was certainly not her intention to agree to large sums of money being spent, only to discover that he was siphoning off pieces of it for himself.

Whenever he had trouble getting approval, he went to Harvath and Harvath in turn went to Ryan. It was a game she didn't take kindly to—something akin to a child playing both parents. Harvath, though, was always a vocal supporter and, when necessary, defender of Nicholas. He usually got what he wanted and nothing, so far, had gone wrong.

Be that as it may, Ryan maintained a detached, professional *trust-but-verify* position when it came to the company's finances. It was one of the leading reasons Harvath was happy to have her sitting in the corner office. He'd go crazy if he had to deal with those kinds of issues every day.

Looking down at his watch, he saw that it was time to get going. "I'll be back in a little bit. Need anything while I'm out?"

Nicholas studied the notepad on the table in front of

him and replied, "Yes. I could use a lot more time, a lot more money, and a lot more luck than either of us deserve."

"Couldn't we all," he replied, standing up and reaching for his jacket. "I'll see what I can do."

Walking outside to one of the team's vehicles, Harvath said a silent prayer that the man he was going to pick up could provide the one thing they needed the most—a miracle.

CHAPTER 55

"Do you want the good news first? Or the bad news?"

Harvath hated conversations that began this way. "I've had a rough couple of days. I could use some good news. Let's start with that."

Dr. Matthias Vella was an unassuming man in his fifties—slim, with dark hair and glasses. He buckled his seat belt as they pulled out of the airport. The enormous amount of equipment he had brought with him on the private jet barely fit inside the team's van.

A PhD in psychiatry and neurochemistry, Vella ran a privately contracted black site. It was located in a windowless, subterranean facility on Malta, nicknamed the Solarium. Their business was top-secret interrogation and high-value detainee detention.

Vella's specialty was the study of the neurological processes of interrogation. He was particularly interested in what could be done via chemical and biological means to speed it up.

Removing a folder from his briefcase, he opened it and said, "We ran your guy past our Russian friend Viktor Sergun."

"Did he recognize Gashi?"

"Immediately. But his name isn't Dominik Gashi and

he isn't a Kosovan refugee. His name is Ivan Kuznetsov. He's a GRU operative."

"Anything else?" asked Harvath.

Vella shut the folder. "A little bit of his military background, some of the previous operations he has run for the GRU. Nothing particularly valuable."

Harvath had been correct. Their prisoner did work for Russian military intelligence. That was an important confirmation. Having a name was a good step forward. He would put Nicholas on it as soon as they arrived back at the compound.

The fact that Sergun could only provide modest background information on Kuznetsov, though, was a disappointment. Harvath knew that the more material Vella had, the better and faster the interrogation would proceed.

"What's the bad news?"

"The bad news," said Vella, "is that you're handing me a subject with multiple bullet wounds, who has *maybe* been stabilized."

"So?"

"So remember what happened in Syria?"

Harvath did remember. He had tried to remotely conduct an interrogation using Vella's techniques. The subject had an underlying heart condition and had died during it.

"What about it?" Harvath asked.

Vella rolled his eyes. He knew Harvath wasn't this obtuse. "Come on, Scot. You know why we do a full medical workup before we start one of these things. Heart rates spike, adrenal production goes into overdrive, cortisol levels skyrocket. The stress response is just off the charts. Kuznetsov might not be able to handle it."

"What are you proposing?"

"I'm going to have to dial it back—a lot. At least initially, until I see how much he can handle. In other words, there's going to be a delay."

"How much of a delay?" asked Harvath.

"Depending how much of the formula I can administer, it could be days. Maybe a week."

"That's not going to work."

"I'm giving you a worst-case scenario," replied Vella, who caught himself and said, "Actually, *death* is the worst-case scenario. What I'm giving you is a potential timeline."

Harvath knew that a lot of what Vella did was still in its infancy. It wasn't something that could be widely studied and peer reviewed. It was, in essence, a dark art that wasn't talked about or shared.

He had brought the man in to speed things up, not to coddle their prisoner and slow things down. But at the end of the day, Vella was here because he was a professional, with a very specific set of skills, which Harvath respected. What's more, Kuznetsov's death would certainly bring things to a halt.

"Do what you have to do," he told the doctor. "But do it as fast as you can. We're running out of time."

When they pulled back into the compound, Harvath called the team out to help Vella unpack and to move all of his equipment into the main building. They then drew up a shift schedule for guarding the property and assisting in the interrogation.

With those tasks complete, he returned to the guesthouse to check on Nicholas and give him the limited dossier that Vella had prepared on their prisoner, Ivan Kuznetsov.

"Did you bring any of the things I asked for?" said Nicholas without turning around.

"They were out of time and money at the store, but I was able to find you a lead," he replied, setting the folder on his desk.

The little man stopped what he was doing on his computer to take a look at it. "This isn't a lot to go on."

"We've got a real name. That's more than we had a half hour ago. See what you can do."

Saluting, Nicholas turned back to his computer, opened a new screen, and went to work.

Harvath grabbed one of the encrypted laptops the little man had set up and carried it to his room. It was early afternoon back in the States and he thought he would try to reach Lara.

He shot her an email, then plugged his earbuds in and opened the video conferencing program The Carlton Group used.

Moments later, a screen appeared with her face in it. She was at home, in their study, wearing one of the low-cut sweaters he loved. Her long hair was swept to one side. She looked gorgeous.

"Hey," he said. "What are you up to?"

Lara adjusted her laptop so he could see the TV and the news coverage of the Istanbul bombing.

"Should I even ask where you are?" she said, turning the laptop back around.

He smiled. She not only understood him, she understood what he did, and that he couldn't always talk about what he was up to.

"Nowhere near Turkey," he replied. In the background, he could see that she had a fire going in the fireplace. "That cold back home?"

"Cold enough. And overcast. How about where you are?"

"Could be worse. How are things at home?"

"Good," she replied. "We miss you."

Harvath smiled again. "I miss you, too. Where's Marco?"

"Taking a nap. He woke up way too early this morning."

"What'd you do for breakfast?"

"I offered to make pancakes, but he said he didn't want 'mommy' pancakes, he wanted 'Scot' pancakes. So we had eggs instead."

"Tell him I'll cook up a huge stack when I get back," he responded.

"Any idea when that will be?"

Harvath shook his head. "Hopefully, soon."

Lara appeared about to reply when she heard something and turned to look over her shoulder. "Speak of the devil," she said, turning back to the camera. "Guess who I think just woke up."

Harvath laughed. It wasn't the first time Marco had interrupted an intimate moment. "Go check on him. I'll catch up with you later."

"Before I let you go, I talked with Lydia last night."

"About what?"

"I called to catch up and she told me Reed isn't doing well, that he's getting worse."

The gravity of the situation was evident in Harvath's voice. "I know," he replied. "She told me, too."

"Promise me we'll go see him when you get back."

"I promise."

Marco could be heard in the background calling for her.

"I love you," she said, blowing him a kiss. "Stay safe."

"I will. I love you, too," he answered, as she logged off.

For a moment, he sat there, just looking at the blank screen. In his mind, he pictured her path from the study to the small guest bedroom they had converted for Marco. He really did miss them both. He missed the Old Man as well. He felt the guilt again of not being there for him, but he also hoped the Old Man would understand the importance of what he was doing and why he needed to do it.

Over the next couple of minutes, he allowed his thoughts a little freedom before putting them in a far corner of his mind and walling them off.

Hopping back over to his email, he checked to make sure there were no requests from Ryan. He didn't see any.

Opening a new message, he sent her a quick update to let her know that Vella had arrived, that he was proceeding with "caution," and that Nicholas was running down the name they had gotten from Sergun. He told her he'd update her with more information when it became available. After reading it over, he hit Send.

Having checked in with his home and office, he had a decision to make. He could go downstairs and check back in on Nicholas, go across to the main building and check on Vella, or leave them both alone and trust them to do the jobs they were being paid to do. He chose the last option and to have confidence in his people.

"Hire the best and set them loose," the Old Man had once said to him. "Don't be a pain in the ass unless you have to be. Let people know what you expect of them, and then get out of their way. Allow them to surprise you."

It was good advice. And while some of it had sounded

like a string of platitudes from a motivational seminar, the Old Man knew how to manage people.

Though he could be gruff at times, there wasn't a single person who Harvath wouldn't go to hell and back for him. That was the kind of loyalty he inspired.

Committed to leaving his team alone, Harvath set his laptop aside on the bed and picked the book about Hemingway's being a Russian spy back up from his nightstand.

Whether it contained any secrets about the Russians that might be valuable today was anyone's guess.

What he hoped it would do was take his mind away for a while and give it a chance to rest. He had learned long ago how to make tough decisions under pressure, but sometimes, when he stopped thinking about things was when breakthroughs occurred.

Operating on only a few hours of sleep, he made it through about two chapters before his eyes got so heavy that he couldn't keep them open and he was out.

CHAPTER 56

When Harvath heard Staelin's voice, it was just after 4:00 a.m. He was lying, still fully clothed, atop his bed with his book on his chest.

"What is it?"

"Vella," said Staelin. "He told me to come and get you."

Shit, thought Harvath as he quickly got out of bed. *This couldn't be good news.* "What happened? Is Kuznetsov okay?"

"Who?"

Harvath had forgotten that Staelin hadn't been given the update. "Dominik Gashi's real name is Ivan Kuznetsov."

"Whatever his name is, Vella wants to talk to you about him. It sounds like maybe he wants to make a deal."

A deal? Harvath was highly skeptical, but stranger things had happened, especially when it came to the Russians. Many had watched their politicians and ex–intelligence officers become billionaire oligarchs, only to want a piece of the action for themselves. It was worth at least listening to what he wanted and, more important, what he had to offer.

Grabbing a bottle of water from the fridge, Harvath left his coat behind and followed Staelin across the motor court over to the main building. He took the stairs down to the basement, which had been transformed into a miniversion of the Solarium back on Malta, and was where they were interrogating Kuznetsov.

There were all sorts of medical equipment, video cameras, monitors, and a computer work station.

Kuznetsov was hooded and bound to a chair. Harvath recognized the hood. It had a special pocket in front into which Vella placed strips of cloth soaked in his special compound. He had let Harvath take a quick whiff of it once. It was like liquid fear.

Like the smell of fresh-baked cookies or bread, scent had a way of bypassing the conscious, rational part of the brain and going straight to where our memories were stored. Vella believed a similar mechanism could be used in interrogations. He had spent years studying, and testing, how scent could unlock certain pathways in the brain. In particular, he had been focused on how it could be used to break a subject, so that he was no longer able to resist and would reveal the truth.

Harvath looked at the bright halogen work lights that had the Russian lit up from the front and the sides.

"I have headphones on him," said Vella, "so he can't hear us right now."

"What did you need to talk to me about?"

"He wants to make a deal."

"What kind of deal?" asked Harvath.

"He's willing to give up everything he knows."

"And you believe him?"

"Come look at this," replied Vella as he gestured toward his computer.

Harvath joined him and watched as he played back

a short piece of video. Underneath it were a series of graphics, similar to a polygraph, but more sophisticated.

Pointing to several of the lines, the doctor said, "If there was even the slightest hint that he was being untruthful, it would show up here. He couldn't be in this range if it was a ruse. He's telling the truth. He wants to make a deal."

"Maybe he's just tired."

"The more fatigued he gets, the more difficult it is for him to hide from me. That's why I don't let them sleep."

"Maybe he's just stringing us along in order to get pain meds. Have you given him any?"

"He's definitely in pain," said Vella, "but I haven't given him anything for it. You've watched me do this before. You know how this all works."

"I'm just making sure," replied Harvath. "This is an option I wasn't expecting."

"This isn't an option. It's an *opportunity*. He's ready to give you everything he has. I have been going at him for almost eight hours. Believe me, this is legitimate. It's also why you brought me in; to speed things up."

Harvath knew this kind of thing happened, but it wasn't exactly his area of expertise. He had a lot more experience with turning Muslim terrorists against one another than he did negotiating with Russian intelligence officers to leave their service.

"Was he promised anything?" Harvath asked. "What did you tell him, *exactly*? And what did he tell you?"

"I started with the standard stuff. I told him he was a prisoner of the United States and was not going back to Russia, ever. His stress levels at this point were already pretty high and when he asked me where he would be taken, I told him Gitmo. That didn't do anything to relax him, but when I told him he'd be placed in with the Muslim population, things really started to blast off."

Harvath wasn't surprised. Russia had made a lot of enemies in the Muslim world. Putting Kuznetsov in with hardened Al Qaeda operatives, who remembered all the bad things the Russians did in Afghanistan and elsewhere, would probably be worse than executing him.

"You'll be surprised to know that he carries several grudges about the Russian military in general and the GRU specifically," the doctor continued.

Right, big surprise. The Russian military was a pretty corrupt organization. What's more, Russians were spectacular grudge-holders. Harvath liked to tell a joke about an angel appearing to three men—a Frenchman, an Italian, and a Russian. The angel tells them that tomorrow the world is going to end and asks what they each want to do with their last night on earth. The Frenchman says he will get a case of the best champagne and spend his last night with his mistress. The Italian says he will visit his mistress and then go home to eat a last meal with his wife and children. The Russian replies that he will go burn down his neighbor's barn.

"Gotland was a huge failure," said Vella. "He knows he will be blamed for it and that the GRU will take it out on his family, so that it serves as a lesson to other operatives. He wants asylum for himself and his family."

"He wants to live in the United States?" Harvath asked.

Vella shook his head. "No. Italy. Florence, to be exact."

"At least he's not picky," Harvath said with a grin.

"I didn't push back on it. It represents something to him. I figured I would let you make the call. One would suppose that if he could help turn over evidence linked to the bombing in Rome, the Italians might cooperate."

The Italians also had a thing about American intelligence operatives who snatched people and rendered them to foreign countries. He didn't know if that was a road he wanted to go down, but for right now it didn't matter.

The Swedes would also need to be massaged. Kuznetsov had killed a Swedish intelligence officer and had sliced open a cop. It would be hard to let a guy like that ride off into the Italian sunset.

Espionage, though, was a dirty business. Sometimes, unsavory deals had to be struck with bad actors—especially when it meant preventing a war.

"Anything else I need to know before I talk with him? What are his grudges against the military and the GRU?"

Vella glanced at some notes he had made. "He was born into a lower-class family. Despite being highly intelligent, he thinks the Russian military, and especially the GRU, have prohibited him from reaching the rank and responsibility he rightly deserves."

"So he's got a Fredo Corleone complex," Harvath replied, referring to the middle brother in the Godfather saga.

"He seems to realize that if he's going to make any sort of a deal at all, now is the time to do it."

It made sense, but from what the Old Man had taught him about his days of brokering deals with Soviet defectors in the Cold War, these things usually required a lot of back and forth. The talks were often complicated and prolonged. The veracity of the information the defectors provided had to be confirmed and always checked against multiple sources.

But those were different times and a *much* different

scenario. Kuznetsov wasn't some embassy walk-in. He was a prisoner—one with a limited amount of bargaining power and one against whom the clock was ticking.

By the same token, though, the clock was also ticking for Harvath. He desperately needed information and, like it or not, his best option was to try to cut a deal. As Vella had correctly pointed out, he had been given an opportunity. He needed to make sure he did everything he could to take advantage of it.

Working together, he and Vella set up the room exactly the way he wanted it. The conversation would still be videotaped, but he didn't want it done under the harsh glare of the halogen lights. Harvath wanted to sit across from the Russian in order to read him. Vella's machines were one thing, but Harvath put his ultimate confidence in how he felt in his gut and what he could see with his own two eyes.

He called upstairs to Staelin and asked him to brew him some coffee and to bring it down along with some bottled water for their captive.

Kuznetsov, being Russian, might also want a smoke. Harvath knew that Vella used cigarettes as incentives with detainees and sure enough, the man had brought along several packs. He placed one on the table along with a small box of matches.

When everything was exactly as he wanted, Harvath walked over to Kuznetsov and removed his hood.

CHAPTER 57

As Kuznetsov blinked, trying to readjust his eyes to the light, Harvath removed the headphones. Sheets had been hung from the ceiling to create a small, enclosed space, preventing the Russian from seeing the rest of the room. He was still tied to the chair, but now there was a table in front of him with a pack of cigarettes on it.

Across from him, drinking a cup of coffee, was the man who had shown up at the beach house dressed as a Swedish policeman—the same man from the hospital security camera footage that Johansson had copied for him.

"Mr. Kuznetsov, I am here because I understand you are interested in cooperating with us," said Harvath.

"I am interested in arranging a deal," he replied.

"I must be honest with you, I'm not particularly fond of deals."

The Russian forced a painful grin. "Imagine how I feel."

"How is it you speak, English?"

"May I have a cigarette?"

Harvath tapped one out of the pack and held it up to the man's mouth. Kuznetsov leaned forward and took it between his lips. Harvath then took out a match, struck it against the box, and lit it for him.

The Russian attempted to take a deep drag, but the pain from his shoulder caused him to cough. The coughing only increased his pain.

Once it had passed, he tried again—this time taking a much more shallow pull.

"Mostly, I taught myself English. I like to read. I also took some classes while I was in the Russian Army and then in my following position."

"With the GRU."

"Yes," said Kuznetsov.

"What can you tell me about your position with the GRU?"

"I am an intelligence officer."

"Where were you assigned before Gotland?" asked Harvath.

The man took another drag before replying. "Let me see," he said, compiling a list in his head. "Bulgaria, Romania, Hungary, Poland, Belarus. Many places."

Three of the countries jibed with what Sergun had told Vella. That was a good start.

"And what was your job when you were in those countries?"

"My job was to do whatever they asked me to do."

"For the most part, what was it that they asked you to do?"

"I recruited spies and built espionage networks."

The Russian took another puff on his cigarette and then indicated by nodding his head that he wanted it removed from his mouth.

Reaching out, Harvath took it and set it on the edge of the table.

"Is there anything to drink?" Kuznetsov asked. "Perhaps you have some more coffee?"

"You may have some water, but first you need to answer some more questions for me."

"I am in much pain. Can you give me something for it?"

"Yes, I can," said Harvath, "but not yet."

"What are the questions you want to ask me?"

"Who is your superior?"

"Colonel Oleg Tretyakov," the Russian replied.

Harvath took a sip of his coffee, but kept his eyes locked on Kuznetsov's face. By all indications, he was absolutely telling the truth.

"And Tretyakov is the one who sent you to Gotland?"

"Yes."

"For what purpose?"

"To recruit spies and build an espionage network," the Russian replied.

"And what was the ultimate goal of this network?"

"To assist the Russian military in a potential overtaking."

"Overtaking?" asked Harvath.

"Invasion," said Kuznetsov, clarifying what he meant.

Nodding his head toward the cigarette, he indicated his desire for another puff. Harvath picked it up and allowed the man to take one, and then returned it to the edge of the table. He wanted a clear, unobscured view of his face for his next question.

"Are you familiar with the anti-NATO attacks that have happened in multiple European countries?"

The Russian nodded. "Yes, I am."

"What can you tell me about them?"

"First I would like some water. Please."

Standing, Harvath reached behind the nearest sheet

and Vella handed him a small bottle. Unscrewing the cap, he walked over to Kuznetsov, placed the bottle against his mouth, and tilted it back so he could drink. The man drank the entire thing.

Harvath set the empty bottle on the table and sat back down.

"Several hours ago, they let me piss. There was blood in it. I need to be taken to a hospital."

"Tell me what you know about the attacks," Harvath demanded.

"No," said the Russian. "First we make our deal. Then we talk about everything else I know."

"What is it that you want?"

"I want my family out of Russia," the man said.

"How many are in your family?"

"Nine."

"*Nine?*"

"*Nine,*" Kuznetsov repeated.

Standing again, Harvath walked over, parted the sheets, and requested a pad and pen from Vella.

When he sat back down, he said, "Give me their names, ages, and relationship to you."

The Russian operative had a wife and four children. He listed their names and ages. The other four family members were his parents and his wife's mother and father.

Harvath held up his hand. "I can only negotiate in regard to your immediate family."

"Our parents must leave Russia as well. I cannot allow them to be punished for what I have done."

Harvath tapped his pen against the pad of paper for several moments as he pretended to think about it. "I will see what I can do, but it will depend on how helpful you are to me. With each minute that passes, the information you have becomes less valuable, and my people will be less willing to make a deal."

Kuznetsov smiled. "Really? I think it is just the opposite. With every minute that passes, my information is more valuable and your people should be more eager to make a deal. Time is a very precious commodity."

"Like I said. I will see what I can do. In the meantime—"

"In the meantime," the Russian interrupted, "I would like something for this pain. And while I am waiting for that, you can contact your people to confirm that you will be getting my entire family out of Russia."

"Nine people," said Harvath. "That's not going to be easy."

"I'm sure the all-powerful American government can find a way."

"I will ask, though I cannot promise where you all will be relocated to."

"Italy," said Kuznetsov. "That's where we want to be placed. Florence."

Harvath was tempted to ask him why Italy and why Florence, but the truth was that he didn't really care. It also wasn't up to him.

"I cannot speak for the Italian government, but I can put in a request to my government to speak with the Italians on your behalf. That is, of course, if what you have to tell me is worth all of the trouble and all the expense of doing all of this."

Kuznetsov smiled. "It will be. Trust me."

Harvath smiled back. "What's the old Russian saying? Trust but verify. You're going to have to give me something I can give my people to convince them."

The Russian paused, considering how much to reveal in order to secure this deal for himself and his family. Finally, he looked at him and said, "The man you are looking for is Colonel Oleg Tretyakov. Chief of GRU Covert Operations for Eastern Europe."

"What about him?" asked Harvath.

"He's behind it."

"Behind what?"

Kuznetsov smiled once more. "All of it."

Harvath picked up his pen. Flipping to a clean sheet of paper, he said, "Ivan, listen very carefully. This is your one and only chance to save your family. I'm going to need much more than just a name. Make this worth it. Give me everything you have."

CHAPTER 58

I can see everyone," said President Paul Porter over a secure link from the White House situation room. "Are we all on?"

"Yes, Mr. President," replied Lydia Ryan, from a Sensitive Compartmented Information Facility, also known as a SCIF, at The Carlton Group.

"I'm here," said CIA Director Bob McGee from his secure conference room at Langley.

"I'm here as well, Mr. President," said Harvath over his encrypted connection back at the compound guesthouse in Brussels.

"Okay, let's cut right to the chase," stated Porter. "I reached out to the Italian Prime Minister. He's willing to accept the family in question, but on two conditions. The first is that the Italians do not have to subsidize them. They will grant conditional citizenship for twenty-four months. Basically, as long as they keep their noses clean, they can stay.

"The second condition is that whatever intel the head of household provides, it absolutely has to have a link to outing the perpetrators of the Rome attack. How are we on both of those conditions?"

"Mr. President," replied McGee, "as per financial support for the family in question, there is absolutely money in the budget for that. In fact, it would be our desire to make the funding contingent upon his continued cooperation. We would expect him to provide everything—every operation he has ever worked on, every contact he has ever had, every asset, every means of communication, names in the GRU, any military intelligence he may have, etcetera."

"Understood," said Porter. "What about the second condition?"

"Scot, do you want to take this one?" asked Ryan.

"Sure," he replied. "Mr. President. From what the subject has told me, there is an absolutely straight-line connection to what happened in Rome. If we can get to the next rung on the ladder, we've got the Holy Grail. He has all of the names, dates, places—all of it. We'll not only be able to tell the Italians we got one of the ultimate players, but we should also be in a position to furnish the identities of their own nationals who were involved."

"And if we can deliver this intelligence to the Italians, then the same person in question should be able to tell us who was responsible in-country for all the other attacks, so that we can provide our other allies with that information as well."

"That is correct. Yes, sir. But with one caveat."

"What's that?" asked Porter.

"Any response needs to be coordinated," stated Ryan. "For instance, we can't have the Italians launching their own campaign while the Norwegians carry out their own, separate reprisal. An attack on one member is an attack on all. The response from the alliance should demonstrate absolute unity."

"This is also," added McGee, "an opportunity to repair some of the rifts in the alliance. The bombings in Istanbul have killed nearly three hundred people so far.

The Turks should be granted a lead role in planning and executing any response."

"Agreed," said the President. "I have been watching the footage. It is beyond horrific. They're calling it Turkey's 9/11. I've already called the President to express America's condolences."

"Absolutely the right thing to do," stated Ryan, "but sir, if I may?

"Go ahead."

"As someone who has operated in Turkey, and continues to pay attention to their politics, we need to make sure that even though the PRF has claimed credit, the Turkish President doesn't somehow use this as an excuse for more political purges."

"I completely concur," Porter replied. "Right now, the Turks are the ones I'm most worried about. Things have gotten to the point, I'm afraid, where no matter what we say, if the Russians contradict it, they'll take Moscow's side. We are going to need absolutely watertight, overwhelming evidence to convince them of who was responsible."

"And we will get it," replied Harvath, "All we need to do is isolate that next rung on the ladder. That's where it will be."

"Understood. So what's left? What do you need from me?"

"For the moment, sir," said Ryan, "nothing. Director McGee will work on an extraction plan for the subject's family, while we work on identifying the next rung, as Scot put it, and how to go after it."

"And what's our exposure on Sweden? Am I going to be getting an angry call at some point here from the Prime Minister?"

"I've already reached out to their intelligence director and have taken the hit," McGee responded. "Gunnar wasn't happy, in fact he was very upset that we didn't give him a heads-up. Lars Lund is not going to be easy for them to replace. The police inspector in Visby hospital, though, will recover. On balance, I think the relationship will be okay—especially now that we can confirm who was behind the Gotland cell and what their mission was."

"Keep monitoring it," instructed Porter. "They're an important partner."

"Yes, sir."

"Is there anything else?"

"No, sir," McGee replied.

"All right, then," the President declared. "Let me end by stating something I know we all agree on, but that I want to make crystal clear. I don't want to see another scene like Rome or Istanbul. Full stop. Is that understood?"

There was a chorus of "Yes, Mr. President" before the videoconference was closed. And while Ryan and McGee, by virtue of being back in the States, might have to bear the burden of dealing with Porter face to face, the real weight of his words, and his expectations, fell upon Harvath's shoulders.

With that knowledge fully in mind, he exited the guesthouse and headed back over to the basement of the main building.

He had lived up to his end of the bargain. It was time for Ivan Kuznetsov to do the same.

And if he didn't, Harvath intended to make clear that even God himself wouldn't be able to protect the Russian, or any of the members of his nine-person family.

CHAPTER 59

Tomasz Wójcik was sitting in the Crowne Plaza's trendy Empire Restaurant, enjoying the view over the city, when Pavel Kushner arrived. He was carrying a large, black leather briefcase, similar to what pilots carried.

"You should have started without me," said Kushner as he sat down.

"I did," Wójcik replied. "You're late. I finished eating a half hour ago."

The Belarusian smiled. His friend had gotten curmudgeonly in his old age. He probably wasn't having enough sex. He should have taken him up on his offer to arrange a girl for him. A young lady of lower social responsibility would have helped reinvigorate his manhood.

"Did you have the buffet?" asked Kushner. "Or did you order off the menu?"

"I had a hard-boiled egg, toast, and coffee," the Pole replied matter-of-factly.

"You know what?" his friend replied, eyeing the nearby buffet. "I really think retirement agrees with you. You were much more uptight in the old days."

Wójcik wasn't in the mood. Both of the nights that he had been in the hotel, he had slept like crap. The first night that was because his room had been right next to the elevators, which had chimed all night long. And the second night, after they had moved him, there'd been a bunch of drunks stumbling up and down his floor. He couldn't wait to get out of Minsk and back to Poland.

"So what do you have for me?" he asked.

"I'll tell you in a moment," said Kushner. "First, I need to get some breakfast. I'm starving."

The Pole almost couldn't believe it. His friend had arrived almost an hour late, and now wanted him to wait while he hit the buffet.

"By all means," Wójcik replied. "Take your time."

His facetiousness was completely lost on the man.

Watching as he quickly walked over to the buffet, he had to wonder if Pavel was actually hungry, or if he was just eager to chat up the very large-breasted woman picking up berries, one at a time, with a pair of tongs and daintily placing them on a small white plate.

Signaling the waitress, the Pole politely requested more coffee. He looked at his watch and tried to figure out how long it would take to get home if he was able to leave in the next half hour. Depending on traffic, it was a seven- to eight-hour drive. Kopec had forbidden him to fly. Customs at the Minsk airport was much tougher than at the vehicle border crossing.

Since their meeting Saturday night in Gorky Park, his psoriasis had only gotten worse. No matter how much ointment he applied, it wasn't getting any better. In fact, it had spread. He really needed to decrease his stress.

Pulling out his phone, he searched for the nearest drugstore. He would pick up some petroleum jelly and slather his affected skin before leaving. He hoped that would provide enough relief for him to withstand the uncomfortable drive home.

"Did you see that woman in the knit dress?" Kushner asked as he sat down, his plate piled high with eggs, pancakes, and bacon.

"How could anyone miss her?"

"She's from Babruysk. You know what they say about women from Babruysk."

"Actually, in Warsaw we don't talk about women from Babruysk that often. In fact, it's probably closer to never. Can we get on with our business, please?"

"My dear, dear Tomasz," Kushner replied. "What good is all the money we made, and *all* the risks we took, if we cannot enjoy ourselves?"

"Pavel, we have known each other for many years, so I hope you'll appreciate my being comfortable enough with you to be frank. Knock off the bullshit. Do you have something for me, or not?"

"What I *have* is a prediction for you. Within a year, unless you loosen up, you will be in a retirement home."

The Pole shook his head. "Of all the meetings I have ever had, this is the one I should have brought a gun to. You'd better have more than just a prediction in that briefcase, old friend."

Kushner smiled. "Would I disappoint you, *old friend*?" he asked, opening the case to show him what was inside.

Wójcik removed the file folder from his own briefcase and compared the pictures Kopec had given him to what he was now looking at. It was a perfect match. Kushner appeared to have secured the components from one of the upgrade kits.

"Where did you get that?"

The Belarusian shrugged. "It wasn't difficult. I told

you. There are only a few people in Belarus who could handle something like this."

"Where are the rest of the kits?"

"They're safe."

"I paid you one hundred thousand dollars to locate them," said the Pole.

"Which I did," Kushner replied. "I even brought one here to prove it to you. If you have a buyer interested in the entire lot, I'd be happy to let my source know."

Wójcik looked at him. "So now you're the broker on this deal?"

"As far as you're concerned, yes."

"Who has the upgrade kits?"

"My dear Tomasz, it would be highly unethical of me to divulge that information," said the Belarusian.

Wójcik felt a wave of nausea coming over him. Kopec was going to be extremely angry at this development.

Taking a deep breath, he tried to remain calm. "How about this? Let's go downstairs to my room. I'll take a few photographs of the merchandise, contact my client, and we'll take things from there."

"Can I finish my breakfast first?" asked Kushner.

"Bring it with you," replied the Pole, removing several bills from his wallet and placing them on the table. "I'll carry the case."

Picking up his plate and his coffee cup, Kushner followed Wójcik to the elevator and down to his room.

There, Wójcik produced a small digital camera and took pictures of the components from every conceivable angle.

When he was finished, Kushner shoveled the last bite of food into his mouth, repacked the equipment into his briefcase, and headed for the door.

"Wait a second," said Wójcik. "Where are you going?"

"If your client is interested, you know how to reach me," Kushner replied. "Thanks for breakfast."

Leaving the room, the Belarusian was careful to make sure that he wasn't being followed. He had been warned that Wójcik likely had a tail.

As he disappeared into the stairwell, a man stepped out of a doorway at the other end of the hall. Seeing that the Pole's visitor had left, he removed his encrypted cell phone and composed a message. Oleg Tretyakov would want to know everything that had happened.

CHAPTER 60

H arvath's plan wasn't simple. In fact, it was quite complicated. That meant there were a lot of ways in which it could go wrong.

According to Kuznetsov, Colonel Oleg Tretyakov was in Kaliningrad. Similar to the Vatican's being its own state within Italy, Kaliningrad was an exclave—sovereign Russian territory, a minicountry cut off from Russia—right inside Europe.

Sandwiched in between NATO members Poland and Lithuania, Kaliningrad was tightly controlled and nearly impossible to get into. And, based on what Kuznetsov had revealed, it would be doubly difficult for Harvath.

Kuznetsov had recognized him back on Gotland because of the CCTV footage Johansson had recovered from Visby Hospital. That footage had been forwarded to Tretyakov and had likely been added to every Russian database.

The moment Harvath tried to access any Russian-controlled port of entry and his photograph or facial scan was run, he'd be taken into custody and the GRU alerted.

That meant the only way he could get into Kaliningrad was to sneak in.

He had thought about somehow smuggling the team in via trucks, but the Kaliningrad crossings resembled those at the U.S./Mexico border. There was a heavy dog presence at each one, and they had no problem holding people up for hours as they went vehicle by vehicle, looking for anything out of the ordinary.

The situation along the exclave's rugged coastline wasn't any better. As Kaliningrad was home to Russia's Baltic fleet, the surface and subsurface patrols were extensive and around-the-clock.

With land and sea options out of the question, that left only one other possibility—air.

The plan was to conduct a High Altitude Low Opening, or HALO, parachute jump.

They would exit the aircraft over Lithuanian airspace and glide for several kilometers, popping their chutes and landing in a predetermined location in the Kaliningrad countryside.

From there, they would make their way into the city and search for Tretyakov. Everything up to that point was the easy part. Getting out of Kaliningrad was going to be something else entirely. Harvath had no idea how they were going to pull that off.

The last big exfiltration he had done had been via high-speed boats out of Libya. Their Navy was easy to avoid and had they been forced to, even easier to outrun. The Russians, though, were in a completely different league.

It was said that it could take even longer to get out of Kaliningrad than to get in. Waits for exiting the country could run as long as five or more hours. It was why citizens of Kaliningrad preferred taking the buses, which have their own lanes at the borders.

On top of the problem of how they were going to get out, Harvath also had to plan for what they'd do if a member of the team were injured or captured, or if the authorities became aware of their presence and there was a tightening at the borders and an exclavewide manhunt. The sheer impossibility of it all was almost overwhelming.

It reminded Harvath of the beginnings of the OSS and the incredibly dangerous assignments its teams were sent on behind enemy lines. But at least when they jumped into foreign countries, they had local partisans on the ground whom they could link up with and get help from.

That wouldn't be the case in Kaliningrad. As soon as Harvath and his team touched the ground, they'd be on their own. They'd have to secure their own transportation, do their own reconnaissance, and avoid detection every step of the way.

With the OSS in mind, Harvath decided to reapproach his problem. How would they have handled it?

While they were tough as hell and, when forced, underwent some amazingly grueling treks, they had always looked for the simplest answer first. If an ounce of courage could prevent a pound of hardship, they had gone the courage route.

The easiest places at which to cross over were the designated border checkpoints. Because Jasinski was Polish military intelligence, and because they might be coming in hot, he wanted to exit Kaliningrad into Poland, where she not only spoke the language, but also commanded some authority.

With that in mind, he studied the five Poland/Kaliningrad crossings. Starting at the Baltic Sea, he went one by one, heading east.

For the most part, they were practically interchangeable. They all cut through flat, open rural farmland. Not exactly ideal terrain for a covert crossing. But the very last, easternmost checkpoint was different.

In the Warmian-Masurian Province was the county of Goldap. A third the size of Gotland, its population was only slightly larger than that of the town of Visby.

It was bordered by the Szeskie Hills on one side and the Romincka Forest on the other. And running parallel to its border crossing was a nice, long lake. A third of it was on the Russian side of the border and the other two-thirds were on the Polish side. The minute Harvath saw it, he knew that was how they were getting out of Kaliningrad.

And as if he needed a sign that he had picked the right spot, when he saw the Romincka Forest running down the eastern side of the lake, it rang a bell with him.

Hermann Göring, the corpulent Nazi who oversaw the creation of the dreaded Gestapo and was a prime OSS target, had built a hunting lodge in the Romincka.

At one point the second-most-powerful man in Germany, Göring was sentenced to death by hanging at Nuremberg, but cheated the hangman by ingesting a cyanide capsule.

Of all the things Göring was infamous for, plundering the art of Jewish Holocaust victims, as well as art from museums across Europe, had ranked him at the top of the OSS's Art Looting Investigation Unit's "Red Flag List." From France alone, it was reported that over twenty-five thousand railroad cars of stolen art and treasure had been shipped to Germany. His personal collection had been valued at more than $200 million.

Göring's lodge in the Romincka, where he was believed to have showcased some of his stolen artwork, was known as the Reichsjägerhof Rominten. It served as his headquarters during Operation Barbarossa, when the Nazis attacked and invaded the Soviet Union.

Harvath would have liked to have been around to have seen Göring's beloved lodge burned to the ground.

As it was, he'd have to take pleasure in sticking it to the Russians by using the lake for their escape.

On the western shore of the Polish side was a hotel and health spa. Because half his team would be needed to help coordinate their exfil, and because half were not HALO certified, Harvath decided that's where they would be based. As guests of the hotel, they would have the perfect cover for exploring the lake and the areas around it.

With that settled, Harvath sat down with Haney and began to make an extensive list of everything the operation would require. He started with how much gear each team member could jump into Kaliningrad with, and then worked on honing it down to what was absolutely essential. It was going to be a bitch pulling the equipment together from various American military outposts in the region, but if anyone could make it happen, it was Haney.

He was, of course, disappointed not to be going into Kaliningrad, even though he was HALO qualified. He had suffered a leg injury during their assignment in Libya, and the team couldn't risk his reinjuring it on this jump.

Jasinski wasn't qualified, so she'd be staying back with Haney as part of the exfil element. Because of the water component involved in their escape, Harvath wanted Barton, a SEAL, to stay back and make sure all of it went off without a hitch.

The trio had already been dropped at Olsztyn-Mazury Airport, near the village of Syzmany. Their portion of the gear would be flown in via a military transport plane. Once it arrived, they would hook trailers up to the SUVs they had rented and drive to their hotel on Lake Goldap.

Inserting with Harvath into Kaliningrad would be Ashby, Staelin, and Palmer. Morrison and Gage had remained back in Brussels with Nicholas to guard the compound and keep an eye on Kuznetsov until a CIA security team arrived to fly him to Landstuhl Medical Center for treatment.

Harvath would have preferred to be going into Kaliningrad with more operators, but the bigger their footprint, the greater their visibility. Four would have to do.

As the Gulfstream jet made its final approach into Šiauliai International Airport in Lithuania, Harvath went through everything again. He wanted every possible angle nailed down before they launched. And they needed to launch as soon as possible.

Not only was President Porter anxious for them to get to Tretyakov, but there was also the concern that Swedish intelligence could cover up what had happened on Gotland for only so long. At some point, Kuznetsov was going to miss a communications window and the GRU was going to get suspicious.

Did that mean Tretyakov would move or go into hiding? Harvath didn't know, but he also didn't want to find out. The sooner they got into Kaliningrad, the sooner they could get to him, and the sooner they could get out.

This operation had Harvath concerned on a variety of different levels, not the least of which was the speed at which it was moving. And when you were moving at such high speed, the slightest mistake could turn into the deadliest of events.

CHAPTER 61

Šiauliai International Airport had once been one of the largest military air bases in the Soviet Union. Now, it was home to NATO's Baltic Air Policing mission. It provided for the rapid scrambling of fighter jets and other aircraft to help protect the airspace over Lithuania, Latvia, and Estonia.

As Harvath dropped the airstairs of the Gulfstream, he saw a familiar face waiting for him out on the tarmac.

"Sveiki atvykę!" shouted Carl Pedersen over the sound of the engines winding down. "Welcome to Lithuania."

The Norwegian was dressed in a turtleneck and a pair of well-pressed trousers. He didn't look at all like a man who had raced to find a plane and landed only an hour earlier.

Harvath descended the airstairs and shook his hand. "It's good to see you, Carl. Thank you for doing this."

"Where would America be without Norway?" he replied with a smile. Then, motioning to the man next to him, he said, "May I introduce Filip Landsbergis of the VSD, Lithuania's State Security Department."

"It is a pleasure to meet you."

Landsbergis was a tall man in his early forties with

blond hair and green eyes. He wore a Barbour coat over a gray suit and a simple navy tie. His handshake was firm.

"We appreciate your hosting us," said Harvath.

"Technically, this is a simple NATO rotation," the Lithuanian said, smiling. His English was excellent. "Planes take off, planes land. Who's to say what happens when they're in the air?"

Harvath smiled back. "Understood."

He pointed to a waiting van. "When your team is ready, we have an area set up where they can refresh themselves and wait for the rest of your equipment to arrive. In the meantime, I have reserved a secure meeting room where we can discuss some of the additional items you have requested. My car is this way."

Pedersen joined him and they followed Landsbergis to his vehicle. The drive across the air base only took a couple of minutes.

They arrived at a long two-story Soviet-era building. Even with the landscaping improvements that had been made outside, nothing could detract from how ugly the structure was.

The VSD operative parked his car near the front and led his guests through two glass doors into the lobby. Their meeting room was halfway down a fluorescently lit corridor to the right.

Landsbergis punched a code into a worn keypad, the lock released, and he held the door open so Harvath and Pedersen could enter first.

He flipped on all the lights and walked over to a small minibar. "I can offer you coffee, mineral water, or Coca-Cola. Anyone interested?"

"Do you have anything stronger?" asked Pedersen.

"Not here, I'm afraid. I could make a call, if you'd like."

"No, don't go to the trouble. Coffee is fine. Thank you."

"And for you?" the Lithuanian asked.

"Coffee for me too, please," Harvath replied, stepping over to the windows. They offered an impressive view over the entire air base. "Didn't the Soviets base many of their long-range bombers here during the Cold War?"

"They did indeed. This was one of only six airfields that could accommodate the Myasishchev M-4."

"The Bison," said Harvath, using the NATO designator for the aircraft. "Capable of reaching the United States, but not getting back to the Soviet Union. For a long time, though, the Russians sure had everyone fooled."

"The *bomber gap*," Pedersen stated, nodding. "The West was worried that the Soviets were building hundreds upon hundreds of these amazing jet-powered strategic bombers. In the end, it was all just a hoax."

"An appropriate metaphor for the Soviet Union itself," declared Landsbergis as he finished pouring three mugs of coffee and carried them over to the conference table.

Harvath agreed. Stepping away from the windows, he joined the two men and took a seat.

The VSD operator's laptop was already connected to a projector in the center of the table. Powering it up, he waited for his presentation to load.

"As Carl said, I represent the Lithuanian State Security Department. Even though I am a few years younger, he and I have been friends and colleagues for some time. The Norwegian Intelligence Service has done many favors for the VSD, and I hope you have found that we have always generously reciprocated."

Pedersen nodded.

"American intelligence has also been helpful to Lithuania," he continued, "and we are very grateful for both relationships. In that spirit, we'd like to help you in any way we can.

"We are extremely concerned about the prospect of a Russian invasion. Currently, Lithuania is undergoing a savage Kremlin-backed disinformation campaign, meant to sow discord and weaken our country. Our fear that this may be a prelude to war has been discussed between America's UN Ambassador and ours. It is the express opinion of the United States that we should not change our military posture for fear of tipping off or provoking Moscow. We understand this position.

"That being the case, we do not wish to sit idly by and wait to see what happens. America is our friend and ally. We also believe we should be involved in any fight that helps to protect and preserve Lithuania.

"Obviously, we cannot do this in any overt official capacity. If the Russians discovered that we had assisted, that could serve as a severe provocation and goad them into war.

"Anything we do will have to be covert and offbook, but rest assured that I understand fear is a two-way street. As we fear the Russians' learning about our involvement with you, you fear the Russians' learning about your involvement with us—and subsequently your mission into Kaliningrad.

"While I'd like to believe that the Lithuanian State Security Department hasn't been penetrated by Moscow, history and common sense would suggest otherwise. No one in the VSD but me will know the details of your plans. And even then, for operational security, I will not know everything."

The Lithuanian took a pause as Harvath looked at Pedersen.

"Without him," said the Norwegian, "I don't think you have a chance. With him, fifty-fifty. Maybe even sixty-forty."

"Actually," clarified Landsbergis, "based on what Carl has explained to me that you need, I think we can help improve your odds even more."

"Show me what you have in mind," replied Harvath as he sat back in his chair, raised his mug, and took a sip.

The VSD operative directed his attention to the front of the room and activated the first slide in his presentation.

CHAPTER 62

"O ne minute!" the jumpmaster at the ramp of the brand-new C-130J Super Hercules yelled to Harvath.

The aircraft was part of the Eighty-sixth Airlift Wing at Ramstein Air Base in Germany. Under authorization from United States European Command, the heavy-duty transport plane had been loaded with a very expensive and very specific shopping list of gear and flown to an air base in Lithuania.

There, four Americans had been standing on the tarmac waiting to meet it. When the aircraft came to a stop, they quickly climbed aboard and kicked the tires of every piece of gear that had been shipped to them.

The American team leader bought dinner for everyone and then spent a good two hours with the crew going over weather conditions, wind speeds aloft, altitude calculations, and other equations. He was one of the most thorough "customers" they had ever given a ride to.

"Thirty seconds!" the jumpmaster yelled.

The team had already double-checked each other's gear and then had checked again. Standing at the ramp with their wingsuits, low-vis helmets, night-vision goggles, and oxygen masks, they looked spooky—like four dark superheroes out of some postapocalyptic comic book.

"Ten seconds!" the jumpmaster yelled.

They were all assembled near the edge of the ramp now. The wind was practically deafening, and it was much colder than it had been a few feet back. Technically, they were about to jump into Russia.

Harvath raised his gloved fist and gave everyone a bump. He'd be the last one out in case anything went wrong.

Ashby would go first, followed by Palmer, then Staelin, and finally Harvath. Had they clumped together, they might have created a significant radar signature. So instead, they were to take different glide paths to the same broad drop zone.

In their packs, they carried suppressed pistols, radios, individual med kits, a ton of cash, maps, and some compact, very high-tech equipment. President Porter, Bob McGee, and Lydia Ryan had wanted to ensure that they were as self-sufficient as possible.

"On the green!" the jumpmaster yelled, pointing to the light near the ramp. "On the green!"

Harvath glanced one last time at the infrared lights on the backs of everyone's helmets. They were all working. He'd be able to track them all the way down.

"Five, four, three, two, one!" shouted the jumpmaster as the light turned green. "Go! Go! Go!"

One by one, the team dove, headfirst, off the ramp at the rear of the aircraft and tumbled through the bitterly cold night sky.

Quickly righting themselves, they extended their limbs, spread-eagled, and began to glide.

Harvath, like the other team members, watched the

computer strapped to his wrist. It provided a range of important data, including altitude, speed, direction, and distance to target.

He had jumped with a wingsuit a handful of times before, but had done so in relatively controlled environments without much gear. The added weight they were now all required to carry had been a big source of back and forth with the flight crew, as they tried to decide where and when to green-light the team to jump.

Sailing through the moonless pitch-black, the only thing Harvath could see through his NVGs were the lights on his team's helmets as they floated through the darkness ahead of him.

Per the course they had charted, they anticipated being in Lithuanian airspace for several minutes before they crossed into Kaliningrad's.

Looking at his wrist, he did a quick bit of math. There'd be an alarm reminding them when to pop their chutes, but he didn't want to depend on a computer. That wasn't how the OSS would have done it.

Adjusting his trajectory, he continued to glide. There was absolutely no other feeling in the world like it.

He continued to check his speed, stunned at how fast they were moving. The pilots had said there would be a favorable wind, but this was amazing.

A minute and a half later, he looked at his wrist and saw they were about to cross into Russian airspace.

Ahead, he could see each helmet already curving left. They were all precisely following the flight path. According to NATO analysis, there was a gap in Kaliningrad's radar system. By hitting it one at a time, they could slip through the crack without anyone knowing. Harvath followed their lead and adjusted his course to match.

The altimeter spun wildly, like a countdown clock on speed. The drop zone was coming up fast.

They had picked a spot that had "looked good," but that could have, for all they knew, belonged to some trigger-happy Russian farmer. According to the Lithuanians, it was a rotating livestock pasture that wasn't currently being used.

Giving his altitude and location one last check, he flared his wingsuit to help reduce his speed and popped his chute. The large black canopy burst into the air and unfurled above him.

He grabbed the toggles and steered himself in just as the alarm on his wrist computer vibrated. Below him, he marked the positions, and speeds, of everyone else. All of their chutes appeared to have deployed, and they were expertly navigating the final distance to the ground.

Just before he reached the grass, he pulled down on the toggles and flared his chute, slowing himself down as he had done with the wingsuit.

Bending his knees, he touched down and jogged forward to dissipate the energy of his landing.

It was textbook. Perfect, even. As his canopy collapsed behind him, he did a quick visual check to make sure everyone else had landed safely. They had.

Wriggling out of his harness, he felt something soft underfoot. Looking down, he saw what it was—cow shit. *Fresh* cow shit.

The pasture wasn't out of rotation, it was in use, and recently so. That was a bad piece of intelligence from the Lithuanians. He prayed it would be the only one.

CHAPTER 63

They met at the Riggsby bar in the Carlyle Hotel at DuPont Circle. Ryan wore an emerald-toned dress that matched her eyes. Kopec wore a black, ill-fitting suit that matched his mood.

"I'll have a Manhattan, please," she said, as the waitress took her order and disappeared.

Kopec, as was his habit, had arrived before her and had started without her. He had been halfway through his second cocktail when she entered the bar.

Though it was only a few years old, the Riggsby looked as if it had been around since the 1940s. With its forest green walls, old-school furniture, and keyhole entryway, it was a passage back to a bygone era.

A plate of sardines sat on the table and Kopec nudged it forward, indicating Ryan should help herself.

"I'm fine, thank you," she replied.

"That must be how you stay so skinny."

He was maudlin. The booze was probably part of it, but there was something else going on.

"What do you have for me, Artur?" she asked.

Removing his phone, he pulled up a series of photographs and slid the phone across the table to her.

Ryan scrolled through the photos. "Where did you get these?"

"My contact in Belarus was able to access one of the kits," he said. Technically, it was his contact's contact, but she didn't need to know that.

"That's wonderful. Where are the rest of them?"

"Somewhere near Minsk, we believe."

"All of them?"

The Polish intelligence officer nodded.

"This is very good news. Who has control of them?" she asked.

"We don't know. They're using a cutout, a middleman."

"Then how do we get them back?"

"You must purchase them."

Ryan glared at him. "Purchase them?" she snapped. "The hell we will. Those are property of the United States government. We're not paying someone to give us back what's rightfully ours."

"You don't have an alternative."

"Like hell I don't. I'll send a team in and we'll take them back ourselves."

"A paramilitary team. On a direct-action assignment."

"Yes," she replied. "Exactly."

Kopec shook his head sadly.

"I paid you a lot of money to track those kits down, Artur. It wasn't your job to set up a purchase." Pausing, she then asked, "Are you trying to rip us off? Because if you are, I promise you, we're going to have a big problem."

"Lydia, please. Of course not," he protested. "The kits were stolen and now they're in the hands of another party who wishes to sell them."

"I want the identity of the cutout."

The Polish intelligence officer threw up his hands. "Why? He's not going to reveal his source."

"You don't know that. We could buy him off. It'd be cheaper than buying our merchandise back."

"And then what? Steal the kits, maybe kill the person or persons who have them?"

"You don't need to concern yourself with what happens next."

"He's *my* source, Lydia. He'd be as good as dead. You don't understand how things work in Belarus."

"To tell you the truth, Artur, I don't care. I want those kits back, damn it."

In the entire time he had known her, he didn't think he had ever heard her swear before. Granted, the United States had to be losing its collective mind over this issue, but the stress really seemed to be getting to Ryan. It was time to lay his cards on the table.

"There might be one scenario under which I would be willing to give you my source."

Ryan, whose Manhattan had just arrived, was about to take a sip. "Name it," she said.

"You must give me Matterhorn."

"Jesus Christ, Artur. How many times do I have to tell you? I don't have him. I don't know who he is. I don't know where he is. Only Reed Carlton knows. And he's not exactly in any shape to talk."

"Or so you say."

Her eyes went wide. "You don't believe me?"

"I'd like to see him for myself."

"And I explained to you why that wasn't possible. He has been classified as a risk to National Security. This isn't like visiting the old folks' home, having a cup of tea and a sweet chat, then leaving. He is in bad shape and he could say anything."

"I'm willing to risk it."

Ryan laughed. "*You're* willing to risk it. That's cute. These are American secrets and American national security we're talking about, not Polish."

"Matterhorn *is* a matter of Polish national security as far as Poland is concerned."

A long, cold silence fell over the table. Ryan picked up her cocktail and sipped from it, trying to decide what to say. What Kopec did next, though, stunned her.

Standing up, he placed a hundred-dollar bill on the table. "When you're ready to get serious about your upgrade kits, you know how to reach me."

"Don't do this to me, Artur," she implored. But it was no use. Without so much as *good-bye*, the Polish intelligence officer turned and left the bar.

CHAPTER 64

After burying their parachutes and wingsuits, Harvath and his team spent the rest of the night in an abandoned barn on an adjacent property. Their weapons loaded and hot, they took turns on watch. Harvath went first.

As everyone else settled in to sleep, he found a spot that allowed him to observe the dirt road outside. Settling into a comfortable position, he reached into his med kit, grabbed several anti-inflammatory pills, and swallowed them down.

HALO jumps were always painful. It didn't matter how much he tried to slow down by flaring his wingsuit. When the canopy unfurled and the drag kicked in, there was an instant *snap* that shocked the body. Like a dog who decides to chase a cat and doesn't know he's on a tether until he reaches the end of it. It hurt like a son of a bitch.

Outside the barn, Staelin had rigged a perimeter of IR security cameras that would alert them to any approach. The feeds were accessible via a tablet that Harvath was using to review their limited mission intelligence.

From an information perspective, this was an incredibly bare-bones operation. Kuznetsov had told them where Tretyakov lived and worked. He had also provided some information about his routine and potential likes and dislikes. Very little of it was actionable. But what there was, Harvath had decided to act upon.

The GRU colonel was single. He had no known girlfriend, or boyfriend. It was not known if he had any pastimes, any hobbies, or any vulnerabilities such as drinking, prostitutes, drugs, or gambling. For their purposes, he was a black hole.

Harvath had done more with less before, but that didn't mean he liked it. In a perfect world, you would set up surveillance on the target for weeks, if not months. You would study his every move; learn all of his habits. You would know him better than anyone else. You would know his hopes, his fears, his dreams, and his weaknesses.

And by doing this, you would learn the best and most effective place to hit him. Someplace that was routine in his day. Someplace where he felt safe. Someplace where he felt invisible and could let his guard down.

There was only one place, outside home and work, that Kuznetsov could remember Tretyakov having a fondness for. It wasn't a bar, a restaurant, or even a specialty tobacconist. It was an island, almost dead center in the middle of the city, accessed by a bridge covered in padlocks.

Kuznetsov had met his GRU superior for a meeting there once. He had remembered Tretyakov remarking that it was within walking distance of his apartment and his office, and that it was where he went when he needed to think.

If only there was a way to force him, to stress him out enough that he would retreat to the island to think, Harvath had reflected.

But a trip to a pretty park somewhere to gather your thoughts was too random. It wasn't like seeing a mistress or visiting a grave on an anniversary. There was no telling how long they could wait for something like that to happen. They would have to pick another place. And they would have to be creative. Every cautious, well-thought-out, well-reasoned, normal thing you would do in a situation like this was out the window.

Harvath was convinced, though, that if they could avoid the gravitational pull of chaos, if they could stay outside the boundaries of Murphy's Law, if they could do that just long enough, they might be able to get the job done.

They passed the night without incident. Before sunrise, they were dressed like tourists, with backpacks, maps, and cameras, waiting to get picked up.

They ate a cold breakfast of water and protein bars. When it was time to move, Harvath gave the signal.

Despite the mistaken report on the status of the cow pasture drop zone, Filip Landsbergis of the VSD had provided some valuable assistance.

A quarter of a mile away, a Lithuanian semi truck importing a refrigerated trailer full of fresh fruit and vegetables sat by the side of the road waiting for them.

Its driver, a gruff man immune to pleasantries, told Harvath and his team to hurry up and get in. Russian patrols were random and all over the place. He likened Kaliningrad to a police state. You never knew where or when you'd be forced to deal with the authorities.

They did as he asked and climbed inside. The temperature felt to be in the thirties. He pointed out a stack of blankets and a power strip for charging any devices before he closed and locked the door.

The team broke out their headlamps and helped themselves to fresh apples and oranges as Staelin recharged the IR cameras and tablet.

The ride would be a couple of hours. Grabbing one of the blankets, Harvath found a place he could stretch out and tried to catch up on his sleep. With everything they had in front of them, this would very likely be the last real chance he had.

CHAPTER 65

On the outskirts of Kaliningrad's capital city, the truck pulled over and the driver opened the rear doors. He handed Harvath an envelope with tickets for the tram and then told his passengers to get lost.

"Nice guy," said Staelin, as they watched him close up the trailer, hop back into the cab, and pull away.

"That *nice* guy's father, two uncles, and grandfather were Forest Brothers," said Harvath, referencing the Baltic partisans who organized a resistance movement and waged guerilla warfare against the Soviet occupation throughout World War II and after.

"And he comes from great stock," Staelin added, upgrading his assessment of the man.

"He's also our ride out of here," said Harvath.

"My respect for him continues to grow."

"As it should," said Harvath, putting his game face on. "Okay, listen up, everybody. We are deep in Indian country and there is no cavalry. We have one job and it is to snatch Tretyakov and get him into Poland. Anything less than that is mission failure. Do you understand me?"

One by one, they nodded. All of them understood.

"Good. See you at the rally point. Let's go."

With that, they broke into teams and went in separate directions. Ashby and Staelin headed south. Harvath and Palmer headed west.

"What's the plan?" the young operative asked, as Harvath checked his map and decided the best route to take.

"Well," said Harvath, "at the most basic level, we were hired to kill people and blow things up. But let's see if we can avoid that this time. We've managed to get in without anyone knowing. If we can get the job done and get out the same way, this will have been a major success."

Chase pretended to make check marks on an imaginary pad. "So that's *no fun*. *No fun*. And *no fun*."

"Funny how you can't spell 'paycheck' without *no fun*."

"Actually—" Chase began, but Harvath interrupted him.

"Our tram is coming. Put your earbuds in and follow me."

Chase did as he was told and they caught the main tram heading into downtown Kaliningrad.

Wearing earbuds was an operational habit they had gotten into. Not only were they able to talk to each other, but it helped them tune out the locals. As long as it looked as if they were listening to music or chatting on the phone, no one attempted to engage them.

They rode the tram into downtown and got off near a former Nazi underground bunker that had been turned into a museum. On foot, they headed for Tretyakov's neighborhood.

As they walked together, Harvath took the opportunity to train Chase—pointing out CCTV cameras to avoid, places to shake a hypothetical tail, and spots where you could dispose of evidence or hide items and come back to get them later.

He had spent a lot of time working with Sloane, but

not as much with Chase. It felt good to be in the field with him—to see how he operated in a foreign environment, how he reacted to unusual input.

For the most part, he was fantastic. He knew his stuff and he was incredibly observant. He still, though, got things wrong—and Harvath knew exactly why.

Like Sloane, he was smart, funny, and incredibly talented. But also like Sloane, he was still green. Despite all his combat deployments, all his time behind a trigger, there was still an immaturity to him. And he wore it like a beacon pinned to his chest.

Killing bad guys—be they mujahideen, hijackers, warlords, or drug kingpins, was one thing. Blending into a normal, everyday scene—as he was doing right now—killing high-profile targets, professional assassins, and unassuming ex-military bodyguards was something completely different.

Chase was exceptional at taking out unsophisticated killers in their own backyard, but now, he had to become the best at taking out sophisticated ones in his.

The West was under attack and it was full of them. The war was changing. He and Sloane were the future. So was Jasinski, if she was truly onboard.

When they got to Tretyakov's apartment building, Chase asked, "What now?"

"Now," Harvath replied, "we keep walking. No matter what happens, you never stop in front of a target."

They kept going until they arrived at a corner with a small German café serving breakfast.

Before the Soviets had invaded in the 1940s, Kaliningrad had been part of Prussia. Today, German tourists were a huge part of their economy and there was a café, bar, or restaurant catering to them in every neighborhood, if not on every block.

"How's your German?" Harvath asked as they took a table outside with a view of Tretyakov's building.

"Terrible."

"I've got this, then," said Harvath, as a smiling waitress came over with menus and coffee.

Smiling back, he spoke to her in his passable Russian, but added a German accent. He sounded like a tourist attempting to speak the local language. The waitress humored him.

She asked where he was staying and, having done his homework, he was able to cite a nearby neighborhood and talk about renting an apartment via a popular Internet app.

As they drank their coffee, the pair looked for other places they might use for surveillance. They could only sit here for so long without drawing attention.

Chase pointed out a boarded-up building down the block. By the looks of it, its roof might have a halfway decent view.

More important, it would allow them to get off the street. According to Kuznetsov, Tretyakov liked to walk to work. The last thing they needed was to bump into him—especially since he might recognize Harvath.

Once their food arrived, they ate and paid their bill. The sooner they were out of sight, the better.

What's more, Harvath was eager to get a closer look at Tretyakov's apartment. He was starting to form a plan, which he hoped would allow them to snatch the GRU operative without anyone even knowing he was gone.

CHAPTER 66

Harvath and Palmer entered the abandoned building by removing a board from one of the rear windows and headed all the way upstairs. The roof, as they had hoped, had a decent, though partly obstructed view of Tretyakov's apartment.

Sending out a text, they told Staelin and Ashby where to find them. Then they set up a small camera and took turns watching the ebb and flow of people, hoping to find a pattern.

Unfortunately, there was nothing special or predictable about any of the traffic. They saw a babushka—a little old woman who was likely the custodian—go in and come out several times from the building, sweeping and handling other menial labor chores.

In the Soviet days, babushkas were often informants who gladly passed on even the slightest pieces of gossip to the authorities. They were quick to report any unusual activity. She would need to be avoided.

And while she probably had keys to all the apartments, Harvath wasn't interested. He could get into them without her. What he needed was information. What time did Tretyakov normally leave? What time did he normally come home? Did he entertain during the week? Did he own a vehicle?

All they had was where he lived, where he worked, and an outdated photo Nicholas had been able to uncover.

"Got him," Chase suddenly said.

Harvath, who had been preparing to burst an encrypted SITREP back to the United States, looked over the edge of the roof.

In his suit and overcoat, with a leather briefcase slung from his shoulder, he looked every inch the unassuming businessman or government worker.

He paused for a moment on the sidewalk, chatting amiably with the babushka, who had followed him outside with a piece of mail.

He smiled at the old woman, but his eyes swept the street, scanning for anything unusual or out of place. He was alert, but relaxed, about to conduct his morning ritual of walking to work.

"Where are you going?" Chase asked as he saw Harvath get up.

"I'm going to follow him."

"Are you nuts? He knows what you look like. If he even feels you on him, it could blow this whole thing."

"He won't feel me," Harvath reassured him. "He won't even know I'm there."

"What am I supposed to do?"

"Stay here and watch his building."

Chase shook his head. The decision felt impulsive to him. It was a huge risk and he couldn't begin to fathom what Harvath thought he might gain from it.

Heading downstairs, Harvath climbed back out the rear window and came around the side of the building. Very carefully, he headed up the street after Tretyakov.

Most carnivores have a finely honed prey drive. It is the instinctive impulse to hunt and capture their food.

The better the hunter, the better it is able to sense when it is being hunted. It was the same for human beings.

Most people, though, had deadened themselves to their instincts. They had stopped listening altogether. When their gut told them something was wrong, they rationalized the warning away. When the danger finally made itself too obvious to ignore, it was often too late to react.

Humans who hunted other humans had a highly developed prey drive. They could sense the presence of other hunters long before they could see them. Chase had been right to warn Harvath.

What Chase hadn't fully learned yet, though, was how to mask the signals that other hunters pick up on. There was an energy, an intensity, that took over the moment the prey drive kicked in. As the hunter locked on to his quarry, it was like projecting a tractor beam.

The key to staying hidden was to unplug the beam, to turn it off by denying it any energy. It was a rather esoteric process. Chase jokingly referred to it as "The Force." And while Harvath didn't have a term for it, the best explanation he had ever found for it was in a book about Zen mysticism. Essentially, he removed his ego from the process. The hunt was neither good nor bad. Its outcome would be what it would be and was therefore, out of his control.

The ability to remove himself was what made him such an effective predator. Combined with the skills he had learned from the Old Man, he had risen to the very top of the pyramid. He was an apex predator, a hunter of other hunters.

One of the most important things about being an apex predator was to try not to appear like one. Once other predators noticed you, they immediately took interest and wanted to know what was going on.

So, like sheep around the world, he took out his phone and pretended to be looking at it as he walked. With his shoulders hunched and his head down, he fit right in with everyone else.

Just based on the time of day, Harvath had assumed Tretyakov was headed to his office, but as they neared the river, he watched him take a detour.

Up ahead was a short bridge covered with padlocks. On the other side was Kneiphof, the twenty-five-acre island Kuznetsov had told him about—Tretyakov's "quiet place" where he sought refuge when he needed to get away from the office.

It seemed odd to be starting the day there, but who could say? Perhaps he just enjoyed passing through on his way to work.

As he watched the man cross the bridge, he unslung his backpack and removed a brightly colored guidebook. He opened to the section on Immanuel Kant and Königsberg Cathedral. Then, once he felt he had given the GRU officer enough of a lead, he began following him again.

Aside from a smattering of vagrants and occasional people cutting through, either on foot or by bicycle, the park was relatively quiet.

The scent of the river was strong and unpleasant. Harvath could only imagine what it was like at the height of summer. But despite that, the island appeared to be an enjoyable, and likely a popular place. It was filled with trees, there were open places to sunbathe or play soccer, there were plenty of benches, and in addition to the cobbled boulevard that ran up the center, there were a multitude of walking paths that branched off in all directions.

Harvath watched as Tretyakov passed the cathedral and the Kant tomb, then took a path that branched off to the right. At the first bench he came to, he sat down.

Placing his briefcase on his left side, he took out the envelope that the babushka had given him. Opening it, he removed the letter from inside, and began to read.

At that moment, another impulse fired from deep inside Harvath's brain. Looking around, and not seeing anything suspicious, he decided to take Tretyakov right there in the park.

CHAPTER 67

Harvath walked up and stopped right in front of Tretyakov. For several moments, the Russian didn't even bother to look up from his letter.

Once he did, he spoke in English. "Mr. Stephen Hall, I presume," he said, using Harvath's alias from Gotland.

"You can call me Steve."

Returning the letter to its envelope, Tretyakov placed it in an outer pocket of his briefcase and studied the man standing in front of him.

"It's a little early in the morning for that, isn't it?" the GRU officer asked, eyeballing the empty vodka bottle Harvath had fished from a nearby trash can.

"This isn't for me. It's for you. In fact, you're going to be holding on to it in a moment."

"You think so?"

Harvath nodded. In his pack was a syringe of ketamine, known for its use as a horse tranquilizer. He had planned on hitting him with the Taser and then injecting him with the ketamine to make it look as if he had passed out drunk. As soon as he had him incapacitated, he would work on getting him out of the park and back to the abandoned building.

"Mr. Hall, or whatever your real name is, I'm afraid I cannot help you."

The man was incredibly calm. He sat on the bench as if he didn't have a care in the world. Though Harvath hadn't shown it to him, he assumed that the hand he couldn't see, the one hidden in his right coat pocket, was grasping a weapon.

"I think you're going to be a lot of help to me," said Harvath, pulling out his Taser.

"Close in. Now," Tretyakov ordered in Russian.

The sudden switch from English jarred Harvath. Instantly, his head was on a swivel.

Four vagrants were now headed toward him from different directions, as were two more "passersby." All had weapons drawn. It was a trap.

"Sometimes, things are too good to pass up," said Tretyakov. "Like a GRU colonel, sitting alone, on a bench in a quiet section of a quiet park."

"There's no way you could have known I was coming."

"I didn't. It was a *hunch*, I believe you Americans call it. When Ivan failed to make contact, we assumed the worst. We knew eventually he would be broken. We just didn't know when. I must thank you, though."

"For what?"

"I didn't think we would catch you so quickly. We were worried we might have to carry on this ruse for quite some time."

Harvath shook his head. "Only six men? That's all?"

"Apparently, that's all we needed."

When the first of the GRU operatives, a bald, muscular man with a scar along the side of his head, got within striking distance, he took Harvath down hard.

Wrenching his arm behind his back, he placed him in handcuffs, left him on the ground, and patted him down.

Relieving him of his Taser, he tossed it to a colleague who was going through his backpack.

Harvath heard the Russian word for *spy* several times as they laid out all of the contents, including his weapons, on the bench and examined them.

The man patting him down took his phone, his watch, his flashlight, all of his cash, and the two knives he was carrying. He then stood guard over him, placing his boot on top of his neck and pushing down with an unnecessary amount of force in order to create the maximum amount of pain possible.

It radiated throughout his skull. He had never felt anything like it.

Just as his vision was beginning to dim, Tretyakov yelled for the goon to knock it off.

The man dialed it back from an eleven to an eight. The pain was still white-hot. If he kept at it, Harvath was going to end up with permanent damage.

Tretyakov had to yell again. This time, the man obliged, removing his boot completely from Harvath's neck. Then, when his boss wasn't looking, he dug it into Harvath's left shoulder blade, creating an all-new kind of agony.

As exquisite as the pain was, Harvath didn't give the asshole the satisfaction of making a single sound.

Finally, they replaced everything in the backpack and Tretyakov gave the command to get Harvath to his feet. Asshole used the handcuffs to do it, adding even more injury to Harvath's shoulders, particularly the left one. They then walked him back in the direction from where they had come.

At the cathedral, they turned left and walked toward the back, where several cars were parked.

The brutality of the Russians when it came to interrogations was legendary. If what had just happened to him was any indication, and he had every reason to believe it was, the nightmare hadn't even started yet.

Everything he had ever been taught about escape and evasion flooded back into his brain. He knew that he had to keep his wits about him. If he lost his head, he might miss an opportunity.

Already, he had managed to reach down to the hem of his coat, tear the inside seam, and remove the plastic handcuff key he had sewn inside. All he needed now was an opportunity.

It would probably come once he was inside a car. Judging by the group of vehicles he was being led toward, they were all sedans. That meant the GRU team would have to split up. It also meant that Harvath would have fewer guards to deal with.

Stepping into the parking area, Harvath took a deep breath and tried to loosen his body. Extricating himself was going to be incredibly difficult. And, depending upon whether there were cars ahead of or behind his, he would probably have only seconds to decide which direction to run.

His chances for success were not good. Not only that, but all he could do at this point was escape. There was no way he could also take Tretyakov.

The operation was a failure, and it was his fault. Had he waited, had he not been so impulsive, it might have succeeded.

As these thoughts raced through his mind, Harvath didn't realize that he had slowed down and was shuffling across the pavement.

The bald goon gave him a shove and that was when it happened. There was a crack, followed by a spray of blood as one of the GRU operatives went down.

CHAPTER 68

Harvath had time to unlock only one hand. Whipping his arm hard to the left, he used the open handcuff like a mace and tore a giant gash right across asshole's forehead, nose, and cheek.

As the man's hands flew to his face, Harvath pulled the GRU operative's pistol from his holster and shot him twice in the chest and once in the head. Turning to the next operative, he did the same.

He turned to engage a third, but before he could, the man took two rounds to the head and dropped dead to the ground.

Looking around him, Harvath counted six bodies. There was blood and brains and bits of bone everywhere. As quickly as it had started, it was over. The GRU had been caught out in the open, without any cover or concealment. Each of the operatives had gotten his ticket punched.

The most important GRU person, though, was gone.

"Hurry!" Chase yelled, as he, Staelin, and Ashby stepped out from behind the vehicles. "Tretyakov took off!"

Harvath had no idea how they had gotten there, or how they had set up such a quick ambush, but now wasn't the time to ask.

Spinning around, he could see Tretyakov disappearing into the park's trees.

The man had shed his briefcase and was running fast. Even with the head start, Harvath was confident that he could catch him, and he took off running.

This was what he had been training for. All the squats, all the hellacious early morning runs, all the wind sprints, and all the Hulk Sauce—it all came down to this. He had pushed his body to the limit so that when it counted most, he could prove he was not only still in the game, but deserved to be here.

With every stride he grew closer. Tretyakov didn't stand a chance. Short of turning around and firing a gun at him, which he would have done by now if he could, Harvath had him.

Twice, the man had looked over his shoulder and the fear was evident in his face. Gone was the cool customer on the bench. He had been replaced by a scared animal, running for its life. The apex predator was in his prime and was about to prove once again why he occupied the top of the pyramid. Harvath had never felt as alive, as purposeful, as he did at that moment. He had this, and a smile swept across his face.

Then he heard the roar of a car engine, followed by a quick double-tap on a horn. As Sloane raced past him in one of the GRU sedans, she winked and flashed him the thumbs-up.

Rocketing ahead of Harvath, she caught up to Tretyakov, jerked the wheel quickly to the right, and sent him tumbling across the ground.

When he got to them, she already had him Flex-Cuffed.

"You can make goo-goo eyes at him later," she cracked,

as he stood there, mouth slightly agape. "Come on. Help me get him into the car."

Harvath obliged, and after seat-belting him in, hopped in the back with him.

"We gone," stated Sloane, peeling out before Harvath's door was even closed.

"Has anybody discussed a plan?" asked Harvath, as she pinned the accelerator to the floor.

"The plan is that we get the hell out of here."

Across the river, Harvath could see the flashing lights from approaching police cars. "Good plan," he said.

Sloane blasted past the cathedral, where Staelin and Palmer peeled out in another GRU sedan right behind them.

"Any other sights you wanted to see before we left town?" she asked.

"Nope," replied Harvath. "All good."

"Okay. Buckle up."

Harvath fastened his seat belt as she sped across the bridge, pulled up her emergency brake, and drifted into a hard left turn.

The maneuver spat them out onto a wide boulevard and she dropped the hammer.

Weaving in and out of early morning rush-hour traffic, she traded paint with buses and all sorts of other vehicles. No matter how dangerous each prior move that she made was, she found a way to top it.

Glancing out the rear window, Harvath saw that, amazingly, Chase was right behind.

"Do you two have some sort of ESP?" he asked.

"Google maps," she said, nodding at her phone, which she had jammed into the dashboard in front of the speedometer.

"Where the hell's our destination?" he asked, as she barely threaded the needle between two semi trucks.

"We're going to the pickup point."

"Negative," said Harvath, from the backseat. "Not until we have swept the cars."

In the rearview mirror, he could see her roll her eyes. "The Russians can't even afford new combat boots for all their troops," she said. "You think they'd waste money on tracking GRU vehicles? In *Kaliningrad*?"

She made a good point. Nevertheless, Harvath wanted to be sure. "Once we're outside of town, pull over. I'm going to check."

"I'll see if we can find a roadside shrine where we can light some candles, too," she replied, downshifting and swerving around a tour bus.

Harvath looked at Tretyakov, who had wisely kept his mouth shut—but perhaps not because he had any choice. His face was badly battered from the fall he had taken, and based on the swelling that was setting up, Harvath wouldn't have been surprised to learn that he had broken his jaw.

"Tight squeeze!" Sloane yelled from the front seat as she maneuvered between a tram and a delivery truck, knocking the mirrors off on both sides.

Two blocks later they reached the on-ramp for the main route that led west out of the city. Sloane hit it hard, but immediately slowed down as she merged with the traffic.

"Everyone, keep your eyes open," she said, partly to Harvath and partly to Staelin and Palmer, whom she had on speakerphone in front of her.

The cops Harvath had seen approaching back by the river had probably gone right to the island and were try-ing to figure out what had happened. The rest of the police force, though, was likely hearing from angry drivers who had called in about two black sedans that had caused damage to multiple vehicles.

The good news for Harvath and his team, though, was when the police ran the license plates, they would come back as GRU and nothing further would be done, no officers would be dispatched to investigate. Only later would they realize that the vehicles had been stolen. And by then, it would be too late for the Russians to do anything at all.

CHAPTER 69

They kept pushing west until Harvath, who had been glued to the rear window, watching to make sure they weren't being followed, felt comfortable enough to give the okay to pull off the road.

Up ahead was a small, run-down truck stop and Sloane suggested they stop there. Harvath concurred.

Around the back was a pair of beat-up old Dumpsters and a crappy, out-of-service car wash. That was where they parked.

Getting out of the cars, they kept their eyes peeled for trouble as they stretched their legs.

"What the fuck were you thinking?" Chase demanded, as he approached Harvath.

"I had a bird in the hand," he replied. "I wasn't going to let him go."

"A bird whose nest we had under observation," stated Sloane.

"Sometimes birds don't come back to their nests."

Chase shook his head. So did Sloane. Staelin was unavailable for head shaking as he had walked over behind the car wash to take a leak.

"We've got Tretyakov," Harvath declared. "That's what matters."

"The ends justify the means," said Chase. "Is that what you're telling me?"

"In this case? Absolutely. When you get a shot, you take a shot. It's that simple."

"You're lucky we were there."

"I *am* lucky," Harvath admitted, not afraid to say it. "Very lucky. But what the hell were you doing there in the first place?"

Chase was neither ashamed, nor embarrassed. "I thought you made a really bad call. So when you left the roof, I decided to follow you."

"Bullshit. I would have known you were behind me."

"Not if I was using the Force."

Again with the Force, thought Harvath. But there was no arguing with the fact that Chase had indeed followed him, and that Harvath hadn't even realized it. Perhaps his skills were much farther along than Harvath had been giving him credit for.

Even so, he wasn't thrilled with Chase's decision to abandon his post on the rooftop. Harvath had been the ultimate rule breaker, it was the foundation of who he was, but now that he had one foot in management and was responsible for people beneath him, he needed his orders to be followed without exception. *Hypocrisy at its best*, he realized.

"Next time I do something you think is dumb," said Harvath, "don't you do something dumber. Okay? In the meantime, thank you."

Chase hadn't been expecting a thank-you. "Seriously?"

"*Seriously,*" Harvath answered. "Thank you."

"You're welcome," he said, and then added, "You also need to thank Ashby and Staelin. They hauled ass to get there. We had no idea what you were up to, but we wanted to have your back in case something went down."

Harvath thanked Ashby, and when Staelin reappeared, zipping his fly, he thanked him as well.

"You bet," the Delta Force operative responded. "'Gunfight in Kaliningrad' is going to make a killer band name."

Harvath smiled. "Make sure to save me a T-shirt."

Staelin nodded and, remembering he had something for him, reached into his vehicle and pulled out Harvath's backpack. "Your phone and the other things they took from you are in there, too."

He was doling out a lot of thank-yous, but he had a top-notch team and they deserved every one of them. The presence of mind to clean the scene like that was a testament to their professionalism. "Thank you," he said.

"You're welcome," replied Staelin. Looking at the damage on both cars, he added, "We need to get rid of these vehicles."

Harvath agreed, but first he wanted to confirm they weren't already being tracked.

They swept each of the GRU sedans and didn't find any tracking devices. That was the good news.

The bad news was that their pickup point was at least forty-five minutes away. And that was if they took the most direct route. The direct route, though, wasn't an option. Not for them.

If it hadn't happened already, police and military throughout the exclave would soon be alerted. Patrols at the border would be stepped up, as well as along all the roads.

The longer they were out in the open, especially during the daytime, the greater the likelihood was that they were going to get caught. They had to go into hiding—now.

Glancing over at the defunct car wash, Harvath got an idea.

There had been just enough room to get both cars inside and still close the metal roll-down door. Harvath used the derma-bond from his med kit to make the broken lock look as if it had never been touched.

They each still had water and protein bars, and there were drains in the floor should anyone need to relieve themselves.

Though no one felt like sleeping, Harvath still posted a guard rotation. It was important that they be prepared for anything.

The next thing he needed to do was burst an update and request a change in the pickup point and the time.

He didn't like risking the exposure, but inside the windowless car wash, without an unobstructed view of the sky, he wouldn't be able to get a signal.

He had Sloane, with her suppressed H&K VP9 pistol, cover him as he placed a small, vehicle-mounted satellite antenna outside and then surreptitiously ran the cord back inside.

It was a calling card that, if discovered, would announce their presence, but he didn't have a choice. Without comms, they were dead in the water.

Retreating inside, he attached the antenna, burst the message to Ryan, and then shut everything off.

Under the guise of combating terrorism, Moscow monitored satellite communications throughout Russia and its territories. While terrorism was a legitimate concern, the effort was more about controlling free speech and blunting espionage. Whatever was being said, at any time, anywhere, the Kremlin wanted to know it.

The position was so draconian that even foreign visitors were mandated to purchase Russian SIM cards for their satellite phones or face fines and potential imprisonment.

Compressing his message and sending it in a short, fast burst was designed to avoid detection and have the lowest probability of intercept. Even if the Russians noticed, there'd be no way for them to trace it.

With the message sent, all they could do was wait. They were used to it. Being good at waiting made you good at the game. And they needed to be good at the game if they were going to get out of Kaliningrad alive.

In fact, they were going to need to be great.

CHAPTER 70

Mike Haney sat down on the outdoor terrace of the Hotel Mazurach, ordered a beer from the waitress, and once she was gone, filled Barton and Jasinski in on his brief reconnaissance operation.

"I'm actually more worried about the Polish side of the border than the Russian side," he said. "Based on what I could see, they're using a lot of high-tech equipment to detect illegal crossings—lasers, infrared, that kind of thing. There are also foot and vehicle patrols, including four-by-fours."

"That's because Poland acts as a border for the EU," said Jasinski. "They've put a lot of money into security here."

"You can say that again. All the buildings are brand-new. The difference between the Polish side and the Russian side is pretty stark."

"How about the lake itself?" asked Barton.

"That's the good part. All they have is a line of buoys marking the border. And a bunch of signs that say Do Not Cross."

"Yeah, I'm not a very good reader."

"Me neither," said Haney. "Especially at night."

"How about patrol boats?" said Barton. "Did you see any? Either Russian or Polish?"

"There's no visible presence from either out on the lake, but that doesn't mean they don't exist. The Polish Border Patrol has a lot of cameras, though, so I imagine they're keeping an eye on the water. But the Russians? Everything I could see looked pretty low-tech."

"Did you get pictures?"

Haney smiled and patted his camera. "Tons. We'll put them on my laptop and I can show you up in the room."

"Great," Barton replied, as the waitress set down Haney's beer and went to take another table's order. Once she was out of earshot, he continued. "As soon as it gets dark, we can start moving the equipment into place. Monika, you'll come with me."

"As a linguist only," Jasinski replied. "I don't have any jurisdiction over the border."

"I'm sure if you had to, you could be pretty persuasive," said Barton.

Haney shook his head. Barton would never need Viagra because his erection was permanent. The guy was a walking hard-on, and he'd been eyeing her since they first met.

"What about my idea for a distraction?" Haney asked, bringing the conversation back to the operation.

"For the record," she stated, "I'm against any destruction of Polish equipment or property."

"Duly noted. How about off the record?"

"Off the record, you'd have to be sure to take out any of their backups, or else what's the point?"

Haney nodded and raised his glass. "So, it's settled, then. You and Barton handle the equipment. I'll be the official pain in everyone's ass and handle the sabotage."

Raising their drinks, Jasinski and Barton clinked glasses with Haney. If everything went well, they'd be back in twelve hours with the rest of the team, doing the exact same thing.

But when it came to complicated assignments, especially one this complicated, things rarely went according to plan.

CHAPTER 71

When his next communications window opened, Harvath downloaded Lydia Ryan's message. To her credit, she had kept it short, sweet, and to the point.

Per his request, the pickup location and the time had been changed. All they needed to do was to stay out of sight until then.

That was going to be no problem. With Sloane covering him once more, he took down the antenna and brought everything back inside the car wash.

Staelin, who served as the team's de facto medic, had been examining Tretyakov. "I think you're right," he said when Harvath came back in. "I think his jaw is broken. He's not going to be able to exfil with a broken jaw."

"Don't worry about the exfil," said Harvath. "I've got it all taken care of. Everything's going to be fine."

As team leader, it was his job to reassure and to instill confidence in his troops. Privately, though, his concern was growing. Twice in the last two hours, a police vehicle had done a sweep through the truck stop.

The first time it was just a slow roll. The second time, they stopped, got out and looked in the Dumpsters.

For their protection, Tretyakov had been carefully duct-taped at the mouth and bound even tighter. They couldn't risk his giving them away.

Harvath decided to double the guard, posting someone at each end of the car wash, even though only one of the roll-up doors had a gap big enough to see through. They might be blind at one of their entry points, but they didn't have to be deaf.

As he had expected, the alert appeared to have gone out. Since their vehicles had been spotted barreling west out of the city, it wasn't a surprise that the authorities were checking this truck stop. They were likely checking all truck stops, as well as rest stops, bus depots, and train stations, in addition to countless other locations.

All Harvath and his team could do right now was to sit tight. Though it felt like an eternity, very soon they'd be on their way and one step closer to home.

When the appointed time neared, Harvath went back and forth about whom to put outside. Sloane was the obvious choice, as a good-looking woman was probably not what the cops were looking for. But a good-looking woman loitering at a truck stop created a whole different sort of potential trouble for the team.

That wasn't to say she couldn't handle herself—she absolutely could—but it might very quickly turn into a problem. Instead, Harvath decided to send out Chase.

He didn't need to be told to make himself scarce. He was functioning as a lookout. If he could do so from a concealed position, all the better.

He found an excellent position behind a stack of discarded pallets. From there, he could see most of the eastern side of the truck stop. That was where the pickup was supposed to occur.

The only problem with his position, besides its limited field of sight, was that it afforded no avenues of escape.

When the police came back through a third time and decided to do an even more aggressive search, Chase realized it wasn't just him who was in trouble, but his whole team.

It didn't take the cops long to find him. Yelling in Russian, they told him to step out from behind the pallets.

He obliged them, but just partly, stepping out from behind the stack of pallets only enough to reveal the left side of his body.

When the first cop moved to call it in over his radio, the second cop, standing next to him, went for his gun. That was when Chase fired.

His suppressed Glock had been in his right hand the entire time. Firing through the open space in the pallets, he killed both of the Russians instantly.

Harvath was the first one out of the car wash to help him scrub the scene.

"I'll handle the bodies," he said. "You figure out how we get one more vehicle inside."

It was the kind of puzzle the Army gave to its Green Beret recruits—like Jeeps with only three wheels that need to be moved right away to a life-or-death location.

Rushing back inside the car wash, Chase surveyed the scene and quickly realized that if they slanted the vehicles, they could squeeze one more in, which is exactly what they did.

By the time Harvath had put the bodies in the back of the police car and had driven it up to the car wash, a space was ready and waiting for him. Once again, Chase was proving how capable he was.

The vehicle secure and no one the wiser, Harvath sent Chase back out to resume his post.

Inserting a fresh magazine into his weapon, he did as he was told and headed back outside.

Twenty minutes later, their ride arrived. He had backed in, along the east side, so as to make it as easy as possible for Harvath and his team to climb up into his trailer without being seen.

"You, too," the Lithuanian truck driver from earlier that morning said.

Harvath shook his head. "Nope. I'm riding with you. Let's go."

It wasn't a request. The driver shook his head and, after closing the trailer doors, came back around front and hopped up into the cab. Harvath joined him on the passenger side.

"I was almost home," he said, putting his rig in gear and pulling out of the truck stop. "Then I get a message that I must turn around and come to get you."

"We appreciate it," said Harvath. "Thank you."

"Tell me the Russians will be unhappy."

Harvath smiled. "I think the Russians will be *very* unhappy."

The old man smiled back.

They rode together without speaking. As the Lithuanian listened to his radio, Harvath put his head back and closed his eyes. He needed to rest up. Their exfil was going to suck.

When he felt the truck slow, he opened his eyes and looked at his watch. He had been out for well over an hour. "Where are we?" he asked.

The driver pointed to the sign. "Ten kilometers from the Polish border. This is as far as I go."

Harvath thanked him and, climbing down from the cab, accompanied him around back to let his teammates out.

The driver had several cases of bottled water and encouraged them to take as much as they needed.

Staelin made a point to take the driver aside and thank him personally. "You come from a family of warriors. It is an honor to know you. Thank you for helping us."

Normally in a situation like this, Staelin would have handed the man one of his military challenge coins. This was a covert operation, though, and they weren't carrying anything that could identify them as Americans.

But in his boot was a small backup knife designed for Delta operators called the *Sgian Dubh*. Bending down, he removed it and handed it to the man.

The Lithuanian was touched and tried to refuse it, but Staelin insisted.

Reaching into his pocket, the man pulled out an aged pocketknife. It had been hand-painted with some sort of a religious icon, probably a saint.

It was apparent that he had owned it for a long time.

Staelin tried to refuse the gift, but the man insisted, so he relented, accepting it graciously.

"Ready to roll?" Harvath asked, interrupting the moment between Staelin and the descendant of the Forest Brothers.

"Yup," said the Delta Force operative. "Good to go."

One by one, the team all shook the truck driver's hand, thanking him. Then he climbed into his cab and drove off while they disappeared into the woods and got ready for the most dangerous part of their mission yet.

CHAPTER 72

O n behalf of Lithuanian Intelligence, Filip Landsbergis had done an exceptional job. The cow pasture drop zone notwithstanding, everything else had been perfect. He had provided a critical part of the operation, getting Harvath and his team into and out of enemy territory.

Landsbergis's final piece of intelligence had been about where the team was now headed.

Across from the border checkpoint, along the shores of Lake Goldap, was a Russian campground. For all intents and purposes, it looked like a wonderful place to take a family. It had cabins, picnic tables, showers, toilets, a dining hall, a trading post, and a stage for skits. But for all its outward appearances, in reality, it was an underground railway stop for Russian spies.

As they moved into and out of Poland, Lithuania, and other adjacent NATO countries, many of the spies came to the campground to unwind and be debriefed. It was a hangover from the KGB days when vacation camps had been created to provide inexpensive holidays for officers of good standing.

There was plenty of cheap booze and even cheaper women, rotated in from neighboring Belarus a month at a time.

American movies, dubbed in Russian, played in the

theater while meals that sounded classy, but were actually very low-rent, were cooked up in the vermin-infested camp kitchen.

Over at the Russian border patrol checkpoint, the officers had been instructed to ignore the alcohol-fueled parties as well as anything else that took place at the camp—if they wanted to keep their jobs.

But those kinds of things usually happened at the height of summer. Now it was off-season. Activity at the camp might just give the border guards something to pay attention to. It could go either way.

Covering the distance to the camp was made difficult by Tretyakov's unwillingness to walk. They would shove him forward and he would cooperate for a few steps and then he'd go back to shuffling his feet.

Harvath reached over and placed his fingers beneath the man's injured jaw. The area was so sensitive that the Russian's entire body seized, his eyes began to water, and he came right up onto his toes.

It only took once to secure his compliance. There was no more slowing the team down after that.

From where the Lithuanian had dropped them off, it was a full ten kilometers to the border, but only three klicks to the campground.

They proceeded in a staggered formation, with their night-vision goggles on and their suppressed weapons hot, ready for anything.

Their hope, of course, was that they wouldn't encounter anything; that they would just move quietly through the campground and no one would know they had ever been there.

That hope, though, was dashed the moment they set foot on the property. Coming up the road from the main camp building was a small Russian military unit.

Sloane was on point and gave the signal for the team to melt into the woods. There, they all froze and didn't make a sound.

Harvath had Tretyakov lie on his stomach. Crouching next to him, he placed his fingers under his jaw, a subtle threat of what would happen if the GRU officer tried to call out through the duct tape over his mouth, or if he made any sound at all.

They waited for what felt like an eternity for the soldiers to pass. There were eight of them, and they were heavily armed.

From where Harvath and his team were hiding in the trees, it was impossible to make out whether these were regular troops augmenting the border patrol, or if they were a more specialized unit. Harvath didn't want to get close enough to find out. Getting Tretyakov off the ground, they pressed on.

They had only been back on the road for a few moments when they heard a vehicle coming from behind them and were forced to return to the woods again.

It was a truck carrying additional Russian troops, and it was headed into the camp.

Damn it, thought Harvath. *They're flooding the zone.*

Whether the troops were just bivouacking at the campground between shifts at the checkpoint or were being spread out in a more organized fashion along the border, it didn't matter. They were standing between the team and their exfil.

Staelin came over and crouched down next to Harvath. Keeping his voice barely above a whisper, he said, "I'm guessing the plan didn't involve the campground being full of Russian soldiers."

Harvath shook his head. "If I'd known, I would have brought more hot dogs."

"What do you want to do?"

"I want to avoid contact at all costs. I'm not really in the mood for another gunfight."

"Agreed," Staelin replied. "So do we try to go around them?"

For the time being, it seemed like the only possible answer, and Harvath nodded. Getting Tretyakov to his feet, they changed course and pushed deeper into the woods.

It made for even slower going. The ground was uneven and there were plenty of hidden hazards—rocks, roots, and downed branches to trip them up. But it wasn't as if they were swimming in options. They had no choice but to push forward.

If they could get to the other side of the campground, there would be a small clearing to cross, and after that, Harvath prayed, nothing preventing them from getting to the water. Then, once they had reached Lake Goldap, they could head for Poland, and freedom.

But no sooner had the thought entered his mind than Sloane heard something up ahead and gave the signal for the team, once more, to freeze.

CHAPTER 73

Harvath tightened his grip on Tretyakov, just as a barrage of gunfire erupted around them. "Contact left! Contact left!" Sloane yelled.

Somehow, somewhere in the woods, the Russians had spotted them. Immediately, the team returned fire.

"Move! Move! Move!" Harvath ordered.

Everyone, including Tretyakov, kicked it into gear.

The wild, indiscriminate shooting seemed to be coming from every direction. The Russians were not only undisciplined, but were also going to end up killing one of their own.

At that moment, Harvath heard a cry from Tretyakov's duct-taped mouth and saw him drop. He had been shot in the back of the leg.

Slinging his weapon, Harvath helped him back up and forced him to keep moving. It was obvious that the Russian soldiers weren't planning on taking any prisoners.

Whether they knew Tretyakov was with them was immaterial. They were throwing so much lead in their direction that there was no way they could expect anyone to survive.

Raising his Rattler in his right hand, Harvath fired off a burst to their three o'clock.

The soldiers pursuing them from that side responded, and Tretyakov was shot again—this time in his upper arm.

"Fuck!" grunted Harvath.

They needed to find cover fast, or they were all going to be cut to ribbons. There were just too many guns on the other side of this fight.

Through the branches up ahead, Harvath spotted what looked like the remnants of an old stone foundation—maybe from a caretaker's cottage or a previous lodge of some sort.

"There!" Harvath shouted, directing his team to it.

They all scrambled or leaped over the foundation wall. Harvath helped Tretyakov as Chase and Sloane laid down cover fire.

Finally getting up and over, Tretyakov landed hard on the other side, followed by Harvath.

"If I had known we were going to be taking on the whole Russian Army," said Staelin as he changed magazines, "I would have brought along a little more ammo."

Like Tretyakov, Harvath's exfil plan was shot to shit. All the work Haney and Barton had done staging dry suits, full face mask SCUBA gear, and propulsion devices was out the window.

Even if they could get to all of it, it was highly unlikely they could successfully transport Tretyakov, underwater, to the Polish side of the lake where the boat was waiting.

He was going to have to come up with another plan. And right now, there was only one plan he could think of. Activating his radio, he hailed Barton.

• • •

"What the hell is that for?" Jasinski asked, as the SEAL flipped open the Storm case and removed a Mark 48 belt-fed machine gun.

"It's for you," he replied, quickly attaching it to its mount. "Did they teach you how to load and fire one of these things in the Polish Army?"

"What are you trying to do, start a war?"

"Actually," he replied as he opened three ammo cans and then fired up the engine, "I'm trying to stop one."

Down the lake, they could hear the withering fire that Harvath and the rest of the team were under.

Hailing Haney over the radio, Barton said, "Good to go, on your mark."

"Roger that," Haney replied, "stand by."

The SEAL looked back at Jasinski through his night vision. He could see that she hadn't yet loaded the weapon. "If we don't go, the Russians are going to kill them."

When she still didn't do anything, he pushed past her, loaded a belt of 7.62 ammunition, and charged the Mark 48.

When Haney's voice came back over the radio and said, "Now!" Barton told Jasinski to hold on as he pushed the throttle all the way forward.

The engine of the Rigid Inflatable Boat roared to life as they raced down the water toward the buoys and the demarcation line between Poland and Kaliningrad.

The closer they got, the louder the gunfire became. Barton prayed that they would make it there in time.

Up ahead on the western shore of the lake, he could see the Polish side of the border crossing. He could only imagine what the officers there were thinking as the gun battle raged across the water from them.

"Time to turn out the lights, Mike," said Barton, as he could see the buoy line rapidly approaching up ahead.

"Five seconds," Haney replied.

And like clockwork, five seconds later there was a detonation at the electrical substation, followed by smaller detonations at the generators that provided backup power for the Polish border crossing.

At the buoys, Barton stopped only long enough to use a pair of bolt cutters to sever the line, before once again throwing the throttles all the way forward.

"Norseman," Barton said over the radio. "We are inbound to you. Sixty seconds."

The soldiers, having zeroed in on the position of Harvath and the team, had discovered some semblance of discipline and were pushing in with a coordinated attack in order to flank them.

"We're not going to have sixty seconds," he replied over his radio. "We're low on ammo and about to get overrun. Tossing out strobes. Hit them as hard as you can."

With that, Harvath activated two IR strobe lights and tossed them as far as he could in the direction of each advancing group of soldiers.

Harvath, Ashby, Palmer, and Staelin then took turns trying to hold them off. They were all on their last rifle magazines.

Barton had the RIB moving as fast as it would go. Approaching the shoreline of the campground, they could see muzzle flashes in all directions. It was absolute bedlam.

Then, through the chaos, they pinpointed the strobes. There were at least fifty Russian soldiers advancing on the team's position.

Barton swung the boat to the side and slowed so that Jasinski could strafe the Russians.

"Light them up!" he yelled.

For a moment, she paused. But before he could re-peat the command, she opened up with the Mark 48 and swung it back and forth, cutting down every Russian in sight and littering the woods near the beach with their dead bodies.

Back behind the stone foundation, Harvath and the team hunkered down as the heavy rounds from the machine gun crackled all around them.

When Jasinski had run the weapon dry, Barton came back over the radio and told the team to keep their heads down—they were reloading and about to make another pass. Seconds later, the Mark 48 lit up the woods again.

When Barton came back over the radio, he said, "On the beach in twenty seconds."

Transitioning to his pistol, Harvath looked at the team and said, "Time to go."

Staelin transitioned to his pistol as well and helped get Tretyakov to his feet and down to the shoreline.

There was sporadic gunfire, as more Russians came through the woods, but Sloane and Chase handled it, dispatching several more soldiers.

By the time they got to the water, Barton was already there.

Loading Tretyakov, Harvath climbed in, followed by Staelin. Chase and Sloane helped push the RIB off the shore, and then hopped in and joined the rest of the team.

As Barton punched the throttle, Staelin began applying pressure to Tretyakov's wounds. Harvath offered to take over on the Mark 48, but Jasinski waved him off. Going hot, she lit up the Kaliningrad shoreline one last time as the RIB disappeared into the darkness toward the freedom of Poland.

CHAPTER 74

A rtur Kopec was still stunned. He didn't know how Lydia Ryan had done it, but the missile upgrade kits were gone, off the market.

When he asked her about it, she had simply shrugged and said, "We found a workaround." That was it. She hadn't offered any further explanation.

He had asked his man Wójcik to query his source, but Kushner didn't know what had happened either. His source had been as vague as Ryan.

To her credit, though, Ryan had kept her word and had arranged a final visit for him with Reed Carlton. The old spymaster was a shadow of his former self. He had lost weight and had aggressively aged.

Due to the combination of severe dementia, and medications for comfort, Carlton was really out of it. So much so that Kopec wasn't sure if his old colleague even recognized him. He had come expecting to spend the entire day together, but instead decided to leave before lunch and catch an earlier flight back to D.C.

He wasn't surprised that the visit had been supervised. Because of all the national security issues, Ryan had made it a condition. What did surprise him was who had done the supervising.

Scot Harvath was Carlton's protégé and heir apparent. Kopec had met the operative only a handful of times and had always liked him. He felt as if they had a bond. Though he was younger, he understood the great game and what was at stake.

In fact, Harvath had spent a portion of their time together confiding in Kopec. Ryan, it turned out, had not been very forthcoming at all. Carlton's rapid memory loss had crippled their organization. There was all sorts of information about spies and double agents that had been lost.

Unlike Ryan, Harvath wasn't hopeful that the material would turn up in some yet-to-be-discovered journal somewhere in the man's personal effects.

The most devastating thing, Harvath shared, was that in addition to Matterhorn, there were two more high-level spies feeding the Russians disinformation whose identities would be taken to the grave with Carlton. It was a massive blow to NATO's anti-Russia efforts.

There was much more that Kopec wanted to discuss, but he was cautious not to overstay his welcome. Harvath looked as if he had been through hell. Obviously, losing Carlton was taking its toll.

They agreed to meet for dinner back in D.C., and Harvath walked him to the door.

"I'm sorry he was unable to interact," he said. "I know you had a long friendship. I'm sure he appreciates you coming all this way."

Kopec smiled and extended his hand. "It is what friends do."

Harvath shook his hand.

"I hope you and I can be friends," the Pole said. "I think there's much that we can do together."

"I'd like that," said Harvath. "Very much."

"Then it's settled. We'll see each other back in D.C."

Harvath nodded and watched as the aging intelligence officer walked down the red brick path to his waiting Town Car.

After Kopec climbed in and the vehicle had pulled out of the drive, Ryan came up behind him.

"How did it go?" she asked.

"Exactly as the Old Man predicted."

She smiled, "Artur has no idea he's Matterhorn, does he?"

"Nope," said Harvath. "That's the genius of the Old Man. As soon as he learned Kopec was a spy for the Russians, he began devising a way to exploit him. You and I just took it to the next level."

"I played the part given me," Ryan replied, downplaying her role. "You're the one who took everything to the next level. Do you think he has any clue that there are no Gryphons in Europe? That even the upgrade kits were phony?"

Harvath couldn't be sure. His whole plan had been to buy time; to knock the Russians off-balance and force them to reassess their attack. He had just needed long enough to figure out what the invasion would look like so NATO could put the right assets into the Baltics to stop it.

"Speaking of which," she continued, "General Dynamics says we can keep the fake upgrade kit their R&D department built for us."

He smiled. "It'll look great in the conference room."

"It'll look better in your office."

Harvath nodded and made a mental note to send

them a special thank-you. Having something to prove the alleged existence of the kits, and thereby the missiles, was critical to his plan. The Russians didn't have to buy it 100 percent. They just had to be worried that land-based cruise missiles, some possibly nuclear-tipped, might have been waiting for them if they tried to invade.

Looking out the living room's large bay window toward the lake, Ryan saw Lara coming back from her walk. Nodding in her direction, she stated, "You two should spend some time together."

"We will," said Harvath, as he walked over to the sideboard and poured himself a bourbon. "Let's finish up our business first."

Ryan's laptop, a stack of file folders, and myriad papers were strewn across the coffee table. "Welcome to my office," she said, offering him a seat.

Harvath pulled out a chair and sat down. "Where should we start?"

"How about we start with why Barton didn't fly back with the team."

"He met a nice Polish girl, but it'll never last. She's too smart and has much better taste."

Ryan's smile broadened once more. "Jasinski turned out to be a good choice."

"She was excellent," said Harvath. "I'd work with her again in a heartbeat."

"The Supreme Allied Commander had a lengthy debrief with her and the feeling's mutual."

"What are you hearing from the Baltics?"

"I've got good news," Ryan replied, "and then I've got good news. Which do you want first?"

"How about we start with the good news?" he said, smiling.

"Nicholas knocked it out of the park. He publicly exposed every fake Twitter and Facebook account that the Russians, through their hacker group Fancy Bear, were using to stir up dissent. He also managed to insert an undercover-style journalism team into the Troll Factory with hidden cameras.

"All of the television stations in Lithuania, Latvia, and Estonia are running specials exposing how the Russians were trying to weaken them from within."

"His sleeves are short, but there's always something up them."

Ryan laughed and continued. "As you know, as soon as you dropped off Tretyakov, Vella went to work on him."

"How has that been going?"

"Very well. He has been able to extract a lot of information about how they had planned to invade the Baltics."

"Had planned?" asked Harvath. "Past tense?"

"The Russians have canceled their training exercise and are actively repositioning much of their military equipment out of the theater."

"They know we have Tretyakov."

"They know someone has him," Ryan replied. "And that's all that matters. Based on what we have passed along to SHAPE, NATO is already taking steps to shore up the weak points the Russians had planned to exploit in the Baltics."

"That's great news."

Ryan agreed. "Yes it is. You and your team did a fantastic job. But before we celebrate, there's a bookkeeping item we need to discuss."

"What is it?"

"Chase and Sloane's expense report from Belarus."

"What about it?" Harvath asked, slowly remembering that this was a part of his job he really didn't care for.

"They were supposed to pretend to steal the crates of alleged missile upgrade kits and then use the Old Man's contact to smuggle them into Belarus."

"Which they did."

"Did you know that after dumping the bricks we used to weigh down the crates, they took all the smugglers out for champagne and steak dinners in Minsk?" she asked.

Harvath laughed. "I didn't know that, but good for them. We should give them a bonus for initiative. That's a valuable relationship we need to maintain."

Ryan didn't necessarily disagree. Faking the theft of the missile upgrade kits had been a key part of their strategy. Allowing the Russians to see the U.S. and Baltic Ambassadors in a heated exchange at the UN was also part of their plan.

It was all over now, though. The ends, as Chase had said back in Kaliningrad, had justified the means. Their assignment was to avert an Article 5—and by all accounts they had done that.

"There's one other thing," said Ryan, as she removed a sheet of paper and slid it across the table to him.

"What's this?"

"The names of every cell leader across Europe in the People's Revolutionary Front organization."

"Tretyakov gave this up?" he asked.

"It came direct from the Solarium," Ryan confirmed. "The list is yours if you want. Full expense account. No time limit."

Harvath looked at the names and the list of European cities. Then he lifted his head looked out the window at Lara.

"I'll take it," he said.

Ryan was surprised. "You will?"

Pushing the list back across the table, he smiled and said, "No. Sloane and Chase should take it."

"Are you sure?"

"I'm positive," he replied. Like it or not, he was the spymaster now. "Give them a limited expense account and three weeks to finish the job. It's time to turn them loose and to see what they can do."

"Does that mean you're going to stick around?" asked Ryan.

"For a day or two," he said with a wink, as he stood up from the table and walked out the door to be with Lara.

But outside, something was wrong. He could see it in her body language as he walked toward her. Before he even saw the shooters, he knew what had happened. Kopec had betrayed them.

"Run!" Lara screamed.

ACKNOWLEDGMENTS

I always start out the acknowledgments with a special thank-you to the most important people on my list—you, the **readers**. Thank you not only for reading and enjoying my novels, but most of all for the wonderful word of mouth. There is no greater honor you can pay a writer than to recommend one of his books.

I also want to thank the fabulous **booksellers** around the world who carry my novels and introduce new people to them every day. Yours is truly a noble profession, which allows all of us to share in the love of books.

One of my greatest honors is being able to spend time with the selfless men and women engaged in the worlds of espionage, counterterrorism, special operations, law enforcement, and politics. Many of them provided assistance for this novel, and to them I am extremely grateful. Thank you.

My lifelong friend, **Sean Fontaine**, had no idea *Spymaster* would be dedicated to him. Thank you for everything over the years, Sean, but most important, thank you for your friendship and the fearless service you have rendered our country.

James Ryan, another dear friend, picked up the phone every time I called and always had answers for me. Thank you for your friendship, your patriotism, and the deep dives into many of the subjects in *Spymaster*.

I also want to thank **Richard Grenell**. Ric and I have been friends for many years, and his help with the novel is much appreciated. Thank you for your service, your patriotism, and your friendship.

On the first night of the Los Angeles riots, I stood on a rooftop there with a group of strangers, watching the city burn. Unbeknownst to me, I would be brought back together with one of those strangers two decades later. **Robert O'Brien** is an amazing patriot and an outstanding font of expertise in regard to military and foreign affairs. On the day I finished the manuscript for *Spymaster*, a pair of OSS cuff links appeared on my doorstep. I don't know how he knew, but he knew. Thank you for your friendship and all of your help with *Spymaster*.

Chad Norberg is another longtime and extremely valued friend, whose dedication and service to the nation never cease to humble me. He is scary smart, very funny, and always available to lend a hand; I thank him for his years of friendship and the help he provided on *Spymaster*.

The incomparable **Rita Cosby** and my amazing Polish publisher, **Sonia Draga**, provided me with some very important on-the-ground insights into Poland. I am grateful to you both. Thank you.

Former National Security Agency analyst, and now journalist, **John R. Schindler** couldn't have been more helpful when it came to information about the Baltic States, Russia, NATO, and hybrid/special warfare. His fearless assessments of the threats the West faces are must-reads. Thank you, John.

U.S. Navy SEALs **Jack Carr** (ret.) and **Pete Scobell** (ret.) were once again both available and incredibly helpful whenever I had questions. I thank you both for your service, your assistance, your patriotism, and your friendship.

The older I get, the better I am trying to become in all areas of my life. The key to accomplishing such a goal is to surround myself with the best possible people. **Brian Williams** is one of them. His example as a husband, father, and warrior serves as inspiration to me. I am honored to call him my friend and appreciate his help with the novel.

My good pal at Axon, **Steve Tuttle**, is always helpful and always available when I reach out to him—even on a Sunday. Thank you for your help, Steve, as well as your wonderful friendship over these many years.

Ulrika Nyberg and I became fast friends during my junior year of college when I lived overseas. I cannot thank her enough for all of her help on all things Swedish in this novel. *Tack så mycket!*

The character of the American Ambassador to the United Nations, Rebecca Strum, was named by a generous contributor at a fundraiser for an organization near and dear to my heart. Thank you for your generosity, and I hope you enjoy the character.

I am very proud to say that we have just signed a new, three-book contract with the wonderful people at **Simon & Schuster**. It is an honor, a privilege, and a lot of fun to work with all of them, especially the brilliant **Carolyn Reidy**. Thank you for all that you have done for me.

And speaking of doing things, I couldn't do what I do, year after year, without my spectacular publisher and editor, **Emily Bestler**. You and your team at Emily Bestler Books are not only the best in the business, but you are also an absolute joy to work with. Thank you for your friendship, your professionalism, and all of your hard work!

At Pocket Books, I'd be lost without the fabulous **Jen**

Long and **Lisa Litwack**. It is a pleasure to be working with you and I look forward to the many adventures ahead. Thank you!

The extraordinary **David Brown** is not only my publicist par excellence, but also one of the most wonderful people I know. David, I cannot thank you enough for all that you do for me.

In addition to David, I want to thank the phenomenal **Cindi Berger** and her fantastic **team at PMK-BNC**. You achieve great results by aligning yourself with great people. In the PR world, there are none better. Thank you.

It is a matter of immense pride to call myself a member of the Simon & Schuster family, and I want to thank everyone there, as well as a few who have recently begun exciting new chapters in their lives. Thank you to one of the all-time greats and publishing giants, **Louise Burke**; thank you to the dynamic and charming **Michael Selleck**, and to the wonderful **Judith Curr**.

Thank you to my good friend, the outstanding **Gary Urda**; thank you to another good friend, the fantastic **John Hardy**; and thank you to the marvelous **Jonathan Karp**.

The incredible **Paula Amendolara**, **Adene Corns**, **Janice Fryer**, **Lisa Keim**, **Suzanne Donohue**, **Colin Shields**, **Chrissy Festa**, and **Paul Olsewski**—as well as the marvelous **Gregory Hruska**, **Mark Speer**, and **Stuart Smith**. Thank you for every single thing you have done, and continue to do for me.

My gratitude extends to every single person at Simon & Schuster, especially the remarkable **Lara Jones**, **Tasha Hilton**, **Irene Lipsky**, and **Michael Gorman**.

A special shout-out goes to super-talented **Albert Tang** of the Atria/Emily Bestler Books Art Department and the awesome **Al Madocs** of the Atria/Emily Bestler Books Production Department, and many thanks to copy editor Sean Devlin. A novel is a work of art on so many levels. Thank you for the work you and your **incredible artists** did on *Spymaster*.

The **Atria, Emily Bestler Books, and Pocket Books sales teams** have knocked it out of the park again this year. You all are unbelievable, and I thank you for every single sale.

In addition to the rest of the terrific members of the Atria, Emily Bestler Books, and Pocket Books teams, I'd like to give my thanks to the exceptional **Liz Perl, Saimah Haque, Sienna Farris, Whitney McNamara**, and **David Krivda** for all their help over the past year. Thank you.

Audio books are booming, and I want to thank the entire **Simon & Schuster audio division**, especially the superhero team of **Chris Lynch, Tom Spain, Sarah Lieberman, Desiree Vecchio**, and **Armand Schultz**. I love working with you all. Thank you for everything.

I am never at a loss for words when it comes to describing my dynamite agent, **Heide Lange of Sanford J. Greenburger Associates**. I am so grateful for all that you have done for me. You have not only helped make my dreams come true, you have helped me exceed them. For that, I will be forever grateful. Thank you, Heide.

Heide's stupendous team, including the wonderful **Samantha Isman** and **Iwalani Kim**, keep everything humming. My thanks to everyone at **Sanford J. Greenburger Associates** for another fabulous year!

Every day I am thankful for the friendship and professionalism of the astounding **Yvonne Ralsky**. Asking her to join my team was one of the smartest things I have ever done. Thank you for all things great and small, far too many to list here. My gratitude for you knows no bounds.

To my dear friend and the world's absolute best entertainment attorney, **Scott Schwimer**, I say thank you for another incredible year. Your indefatigable efforts on my behalf are only outpaced by your love and friendship. I am honored to have you in my life.

I always save the absolute best for last. **To my phenomenal** family—thank you. Thank you for your love, your support, and all the things you gave up, or put on hold, so I could finish writing *Spymaster*. This book belongs to you. Without a single complaint, **my gorgeous wife**, **Trish**, kept all interruptions at bay, while **my beautiful children** found countless ways to keep everything on track and running smoothly. This truly is a "family" business, and I couldn't do it without all of you. I love you more than words can say.

Turn the page for a sneak peek
of Brad Thor's new Scot Harvath thriller

Backlash

CHAPTER 1

The transport plane, like everything else in Russia, was a piece of shit. For years, mechanics had swapped out its worn scavenged parts with even older parts. Cracks had been filled with epoxy. Leaking tubes and frayed wires had been wrapped with tape. A crash had been inevitable.

A booming noise, like a bag of horseshoes thrown into a dryer, had been heard coming from the left engine. The pilot had throttled back, but the noise had only gotten worse.

He and the copilot had scanned their instruments, searching for clues, but hadn't found any. Everything, right down to the cabin pressure, had appeared normal.

But suddenly, the interior had begun filling with smoke. Seconds later, the left engine died, followed by the right.

As the pilot attempted to restart them, the right engine exploded. He immediately ordered the copilot to activate the extinguisher. They had to keep the fire from spreading to the rest of the aircraft, even if it meant shutting down one of the engines permanently.

The copilot pulled the fire extinguisher handle as ordered, but they had another problem. The left engine, which had successfully been restarted, wasn't producing enough thrust. They were falling at a rate of more than 1000 feet per minute. Over the blaring of cockpit alarms, the pilot put out a distress call.

They were flying in bad weather over the most remote, most inhospitable region in the country. It was unlikely anyone would receive the transmission.

The pilot never got a chance to repeat his mayday. The avionics and electrical system were next to go.

After trying to get the auxiliary power unit back online, the pilot instructed the crew to prepare for the worst. They were going down. Hard.

All this risk, he thought, *all this danger, just to deliver one man—a man chained in back like an animal.*

A Russian Special Forces team had boarded him with a hood over his head. No one had seen his face. The entire crew had assumed he was a criminal of some sort; maybe even a terrorist. They had been informed that he was dangerous. Under no circumstances were any of them to speak with, or get anywhere near the prisoner.

But that was before they knew the plane was going to crash.

Moving quickly to the rear of the aircraft, the plane's loadmaster approached the large Spetsnaz soldier sitting nearest the prisoner.

"You need to put an oxygen mask on him," he said in Russian.

The operative, who already had his mask on, looked at the hooded prisoner, adjusted the submachine gun on his lap, and shook his head.

"*Nyet,*" he stated. *No.*

Career Russian Air Force, the loadmaster was used to transporting elite operators. He was also used to their bullshit.

"I'm not asking you," he replied. "I'm *ordering* you."

The soldier shot a sideways glance at the intelligence officer sitting nearby.

The plane was losing altitude. The smoke in the cabin was getting worse. The officer nodded back. *Do it.*

The ape reached over, snatched off the hood, and affixed a mask over the prisoner's face. Then he put the hood back on and, satisfied, leaned back in his seat.

"Now unshackle his arms so he can brace for impact," the loadmaster continued. It enabled only a minor altering of the body's position, but in a crash it could mean the difference between life and death. Whatever the prisoner had done, surely he didn't deserve to die, at least not like this.

Pissed off, the soldier glanced over again at the intelligence officer. Once more, the man nodded.

Producing a set of keys, the Spetsnaz operative reached down and opened the padlock securing the prisoner's handcuffs to his belly chain. Grabbing the man's arms, he raised them and placed them against the seat in front of him.

"His feet as well," the loadmaster ordered. "He must be able to rapidly evacuate the aircraft."

The soldier didn't need to look to his superior a third time. The intelligence officer answered for their entire team.

"The only way that man walks off this plane is with one of us," he said from behind his mask.

The loadmaster gave up. He had done what he could and knew it was pointless to argue any further. They were out of time.

"Make sure your weapons are secure," he directed, as he turned to make his way to his jump seat.

But suddenly, the plane shuddered and the nose pitched forward. The crewman lunged for the nearest seat and buckled himself in as anything not locked down went hurtling toward the cockpit like a missile.

With no instruments and no visibility, they were flying blind. The pilot and copilot fought with all their might to regain control of the aircraft.

Fifteen hundred feet above the ground, the pilot managed to pull the nose back up and slow their descent. But with no thrust from the remaining engine, they were still falling. They had to find someplace to land.

Staring straight ahead, peering through the weather, the pilot could see they were flying over a dense forest. Ahead was a clearing of some sort. It might have been a field or a frozen lake. All he could tell was that it appeared devoid of trees.

"There," the pilot said.

"There's not enough length. It's too short."

"That's where we're landing," the pilot insisted. "Extend the landing gear. Prepare for impact."

The copilot obeyed and engaged the emergency landing gear extension system. With no electricity with which to activate the PA, he turned and shouted back into the cabin, "Brace! Brace! Brace!"

The command was acknowledged by the loadmaster, who then yelled over and over in Russian from his seat, "Heads down! Stay Down! Heads Down! Stay Down!"

Only a few hundred feet above the ground, the pilot pulled back on the yoke to lift the aircraft's nose in an attempt to slow it down, but he misjudged the distance.

The belly of the plane scraped across the tops of the tall, snow-laden trees. The left rear landing gear was snapped off, followed by the right.

Just before the clearing, one of the wingtips was clipped, and the plane was sent into a violent roll.

CHAPTER 2

Police Chief Tom Tullis had seen plenty of dead bodies over his career.

But this was a record for him at a single crime scene.

During the height of the summer, the popular resort town of Gilford could swell to as many as 20,000 inhabitants. Off-season, like now, the number of full-time residents was only 7,300. Either way, four corpses were four too many.

Removing his cell phone, Tullis texted his wife. They were supposed to meet for lunch, but that was impossible now. He told her not to expect him for dinner either. It was going to be a late night.

Returning the phone to his duty belt, he focused on the bodies—two men and two women. They had all been shot, either in the head, the chest, or both. Judging from a quick scan of the walls and windows, no rounds had missed their targets. That told him the shooter was skilled.

Interestingly, three of the four victims were armed. One of the women had a Sig Sauer P365 in her purse, the other a Glock 17 in her briefcase. One of the two men carried a Heckler & Koch pistol at his hip. No one had drawn their weapons. That told Tullis something else. Either the victims had known their killer, or they had all been taken by surprise. Considering who the victims were, he doubted it was the latter.

The woman with the Sig Sauer had credentials identifying her as a former Boston Police Detective, eligible to carry concealed nationwide. The woman with the Glock had no such credentials, but in the "Live Free or Die" state of New Hampshire it was legal to carry without a permit. Not that a woman like her would ever have had trouble getting one.

Seeing the name on her driver's license, Tullis had instantly recognized her. She had made a lot of headlines when the President had elevated her to Deputy Director of the CIA.

The gun-carrying male victim had ID that claimed he was an active military member. United States Navy.

What the hell were they all doing here? the Chief wondered. *And who had killed them?*

He suspected that the key might lie with the final victim.

Just off the dining room, facing a large TV, a hospital bed had been set up in the den. In it, shot once between the eyes, was a man who appeared to be somewhere in his eighties. He was the only victim Tullis and his team hadn't yet identified. The Chief had some decisions to make.

Judging from the postmortem lividity of the bodies, they had been dead for at least two days, maybe more. The killer's trail would already be going cold.

As a seasoned law enforcement officer, Tullis knew the importance of doing everything by the book. He needed to secure not only the house but also the grounds around it.

Going the extra step, he decided to shut down the lone bridge that connected the 504-acre Governor's Island to the mainland and to request Marine Patrol units to cover the shoreline.

This wasn't some murder-suicide in which the husband had shot the wife and the pool boy before turning the gun on himself. And it wasn't some drug deal gone bad. This was a high-profile case; exactly the kind of case no town ever wanted—especially a tourism-dependent place like Gilford.

Getting on the radio, the Chief told the dispatcher to send the entire shift. He then instructed her to call in all available off-duty officers. They were going to need as much manpower as possible.

The next step was to alert the State Attorney General's office in Concord. Per protocol, they would mobilize a Major Crime Unit team from the State Police to come up and lead the investigation. Before he made that call, though, he decided to place another.

It wasn't a by-the-book move. In fact, Tullis was way overstepping his authority.

But if it meant protecting Gilford and the town's hardworking men and women who so depended on the tourist trade, that was one scenario in which the Chief was willing to bend the rules.

CHAPTER 3

When the call came in to Langley, the Director of Central Intelligence, Bob McGee, happened to be in a meeting with the Director of the FBI, Gary Militante.

Though the DCI's assistant was hesitant to interrupt, she knew she had to make her boss aware of the call. McGee put it on speakerphone. He and Militante were speechless.

The FBI Director introduced himself, gave Tullis his personal cell phone number, and asked to be texted as many pictures from the crime scene as possible—pictures of the bodies, the IDs, the weapons, all of it. Minutes later, his phone began vibrating.

As the photos poured in, McGee kept his emotions in check. With professional detachment, he narrated whom and what they were looking at, right down to the body in the hospital bed—retired CIA operative Reed Carlton—the man who had founded the Agency's Counter Terrorism Center.

Militante had the same questions as Tullis. "What were they all doing in New Hampshire, and who could have wanted them dead?"

It was a long story, which McGee promised to explain in flight. He wanted a look at that crime scene for himself—and the only way he'd have any legal access to it was if the FBI was attached.

Before he and Militante could leave, though, there was an additional person the DCI needed to reach.

He tried three times, but his calls all ended up in voicemail. *Why the hell wasn't he picking up?*

After sending a quick text, McGee grabbed his jacket and headed downstairs with the FBI Director and their security details for the two-minute ride to 84VA, the Agency's helipad a mile west of Langley.

Boarding their respective helicopters, it was a short flight to Joint Base Andrews, where an Embraer Praetor 600 was fueled and waiting.

The jet was a recent addition to the CIA's fleet. Fast and able to take off using less than 5,000 feet of runway, it was perfect for the trip to Gilford.

When they landed, a phalanx of rented SUVs was waiting for them. The detail leaders hated movements like this—no warning, no planning, and little to no co-ordination with elements on the ground. Nevertheless, both directors had insisted that the trip was necessary and that time was of the essence.

From Laconia Municipal, it was only four miles to Governor's Island. They were met at the airport by Gilford PD and given an escort through town and over the bridge to the crime scene.

Stepping out of one of the SUVs, McGee took a deep breath. The air was cold and smelled of pine. A hint of wood smoke drifted from a chimney somewhere unseen.

McGee looked like a marshal from an old Western. He was a tall man in his late sixties with gray hair and a gray mustache. A testament to his Army career, his shoes were shined, his suit and shirt crisply pressed.

He wore no jewelry other than a Rolex Submariner, a gift to himself when he left Delta Force decades ago and signed on with the CIA's paramilitary branch.

McGee was old-school, known for being tough, direct, and unflappable. He hated politics, which had made him a good choice to head the CIA.

The nation's once proud intelligence service was being choked to death by bureaucracy. It was packed with talented people willing to give everything for their country, but they were being held back by risk-averse middle managers more concerned with their next promotion than with doing what needed to be done.

Familiar with the Agency from the ground up, the President had put McGee in charge of cleaning out the deadwood. And he had gone after it root and branch.

But McGee had quickly realized that mucking out the Agency's Augean stables was indeed a Herculean task—one that was going to take much longer than any of them had envisioned.

In the meantime, the threats against America were growing—becoming deadlier, more destabilizing, and more intricate.

As red tape slowed Langley down, America's enemies were speeding up. Something needed to be done—something radical.

With the President's approval, McGee had agreed to a bold new plan—as well as a major sacrifice.

The plan was to outsource the CIA's most clandestine work. It would go to a private intelligence agency outside the bureaucracy's grasp. There, safe from government red tape, sensitive operations could receive the support and commitment they deserved.

It was viewed as a temporary fix while Langley was

undergoing its gut rehab—a rehab that would have to go all the way down to the studs.

The private intelligence agency charged with taking over the darkest slice of the CIA's pie was The Carlton Group, started by the aforementioned, now deceased, Reed Carlton.

And as to McGee's sacrifice, another victim at the scene represented it.

With his blessing, Lydia Ryan had left her position as CIA Deputy Director in order to run The Carlton Group.

That was the backdrop against which Bob McGee stepped out of the SUV, breathed in the frigid New England air, and prepared himself for the horror he was about to see inside.

Tullis met the two directors at the front steps and solemnly shook their hands. Then, after having them sign into the crime scene log, he distributed paper booties and latex gloves. The protection details didn't get any. They would have to wait outside—the fewer people coming in and out the better.

The Police Chief was about to show the two men inside, when one of his officers came up carrying an evidence bag.

"We found something back in the trees near the end of the driveway," the patrolman said, holding it up. Inside was a phone.

McGee recognized it immediately. Or, more specifically, he recognized its cover.

Made from a rigid thermoplastic, the distinct Magpul cellphone case was popular with military operators. Its styling mimicked the company's ruggedized rifle magazines. On the back, a distinct Nordic symbol had been added. The Chief stepped off the porch for a closer examination.

As he did, the FBI Director saw the look on his CIA colleague's face. Slowly, he mouthed a name. *Harvath?*

McGee nodded.

Their bad situation had just gotten worse.